MW01611164

THEFT BY CHOCOLATE

Luba Lesychyn

DEDICATION

With deep love, to my parents, Paulina and Bohdan Kulchyckyj, whose sacrifices and endured hardships leave me profoundly grateful for the life I have led.

A Note on Chocolate

Chocolate is one of the most addictive "food" substances available as it contains the following high number of addictive substances:

Refined sugar.
Caffeine.
Cannabiniods.
Theobromine.

Gruben, Prof. Rozalind, "Understanding the Nature of Food Addictions," Living Nutrition, Volume 14, 2003, pp. 26-27.

CHAPTER ONE

I scrambled beneath the humbling granite archway that framed the Royal Ontario Museum's staff entrance, water dripping from me as if I had just slipped out of the shower. The quivers that waved through my body triggered an uncomfortable realization, not that I was cold from my drenched state, but that I'd transitioned into the first stage of chocolate detox. I hadn't had a crumble of the substance for at least eighteen hours.

The tinted glass of the door before me mirrored a startling reflection − 'harrowing' would have been a kind descriptor. The morning had started as a good-hair day, but the flash-flood rains that had caught me sans umbrella put a different spin on the do. So not fair. Why was it that Audrey Hepburn looked positively radiant after being soaked in a torrential downpour in *Breakfast at Tiffany's*? I looked like *Breakfast at Wal-Mart*. Mind you, I didn't resemble Audrey Hepburn at the best of times except perhaps for the dark, doe-like eyes I shared with the Hollywood icon.

I tilted closer towards the glass, raised my index fingers to the corners of my eyes and elongated the fragile skin upwards planing out the subtle crow's feet. Maybe I did have a bit of Hepburn going on. The image grimaced back at me. Who was I kidding? The Hepburn I was channeling was

Katharine when she was fished out of the Ulanga River in *African Queen*.

"Are you going inside or are you planning on staring at yourself all day?"

Embarrassed that my self-deprecation had been interpreted as vanity, I rotated towards the person with the after-hours-club voice. The young woman I faced sliced away any traces of my self-esteem in a nanosecond, bulldozed past me, and vanished behind the second set of doors.

I mustered a handful of dignity only to lose it after slipping and lurching on the stone floor opposite the security control room. Through the triple-glazed, bullet-proof glass, there was a beehive of activity. Security command central was crammed full of people, and I discerned guards who didn't usually work the morning swing. The news must have broken over the weekend. But I had eyeballed all the dailies before stepping onto the subway – *The Globe and Mail*, *The National Post*, *The Toronto Star*, and even skimmed the free Metro paper, but none referred to the disappearance of the porcelain Tang horse from the Chinese gallery the previous Friday.

One more set of doors steered me to the main security checkpoint where a boyish newbie guard was planted behind the counter of black polished laminate. I instantly dove into his eyes. Emerald green pools like that are a rarity. The combination of those eyes with his dirty blonde faux bed-head was an irresistible combination. His neck was a tad thick, but I suspected there was a body-builder's frame hidden beneath the uniform.

"Good morning." I hoped my voice would drown out the sound of my heart palpitating.

4

"Good morning, ma'am. Looks like you forgot your umbrella today."

Ma'am? Seriously? Clearly my cougarishly-tight skirt wasn't fooling anyone. "You can call me Kalena. And I suggest you drop the word 'ma'am' from your vocabulary, at least around here." I was doing him a favor. He could lose his head if he used that term on one of our resident feminazis.

"Uh...noted. My name's Marco...Marco Zeffirelli."

"Like the director?" Franco Zeffirelli's screen version of *Romeo and Juliet* was my all-time favorite version of the story of the star-crossed lovers.

"I thought the Director's name was Carson James."

"Never mind." Eyes you could lose yourself in – yes. Knowledge of Italian film directors – no. I plunked my purse down and rummaged for my ID badge. No point asking a keener if he'd swipe me through. "What's going on in the control room?" I scrounged deeper into my bag with the fervor of a manic dog trying to surface a buried bone.

"They caught the guy that stole that horse."

"Are you kidding?" So far I'd found a bottle of dark plum nail polish and some rogue shavings of chocolate in my bag. I licked my fingers.

"Oh, I wouldn't kid about a thing like that. It's only my third day on the job."

"Sooooo, who was it?"

"One of the contract construction workers. Have you found that ID yet, ma'am, I mean, Kalena?"

"How did they catch the guy?"

"Seems he was a suspect in the theft of that small Group of Seven painting from the Art Gallery a couple of months ago? They've been keeping an eye on him. The perp's a total amateur."

5

"Why do you say that?"

"International art thieves go for big-ticket items. Like that opal collection that went missing from here."

"That was almost thirty years ago." My eyebrows arched into an unnatural point. Was this kid even born when the gems went missing from the Royal Ontario Museum? "You seem to know a lot for someone who's been on the job for only three days."

"Personal interest of mine, art theft, that is. The crime's second only to drug trafficking. About $6 billion worth of art is stolen every year."

"Who knew?" I spied the woman who'd almost bowled me over moments earlier as she whizzed through the corridor bordering the rear of the security desk.

"By the way, do you know the woman that came through here just before me?"

"The one who's a lead singer for a death metal band?"

I tried to suppress a chortle, but failed. "I think you profiled that one pretty accurately."

"It's not a profile. I saw her front a band a couple of months ago. She's the new IT Help Desk person – still has her temp badge. Doesn't really have customer service written all over her, if you ask me."

Finally, my fingers landed on a familiar plastic shape. I whipped my hand out of the bowels of my purse as though withdrawing it from an alien's guts. Out fell my BlackBerry as well as heaps of gold foil wrappers that feathered the security log book.

"Ferrero Rochers for breakfast again?"

I budged my head towards the repulsively familiar voice and was walloped by a blast of Gucci cologne. "Good morning to you too, Richard." I scooped up the week-old chocolate wrappers and with a deft sleight of hand they disappeared back into the depths of my bag.

"That's a great suit, sir. Is it Cavalli?" said Marco.

"Who are you?" said Richard.

"My name's..."

"It was a rhetorical question." Foam was forming in the corner of Richard's mouth. "I didn't really expect an answer."

Marco's face soured. Poor kid. Nothing like being verbally bitch-slapped first thing on a Monday morning.

Richard Pritchard was my former boss and current Director of Exhibits and Programs. When he was recruited to head the division in which I'd worked for almost fifteen years, it was as if a gnarly chunk of metal had been thrown into a finely tuned piece of machinery. I fled the toxic environment as quickly as possible and joined a newly created department called Museum Consulting Services.

Richard slid back the finely-woven sleeve of his jacket and eyed his Movado. "Running right on time as usual, I see."

I elevated onto my tiptoes and transfixed my gaze to Richard's forehead. "If I were you, Richard, I'd request a refund for the Rogaine. I really don't think it's doing the job."

Richard whipped up his hand, skimmed over the peach fuzz at the front of his skull and immediately dropped his arm as if all life force had been drained from the limb. Blood slowly rose up his neck and began flushing his face from the chin up, like red-tinted mercury rising up a thermometer. I dipped my chin and turned my face sufficiently to give Marco a discreet you-owe-me-one wink. He responded with a Cheshire grin.

"You might be interested to know I'm meeting your boss and Brenda in twelve minutes and fifty-six seconds," Richard said, "and we're expecting you to take notes."

"I'm aware of that," I said, sporting a saccharine smile.

"You must be telepathic then seeing as Stewart and I arranged this meeting minutes ago."

"Please don't spit on me." With the palm of my hand, I swiped my cheek. "Stewart sent me a text." I grabbed my BlackBerry from the counter, slid my thumb over the dead battery indicator light, and waved it past Richard's face as though swatting a fly.

"You'd better hurry—"

"Yes, I'd better." I swiped my ID card through the electronic reader releasing the lock and cycloned my way through the doors to the curatorial center where the Museum's offices and collections are housed. Richard bellowed something after me, but it was lost in the wake I left behind.

With determined grace I circumnavigated the first corner, ensuring I was out of Richard's sightline, then idled at Information Technology's door. Through the window I spotted the overly-made-up death metal vocalist. But there was no time to waste. If memory served me well, there was a chocolate bar stashed in my desk. There was still time to inhale it before the meeting with Richard.

I sprinted through a maze of hallways like a thoroughbred bolting for the win, past Carpentry and Taxidermy, and galloped past the Museum's own weapon of mass destruction, the daunting fumigation chamber used to exterminate insect stowaways catching rides on incoming artifacts and animal specimens. My high heels tap-tapped against the worn tile floor, mimicking the sound of machinegun fire. I rounded the next bend with an indelicate skid almost colliding into a technician from the Egyptian Department. Planted in the middle of the narrow corridor, she was talking to the Museum's chief librarian, Walter Pembroke. They hovered over a cart of small mummified creatures – probably cats or baby crocs.

"Whoa! Sorry about that," I said and swerved around the pair and barreled onwards.

"Kalena, have you returned *The Art Newspaper*?" Walter hollered.

I decelerated to a trot. *The Art Newspaper* was the museum and art world's answer to an entertainment rag reporting on who bought what for how much, exposing galleries that had inadvertently purchased forgeries and headlining the most recent museum thefts. "Soon, I swear."

Parting my way through a last set of doors, I emerged into a public gallery lined with boulder-sized rocks, minerals and gems to whose beauty I had long become desensitized. I came to a slow halt, panting as though I had just climbed the stairs of the CN Tower. A sign with the words 'Museum Consulting Services' finely etched into a brass plaque hung on the stone wall at eye level. Home at last.

The department was the brainchild of my boss, Stewart Anderson, who had modelled it after a local private firm that provided consulting services to museums internationally. Stewart persuaded the Museum's new Director and Board of Governors that a consulting branch within the institution could offer expertise on everything from designing a new gallery to building a museum from scratch and turn a much-needed profit for a Museum whose funding sources were increasingly shrinking. He was given carte blanche on the condition the new department earned enough to cover all salaries and operating costs and made revenue to spare.

Stewart knew I had been integral in developing another Museum department from scratch, and he wanted someone who could produce administrative protocols and maneuver with ease through the Museum's tangled bureaucracy. He was relying heavily on me and our senior consultant, Brenda Lockhart, to achieve the department's mandate. And all of us bore Atlas's burden daily.

I twisted the doorknob to the office with the tremble of a heroin junky plummeting from a high. "Hey, Brenda."

"Morning," she said, without releasing her stare from her computer monitor.

I whipped off my soggy plaid trench and set my purse down beside the picture of my cat. Sweet old thing had died shortly after my second husband moved out. She had been as brokenhearted as I was. I flung open my desk drawer. Where was that chocolate bar? Crap. I had forgotten I had consumed it as an afternoon snack on Friday. Chocolate withdrawal was obviously affecting my memory. What the hell was I going to do? I couldn't go to a meeting with Richard in this fragile state and risk coming undone in front of him.

"Were you at the gym this morning?" Brenda tilted her head upwards at a newsroom-like row of clocks labeled London, Lisbon, Hong Kong and Toronto. The time for Toronto read 9:25.

"No. I woke up too late for my body combat class this morning. My alarm clock's messing with me."

"Uh-huh."

"Honestly, there's something screwy going on with the volume on my radio alarm, and I didn't hear it go off. Anyways, have you talked to Stewart yet?"

"The usual crack-of-dawn briefing." Brenda typed so furiously I thought her keyboard was going to split in half. "Don't worry. Stewart loaded up at Heathrow with Thornton's including your favorite chocolate-smothered toffee."

"Aww, really?"

"You know he always does. You can pick it up when you see him. He called down a few minutes ago and said he needs you in his office prr-onto."

"I know, I know. I ran into Richard on the way in, and he told me we're meeting. Said I was supposed to take, uh...notes, like suddenly I'm uh...a...secretary or something."

Brenda swiveled around in her Herman Miller and peered at me suspiciously over the rim of her round metal-framed specs. With her banged bob of red hair and her penchant for wearing flats and skirts whose hems fell below the knee, she reminded me of a 1920s flapper. "Richard's neurons are misfiring again. Stewart didn't say anything about me joining the hot air fest. But you better do something with that hair of yours. Freakishly scary."

I whipped a mirror out of my purse. "Oh, give me a frigging break." Between the rain and the mad dash from the staff entrance I had a veritable vermin's lair on my head. "I can't believe people I work with have...uh...seen me like this."

Brenda hopped to her feet as though she'd been auto-ejected from her chair. "You're exhibiting symptoms of fuzzy brain. You haven't had any chocolate yet today, have you?"

"I thought I had a candy bar in...uh, my desk—"

"Just coif the do, and I'll be right back."

By the time I had stroked a comb through my unnaturally blond hair and twisted it into a stylish updo worthy of a television commercial for a miracle hair clip, Brenda returned with a tin of Harrods' cocoa and a spoon. She pried the metal lid off and scooped out a heaping portion of the posh British blend. "Go ahead. You know you've done worse." She forced the spoon into my hand, and I downed the dry cocoa like an obedient child.

The instant the rich powder hit my tongue I felt a warm, steady rush invade my body like an electrical current moving in slow motion towards my extremities. The body shudders subsided, and my hands steadied. When I returned to Planet Earth, I stepped towards Brenda to give her a hug, but she backed away and raised her hand.

"Don't mistake my actions for some kind of team effort. Now get the hell out of here." She cracked a sliver of a smile, grabbed the backs of my shoulders, and sent me flying out the door. "And don't you dare tell anyone about what I just did for you. It would ruin my reputation around here as a hard-nose."

"I signed a confidentiallty agreement when I was hired, didn't I?

"Right."

"Hey, do you know anything about those opals that were stolen from the Museum?"

"There's no time for chitchat."

"Do you?"

"Oh, God, that was like decades ago. It happened during the staging of a special exhibition. The cops never caught the thief, but the opals turned up years later in a market in Hong Kong. Now get your ass upstairs."

Brenda was right. There was no time to lose, and I broke the land speed record hightailing it to Stewart's office in the executive's suite on the third floor. As I was about to tap on the doorframe, Stewart spotted me.

"Come in, come in." Stewart's prematurely silver beard and hair gave him a bit of a jolly Santa vibe. He was a gentle giant who probably could have been an awesome football player had it not been for the total lack of aggression in any

12

cell of his body.

"Welcome back, Stewart." I suddenly sounded raspy. Damn. Some of the cocoa I had knocked back was lodged at the top of my esophagus.

"Thank you. It's good to have my land legs for a while."

My eyes darted around the room. "I see you've rotated your art again. Just how big is that, heh, African collection of yours?" I counted on a few more coughs to clear my obstructed throat.

"According to that lovely wife of mine, too big."

A giggle got trapped in my throat and came out as a cough.

"Are you all right? Shall I get you some water?" said Stewart.

I gestured no with my hand. "Richard will be here any second...and I have a confession. I had a bit of an ugly encounter with him at the staff entrance. He brings out the worst in me," I said like a Janis Joplin sound-alike.

"He does have that effect on people. But you have to learn to separate the persona from the position. He is, after all, a senior manager. And this meeting we're about to have, if Richard ever makes an appearance, is at Carson's request."

Odd, I thought. Rumor had it that the Director and Richard were on the outs lately. Richard must have groveled his way back into Carson's good graces. Before I had a chance to speak further, a thundering knock startled both of us.

"Hello." Richard wriggled his thick form through the partially open doorway. "I took the liberty of inviting someone else to join us." He forced the door wide open to expose Veronique Bouvier, Richard's embarrassingly inept sidekick and head of Exhibits. She was the personification of a French Poodle. Tall with lanky limbs, she always wore Nehru-collared suit jackets with faux-fur cuffs. To this kooky wardrobe staple she regularly paired an Hermés scarf snugly wrapped around her head, as if attempting to hold in her melting brain. Her mousy brown locks erupted into curls above the designer bandana.

"*Bonjour*," Veronique said.

"Is there anyone else hiding out there?" Stewart said.

"*Mais, non*. But where's Brenda?"

"She's working to deadline on a study for a planetarium in Lisbon," said Stewart.

"But…" spluttered Richard.

"I can't afford to pull her away for anything right now. Luckily we have Kalena on our team."

Richard and Veronique shifted their scrutiny towards me just as I declined my chin, hoping to dislodge the cocoa from my throat.

Veronique spoke up. "But we need someone with Brenda's—"

"Veronique, let's get on with this. I'm meeting with the Director in fifteen. And your tardiness has already cost us some time," Stewart said.

Veronique withdrew into pout mode, and Richard seized the lead. "Veronique and I have been approached by the San Francisco Museum of Art and Science to host *Treasures of the Maya*. The last venue on its tour pulled out at the eleventh hour, and they're seeking another institution to round out the tour in this part of the continent."

Aware that the Museum had not presented a blockbuster of this magnitude for some time, my jaw almost unhinged. The sudden intake of air resulted in a silent burp, and a powdery brown vapor escaped, forming a small dark cloud in front of my face. I fanned the cocoa haze as unobtrusively

14

as possible, but detected Stewart peering at me from the corners of his eyes. He abruptly clapped, spooking us all and attracting the full attention of Richard and Veronique. "Yes. *Treasures of the Maya*….currently packing in huge crowds across the States."

I massaged my irritated throat. "But what does this have to do with Museum Consulting? Why aren't you taking this to the Exhibits Planning Committee?"

Richard white-knuckled the arms of his chair. "It would be impossible to mount this exhibition through normal protocols given the time constraints. But Carson's keen to bring the show here at any cost, and your operation can bypass the Museum's bureaucratic encumbrances."

"Clever." Stewart inhaled deeply. "And what about admissions revenues?"

"The profits will cover all your expenses, and a percentage of the net will go into your coffers for future endeavors. It's a win-win situation for everyone."

Stewart drew his palms together in prayer position and rested his bearded chin on his fingertips. I knew he was analyzing the scheme faster than a team of consultants and had likely worked out some rough profit margins.

"*Exactement.*" Veronique's penchant for haphazardly tossing in French phrases as a way of reminding everyone she was the daughter of French diplomats annoyed me to the nth degree.

"One of the exhibit's signature artifacts is the oldest piece of chocolate in the world," said Richard.

My eyes expanded to saucer proportions. The oldest piece of chocolate – how cool was that?

"But the big-ticket item is a magnificent gold jaguar mask," said Richard.

Big-ticket item? That was the phrase Marco had used earlier.

"You've piqued my interest." Stewart sank back into his chair. "And I presume the SFMA knows nothing of our recent security breach? Otherwise they would demand extraordinary insurance coverage negating all profits."

"The Tang horse? No," said Richard. "The incident has been fully cloaked. It's one of the advantages of having a Director who was a former media mogul. He's managed to gag the papers, and with no insurance claim having been filed, there's no public record of the pilfering. As far as those who know anything about it, it was a temporary displacement."

The activity I witnessed in the security control room was making more and more sense. Cover-up was the operative word.

"But we need an experienced person to manage mounting the exhibit. If Brenda is *occupé*, perhaps—"

"Kalena will direct the project," said Stewart.

"Who?" Did I hear him right?

"This is no time for modesty, Kalena. Your administrative experience in Exhibits combined with your history background will be invaluable. And you do share a love for chocolate with the Maya." Stewart winked. "More importantly you have a record of expediting difficult tasks."

"Kalena?" Richard was a ghostly beige.

"You can count on me." I sensed beads of sweat forming in my armpits, but Richard had pressed the wrong buttons, and I wasn't about to back off.

"I must cut this short now," said Stewart. "Carson is booked with back-to-back meetings, and I can't keep him waiting."

Richard and Veronique leapt from their chairs like

school children who had been dismissed from class. The two exited the office, and Stewart closed the door behind them. "It's time for you to spread those wings of yours."

"Yes, sir, but I'm not sure I —"

"We'll talk about this further after I've cleared up some critical matters. Geoffrey's flying in tomorrow, and I have some major number crunching to perform before his arrival."

"Geoffrey's coming to town?" I felt a tingling in my sacral chakra. The debonair Geoffrey Ogden, Stewart's former school chum, ran our London office.

"He's just met with the Lisbon clients and is coming to meet with Brenda and me." Stewart reached into his desk drawer and gently flipped a bag of Thornton's chocolate-smothered toffee into my palm.

"Thanks, Stewart." I clutched the foil pouch to my breast.

"You're welcome. I hope this keeps you out of the cocoa provisions."

I felt my cheeks turning pomegranate. "Won't happen again."

"I've never seen anyone exhale a cloud of chocolate vapor before."

"I have a reasonable explanation — sort of."

"You'll have to tell me about it another time." Stewart thrust the door open. "Grab that copy of *The Guide to Travelling Exhibitions* — second bookcase on the right, third shelf down. And get any relevant literature from the library as soon as you can." Stewart vanished into the hallway before I could draw another breath.

I snatched the book and a dog-eared photo of Stewart and Geoffrey slipped out. Stewart looked quite the nerd in head-to-toe Tilley gear. He was voluminous and pasty in comparison to the trim and sun-kissed Geoffrey as they stood in front of the cliff-embedded Treasury of Petra in Jordan. They were *The Odd Couple* of business partners. Stewart had grown up in a small farming community outside of Toronto while Geoffrey hailed from upper-crust Brit stock. Last I heard, Geoffrey was dating a super-model or was it the Parisian architect of the moment?

I tipped the photo inside another book and decamped with the Thornton's toffee in hand. But I wondered why Richard had approached Stewart with *Treasures of the Maya*. His explanation seemed irrational, and I wasn't buying it, especially since Richard had made no secret of his opinion that our department was doomed to failure. As I cruised back to the office, the phrase 'big-ticket item' kept playing in my head like a bad song you couldn't forget.

CHAPTER TWO

"Why are you walking like that?" Brenda said, standing outside the office door gawking at me as I waddled duck-like towards her.

"I went for a run last night. Guess I overdid it," I said.

"You're becoming OC when it comes to this fitness crap. Have you thought about clipping your chocolate intake instead?"

"I'm not obsessive-compulsive. Besides, the jog wasn't a guilt workout."

"Uh-huh," said Brenda.

"I was in serious need of some stress relief after yesterday's turn of events."

"Do you think bringing *Treasures of the Maya* to the Museum is out of your league?"

"Uh, YES."

"I think you're right," said Brenda.

I deflated like a balloon that had been pin-holed.

"Let's be realistic. It's a huge job."

"I know. I know," I said.

"And I can't help out. The Lisbon project's fucking draining me." Brenda checked her watch. "Shit. I have to meet with the resident astronomer before someone realizes we closed down our planetarium five years ago, and we no longer need an astronomer on staff."

Brenda darted off with the verve of a sprightly young

19

hare while I trundled into the office like an octogenarian on Valium making it to my desk just in time to pick up an incoming phone call.

"Museum Consulting Services," I said.

"Good morning, Kalena."

"Stewart?" I was a little puzzled as the phone's display indicated the call was coming from the Museum's front desk."

"I'm at the main entrance with Carson and the contingent from Hong Kong. They're a day early, and I'm booked with the Museum's lawyer, and Carson can't stay either...I'm counting on you to give them a tour."

"Uh, okay."

"If you could meet them in the main Rotunda in about ten, Carson will be eternally grateful."

"Sure thing," I said.

"Most excellent. You can let me know how it goes later. Good luck."

I hung up and whimpered as I took another step. How on Earth was I going to navigate the Museum without looking as though I had just had both hips replaced? Some chocolate might diminish the pain, I reasoned most illogically. I ransacked my desk and hit upon the foil package of Thornton's. There was one last stone-sized piece of the chocolate-covered toffee remaining, and I tossed it into my mouth. As soon as I bit into it, every tooth became embedded in the sugary mass, and my mandibles locked tighter than a shark's grip on a freshly caught seal. Oh, lord, this candy had better melt before I rendezvoused with the Director.

I doddered through a long atrium that took me into our Earth Gallery. Tucked beside a colossal reproduction of a volcano, I clocked two silhouettes resembling a giant ruler and

20

an over-sized pear on legs – Veronique and Richard. With a few minutes to spare, I thought I might ask them for further details on the exhibit. But as I shuffled closer and became mindful that my jaws were still clamped shut, I reconsidered and decided to save the conversation for a time when I could actually communicate. Rather than forging towards the pair, I detoured behind the volcano, back around the deep folds of the artfully painted pyramid of light-weight concrete and metal mesh.

"*Peut-être* it will be better with Kalena on the project."

My ears radared in on Veronique's voice like a bat that had caught the scrambling of a mouse.

"You always said she had a *tête de linotte*," continued Veronique.

"How could I 'always say that' if I don't even know what that means?" barked Richard.

"Sorry, I thought you knew that expression – bird brain. You always said she was a bird brain."

"She is. But she'll be watching me like a hawk, looking for any irregularities. And the whole Museum is already on high alert because that imbecile construction worker decided to decorate his living room with one of our Chinese artifacts. Things are going to be tighter around here than after the last major theft at the Museum."

"That was long before you started working here," said Veronique. "How do you know how things were then?

"Trust me. I know."

I felt as though the breath had been vacuum-sucked from my lungs. Were they talking about the opal theft? Unexpectedly one of my thighs cramped, and I inadvertently slid my foot forward, stubbing the point of my shoe on a section of the artificial lava flow."

"What was that?" said Richard in a hushed tone.

"*Je ne sais pas.*"

"Welcome to the Royal Ontario Museum's Dynamic Earth Gallery..." suddenly boomed an iconic voice from the mini-theatre located within the volcano.

"Damn that ridiculous auto-timer," said Richard. "I thought it was set to begin after the Museum opens."

"The beginnings of the planet date back millions of years..." resumed the video.

"Let's get out of here," said Richard. "And contact the AV technicians immediately and have them correct that timer. It's a complete waste of energy."

"*Oui, oui, oui.*"

Relief flooded my body. Who knew that one day I would be rescued by Christopher Plummer's narration? He still made me weak-kneed every time I watched *The Sound of Music*. The voice-over narrative from the volcano's theatre continued to chronicle the formation of the planet and when the sound of Richard's and Veronique's footsteps waned in the distance, I boogied down the narrow atrium. Up ahead I spotted Carson surrounded by a small contingent of people.

"We have more than ten million objects in our collections," I could hear Carson say as I approached the guests from Hong Kong. He noticed me and motioned to me to move closer. "Isn't that right, Kalena?"

"Mm-huh," I mumbled. Are you kidding me? The toffee had still not softened enough for me to speak. Carson introduced me to the director of the Hong Kong Museum of Natural History and, in turn, to the rest of his courteous associates.

"Our colleagues from Hong Kong are very interested in our science collections and, in particular, the gem rooms."

Carson articulated every word very slowly.

"O—" I said. The toffee was finally liquefying, and I succeeded in making a small round shape with my mouth.

"After you've toured the gem rooms, please escort the group to Mineralogy. I can meet them there, and we'll proceed to lunch."

"Shertainly, shir. Leave it with me." Carson was a tad hard of hearing and too vain to wear an aid, so I prayed he hadn't detected the toffee slur.

Like a well-trained Border Collie, Carson herded the group into the main hall. As they stood mesmerized by the monumental cases filled with some of the Museum's most magnificent treasures, Carson took me aside and murmured, "They're considering hiring us to consult on their new gem gallery. So, impress, impress."

"I'll do my best to dazzle, sir." The toffee garble had dissipated just in time.

"Good, good...You know, I'd never noticed you walked with such a pronounced turnout. You must have studied ballet in your youth."

"Uh, yes, sir." Hip hop and rock jazz were more like it, but that was in recent years, and I was not about to confess that my penguin stance was the consequence of overly zealous exercise.

"Well, you and Richard have something in common then," Carson said.

"Richard Pritchard?"

"He's still very active in promoting the National Ballet."

"Richard Pritchard?" An image of the butterball in spandex and on point gave made me a bit nauseous.

"I'll catch up with you later." Carson bowed his head and departed. His salt-and-peppered hair and grey worsted suit dissolved into the stone of the Museum's walls and floors.

I wobbled in front of the group and guided them to-wards our acclaimed gem rooms which, although a fraction of the size of the Smithsonian, were still quite magnificent.

As we slowly journeyed in the direction of the rooms designed to simulate vaults, the director of the Hong Kong Museum inched towards me and spoke with a muzzled tone, "We are most grateful, Mrs. Kalena, especially considering the history between our museums."

"History?" What was he talking about?

"I assure you our museum's purchase of your opals oc-curred only after authorities cleared all matters. Everything was, as you say here, on the up-and-up."

"I'm sure it was." 'Clueless' was branded on my fore-head.

"But let us forget about these unfortunate events and move forward."

"Absolutely," I said. "We're very enthusiastic about working with your museum and moving forward."

CHAPTER THREE

Had anyone seen me descend into the chair as though a crane were docking a crate of volatile explosives, one would have surmised I was suffering from a debilitating case of hemorrhoids. Fact was that my quadriceps were still flaming. But once seated, relief was achieved, and I began to flip through the binder of newspaper clippings.

Tucked away in a quiet recess of the Museum's library I scrutinized the one and only article I had found concerning the opal theft. I would have thought this material would long have been digitized or at least microfiched. Unfortunately, I was stuck with a jaundiced piece of newspaper upon which someone must have spilled a cup of coffee. Whole sections of the copy were illegible and only a few discernible words remained of the photo caption beneath the snap of a spectacled man-boy sporting a tie secured so tightly, his neck looked like an upside-down muffin. The caption read '…the Museum's chief administrator holds uncut opal left by thief…were stolen from show case at…'

I had seen the face in the picture somewhere before. Was this person still employed by the Museum? I needed one of those computer graphic programs that could age a person and predict what they might look like thirty years later.

From the amount of decipherable text in the story, I was able to establish the theft had occurred sometime between late January 7 and early January 8, 1981. A large number of the staff had been preoccupied mounting an exhibition on Italian maiolica, brightly colored tin-glazed pottery dating from the Renaissance. At the same time, the Museum had recently laid off some of its security staff. The case that held the gems had been disarmed by the thief, and because the area was being patrolled only every two hours, the disappearance went unnoticed for some time. The investigators were most puzzled at the thief's choice to abscond solely with the opals and to leave behind gems of significantly greater value. 'Presumably, he took only his personal preferences,' read the article.

Over seventy opals were stolen from a collection that had been acquired in the late 1940s. Oh, now this was interesting – 'The Museum stood to recoup a substantial amount of money if the opals weren't recovered.' I scanned further down the page – no reference to an inside job. Surely, they must have considered...wait, what was this? The police found some kind of mark. I squinted as though doing so would help me see through the darkest part of the coffee stain. Some kind of mark that might have been the brand of...what? Damn, I couldn't make out this section of the article.

"Excuse me."

My heart felt as though it had been ripped out of my body by an organ snatcher without the use of anesthesia. "Walter! For crying out loud, you scared me out of my skin."

The clichéd meek librarian had apologies written all over his face. "I was trying to be unobtrusive."

"Good job!" With my heart still pounding as if being beaten by a Japanese Kodo drummer, I slunk back into my chair copping a glimpse of Walter's soft-soled Wallabees. 'Ugliest shoes in the world...as if stitched together by elves,' I remembered once having read in a fashion blog ranting about the revival of hideous footwear including Crocs and Chung Shi sandals.

Walter dipped his gaze to the open binder on my desk, and I thwacked the cover shut with a hypersonic force.

"I see you're doing some kind of research." Walter removed his pop-bottle-bottomed glasses and cleaned them with his jacket lining.

I was blindsided by the Superman features lurking behind the Clark Kent façade. "I'm…I'm looking at press on some recent blockbuster exhibitions."

"But those binders contain articles from the eighties. There are more recent clippings—"

"It's okay. I have to get back to the office." I started to shuffle the papers on the desk, but stared with the intensity of a cobra at Walter. He had returned his magnifiers back to his face. "Have you considered contacts or laser surgery?" I said.

Walter suddenly looked as though he had been told to put his dog down. "I'm in that infinitesimal percentile that is unable to wear ocular corrective lenses or undergo surgery to the cornea."

"Oh, sorry. I was just curious. Anyway, according to *GQ*, geek chic is in again." I forced a dippy smile.

"What are you implying?" Walter slipped his glasses off again and inspected them.

"Nothing. They're very…attractive." The optician who recommended the glasses must have been sight-challenged themselves.

"I purchased them at Honest Ed's."

"I see."

"I sense you are not impressed."

27

"Oh, but I am." Who buys glasses from a bargain ware-house store?

"Your charming colleague had a parallel reaction to yours."

"Stewart?" I said.

"Brenda."

Brenda, charming? She did have an uncanny ability to turn off the trailer-trash mouth and substitute it with Havergal College polish in an instant. Still, charming wasn't an adjective any other staff would use to characterize Brenda.

"And she can be quite a spitfire."

"I really do have to go."

"Oh, by the way, thank you for returning *The Art Newspaper*, but it's a bit redundant now. The new issue has arrived." Walter pulled out a small, vellum-like parcel from his jacket pocket.

"Shut up!" I screamed. Walter looked petrified. "It's an expression, you know, like 'holy cow.'"

"Unusual. I must check the origin of the phrase."

"May I take the new issue?"

"I'm afraid that is not possible. I peruse it on the Direc-tor's behalf before it goes on the shelf – in case the Museum has been mentioned." Walter eyeballed his watch. "Per-haps...I could allow you to browse the issue until closing."

"I'll put these clippings back on the shelf for now." I picked up the binder exposing a gargantuan Toblerone choc-olate bar underneath. Walter transfixed his gaze on a sign at-tached to a nearby pillar – 'No food or drink permitted in the library.' I pitched the mega-chocolate bar into my handbag, pulled out a packet of wet wipes, gave my fingers a dab and flung an irreverent smile at Walter.

28

The librarian handed *The Art Newspaper* to me like a relay runner reluctant to pass on the baton and then evanesced into the shadows of the library without even a nod. What a fruitcake. Thank heaven I had not accepted that library science scholarship when I was choosing my career path; otherwise, I might be wearing Wallabies and lurking in library stacks, desperately seeking human contact. The horror! The horror!

* * * * *

As soon as Walter was out of range, I whipped out the Toblerone. It was a box of One by One, containing several different flavors of chocolate, each individually wrapped in color-coded metallic foil. I decided to sample the 'White One.' Although white chocolate contains no cocoa mass and technically is not chocolate, there was nothing as delectable as a confection made with twenty percent cocoa butter. The white mountain-peak-shaped chocolate tickled my taste buds to the max.

I turned my attention to *The Art Newspaper*. It always transported me into the glitzy world of jet-setting art lovers and aficionados. With a general lean towards the sensational, this issue was no exception. 'Museums Beware: *Il Gattopardo* is on the Hunt Again,' the front-page headline read. Exhilaration surged through my body, but I wasn't sure whether the white chocolate or the juicy story was the source of my buzz. I read on as if soaking up a piece on the latest celebrity breakup.

'One of Europe's most infamous art thieves is on the prowl again, claims a confidential source.

Though Interpol has failed to capture one of the most successful criminals of the later twentieth century, evidence suggests that *Il Gattopardo* has come out of hiding.

Key pieces from several major private collections in Paris have gone missing and the only clue left behind in each robbery was *Il Gattopardo's* classic signature, a set of leopard-like scratches on a nearby wall.

Police in France, Germany and Italy have been fumbling, à la Inspector Clouseau, in search of this elusive real-life Pink Panther. Our source suggests that *Il Gattopardo* may be heading to North America to mark new territory.'

It was hard to believe such characters existed in reality. My only exposure to such smooth operators was to the likes of Cary Grant's cunning character in *Alfred Hitchcock's To Catch a Thief*. Cary Grant – there were no real modern-day equivalents in Hollywood these days. I continued skimming through the remainder of *The Art Newspaper* and got sidetracked by the pieces on high society balls and fundraisers and the photos of socialites wearing McQueen and Galliano.

As I neared the end of the periodical, a small headline caught my attention – '*Treasures of the Maya* Lands in Canada.' Shocked, I continued reading.

'The San Francisco Museum of Art and Science need look no further for a new venue for its spectacular traveling exhibit. Following on the heels of Cincinnati's sudden withdrawal from the tour, Toronto's Royal Ontario Museum has stepped in as the new home for the blockbuster show...'

Considering *The Art Newspaper's* lead time must be weeks ahead of its distribution date, Richard was the only person who could have disclosed the story to the rag. He had clearly been scheming on bringing the exhibit to Toronto for some time. But this kind of media leak before the Board had even approved accepting the blockbuster could get Richard into deep water. Why would he risk it?

Chapter Four

After I had shredded the empty Toblerone box and chucked it into the trash, I stashed *The Art Newspaper* between my file folder and zigzagged my way through the desolate stacks of the library. At the exit Walter was behind the counter deep in conversation with Death Metal Chick. With her big and bountiful charcoal mane, she looked as if she were capable of swallowing the dandified Walter behind whom she stood while pointing at a computer screen.

Through the glass wall that separated the library from the galleries, I witnessed security guards stream past like drones. The building was closing and the officers were sweeping it of visitors. If I didn't escape the library momentarily, I would have to cross through alarmed galleries to reach my office. I had only one recourse – bolt. I flashed across the open area, contraband in hand and sped like a demon on fire from the library. As the door swished behind me, I dared not gander back to see if Walter had witnessed the getaway.

The first public announcement warning of the Museum's pending closure echoed through the galleries, propelling surges of guards up stairwells and waves of visitors towards the main entrance. I burst into the office expecting to find Brenda slaving away, but she was nowhere in sight. There was, however, something on her desk that hooked my attention – its nectarous aroma wafted in my direction triggering a sense-memory of Paris.

I drew closer...and closer...and closer towards the exquisitely wrapped delicacy. It was a chocolate truffle. Not just any truffle. It was a Jeff de Bruges made by a chocolatier whose Belgian chocolate delights were available only in Paris and in a few select countries overseas, Canada not being one of them. Surely whoever had left this truffle intended to deposit it on MY desk, not on Brenda's. I extended my hand towards the truffle when the office door flung open and slammed into the adjoining wall.

"Geez, sorry about that," said a male voice.

I one-eightied and exhaled a sigh of relief upon seeing Marco, the fledgling security guard. "They've put you on closing rounds, I see."

"Second time now."

"A pro."

"I scoped the other side of the building yesterday at closing." Marco conducted a stationary audit of the room with the subtlety of crackerjack spy Jason Bourne. "This office is pretty swanky compared to the rest of the offices I've seen."

"We host a lot of outside clients and VIPs, so my boss wanted it to be a cut above. All the artwork belongs to my boss."

"The masks are awesome."

"But the Turkish rug," I said, pointing to an opulent Kayseri piece á la *Wheel of Fortune's* Vanna White, "that's mine."

"Why isn't it in your home?" said Marco.

"I'm living in a shoebox and don't have room for it."

"Refused to take anything in the divorce settlement, huh?"

This kid should be working for Interpol. But my personal life was none of his concern. "I'm trying to keep my carbon footprint as small as possible, actually."

"Interesting."

"How did you know I was divorced?" I said.

"Just a guess. I didn't see a wedding ring. And I can't imagine someone like you not having been previously snapped up."

Was that a compliment?

Marco perused the shelves behind my desk. "You have a lot of books on art."

"Italian Renaissance, mostly. I did my Master's thesis on art patronage in Northern Italy."

"Really? My mom was from Northern Italy."

"Do you speak Italian?"

"A little," said Marco.

"Do you know the word *gattopardo*?"

"That's the name of the thief they suspect of taking our opals. The word means leopard."

My eye lids retracted. "What do you mean?"

"It's a large member of the cat family—"

"I know what a leopard is. What do you mean *Il Gattopardo* stole the opals?"

"That was one of the theories. They found some unusual scratch marks on the case that housed the opals. But if it was The Leopard, it was the one and only time he hit a museum on this side of the pond. The investigators at the time thought our thief was a copycat who had his own peculiar motives for taking the opals."

O...M...G. That was the information in the newspaper article I wasn't able to read because of the damaged paper. As I was about to grill Marco further, the office door opened, and Brenda stepped in.

"Oh!" Brenda iced up at the sight of the security officer.

"Brenda, this is Marco. He's a new guard here."

"Welcome to our nightmare," said Brenda as she swished past him.

"It's not so bad," said Marco. "But there seem to be a lot of, well, unusual people who work here."

Brenda tossed me a smirk. "That's an understatement."

Marco checked the bank of clocks on our wall. "Oh, man, I've got to rocket to the next office. Are you two going to be here much longer? I need to make a notation in my closing report."

"Consider me history," Brenda said.

"I'll be another half hour or so. I'll call the control room when I'm ready to leave," I said.

"Great. *Ciao*, ladies." Marco vanished as quickly as he had appeared.

Brenda swiveled her head towards me like a slow-moving oscillating fan and batted her eyelashes. "Does Kalena have a new Italian friend?"

"Give me a break. I'm old enough to be that bambino's mama."

"Get 'em young and disease-free," Brenda said.

I rolled my eyes. "He probably still lives with his parents."

"You realize what you're doing?"

"What would that be?" I said.

"You're cutting out a whole demographic of possible suitors."

"I don't need a 'sui-tor' who just learnt how to tie his shoelaces."

Brenda's phone rang, and she darted towards it. She

spied the Jeff de Bruges truffle and casually swept it into her drawer. "Hi, mom...Yes, I'll be outside in a sec...I swear. Just hold on. Bye."

"A wonderful evening of mother-daughter bonding ahead?" I giggled.

"That woman is going to unhinge me. I swear, she's on a one-woman mission to eradicate workaholism." While Brenda slipped on her coat, a public announcement sounded from the gallery outside our office. It was the final message advising visitors to leave the Museum.

"Gotta split. Mum's got the old BMW running out front, and I don't want her to die from fumes. And don't forget Geoffrey's coming by in the morning."

"How could I forget about 'our man in London?'"

Brenda popped out the door leaving me *tutto solo.*

* * * * *

So, *Il Gattopardo* may have stolen the Museum's opals, eh. Or was it a copycat? I decided to Google the alleged culprit, but when I yanked out my computer keyboard drawer, it jammed. Stupid contraption – it always ceased at the most inopportune times. After having grabbed a screw driver from a tool box we kept on hand, I hiked up my little black dress and slid onto my back underneath the desk. I was loosening a screw when the office door opened. Now what?

"*Voilà,*" Veronique said.

I drew my knees into my chest and stiffened.

"I told you Kalena would be long gone. I'm sure she had a two-hour lunch as well," said Richard.

Are you kidding me? My hand clenched the screwdriver. It would make a fine weapon.

"I suppose you'll have to make the calls to the west coast museums," Richard said.

"*Moi*? Now?" Veronique whimpered.

"You heard Carson. He wants the *Treasures of the Maya* stats before the Board meeting. Let's go. I still have to check if the library received the latest copy of *The Art Newspaper*. If it reaches anyone's hands before we meet the Board, we jeopardize getting the green light for the exhibit."

I could feel my face blanch. Did I leave *The Art Newspaper* on my desk?

"Do you think that's *possible*?" said Veronique.

"Yes. And without that approval all our planning will have been for naught. And need I remind you how much we all have at stake?"

"*Oui, oui*, Richard. It will make a big difference to all our lives."

The door creaked open and closed. The air was inert once more. My thighs spasmed.

CHAPTER FIVE

It was some minutes before circulation returned to my legs and I was able to crawl out from under the desk. I pulled my dress back into place and yelled out loud, "Shiiiiiiiit!" The residual numbness in my body was replaced with nausea.

I dove towards Brenda's desk and heaved open the top drawer. It was dotted with a dozen Jeff de Bruges truffles. WTF? If she had all this chocolate in her desk, why had she force-fed me cocoa powder like a *foie gras* duck on a sugar diet before my meeting with Richard the other day?

My eyes glazed over while staring at the truffles and the delicacies grew dwarfish heads and limbs. They screamed up at me, "Eat me! Eat me!" I slammed the drawer shut to muffle the shrieking. How could I steal chocolate from Brenda? No, just couldn't do it.

I scooped up Brenda's phone and keyed in a number with trembling fingers. "Hi. It's Kalena Boyko in Museum Consulting," I said to the security guard on the other end of the line. "I'm on my way out of the office, so if any alarms signal in the Mineralogy Gallery, it's just me passing through."

"You'll have to stay put in your office until we get a floater to escort you," said the female officer.

"What are you talking about? I've always exited on my own."

"Part of the new security procedures. Staff aren't permitted to cross through gallery spaces while the Museum's closed, at least not until the new surveillance upgrades are installed."

"I see...Okay, I'll wait here...But I'm in a hurry."

"The floater's near your area. I'll radio the guard right away."

"Thanks," I said and hung up.

I gathered up my things and waited in the hallway at the edge of the gallery. The lighting created by the snakelike fibre-optic fixtures that lit up the myriads of translucent minerals cast eerie shadows on the stone walls, and I was spooked by a movement at the end of the atrium. It turned out to be a security guard, and he gestured to me from afar to proceed across the gallery. Was this the security department's idea of an escort?

When I arrived at the control room several minutes later, I realized I would have to sign out. Richard and Veronique would be logging their departure after me and they might notice what time I'd checked out. Veronique was too daft to make the connection, but Richard might clue in that I was in the building when they dropped by the office. What if he thought I had been hiding in the back room? What if—

A unibrowed officer behind the thick glass partition bellowed into a microphone, "Are you going to sign out or what?"

"I don't suppose we could forget this formality just this one time?" I said.

The creepster channeled a glacier and pointed to the pen beside the journal. No sense of humor. I snatched the pen, scribbled my name and exit time as illegibly as possible, then fled the Museum as if hungry hyenas were at my heels.

* * * * *

Once in the comfort of my own neighborhood, I picked up some vegetarian Pad Thai from a local haunt. My eyes sparkled when I was handed a free three-pack of Lindt's Lindor chocolates with my take-out order. Bonus! When I finally plunked myself in front of the TV with dinner and a pair of chopsticks, I surfed the movie stations for some escapist fare and landed on a favorite – *How to Steal a Million* with goddess Audrey Hepburn and the king of comebacks, Peter O'Toole. 'A romantic comedy about a woman who steals a statue from a Paris museum to help conceal her father's art forgeries (1966)' read the digital TV guide description.

Before tuning into the movie, I had managed to temporarily shove the memory of Richard and Veronique's conversation to the recesses of my mind. But *How to Steal a Million,* thrust it back to the surface. How would *Treasures of the Maya* change Richard's and Veronique's lives? Were they looking to steal a million or, in today's terms, multi-millions to keep Richard in Armani for the rest of his life? For that matter, something like the gold jaguar mask could keep the entire population of Lichtenstein in Armani. And these days there was a plenitude of gazillionaires who would give up their souls for a piece like that. My brother had told me about Russian mobsters he had met in business meetings who had private art rooms whose contents were of dubious provenance or on the list of banned or restricted trade items. And these sociopathic owners lacked any fear of legal repercussions. Were Richard and Veronique in cahoots with some ne'er do wells? Their ethics were certainly questionable, but were they criminals?

Brain-drain was settling in, and I was ready to call it a night. I chop-sticked the last of the Pad Thai and changed into a stretchy lace camisole and yoga shorts. Since my thighs were still a tad sore, I began to massage them. But there was something strange about their texture. They looked rippled and bumpy. I leapt to my feet and illuminated every light in the room and grabbed a substantial pinch of leg flesh. How was this possible? I was at the gym almost every frigging day. But there was no doubt about it – my legs were infested with cellulite. Was this some kind of cruel joke? I had turned forty, my second marriage ended just weeks later and now I had legs chock-full of cellulite. Damn it – where had I buried those Lindor chocolates?

CHAPTER SIX

The next morning, I tumbled over to the side of my bed and tuned into pop iconoclast Marilyn Manson singing his deafening cover of the Eurythmics' *Sweet Dreams*. I slammed my hand on the radio alarm clock, ending the cacophonous wake-up call and pushed aside a few panels of the weathered vertical blinds covering the window beside my bed. Threatening clouds steamrolled in towards Toronto off the lake. On a low-pollution day, Hamilton, the city in which I had grown up, could be seen across the bay. The smoke stacks from its infamous steel mills, now defunct for the most part, served as a regular reminder of the leap I had taken, over twenty years ago, from small-town life to a thrilling world in a bustling metropolis. Okay, some days were more thrilling than others.

The thick plastic blinds swung back into place, and the digital clock's luminescent green numbers brightened in the dimness. The blood in my body shot to my heart, leaving me in a state of shock. It was eight o'clock.

How had that happened? The alarm had been set to 6:30, but evidently the connection on the volume control had loosened again. With only an hour before Geoffrey was scheduled to arrive at the Museum, all I could think about was wolfing down some chocolate. I raced to my miniscule kitchen where countless quartz crystals hung from the plastic grate covering the enormous fluorescent light fixture over-head. The crystals were supposed to infuse me with positive energy and serenity. Clearly there was a crystal malfunction this morning. I flung open the beige melamine cupboard drawers two at a time, and my heart pumped as the unspeak-able truth unfolded before my eyes – there was not a single ounce of chocolate to be found anywhere. Was my kitchen truly devoid of chocolate? Was the universe so dreadfully harsh? Where were the sniffer dogs when you really needed them?

Although my condo was barely larger than a postage stamp, there were nooks and crannies everywhere. There were hiding places – secret hiding places – secret hiding places where I'd stashed away supplies of chocolate in case of natural or man-made disasters that might leave me ship-wrecked for months at a time. Unfortunately, I pillaged my reserves more frequently than I replenished them. Secret hiding spot? Who was I kidding? How could you conceal something from yourself unless you suffered from a serious memory disorder? Maybe I did have a serious memory disor-der. Maybe I was just seriously disordered.

What about the German chocolate-covered marzipan that Stewart had brought back for me from one of his Euro-pean trips? Surely, I'd not consumed it, especially since mar-zipan made me retch. My sightline landed on the bijou silver tin in which the expensive marzipan had been lovingly pack-aged. A new surge of hope ebbed through my body, but as soon as I picked up the light container the anticipation was dashed by a tidal wave of despair. Still, I opened it up because maybe, just maybe, there was one last remaining morsel. I jimmied the lid off with a knife, but only the chichi foil wrap-

43

pers remained. Had I been in some altered state when I polished off the goods? Or perhaps I'd awoken this morning in some kind of parallel universe where things weren't quite what they seemed.

I tossed the marzipan container aside and macheted through the cupboard containing my baking supplies, not that I baked, but I usually kept some semi-sweet baking chocolate on hand for desperate times. This was a desperate time. Damn, no baking chocolate. But I spied something even better, something considerably sweeter than baking chocolate – organic chocolate chips. The universe was not as brutal as I'd imagined. I flung a handful of chips into my mouth, dashed to the washroom and almost catapulted head first into the bathtub. Botticelli's tranquil Venus floating upon a half-shell smiled back at me from the shower curtain that broke my fall.

After a few splashes in the shower, I rifled through my wardrobe for the perfect outfit for Geoffrey's visit. The closet interior looked like a crayon box with clothes arranged in color groupings – the reds and pinks in one area, the greens in another and the purples, blues and other hues each aligned in the other sections. Despite the colorful palette, my eyes were drawn to the browns – the color of chocolate – very comforting. At super-human speed, I pulled on a brown suede skirt, struggled into a snug mocha turtleneck and tugged on a pair of chestnut imitation snakeskin boots with deadly heels.

I returned to the kitchen in search of something nutritious after I had finished dressing. I slid the blender into the middle of the counter, filled it with spring water, threw in half a cup of vegan protein powder, a tablespoon of Salba, a heaping teaspoon of freeze-dried açai powder and two handfuls of chocolate chips. After all, chocolate was made from a bean. And a bean was a vegetable. So chocolate was a vegetable. The chocolate chips spun around like asteroids in the far reaches of the galaxy and clanged against the glass pitcher as the blender kicked into high gear. There was no time to wait for the tiny nuggets to disintegrate, so I poured a large tumbler of the chunky beverage and chewed as I gulped down the liquid breakfast. The clock on the stove read 8:31. I could still make it!

Once out of my building and on the street, I hailed a taxi. "The ROM," I shouted, startling the driver. Inside the car, my spiked heel pierced a newspaper on the floor and, as I plucked it off, I recognized it as a trodden copy of *The National Inquisitor*. There, in large black type set against a fluorescent yellow background was the alarming cover story title – *Stars with Cellulite*. Below, large red arrows pointed to dimpled thighs and exposed butt cheeks of numerous celebs in revealing bikinis. I peeked at the cabby's rearview mirror and discreetly tucked the newspaper into my bag for closer inspection later.

When I arrived at the Museum, Marco was on duty at the Staff Entrance. *"Buon giorno,"* he bellowed before I stepped fully through the door.

"Buon giorno." I looked around to see if anyone had witnessed Marco's zealous greeting.

Marco snatched up a large envelope and covered up a book at the side of his desk. The spine was still visible and the title was a familiar one – *The Arts of the Italian Renaissance*. "Cool outfit...by the way," he said.

"Uh, thanks." I'd have to find an appropriate moment to tell Marco how old I was and nip his burgeoning case of puppy lust in the bud.

When I landed at my desk, I had a few minutes to spare before Geoffrey was scheduled to arrive, but it wasn't enough time to make a pit stop at the library. "Brenda," I said, holding up the copy of *The Art Newspaper*, "can you return this to the library for—"

"Not on your life. You're not sending me to do your dirty work. And I do not want to run into that weirdo, Walter." Brenda shaped her hand into the form of an 'L' and raised it to her forehead. "That man's a loser with a capital 'L.'"

"Okay, okay." I chucked the small newspaper between my project files and exited the office, but no sooner had I crossed the hallway then someone's arm slid around mine, giving me a start.

"Geoffrey. Where did you come from?" Geoffrey's cobalt blue eyes gave the magnificent minerals in the gallery some stiff competition.

"I was in desperate need of a delightful companion to chaperone me to Stewart's office, of course."

This man synthesized the suaveness of Sean Connery, Roger Moore, Pierce Brosnan and Daniel Craig all into one heavenly creature. How he'd landed in museum work instead of the movie biz was beyond me. But no one was more grateful than I to have such eye candy in my presence, even if infrequently.

"Brilliant," I said. Geoffrey looked a bit perplexed by my dreadful Bridget Jones accent. Clearly, I was no Renée Zellweger.

When we arrived at Stewart's office, he was on the phone. "Yes, dear. I swear, no more junk food this week...Yes, I have the sandwiches you made right here." Stewart picked up a paper lunch bag and launched it into the trash bin.

46

Geoffrey turned towards me and whispered. "Must be Patsy." I released a ridiculously silly giggle.

"Okay, sweetie, Geoffrey and Kalena are here. Miss you…Yes, shall do."

"Can you believe those two have been married for fifteen years and are still in love?" Geoffrey said to me.

"It's some kind of aberration." I hadn't been able to get past year seven in either of my marriages.

Stewart hung up the phone. "You found your way up, I see, with a little help."

"Indeed. I still find the Museum's halls a little labyrinthine."

"Pretty soon you'll be as familiar with the Museum as your grandfather was," said Stewart.

"Your grandfather?" I turned to Geoffrey, and he looked uncharacteristically tongue-tied.

"Have neither of us ever told you Charles Trick Currelly was Geoffrey's grandfather's mentor? They worked together on some of the greatest digs of their day."

"Really? Our Museum's founder? Wow."

Geoffrey continued in silent mode. Was this a modest side of Geoffrey surfacing?

"They helped assemble some of our major collections," continued Stewart.

"That's some legacy, Geoffrey," I said.

"Hmm, I suppose so…Stewart, we really should get started. I have that afternoon flight to catch."

My heart felt punctured. "But you just arrived."

"Stewart and I wrapped most things up last night. And I have responsibilities back at home."

I envisioned Savannah or Alexandrine or whatever his girlfriend's name was picking up Geoffrey at Heathrow in her

Maserati, wearing the latest Versace. I'm sure she didn't have cellulite. "I'll leave you two to carry on, then."

"Congratulations, by the way," said Geoffrey.

"For..."

"Stewart told me about *Treasures of the Maya*."

"Oh, right," I said.

"It will be good for you to have that kind of experience under your belt." Geoffrey looked at my waist, and I felt a blush blossom. "The success of this experiment will determine if Museum Consulting Services gets into travelling exhibitions in a bigger way."

I flashed a look of panic at Stewart. "Oh, really?"

Stewart nodded. "Blockbuster exhibitions are the bread and butter of museums like ours. If we can develop a travelling exhibition portfolio for our department, well, it would be smooth sailing for us."

"Not to put any pressure on you," said Geoffrey.

"I think I'm going to need a regular supply of Thornton's to get me through this."

"If that's all it takes to keep you motivated, we're getting off easy," said Geoffrey. "But we can do better than Thornton's. A friend of mine owns a fabulous chocolate shop in Brighton."

I could barely restrain myself. "Choccywoccydoodah?" I screeched.

Geoffrey and Stewart leaned back as if blasted by hurricane winds. "Why, yes," said Geoffrey.

"Choccywoccydoodah creates the most fabulous chocolate in the universe including some of the awesome cakes and sweets in the Harry Potter movies and in *Willy Wonka and the Chocolate Factory*." I turned to Stewart, grinning. "It really is a marvelous shop. They make these too-adorable chocolate shoes. And their Buxom Ballerinas — off the cute scale...I'll, I'll shut up now."

Stewart swiveled towards Geoffrey. "Have I introduced you to our resident chocolativore?"

CHAPTER SEVEN

"Sorry about that monologue on chocolate," I said to Geoffrey as we ambled towards the staff entrance.

"No apologies required. I quite enjoyed the enthusiastic outburst. Most refreshing." Geoffrey tilted his head downwards towards my ear. "And thank you for once again acting as my guide in this maze."

"Anytime. By the way, that's fascinating about your grandfather and Charles Trick Currelly. How did they first meet?" I said.

"That's a long, boring story."

"Boring? I doubt it."

"Has your team done any preliminary layouts of the Maya exhibit yet?" said Geoffrey.

That was an abrupt change of subject matter. "Uh, no. I haven't even received the detailed artifact list yet." We rounded a corner of the snaking hallway. Up ahead, Walter lumbered towards us, made momentary eye contact and broke into a run.

"Kalena!" Walter screamed.

"Walter, I was going to drop by the library as soon as I dropped my guest off." I pivoted towards Geoffrey. "Feel free to go ahead, Geoffrey. You don't need me to sign you out."

"Not at all. I suspect this is going to have an amusing outcome," said Geoffrey.

"Not likely." Walter burned a hole through me with his eyes.

While rifling through my file folders in search of *The Art Newspaper*, I was side-swiped by someone who had manipulated the turn on the wrong side of the passageway. It was Richard, and his body slam sent my files soaring, our papers commingling in mid-air. *The National Inquisitor* and *The Art Newspaper* sailed towards the ceiling, as if in slow motion, and dropped to the floor. *The Art Newspaper* was covered by a mass of 8 x 10 photos that had been knocked from Richard's hands, but *The National Inquisitor* lay on top of the heap.

Geoffrey picked up the gossip rag and gasped. "*Stars with Cellulite.* Such salient reading material, Kalena."

I snatched the paper from Geoffrey's hands. "I bought it as a joke. I thought Brenda might get a laugh out of it."

"Brenda reads this kind of trash?" Walter said.

"No...never mind," I said.

Richard rolled his eyes. "This is utterly annoying."

Walter swooped down as if avoiding a soccer ball aimed for his head and scooped up *The Art Newspaper* from underneath the photographs. Did Richard catch that?

"Bye, Walter," I said. The librarian appeared offended at my brusqueness, but I was in no mood for a lecture on library protocol, especially in front of Geoffrey. Based on the blank look on Richard's face, he had not seen what it was that Walter had plucked off the floor. And I wanted to keep it that way.

Walter continued on his route, and the rest of us knelt down like a group of over-dressed mushroom pickers to sort out the melee of papers on the floor.

"These photos are almost as interesting as your *Na-*

tional Inquisitor," Geoffrey said, holding up a couple of photographs of Maya ceramics and of a gold jaguar mask.

I irised-in at the shots. "Are these from *Treasures of the Maya*?"

"Yes...no," Richard said.

"That was a committed response." Geoffrey studied the photographs intensely.

"And you are?" said Richard, grabbing the photos from Geoffrey.

"Geoffrey Ogden. I run the Museum Consulting Services office in London."

"Ogden." Richard's expression approached a snarl. "One of the Mayfair Ogdens?"

"Why, yes? Do I know you?"

"This is Richard Pritchard from Exhibits," I said, straightening up.

Richard and Geoffrey popped up off the floor. Geoffrey's pallor had turned sickly.

"Geoffrey, are you alright?"

"Of course." Geoffrey turned towards Richard. "I understand you're the clever man responsible for bringing *Treasures of the Maya* to the Museum."

"Yes, I am." Richard peacocked his chest forwards. "But I suggest you and your family stay out of the Museum's affairs."

"What are you talking about, Richard?" I said.

"Perhaps your Mr. Ogden can answer your question. I'm running very late thanks to this unnecessary delay." He tucked the photos into a folder and turned to me. "By the way, I dropped by your office last evening, around six, but you weren't there."

"I had a meeting that went on until after closing." I

hated the fact that Richard could turn me into a pathological liar. "What did you want?"

"It's of no consequence. I had to deal with it myself." Richard did an about-face and proceeded down the hall.

"You or Veronique?" Shut up! Why did I say that?

Richard halted, but didn't turn around. I pictured sluggish gears grinding in his brain while he puzzled over my comment. He had not mentioned that Veronique was with him when he visited my office.

"Who is Veronique?" Geoffrey said after Richard was out of earshot.

"His doltish lackey." I grabbed Geoffrey by the arm and dragged him towards the building's exit. "But what was all that about with Richard?"

"I have no idea. Ogden is a common British name. Perhaps he has me confused with someone else."

"Are there many Ogdens in Mayfair?"

"Well, no...Yes. It's of no consequence. Don't worry yourself about the matter."

"Ooookay. But did you notice anything unusual about Richard's photos?"

Geoffrey raised one eyebrow. "For instance?"

"There weren't any labels on the backs of them — just dates marked in pencil with question marks beside them."

"Perhaps they were publicity shots."

"Pictures intended for the media would have been captioned on the back. Plus, those photos were shot by an amateur. They were off-center and looked as if they'd been taken through glass." And if Richard's photographs were 'official' pictures, why had he not passed on a set to me? I was the one who was supposed to be organizing this damn exhibition.

CHAPTER EIGHT

M arco beamed when I stepped into the staff entrance, but his spark vanished as soon as he spotted Geoffrey at my heels.

"You're on your own from here," I said to Geoffrey, "unless you want me to hail you a cab."

"I think I can manage that part on my own." He removed his temporary ID badge from his immaculately tailored suit and placed it in front of Marco. "I believe I return this to you, young man."

Seems I wasn't the only one who thought Marco looked like an adolescent.

"You have that right, sir." Marco seized the badge from Geoffrey and checked it against the visitor log. "Hope you had a pleasant visit, Mr....Mr. Ooden."

"That's Ogden. And, yes, thanks to Kalena my meetings here are always agreeable."

"I'm sure." Marco's ears had turned a vibrant shade of purple.

Geoffrey laid his hands on my shoulders and pecked me on the cheeks. The hairs on my arms stood to attention. "Cheers, for now. But I'll return soon, I promise."

Geoffrey's departure from his usual formal handshake made me feel as if a blow dart had penetrated my throat and paralyzed my vocal cords.

"Kalena?" Geoffrey snapped his fingers. "Are you with

me?"

"Sorry...I think I may have contracted a case of narco-lepsy. Were my eyes closed?"

Geoffrey burst out laughing. "I think I'm going to miss you. But I really must dash." He swirled around with the drama of a flamenco dancer, waved goodbye and left the building.

"Pretty charming, those English guys." Marco's voice drew me back from the ionosphere. "Who is Mr. Aww-gden?"

"Geoffrey runs our London office. And it just so happens that his grandfather played a critical role in founding this Museum."

"Oh yeah, like how?"

"Well, I'm not sure, exactly. Geoffrey's a little tight-lipped about it. I think he's being modest or something."

"Or something else entirely. Anyways, there's ways of verifying that kind of information." Marco's forehead was creased worse than a linen shirt packed in a suitcase for a month.

"I don't think there's any need to verify anything."

"Right...I guess you don't see him very often, living in London and all?"

"He comes here about once a month."

With smile erased, Marco said, "What does his wife think about that?"

"He's not married."

"Guys like that usually aren't."

"Guys like what?"

"The ones who always say the right thing."

"Have YOU ever been married?" I said.

"No, but I'm not as ancient as he is," said Marco.

"Well, if he's ancient that makes me positively prehistoric." The curatorial center door swung open behind me and an accompanying wave of cold air sent shivers rippling up my spine.

"Hi, Marco." It was Death Metal Chick.

"Uh, hi."

The young woman body-scanned me, making me feel as if I'd been caught in bed with her lover. "I don't think we've met. I'm Aurelia – Aurelia Alberti from the IT Department."

She extended her hand and squeezed mine so tightly I thought she'd fractured some bones. "Right. You're the new person on the Help Desk."

"Computer Technical Services Assistant," said Aurelia.

"I stand corrected. I'm Kalena...Department Administrator, Museum Consulting Services."

Aurelia paused as though processing information from an alternate world and turned to Marco. "Have you gone for lunch yet?"

"I'm taking a late one today." Marco wriggled in his seat and looked down at what appeared to be a schedule.

"Can I bring something back for you...coffee, dessert?"

"No thanks. I'm fine. Thanks. Really," said Marco.

"I'm off then. And I guess you have to get back to your office too," Aurelia said to me.

"Yes, I do, in fact. Have a good lunch," I said.

Aurelia batted her Betty-Boop eyelashes at Marco and passed through the doors. She glanced back long enough to give me the evil eye before disappearing around the corner.

"She's quite ravishing and...strong." I felt my hand for broken bones.

"I hadn't noticed the ravishing part," said Marco.

* * * * *

I made my way back to the office where I found Brenda sipping tea.

"So how was Mr. Bond, James Bond?" Brenda said out of the side of her mouth à la Sean Connery.

"Dangerous, as ever."

"Oh no, please don't tell me you've been swept off your feet by Double-Oooh-Seven?"

I dropped into my chair with a thud. "You're a nutter."

"Don't get me wrong. Geoffrey's great to work with, but need I remind you that he makes your ex look like a boy scout? Geoffrey's had more women than the real James Bond...or the fictional one. You know what I mean."

"Yeah, yeah. You don't have to worry about me. Geoffrey's not my type," I said.

"Are you bullshitting me? He's every woman's type — and every man's type for that matter." Brenda gulped back her tea and reattached herself to her computer station.

Geoffrey's attentive behavior had stirred up some serious butterflies. I had not felt that sensation in a long time but his unexpected flirtatiousness perplexed me. Maybe he was coming down with the flu or maybe he was jet-lagged. Or maybe he was in between girlfriends? Whatever the reason, I was sure it was an aberration.

I opened my email and glimpsed a message from Geoffrey sent from his phone. That didn't take long. He must have forgotten something. I double-clicked the envelope and read: 'Managed to catch a cab on my own. I'm so clever, I surprise myself sometimes. ;) Geoffrey.'

Was he on some kind of medication? Or...maybe he noticed I had stopped wearing my wedding ring. That had to be it. He had had a crush on me all along, but was waiting until I was emotionally and officially available. He wasn't a cad after all.

The flurry of heart palpitations ended when a message from Richard marked urgent popped into my mailbox. A double-click opened the email: 'Veronique: Had an unexpected encounter. Come to my office as soon as you're finished with your meeting. R.'

"Oh, brrrrother," I said.

Brenda gawked at me. "What's up?"

"Richard sent me another email intended for Veronique."

"You're going to have to change your name."

Veronique's surname – Bouvier – was right above mine – Boyko – on the Museum's list of internal addresses. Richard's stubby fingers were mouse-challenged, and he occasionally picked my name instead of Veronique's. One of these days, Richard would figure out he had been sending the odd email to the wrong address. In the meantime, I reread his cryptic message. Did Richard's reference to an 'unfortunate encounter' allude to our collision in the hallway? Had he noticed it was *The Art Newspaper* that Walter had picked up from my scattered papers? Or was he perturbed that I had seen his 'secret' photographs of the Maya ceramics and jaguar mask?

Brenda jolted me out of my internal discussion. "So, what did Richard say in the email?"

"Oh, nothing important" I said. Brenda thought the tension between Richard and myself was counter-productive and that our department would suffer in the end if I maligned him. So, I decided not to share the contents of the conversation I had overheard between Richard and Veronique while trapped under my desk. She would think I was a conspiracy theorist and an idiot for hiding like that – and, unfortunately, she was probably right.

Out of the blue, Brenda was hovering over my desk. In my state of reverie, I hadn't noticed her meander to my side of the office. Her hands were cupped closed in front of her. "Are you going to survive?"

"Highly unlikely – I suggest you make funeral arrangements now." I envisioned Brenda, Stewart and Geoffrey dressed in black jalabiyas and seated atop camels at the base of the Great Pyramid of Giza, their robes billowing in the wind as my ashes were strewn over the desert sands.

"Maybe these will help." Brenda opened her hands like a burgeoning flower and released a heap of Jeff de Bruges truffles onto my desk.

My eyes gleamed brighter than the perfectly cut diamonds displayed in the gallery on the other side of our office. "Where did you get those?" I said, ogling the cache of chocolates I had previously seen housed inside her drawer.

"Some freakazoid has been leaving these on my desk, one at a time."

I leered at the truffles again. "You've no idea who–"

"Not a rippin' clue. I'm never around when the person drops them off. At first, I thought you were messing with me by leaving them on my desk. Then I realized you'd never give away any of your chocolate."

"Geez, thanks," I said. "But, why didn't you give these to me the other day, instead of the dry cocoa?"

"I wanted to see if you'd actually down it."

I glared at Brenda. "You're such a pal."

"You have to admit your desperado behavior was pretty, well, desperado."

"I'm so not amused." Who does that to a person? "Have you tried one yet? People have been known to have out-of-body experiences after eating these truffles." I popped one of the truffles into my mouth and let it dissolve.

"Chocolates are your drug of choice, not mine, which is why I don't get why someone's leaving these for me. Someone must have our desks mixed up," Brenda said.

"I think you're right on that count. What are the chances you have a secret admirer?" Regrettably, my co-worker was capable of bringing out the inner evil in me. Brenda's sudden chill was sufficient to stop global warming. "Sorry, payback for the cocoa feeding."

CHAPTER NINE

After my harsh quip, Brenda trudged back to her desk in silence. An apology would only annoy her further, so I adjusted my attention to the Jeff de Bruges truffles. I positioned one in the palm of my hand and sniffed it from several angles, luxuriating in every aroma as if it were a glass of wine. It hinted of orange zest and embodied a suggestion of smoke. The associations were surprisingly simple, yet unusual. I placed the truffle on my tongue and let it melt as slowly as possible. The taste was orgasmic. But fearful that Brenda might go bi-polar on me again and confiscate the rest of the truffles I inhaled the lot in a matter of minutes. The beautiful wrappers floated down, one by one, to my trash bin and blanketed the copy of *The National Inquisitor* I had tossed away earlier. The celebrity cellulite exposé had been intriguing to me, in a pathetic kind of way, but it didn't offer any solutions to those afflicted with dimpled thighs. I decided to see what the Internet had to say about cellulite.

With a billion sites, clearly cellulite was an international crisis, a pandemic for which scientists around the world were looking for a cure. I narrowed the search to 'cellulite solutions' and came up with a more manageable 70,000 references. One heading from a UK website caught my attention: 'Fashion gurus believe new jeans can get rid of cellulite.' Jeans that could battle cellulite? Where could I buy them? I clicked and read on.

Clothing that released serum into your skin? That concept was a bit too sci-fi for me, so I moved on to a site for lingerie that made a woman look good even if she had cellulite. Camouflage was definitely a safer alternative to wearing jeans soaked in pharmaceuticals. I clicked on the link, but was propelled into a site on extreme cosmetic surgery. Graphic images of liposuctions, breast implant surgeries and buttock enlargements flashed across my screen and my computer rang like a pinball machine on speed.

"What the hell's going on with your computer?"

"Dunno, Brenda." The Internet navigator wouldn't respond to my frantic clicking. My computer had been stalling in hang mode for the last week or so and it refused to respond to mouse, keyboard or even a soft reboot. As I ripped the cord from the wall to cut the power, the Director entered the office.

"Good afternoon, Kalena...Brenda."

"Good afternoon, Carson," Brenda said.

I smiled at Carson.

"I wanted to be the first to tell you that the Board has

approved *Treasures of the Maya*."

"Oh, really. Awesome," I said.

Brenda slivered her eyes. Did my 'awesome' not sound convincing?

"We had to do a little lobbying," Carson said, "but we swayed the majority. We will have to ensure, however, that we prove the naysayers wrong."

Translation: Carson would be screwed if I messed up this exhibit. Driplets of sweat dotted my forehead. "I'm on top of it, sir."

"That's what I like to hear, especially since Richard was over-zealous and leaked information to the media about the exhibit coming to the Museum."

"Really?" I said. Guess someone saw the article in *The Art Newspaper* after all.

"I was compelled to do some back-pedaling to explain the papers' knowledge about the exhibit before the Board did, but I believe Richard's intentions were good."

Why was the Director defending Richard?

"I also came here to thank you for the tour you conducted for the contingent from Hong Kong. The situation is looking very positive for a contract with them to design their new gem gallery."

"That is great news, sir." I looked over at Brenda and from behind Carson's back, she gave me a two-thumbs up. She approved of my enthusiasm quotient. "But can I ask you a question, sir?" I said to Carson.

"Most certainly. What is it?"

"While I was conducting the tour, the director of the Hong Kong museum mentioned something to me about some history between our museums."

Carson pulled up a chair and leaned in towards me. "I'm

surprised he brought that up. It was rather uncomfortable between us for many years. I'm not sure if you are familiar with the fact that we were once robbed of a rather spectacular opal collection."

"I did hear about it, yes."

"The thief was never caught, but almost twenty years later the opals turned up in Hong Kong. Unfortunately, they were no longer considered Museum property because the Museum had been compensated for the loss by the insurance company."

"Really," I said, "I didn't know it worked that way."

"I'm afraid so. They landed in the hands of Sotheby's who in turn put them up for public auction. Our mineralogy department hoped to purchase them, but the Hong Kong Museum of Natural History outbid us, and the opals are now part of its collections."

"Seriously?"

"Most seriously," said Carson. "But much time has passed since all of this occurred, and we are trying to mend the relationship."

Especially if that relationship involved a lucrative contract benefitting the Museum coffers.

"And, Brenda, how is the Lisbon project progressing?"

Brenda, who had tuned out of the conversation once Carson had hushed his voice, spun her chair around. "It has my full attention, sir."

"Excellent. Now I must be off. I'm addressing a group of Toronto businessmen at The Empire Club this afternoon." Carson rose. "Wish me luck."

"I doubt you'll need it, but good luck," I said.

As soon as Carson departed, Brenda came over and picked up the plug from my computer. "What was this all about," Brenda said, swinging the cord.

"I was on a website that launched me into some crazy plastic surgery site and pop-ups possessed my computer."

"Fuck, let's hope Big Brother doesn't trace the problem back to you." Brenda raced back to her desk.

"Can you translate please?"

"The site you visited must have breached the Museum's firewall and clogged up the network. It was down to about a quarter of its usual speed. The bad news is IT can figure out the source of the problem...Damn, there it is," Brenda said, eyes anchored to her computer screen.

"What?"

"The email from Big Brother."

I shook my head. "Is there a good-news side to this?"

"It's an all-staff email."

"Huh?" I said, sounding as if my IQ had dropped to two digits.

"Instead of singling you out, which they easily could have done, IT sent out a generic reminder to all staff."

"Let me see that email." I sprinted across the room to Brenda's desk and peered over her shoulder.

'Reminders on What Constitutes the Misuse of our Internet Connection.

Please remember that while using your computer, here at the Museum, there are certain practices that we must ALL follow. We all share one Internet connection (therefore, we have limited bandwidth). The public uses the same bandwidth when they access our website.

Sometimes utilization on this connection is at 100% capacity. When we look into the details of use, we sometimes see internal users taking up much of it.

Just a reminder that we must NOT misuse our computers while here at the Museum for certain things such as:
- *watching/downloading streaming video;*
- *listening to an internet radio station;*
- *downloading and installing software;*
- *downloading music;*
- *viewing websites unrelated to Museum business.*

Please use common sense when using this connection.'

CHAPTER TEN

"Have you heard anything from the IT Department?" Brenda said to me a few days after my 'misuse of the Internet.' We strolled down the bowling-alley-like atrium towards the Museum's cafeteria.

"So far, so good. No direct censure," I said.

"I bumped into Walter this morning." Brenda created an L-shape with her hand and tapped it to her forehead.

"You shouldn't be so mean. He's harmless...and actually quite cute without his glasses," I said.

"Have you been drinking? Anyway, he told me the new IT Help Desk hire messed up one of the library's databases and IT has been working twenty-four-seven to repair it."

"Death Metal Chick?"

"I don't know, but if it weren't for them having to do all that damage control, they may have had time to spank you. You could have been fired for your infraction, you know."

"For surfing the Internet?"

"Uh, yeah, considering it wasn't for work-related purposes."

"Okay, okay. I get it." I checked my watch. "I have to boot it. Richard's probably in the cafeteria already."

"Remember to keep the claws drawn in."

I smirked at Brenda and darted out.

* * * * *

"Will that be together, sir?" said the Museum cafeteria cashier to Richard. She wagged her finger between Richard's half-regular, half decaf-espresso and my iced chocolatino.

"No!" Richard said.

The minxish young woman looked puzzled as she handed Richard change from a hundred-dollar bill. I paid for my items and raced after Richard, zigzagging through throngs of children looking for a spot to sit down in the overcrowded eatery.

"What are all these ankle-biters doing here?" Richard said. "This is ridiculous. Let's go to my office." Richard spun around and sped off again as I trailed several meters behind him.

"We're taking this meeting in my office," Richard barked at his assistant, Deepa.

"But your desk hasn't arrived yet," said Deepa.

"I still have chairs, don't I?"

"Yes, sir." Once Richard stepped into the office and was out of Deepa's view, she raised her arm in a Nazi salute.

"You're going to get caught one of these days," I whispered to her. She snickered and nudged me into his office.

"What happened to your desk?" I said to Richard.

"Ugh. It was so inappropriate. I have an antique desk coming in."

Since when did the Museum's equipment budget cover antique desks? Or was he paying for it out of his apparently bottomless pockets?

I handed Richard a set of documents.

"What's all this?" Richard puckered up his face like a dried up old apple.

68

"The first document's a project schedule."

"What do you want me to do with it?"

"It would be helpful, Ri-chard, if you went through the timeline and flagged any dates that need to be revised or add any milestones I may have missed. I'll forward an electronic copy to you so you can make changes directly to the file."

"I don't have this program installed on my computer. I have people who deal with this for me. Send it to Deepa."

"Whatever." I shook my head rapidly as if that would keep it from bursting. "The next schedule is the list of meetings I've set up with different departments."

Richard picked up the spreadsheet and pursed his skinny lips. He was probably the only person on the planet to whom I would recommend lip enhancement surgery. "After you've met with everyone, draft me a summary report."

"If you're attending the meetings, why should I waste my time doing a report?"

"These dates are set for the next two weeks. I won't be here."

"What do you mean? This is a critical planning phase, especially with the truncated timeline," I said.

"I've arranged a junket to Seattle, San Francisco, Los Angeles, Miami, Cincinnati and New York."

These cities had all hosted *Treasures of the Maya* except for Cincinnati, which was the city that was supposed to have been the last stop of the exhibit until they pulled out. I rubbed my throbbing temple. "Did you ever think it would be useful for me, or at least one of the preparators, to visit the museums?"

"The travel budget won't accommodate a third person."

Third, I puzzled.

"Veronique will be accompanying me."

I'd taken a swig of my chocolatino and almost sprayed it out like a cartoon character. "Are you kidding me?"

Richard handed my documents back to me. "So, carry on. That will be all for now."

I clutched the papers and stomped out of the office. Richard closed the door behind me, barely missing my butt.

"Looks like that went well," said Deepa.

"Unbefuhqinglievable," I said.

"I presume you're referring to his upcoming travel plans. I told him you should be accompanying him, but he insisted on taking Veronique."

"What bonds those two together other than the fact that they are soul parasites?"

"I'm still trying to figure it out," said Deepa.

"And what's with him redecorating his office à la Bill Gates?"

"I can only presume a long-lost relative bequeathed him a fortune. He just bought a house in Rosedale, too."

It took a moment before the oxygen that was sucked out of my lungs replenished and I could speak again. "And he can afford a place in an old-money neighborhood how?"

Deepa raised and dropped her shoulders. "And he's renovating top to bottom, to boot. I have to deal with all the calls from his contractor and decorator."

"Why do you put up with his crap?"

"Same reason most Museum staff stay here – we're unemployable anywhere else." Deepa winked at me.

When I returned to the office, I felt like smoke was still fuming from my nostrils.

"That was a quick meeting," said Brenda.

"Richard's a tool. I don't want to talk about it."

"O-kay. Well, did you hear about the Indianapolis Art

Gallery?"

"No, should I have?"

"Someone carried off one of their prize Rembrandts."

"You're kidding. It must have been worth some serious coin."

"Eight digits," said Brenda.

"Yikes."

"And the thief left some claw marks where the canvas had been hanging. They think some fruitcake European art thief is running rampant again."

I craned my neck forward. "*Il Gattopardo*?"

"What?" said Brenda.

"Oh, nothing...Wasn't Richard in Indianapolis lately?"

"About a month ago. He was there for some conference."

Or scoping out a Rembrandt? That would cover the cost of a house in Rosedale quite nicely. If Richard was up to something seedy to finance his opulent lifestyle, I was determined to uncover his contemptible behavior.

CHAPTER ELEVEN

'Dear Kalena: No further data is available on the theft of the Rembrandt,' read an email I received from Marco several days after the heist in Indianapolis. 'There seems to be a tight lid on the matter which probly means investigators have some leads, but don't want to tip off the thief. I'll make contact if I have any new information to report. By the way, I rented *The Agony and the Ecstsy* the other evening. Charlton Heston played a convincing Michael Angelo.'

What a goof! Did Marco really think watching a historically inaccurate film about an Italian Renaissance artist would score points with me? It didn't. Neither did his typos. But his earnest attempt to dig up some dirt on *Il Gattopardo's* recent job did impress. Unfortunately, my curiosity had to be moved to the backburner for the time being. The endless barrage of *Treasures of the Maya* meetings was depleting the life force from my body. At the same time, the adrenalin surge created by the hyper-activity was occasionally as invigorating as a chocolate rush – well, almost.

The task of staging a travelling exhibit was a massive undertaking. The project needed a 3-D designer to create a layout of the objects and cases as well as a 2-D designer for signage and labels. And, I needed strong curatorial support. Although the exhibit originated at another institution, we typically added objects from our own collection to make a special exhibition even richer, creating a great opportunity to feature some of our own treasures normally hidden in our vaults.

Other meetings on my calendar included those with support departments like Registration, whose staff oversee collections entering the Museum and ensure all artifacts in the upcoming exhibit have been acquired legally; Preparators whose highly skilled staff creates mounts for artifacts and is responsible for installing the precious and often fragile items in cases; and Conservation that oversees environmental conditions for objects on display and repair any damage sustained to artifacts in transit. Marketing, Publicity, Programs, Security and Shipping were all on my list as well.

I tried to allocate Museum staff to the project wherever possible, but many of my colleagues were already overworked, necessitating hiring some outsiders. With our Head of Shops on maternity leave and her assistant on the verge of a nervous breakdown, I agreed to cover the salary of an external buyer whose sole focus would be the exhibition. But being in the midst of the holiday buying season, most retail consultants worth their salt had already been scooped up. Consequently, I ended up with an oddball who agreed to take the job despite her own considerable commitments. By the time I nailed her down for a rendezvous, we had already lost several weeks in a very tight timeline.

On the morning of the meeting, I picked up a voicemail message from the consultant. "Hello, Kalena. It's Gert, Gert Muller, the woman you are meeting with today," she said in a very staccato-like manner that made me pay attention. "I will be arriving at 11:00 sharp as agreed upon. I am very much looking forward to meeting you and working with the Museum. Goodbye. Do not try to call me as I am leaving home now."

While waiting for Gert to make her appearance, I dove into a bag of Sunspire SunDrops. The candy-coated chocolate treats made with unprocessed sugar were a healthier version of Smarties or M&M's and were a staple of my diet. The phone suddenly rang, and I identified myself with my usual greeting.

"Kalena. Is that you? It must be. You just said so...It's Marco, and I have a woman here, a Gert Muller, to see you."

"Thanks, Marco. But she was supposed to meet me at the main entrance."

"She said she went there first, but there was a problem. You'd better come down here right away."

"What kind of problem?"

"I, uh, whoa, boy! Down. You need to sign her in, ASAP. I'll explain when you get here." Marco slammed the phone down.

That was weird. I dunked my hand into the bag of Sun-Drops, took a heaping handful and loaded up a pocket in my trendy little suit jacket. It was navy with white stitching and I wore a pair of cute navy and white slingbacks that matched perfectly. I'm sure the stylists from the reality television program *What Not to Wear* would take one look at me and say I was 'too matchy-matchy,' but at my age it was hard to break free of a lifetime of over-coordinating my outfits.

While hiking towards the staff entrance and munching occasionally on the chocolates, I heard a 'kerplunk.' One of my SunDrops had fallen and rolled down the hallway. Oh well. There were lots more where that came from. At the staff entrance, a petite woman with a mousy brown 'fro' and a complexion that looked as if she'd been drained by a vampire was seated across from Marco. She gripped a leash attached to a Welsh Corgi that was snarling at Marco. The young security guard leaned away from the desk with arms crossed.

"Thank God you're here," Marco said as I entered the security reception area. "This is Gert Muller and Caligula. They've both been signed in."

I extended my hand. "Hello, Ms. Muller. I'm Kalena."

"Please, call me Gert."

Caligula scurried towards me and Gert snapped the leash. "My apologies. Caligula has problems with manners."

"Caligula's a hearing-ear dog," Marco said. "The folks at the admissions desk weren't sure if they could let him in, so they sent these two back here."

I glanced at Gert and noticed she wore a bejeweled hearing aid.

"It is one of mine," she said.

"Pardon me?" I said.

"I design specialty hearing aids. Most people try to hide them. I celebrate assistive devices."

I looked down at Caligula. "You didn't mention you'd be bringing a dog."

"He has become such a part of my life that sometimes I forget to tell people," said Gert.

"Do I need to speak loudly?" I amplified my voice.

"No. My aid works very well. And Caligula tells me when people or cars come towards me. But he still trains."

Caligula's tail wagged and I stooped down to pet him. As though on a four-legged pogo stick he hopped up and down, and Marco raced around the security desk, planting himself between me and Caligula. "It's okay, Marco. I think he's just a little excited."

"Sit, Caligula, sit." The dog obeyed his owner's command and settled down.

I turned to Marco. "Is it okay if we go to my office?"

"I checked with my boss. There's no policy on hearing-ear dogs, but he figured if seeing-eye dogs are allowed in the building, Caligula could come in." Marco rotated towards Gert. "You may want to muzzle him next time."

"Go ahead," I said to Gert. She passed through the doorway, and I whispered back to Marco. "What have you got against dogs?"

Marco pushed up the sleeve of his pale blue shirt and revealed a scar that looked like teeth marks. "A harmless family pet, so they told me...By the way, there was something I wanted to ask you."

"It'll have to wait until later," I said and ran after Gert and Caligula.

The three of us were part way down the hallway when Caligula stopped, sniffed out the renegade SunDrop I had dropped earlier and hoovered it. It seemed Caligula was a fellow chocolativore. But, wasn't chocolate deadly to dogs? Maybe not in such a small quantity, I hoped.

Gert drew on the leash. "I think I may have to return him to drill camp."

When we reached the office, Gert attached Caligula's leash to the closet doorknob, told him to stay and seated herself across from my desk. Brenda was at an off-site meeting, and we had the office to ourselves. Caligula stood up and raised his nose in the air again. I wondered if he had caught the aroma wafting from the full bag of SunDrops on my desk.

Gert snapped her fingers and Caligula dropped to the ground sporting a doggy pout. The consultant then spent the next forty-five minutes reviewing a portfolio of various wares from Mexican jewelry and pottery to hand woven rugs and basketry. She had actually pulled together a broad selection of goods with which I thought our shop's staff would be pleased.

"That's great, Gert," I said wrapping up. "I'm sorry the acting head of Shops couldn't join us today. But you've left us with lots to consider. I'll pass all these materials on to her."

"Very good." Gert planted her feet firmly on the floor and Caligula leapt up. The woman trundled over to the pooch and showered him with sloppy affection. His tail whirred around like a small propeller. I took the opportunity to pop a few more SunDrops into my mouth and to refill my pocket with the chocolate niblets.

"Is it possible to leave through the front door?" said Gert. "I do not think Caligula was very fond of the security guard at the back entrance. Maybe it was his uniform. We are both suspicious of men in uniform."

"Certainly. I'll walk you to the main entrance and you can leave your temporary badge there."

The three of us advanced towards the door in unison with Caligula sniffing at my pocket.

"My dog appears to admire your suit."

More like the chocolate in my pocket. We forged ahead and wove through the galleries, visitors staring as Caligula hopped up and down as if on a moving trampoline and snapping towards my pocket. Out of the corner of my eye, I caught sight of Marco traversing the gallery at a diagonal. Gert clocked him too, veered away from him and inadvertently shoved Caligula into me. The dog reacted by jumping onto his hind legs and as he raised his front ones, he caught a claw on my pocket. In an attempt to liberate himself, he tugged hard and sent a shower of chocolate SunDrops all over the slick polished limestone floor.

Marco throttled towards us like a hyped drug addict and screamed, "Get off her, you beast."

Caligula freed himself from my clothing and cowered between Gert's legs. Marco dove my way, arms waving, and once within reach, slipped on the candies, legs flying into the air until his whole body was parallel to the floor. He dropped with the force of someone quadruple his weight, and his two-way radio smashed on the hard floor, creating a loud cracking sound that reverberated through the cavernous space. Caligula regained his courage and inched forward to gobble up the chocolates surrounding us.

"Ohmygawd, Marco. Are you okay?" I said.

"What is wrong with this man?" hollered Gert. "Stay away from him. He is crazy," she said while yanking Caligula's leash, sending the canine into gag mode. He retched a few times before regurgitating a putrid puddle of half-digested SunDrops.

Marco groaned, rolled onto his side and grabbed his radio.

"Someone help us. This man is verrückt," Gert shouted.

"Verr what?" Marco depressed a button on the two-way and shrieked into the radio, drowning out Gert's wails. "Officer down, officer down. Send for back up in zone one-dash-zero-two. Officer Zeffirelli has been wounded."

A voice rang over the radio. "Repeat, Officer Zeffirelli, repeat."

"Officer down, officer down," Marco yelled.

I didn't know much about the Museum's security lingo, but I was pretty sure that 'officer down' meant the same thing as it did on the streets. In a matter of seconds, every security officer in the building honed in on us and Caligula started barking as if the country was under attack.

Another message echoed from the radio. "Police units are on their way. Is the shooter still in the building?" All the guards in sight, stopped in their tracks.

"What'd they say?" Marco said.

"They think you've been shot," I said.

"Oh shit," said Marco. He lifted his radio, but the fire alarm sounded and a voice came across the loud speakers. "All visitors are requested to leave the building. This is not a test. Please evacuate the building immediately. This is not a test." Caligula began howling and a phalanx of police officers pushed through the main entrance into the gallery, hands poised at their pistols.

Gert picked up Caligula and clutched him in her stubby arms. "We're all going to be killed!"

Marco gazed at me with his gorgeous green eyes. "They respond really quickly around here, don't they?" Marco said, grimacing in pain.

"The Israeli consulate is right across the street. No other tourist site in the city is more prepared for a terrorist attack than we are," I said, smiling half-heartedly.

Marco propped himself up on his elbows. "Just in case this goes down badly and I don't have a chance to speak to you later, my sister gave me some tickets to the ballet, and I was wondering if you wanted to go with me. Do you?"

CHAPTER TWELVE

After Marco was wheeled away in an ambulance and I had escorted the visibly shaken Gert and her trembling companion from the building, I was left behind to meet with our Director of Security, Malik Roumanos. Fortunately, we had an excellent working relationship, and when I explained to him what had led to the city's SWAT team descending upon the Museum, I couldn't have asked for a better spin-doctor. 'The Museum was able to test out its new terrorist response procedures, and security staff successfully evacuated the building in record time' he wrote in his report to the Director. 'Loss of revenue at the admissions desk was negligible as the building was closed less than ten minutes and resulted in only two refunds.'

Nonetheless, poor Marco took the biggest hit on several levels. He had been rushed to emergency at a nearby hospital where he was diagnosed with a 'badly bruised tailbone.' Subsequently, Malik determined Marco's response to the Corgi's 'attack' as overly zealous and deemed his radio language inappropriate. A message such as 'security officer has slipped on floor' would have been more suitable, he had told Marco. Malik had no other choice, with Marco being a recent hire and still on probation, but to give him a disciplinary warning.

A few days after the 'terrorist attack', Richard returned to Toronto, but he evaded my calls and ignored my emails.

He finally surfaced at a staff Lunch n' Learn lecture, a program initiated by the Director's office providing staff an opportunity to showcase its research. The crowd that turned up for the talk on 'The Cretaceous-Tertiary Boundary Controversy' was a mixed cast of characters.

I had no idea what that title meant, but it frightened me that there were people who did, including Brenda. She had accompanied me to the presentation but had decided to do so only after her mother had called to ask if she was taking a lunch break. Walter was also in attendance and sported a new pair of Wallabees. Veronique, who was seated beside Richard, appeared minus the Hermes head scarf and with a new spiky asymmetrical haircut that she must have had coiffed in L.A. or Miami. Aurelia, whose Band-aid skirt I thought was going to split upon sitting down, settled in a row in front of Walter. Every time someone entered the room, she whipped her head around and then glared at me before returning her gaze to the front. What was that about?

Carson introduced the speaker, a perky young thing with passion to spare about her specialized subject matter. She waxed on about the massive extinction of organisms from plankton to dinosaurs and made reference to iridium, a rare element in the Earth's crust. Somehow, the two issues were related, but despite the lecturer's enthusiasm, I nodded off part way through the presentation. Brenda poked me in the ribs as the curator spoke of a monumental collision of an extraterrestrial object with Earth.

A few moments later, Aurelia turned around and waved at someone. I twisted my head slowly and saw Marco duck out the doorway. Aurelia's eyes met mine, and her smile turned into a spooky glare. Had she somehow discovered Marco and I were going to the ballet together in a few days?

When Aurelia suddenly leapt to her feet and zipped from the room, she startled those around her. Had she raced after Marco?

When the curator ended her presentation and the hearty applause from the audience terminated, I darted to a vending machine at the back of the room, tossed in some coins and pressed the button for a Mr. Big chocolate bar. The corkscrew mechanism pushed the last Mr. Big towards the front of the dispenser where it stalled. The winding apparatus continued to rotate, but Mr. Big failed to fall down the chute.

"Hasn't your chocolate addiction created enough havoc around here recently?" Richard snickered like a mad scientist as he stepped towards me.

"Hello to you too, Richard," I said.

"I hear they shut the Museum down and one of the guards was injured."

"Freak combination of circumstances," I said. "By the way, I tried calling you in Cincinnati but couldn't reach you."

"I don't know why not. Deepa had the number to the hotel."

"It seems you never checked in."

"That's ridiculous," said Richard.

Veronique approached us before I could further grill Richard. "*Bonjour*, Kalena. I understand you caused quite a commotion here last week. All hell broke loose, as you English say."

"Depends on one's definition of hell," I said.

Veronique looked befuddled. "There is only one definition of hell, is there not?"

"Interesting hair cut you have there," I said. "What do you call it, neo-punk?"

82

"Do you like it?" said Veronique. "I have received many comments about it."

"I'm sure," I said.

Veronique leaned in towards me. "People say I look twenty years younger."

Richard rolled his eyes, grabbed Veronique by the elbow and dragged her out of the room. Within seconds, Brenda skipped over to me.

"Golly gee, thanks for bringing me to the lecture. I can't wait to share my new knowledge about chondrites and isovalines at my next dinner party," said Brenda.

"Knowing you, you will probably find a way to work it into your conversation," I said.

"Richard looked pretty pissed when he left. You know, the two of you really must learn to play together." Brenda refocused her attention to the vending machine behind me. "What's going on with that thing?"

"It's gone into meltdown mode." I started pounding on the side of the machine when we heard a commotion. It was Walter banging his Wallabeed toes on every other chair as he stumbled down the aisle.

"Hello, ladies. Stimulating lecture, wasn't it?" said Walter, somehow managing to have arrived at our sides in one piece. "I can't wait for next month's event, 'The Persistence of Memory in the DNA of Catfish.'"

"Oprah's creating a show on her network on that exact subject," said Brenda.

"Is that a fact?" Walter removed his glasses, but they slipped out of his hand, and he fumbled like a juggler to catch them. Despite his improbable save, he exuded such embarrassment that we felt tremendously ill at ease.

"I've got to get back to the office and make a call to Lisbon before they shut down for the day," said Brenda.

"I'll be back in the office in a bit," I said. "I'm going to try to get my chocolate bar out of this psycho dispenser."

"Shall I escort you part way?" Walter said to Brenda.

Brenda looked at me with quiet panic. "I, uh, suppose." She pivoted and took a step. Walter followed directly behind her and planted one of his size-tens on the back of her heel. Like a wounded puppy, Brenda yelped and the stragglers in the room turned and stared.

"Oh, my goodness. I'm so dreadfully sorry. Are you injured? Shall I call a medic?" said Walter.

"I'm fine," Brenda said, limping towards the door. She looked back at me and mouthed 'help.'

"Shall I carry you?" Walter said.

"Don't be ridiculous," Brenda yelled. Then, she and Walter almost smashed into Marco in the doorway.

Marco sauntered towards me. "What happened there?"

"A foot-to-foot collision," I said. "This Museum's a dangerous place to work in."

"That fact is becoming more and more evident every day."

"How's the back?"

"It's still a little tender when I sit down," said Marco, "so my boss took me off the staff entrance and put me on rounds the last couple of days. It's easier being on my feet." Marco eyed the snack dispenser, swung around to the rear of it, unplugged the unit and carefully tilted it forward. My Mr. Big fell into the retrieval bin.

My eyes lit up. "Thanks." I snatched up the candy bar. "I believe Aurelia's on the hunt for you."

"I'm sure she'll track me down. I think she was a blood-hound in a previous life. She seems to know my every move," said Marco. "But, I...I wanted to double check that we're still on for Saturday...for the ballet."

"I have to say, you really don't strike me as a ballet kind of guy."

"Busted. But I thought you might be a ballet kind of girl, so when my sister gave me the tickets, I thought..."

"I'm not a girl, Marco. I'm over forty and been married a couple of times." I waited for Marco's jaw to drop, but his expression remained deadpan.

"I know. You met both of your husbands here at the Museum," he said.

"Did you do a background check on me?"

"One of the other guards told me...I couldn't believe it...I mean, you don't look a day over – well, I get the feeling you're fun to hang out with."

"Have you been smoking crack?" I said.

"And you've got an interesting sense of humor."

"Listen. I've never had any *Mrs. Robinson* fantasies."

"Is that someone I should know?" said Marco.

"Older woman Anne Bancroft seduces her daughter's boyfriend played by Dustin Hoffman." I waved my hands. "It doesn't matter. What I'm trying to say is, I usually go out with men twice your age."

"You date sixty-year olds?"

"You're thirty?" I said.

"A couple of months ago."

"I have cellulite."

"So do I."

I couldn't resist giggling.

"I do," said Marco. "I have cellulite-butt. C'mon. Just go

to the ballet with me this once. I've never been."

"I must say I haven't been to a ballet performance in a long time," I said.

"So, we're on?"

"Yes. But it's not a date. I'll meet you at the center, and I'll go home on my own."

* * * * *

"Hello," I said into my cell phone.

"Hello, Kalynechka," said my mother in Ukrainian, cueing me to switch to my mother tongue.

"Oh, Mom, I'm so sorry. I meant to call you back. I had such a busy week."

"We thought maybe you had been murdered."

"You don't have to worry about that happening to me."

"You hear about it all the time. Women living on their own in Toronto die, and no one realizes they're dead until they do not show up for work...Why are you breathing like that? Do you have a chest cold?"

"Is she sick?" my dad said in the background.

I stopped in my tracks. "I am not sick. I was just walking. I am on my way to the ballet."

"The ballet? The tickets are very expensive, I understand."

"A friend is treating me."

"A friend? What kind of friend?"

"Just a friend," I said.

"Pavlo, Kalena has a date...to the ballet."

"No...Mom...no. It's not a date. He's just a friend."

"Well, that's how it starts," said my mother.

"Is he Ukrainian?" my father bellowed.

"Tell him it doesn't matter. It's not a date," I said.

"It would be nice if you married a Ukrainian boy this time," said my mother.

I rolled my head back, my mouth agape to the overcast sky.

"Kalena...Kalena...are you there?"

"I have to go. I don't want to be late."

"Why didn't he pick you up? It's not safe to walk the streets at night in Toronto."

"This Casanova did not pick her up? Does he not own a car?" said my dad.

"Mom, I have to go."

"Okay. Bye, Kalynechka. Have fun."

I tossed my BlackBerry into my purse and pressed on. Despite the telephone interruption, I arrived at the theater a few minutes early. But it was starting to sprinkle rain and my chic cocktail purse, covered in real feathers from a bird to which no harm had been done, I hoped, was too tiny for an umbrella. The box office looked far more inviting, so I headed indoors and tucked myself into one of the lobby's corners.

There was no sign of Marco, so I pulled my BlackBerry back out and tuned in to an old Patricia Kaas album. The smoky voice of the French-German songstress transported me back to happy times studying in the South of France. I'd had quite a crush on the school's film programmer who was a good decade younger than me, but at least we shared a common passion for independent film. What had I been thinking by agreeing to 'hang out' with Marco? I slid my thumb along the top end of the gadget, adjusting the volume and looked up to catch a glimpse of a familiar face on the opposite side of the box office lobby – it was Richard.

Ohmygawd! Ohmygawd! Of all people, I did not want to

run into him. I was pushing myself further into the corner so Richard couldn't see me when Marco sprang out of nowhere, frightening me out of my shoes.

"Hi, Kalena. Sorry I'm a bit late. They wouldn't let me park in the underground lot, so I had to drive around the block a few times looking for a spot on the street."

"What?" I was peering over at Richard.

"Ah, it's a stupid thing. The muffler's trashed, and the car backfired when I pulled up to the attendant's gate. He didn't want to let me in. He said the backfiring might give some of the blue-hairs who park there a heart attack."

"Oh, okay." I slouched down trying to keep out of Richard's sightline.

"Are you feeling all right?" Marco said.

"Yes....No. Actually, I just saw Richard, and I DO NOT want to talk to him."

Marco twisted his head from side to side. "Are you embarrassed to be seen with me?"

I hadn't thought of that. "Uh, no. I just have no desire to see that pill outside of work hours. Even worse, Veronique might be close behind."

"That airhead? She walks around with her lights turned off most days."

"Indeed."

"Let's grab our seats," said Marco. "This place is humungous. I doubt we'll run into him again."

I peeked around Marco. "Wait a minute. He's not here with Veronique."

Marco pivoted, and both of us witnessed Richard give a woman a peck on the nape of her neck.

"I thought he was gay," Marco said.

"ME TOO? Maybe he's bi." I periscoped around Marco

again and ogled the tallish, lean woman. "There's something familiar about her. She kind of looks like a Modigliani Madonna. Maybe we can snap a picture of her."

"Why?" said Marco.

"I know it's going to sound crazy, but I think Richard's up to something diabolical, something to do with the Museum, and this woman could be involved too."

"Like what? A heist?" Marco chuckled.

I paused. "Could be." Marco looked at me incredulously. "Richard's been acting suspiciously lately, and he seems to have wads of money from God knows where. I'll fill you in later, but right now I just want to get a picture of that woman."

Marco whipped out his cell phone. "I upgraded the camera feature on this phone. It takes awesome close-ups."

"Brilliant."

"But what do you plan to do with the picture?"

"Maybe we could take it to Interpol and have her IDed."

"This is Canada, Kalena. We have the CSIS."

The performance center's warning bells chimed. "We don't have much time," I said. "They'll be dimming the lights soon. Oh no! Richard and his friend are heading this way."

Marco plunged towards me, pressing me into the corner with his body. He tilted his head down with his face just inches from mine. Heat radiated through our pores, and we both blushed.

I went up on tippy toes and craned over his shoulder. "Okay, they've passed into the next lobby area."

We raced towards the hall's entry doors and caught sight of Richard's date. She wore a stunning royal blue jacket that was easy to track in the crowd. The couple cruised by the ticket takers, and Marco and I dashed after them.

"The escalator to the right and up two levels," said the female ticket taker.

"Huh?" I looked at the tickets. Our seats were in the nosebleeds, and Richard and Ms. X moved directly ahead to the orchestra level. "This could be a problem." I snatched Marco's arm and dragged him towards the next set of doors. "They won't let us past here with these tickets. You're going to have to do this on your own. I'll distract the usher at the doorway so you can sneak through. Just take the picture and run. I'll wait here."

"You sound like you've done this before."

"I've had lots of practice sneaking into restricted areas of theaters during Toronto's International Film Festival."

I pushed my way in front of Marco, pulled out a catwalk prance from somewhere deep in my psyche and turned over on my high heel just in front of the usher. As I grabbed the railing, the usher came to my rescue, and Marco ducked around him.

"Are you all right, miss?" said the employee.

"These damned heels." Past the usher, I was just barely able to see Marco inside the hall panning the crowd. He halted, ran to the side aisle and raised his phone only to have an usher slam his arm down.

"Did you sprain your ankle?" said the usher.

"I don't think so."

"Where are you sitting? May I see your ticket?"

Suddenly I heard Marco in altercation mode with the usher inside the hall.

"Your ticket, miss?"

"Oh, sorry. Here it is."

"Your seat's in the mezzanine. You'll have to go back out this hallway and take the escalator."

"Now I really feel foolish," I said.

A light flashed from inside the theatre, and I witnessed Marco being escorted by ushers on each arm. Crap.

I fled down the corridor, back into the lobby and around to the other side. The ushers trod towards the coat check area with the prisoner still between them. The trio paused within earshot, but an attendant from the front door approached me.

"Can I help you, Ms?" he said.

"My date's running late. I thought I'd wait here."

"We won't be able to seat you until there's a break in the performance."

"I understand." I turned my attention back to Marco and the ushers.

"Sir, we're going to have to ask you to delete that picture," one of Marco's escorts said to him.

"But it's just a photo of the auditorium," Marco said.

"There are no photographs allowed inside the hall. We've explained this to you over and over. What part did you not understand?"

Marco raised the camera and fidgeted with it as the ushers stared at the LED display.

"Thank you, sir. Now, if you would you like to go back inside, you're going to have to check the phone."

"I don't think so. I'll just leave, thank you very much."

I made a beeline for the exit.

"You're giving up, Ms?" said the usher stationed at the door as I sped by.

"I'll wait outside." I grinned then barreled into the street.

Moments later Marco caught up to me. "Keep on walking – fast."

"What's up?"

"I can restore the deleted photo, but I have to do it before this thing goes into auto pause."

CHAPTER THIRTEEN

M arco and I scooted down the block into the heart of the city's theater district. The street was almost silent now that most people had streamed into various theaters lining the avenue. We spotted a bench ahead and plunked ourselves down.

"I think I got the shot, but give me a second," Marco said. He depressed a couple of buttons on the phone.

"Did Richard and his paramour see you?"

"I don't think so."

"Are you sure? It looked like you stirred up quite a commotion," I said.

"Those lovebirds seemed more interested in snuggling than in anything going on around them," said Marco, fidgeting with his camera. "Success! The shot's been retrieved."

We gazed towards the LED display. The picture was perfectly focused thanks to the built-in zoom. Unfortunately, the person seated in front of the pair completely blocked out Ms. X's face.

"Oh, man. That guy must have moved at the last minute," said Marco.

"Nice try."

"Oh, man, not only did I mess up the picture, but I ruined our evening at the ballet."

"It was my fault. And to be perfectly honest, modern dance is more my thing."

"But we're all dressed up and, well, no place to go. And that purple outfit you're wearing is pretty snazzy."

"You don't think it's too Justin Bieber?"

"He wears dresses?"

"Not that I'm aware of. But purple is his favorite color. Don't ask me how I know that."

Marco howled until air hunger hit him.

"Listen," I said. "I have an idea. There's a rep cinema minutes away, and I've been dying to see Pedro Almodovar's latest movie."

"What movies has he been in?" Marco said.

"He's a Spanish director, not an actor. He launched the careers of Antonio Banderas and Penelope Cruz, and his films are huge."

"Cool."

"This isn't going to be your average Hollywood adventure flick," I said.

"That's okay."

"It's subtitled."

"Uh-huh."

"And it might not have a linear story line," I said.

"Whatever that means, but I'll try anything once. My car's parked a couple of streets over."

I looked down at my feet. After my walk to the performance hall and galloping around the building, they were throbbing.

"You wait here. I'll get my car and pick you up."

"I'll grab a paper and check the movie times."

"See ya' in a few minutes," Marco yelled, already half-way down the block."

I was folding the newspaper when a car horn sounded, and a Gremlin halted in front of me. Who drives a Gremlin?

Hadn't they all exploded by the early 1980s or were those Pacers? I drew near the car. It looked as if it had been painted with a brush, and it was a hideous orange.

Marco popped open the door from inside the car and a large cloud of dust escaped. "Need a lift, miss?"

Giggling, I descended into the seat. At least I would be able to tell my parents my so-called date had a car.

"I'm glad you have a sense of humor," said Marco. "After you said you didn't want a ride, I loaned my sister my other car. I bought this beast at an auction last week."

"Must've been a sweet deal." I looked down at the seat. "Is this denim?"

"This was a special edition Gremlin with a Levi's denim interior." Marco jammed on the accelerator and we sped off.

"Interesting design concept."

"I know it's a little grungy right now, but it's a collector's item. By the time I'm finished with this car, it'll be a beauty, and I'll probably triple my investment."

I stared blankly at Marco.

"Actually, there's a pretty interesting story behind these things," he said. "In the seventies, AMC heard that Ford and General Motors were coming out with a subcompact car, but they couldn't afford to design a new vehicle. So, one of their designers came up with the idea to chop off the back end of a Javelin."

"Ingenious."

"Are you making fun of me?" Marco said with a glint in his eye.

"You deserve it." A huge blast fired out of the car's muffler, and people on the street lurched with fright. We began to laugh uncontrollably when Marco stomped on the brakes. He jammed the car into reverse and screeched into a parking spot.

"Now what?" I said with my heart thumping a million times a second. We were still blocks away from the cinema.

"Stay put. I'll be right back." Marco vanished and came back a few minutes later with a bag from the Rocky Mountain Chocolate Factory.

"I get the impression you like chocolate," Marco said.

I peered inside the bag and my stomach flipped.

"Chocolate-caramel praline candy apples...for the movie. Hope you like 'em."

CHAPTER FOURTEEN

'This morning's body combat class is cancelled' read the sign at the gym's reception desk. Really? What was I going to do about a workout? With the scrumptious chocolate-caramel praline candy apple Marco treated me to on Saturday night followed by a Sunday night chocolate feast I had indulged in, my calorie intake over the weekend was OTT. Over the top sugar intake required an OTT workout to incinerate some major calories.

"I guess you saw the sign," said the receptionist.

"Ya' think?"

"Don't worry. You can take the spinning class instead." The young woman's perkiness was unbearable on a Monday morning.

"Spinning? I have a frigging bike phobia."

"Oh, these bicycles don't move."

Give me strength. I lollygagged en route to the change room and then slipped into a one-piece, knee-length leotard with a sexy open back. The outfit was far too chichi for a spinning class I realized as I caught up to a group of young jocks on the way to the spinning studio wearing nondescript T's and biker shorts. Their cellulite-free thighs gleamed in the early morning sunshine that poured through a band of windows. Once in the room, they raced to their favorite 'horses,' checked the pedals for God knows what, and adjusted the seats.

"First time?" said a husky voice behind me.

I spun around expecting to see a man, but it was Cassandra, the spin class queen bee. The voluptuous Amazon's daunting presence tied my tongue.

"I always get some run-off anytime body combat is cancelled." Cassandra bulldozed me towards a bike. "Just fake it," she whispered.

I inhaled as though it was my last breath ever. How hard could this be? I fed my leg through the bicycle and slid awkwardly to the other side without landing my butt on the seat. Another indelicate hoist and butt-to-seat contact was achieved. Unfortunately, my feet dangled several inches above the pedals, so disembarkation was in order. Was I supposed to swing a leg behind me as if climbing off a real bike or bring the leg through the center and land with both feet at the same time? I opted to swing both legs back like a gymnast dismounting a vault. My feet thudded to the ground, and the regulars snickered. Cassandra glanced my way, gave me a thumbs-up and pointed at the knob on the back of the seat. Yes, I knew how to adjust the height of the seat.

It took some major pushing and tugging, smacking and clanging, but I was finally all set. Cassandra broke into a series of whoops and hollers and led the class like an army drill sergeant. The concept of 'working at your own pace' was clearly foreign to her. By the end of class, an embarrassing puddle of sweat had formed beneath my bike and Cassandra slipped in it when she came over to question me about my blood pressure. She confessed she had never seen anyone turn as red as I had and suggested I see a doctor before spinning again.

"I'd rather contract a deadly disease than participate in

another spinning class," I whispered under my breath while wobbling towards the exit. Feeling quite spacey, I made my way towards the change room.

"Hey, Kalena."

I rotated as if tipsy — it was Marco, looking Hollywood sexy in his workout gear and evidence of a six-pack visible under a snug CBGB's T-shirt. Hot, hot, hot. "Hello there. What are you doing here?"

"After you told me about your gym, I thought I'd check it out and they gave me a free membership for a week. Guess we'll be gym rats together."

"Woo hoo."

Marco examined me with the intensity of a dermatologist checking out a mole. "You look like you're going to pass out or barf or something."

"I just did a crazy-ass spinning class."

"Did they make you hold a hundred-pound weight while you pedaled?"

"Ha...ha." I tilted my gaze towards his T-shirt. "Ever been there?"

Marco looked confused.

"CBGB's."

"Oh...no. Never had a chance. Would've been crazy awesome to have gone to the final show. Patti Smith was the headliner."

"I know, I know," I said. "I love her. *Because the Night* is THE best rock ballad in the history of the universe."

"You have pretty strong feelings about certain things, don't ya'?"

"Do I?"

"Like about Richard."

"I can't argue with that."

"Well, I found out some pretty heavy-duty stuff about Richard."

My ears perked up like those of a German Shepherd that had detected a scurrying squirrel. "I just saw you Saturday. How could you possibly have dug up any dirt since then?"

"When I went home yesterday after the gym, one of our neighbors popped in. His family's been in the security biz for almost half a century. I happened to mention the opal theft, and he told me that heist was the talk of Toronto's security industry for years."

"I thought you said you had some scoop on Richard."

"Richard's father was chief administrator of the Museum when the theft happened."

"NO...FRIGGING...WAY." Richard's father was the man I had seen in the newspaper article I had uncovered in the library. How had I missed the resemblance?

CHAPTER FIFTEEN

"C'mon, c'mon, dish it," I said to Marco. My body felt as if I was experiencing an earthquake of immeasurable amplitude.

Marco glanced at his watch. "I can't right now. I have to get to work."

"There's no way you're going to leave me hanging like this."

"I'm on probation. I can't afford to be late."

I stifled a frown. "I hear ya'. You better run."

"I'll give you a shout on my lunch break."

"You better, or I'll have Aurelia hunt you down."

"Spare me." Marco spun on his heels and darted away.

"Hey, Marco."

"Yeah," he said without turning around.

"Thanks for Saturday." I noticed Marco's stride change. Was that a little happy skip in his step?

After cleaning up, I left the gym and dropped in at the local Shoppers Drug Mart to pick up some energy food. I proceeded to the snack section wondering if the store carried...? Yes, there it was – cranberry crunch trail mix with chunks of chocolate. Through the clear plastic packaging, I noticed the first package was a little lean on chocolate so I moved on to a second and a third, setting each on the shelf below as I moved on to inspect the next.

"May I help you?" said a young Asian woman.

"I'm just picking out some trail mix."

"These are all the same." The woman barricaded herself between me and the shelf.

I retracted. "Usually, but sometimes the chocolate to nut and seed ratio varies."

The woman's expression turned dour. "I'll be at the cash register when you're ready."

I kept three bags of the trail mix and circled around the corner to the next aisle where a can resting beside the pantyhose section caught my eye. 'Spray-On Stockings,' said the package. What a curious concept. I read the label:

'Spray-On hose, designed to provide the look and feel of pantyhose without the discomfort contains:

Hydrolyzed silk-infused leg-befitting ingredients

Caffeine (to treat cellulite)

Green tea extract (for firming)

Moisturizers (for hydrating and moisturizing the skin)'

Leg-befitting ingredients? Someone was actually paid to write such bad copy? But who knew caffeine was an anti-cellulite treatment? Too bad caffeine upset my stomach. But could this stuff truly camouflage my pitted thighs? I whipped a can from the shelf and took it to the checkout counter along with the three bags of trail mix.

"Are these the right ratio?" said the clerk I had encountered in the snack section.

"Yes."

She picked up the can of Spray-On Stockings and studied the label.

"This looks interesting. Does it work?"

"I hope so."

After I had paid for the goods, I made my way to work. En route I could not help smiling about the botched night at the ballet. Following the movie, Marco and I had chatted about Almodovar's offbeat story, Marco had departed in his backfiring car, and I had cabbed it home. The fact was I had had more fun with Marco than I had ever anticipated. Who would have predicted?

Once at the Museum, I drew open the heavily tinted glass door and a couple of young children fell backwards.

"I'm sorry," I said. "But it's not a good idea to lean on this door."

The youngsters looked up at me dazed and confused. I pulled the door open all the way and stepped in. Both the foyer outside the control room and the inner reception areas, were packed thicker than a colony of penguins huddled together in a blizzard. Their teachers were crammed around the reception desk and, opposite them, I could make out Marco back at his usual station. He was, I suspected, trying to communicate to the group that they had come in the wrong entrance and needed to exit and re-enter through the school group doorway. Suddenly I glimpsed Geoffrey waving at me in the far corner of the reception area. What the devil was he doing here? I attempted to forge ahead, but it was futile.

"Okay, kids, we have to go back outside," one of the teachers yelled, sparking a hysteria that passed through the children like a wave. Geoffrey lifted a posh paper bag above the heads of the students and said something unintelligible. In the meantime, Marco rounded up the masses and began evacuation procedures herding the school group.

"We'll get you signed-in shortly Mr. Ooogden," Marco bellowed at Geoffrey.

Geoffrey nodded and yelled out in my direction. "I brought you a..." The crowd became unnaturally silent as

Geoffrey completed his sentence. "Choccywoccydoodah Buxom Ballerina."

"Choccy what?" Marco said.

"Choc-cy-woc-cy-doo-dah Bu-xom Bal-lerina," echoed Geoffrey. The children laughed uncontrollably, and Geoffrey turned an iridescent shade of vermillion.

"C'mon, everyone," Marco said. "Clear the way so that young woman can get her Buxom Ballerina."

"What's 'buxom' miss?" I heard one of the youngsters ask his teacher.

"Never mind," he said.

As the munchkins barreled out the door, I plowed forward while Marco scooted back behind the counter. He handed me the visitor login sheet to sign-in Geoffrey and leaned in towards me. "There's someone I want you to meet at lunch," he said.

"I'll see what I can do." I signed the sheet and handed it back to Marco.

"Kalena," Geoffrey said, stepping around the last of the children. "What an absolute madhouse."

"Did I miss an email? I didn't know you were going to be in Toronto," I said.

"It was a last-minute decision. I thought I'd surprise you."

"I'm delightfully surprised," I said.

"So am I. I'm not sure about the 'delightfully' part," Marco muttered under his breath. "Here you are, sir." Marco passed a temporary visitor's badge to Geoffrey.

"The officer had tried calling Brenda—" Geoffrey said.

"She was out of the office...and so was Stewart," Marco said.

"So, I decided to wait for you to arrive," said Geoffrey.

"I'm sorry you were caught up in that tornado."

Geoffrey opened his mouth to speak, but was interrupted.

"How long will you be in the Museum, sir?" Marco said.

"I didn't know I had to provide an estimated time of departure," said Geoffrey.

"You don't." I swiped my ID through the reader, and Geoffrey and I passed into the curatorial center.

"I do believe that security guard has an interest in you," Geoffrey said as we strolled down the hallway.

"I don't think so."

"And he seemed unusually curious about this." Geoffrey lifted the Choccywoccydoodah bag and slipped the handles into my hand.

"The Buxom Ballerina!" I had almost forgotten about Geoffrey's gift.

"It's custom made."

"Oh, my."

"She's wearing a purple tutu and matching ballet slippers."

I looked down at my fluted aubergine skirt and black silk blouse with aubergine polka dots. "Is it that obvious?"

"You mean besides the purple pens, purple file folders and the purple agenda?"

A blush rose up to my temples. "Thanks so much for this. I feel like I've won the lottery."

"I must say, you're very easy to please."

We reached the stairwell that led to the executive's suite. "Shall we see if Stewart's returned to his office?" I said.

"By all means."

"Um, before we head up there, can I ask you a strange question?"

"The stranger the better." Geoffrey's eyes gleamed.

"Have you heard of *Il Gattopardo*?"

Geoffrey's expression turned serious. "Not you, too?"

"Why do you say that?"

"It seems the entire planet is obsessed with the thief. The media in Europe is having a field day."

"I'm concerned the artifacts in the exhibit might be at risk, especially the jaguar mask."

"I don't think you need lose any sleep over the matter. The security here is impeccable."

I thought of the Horse that had recently been lifted and then returned to its rightful place.

"Would you like to go to dinner with me this evening?"

I looked around. "Me?"

"I have a late flight, and it might be a good opportunity for us to become better acquainted."

Even with the few moments I took to collect myself, the response I blurted out was indecipherable. Thankfully, Geoffrey interpreted it as a yes. "Shall we head up to Stewart's?" I said, fidgeting with the ribbons on the Choccywoccydoodah bag.

Geoffrey nodded, and we ascended to the third floor. Stewart was indeed in his office, and at the sight of Geoffrey, a warm smile came over his face. "Well, I'll be. Where did you come from?"

"Boston, actually. I did try your mobile a number of times but it was disengaged."

"Darned battery is done in. It refuses to recharge. Our IT department is ordering me a new one as we speak. Come in, come in. Your timing couldn't be better. Lisbon's putting some pressure on Brenda to push up the completion date of the report and we need to respond."

"They have been relentless. That is precisely why I engineered this detour to Toronto before heading back to London. There are a few things Brenda and I can do to fast track the research, but I wanted to run them by you first."

I cleared my throat. "I'll leave you two to flesh out your plans to rule the world."

"Thank you for taking time out of your morning," Geoffrey said.

"Always a pleasure," I said, trying to suppress the butterflies in my stomach.

Chapter Sixteen

slipped into the ladies' room and evaluated my clothing in the mirror. Although the eggplant ensemble I wore was stylish and flattering in a schoolmarm kind of way, it was not the saucy administrator kind of outfit I would have worn had I known dinner with Geoffrey was on the agenda. There was no other choice. I would have to dash out and pick up something a little more décolleté to wear on my – dared I say it? – date. I had to look smashing.

Giddy with excitement, I flew back to the office. The door creaked as I opened it, and Brenda's head immediately tilted upwards to the row of clocks hanging on the wall.

"I was up in Stewart's office," I said, tucking the Choccywoccydoodah bag under my desk before Brenda turned around. She did not need to know about Geoffrey's gift.

Brenda swiveled around in her chair and extended her palm.

"Is that another Jeff de Bruges truffle?" I said.

"Uh-huh. It was on my desk when I arrived this morning."

"This truffle courier must have a master key."

"Not necessarily," said Brenda. "The cleaning staff is here at the crack of dawn, and they don't always lock up when they leave."

"Well that doesn't help narrow things down other than

it's someone who arrives at the Museum even earlier than you."

"Or it could be elves…you know…they sneak under the door and catapult the chocolate onto my desk." Brenda tossed the truffle to me.

"*Danke schön.*" I swallowed the truffle and felt as though I had swallowed a Happy Face.

"So, Stewart's back in his office?" Brenda said.

I licked the chocolate residue from my palm. "Yup. And he's with Geoffrey."

"What? I thought Geoffrey was in Boston."

"He was. He decided to stop off here and brainstorm with you on the Lisbon project."

"Thank fuck. The clients want me to present the report in Portugal a month earlier than we'd agreed upon even though they're not giving me what I need to wrap the damn thing up. Hell, they haven't even confirmed the planetarium building site."

I raised my arms as if I had been hammered by gale-force winds.

"Sorry about that." Brenda took a deep breath. "Stewart has me doing some preliminaries on the gallery in Hong Kong, and we don't even have a contract yet. I think worms may have bored into his brain and destroyed the grey matter."

"He wouldn't waste your time if he didn't think Hong Kong was a pretty sure thing. Have you ever known his instincts to be wrong?"

"Not yet. By the way, Registration's been trying to get a hold of you. Anita called me trying to track you down. She probably left you a voicemail message…or two. Your phone's been ringing like bananas all morning."

"The head of Registration is trying to contact me? Now

what?"

"It may have something to do with a curator in New York who tested the age of some of the *Maya* artifacts using a new technique he developed. There's speculation some of the objects in the exhibit might not be genuine."

"WHAT? This can't be happening. Surely the artifacts were properly authenticated long before they went on the road," I said.

"Clay objects can be a little tricky. In order to render a more accurate date, ceramics have to be fired above a particular temperature, and the clay has to contain an adequate amount of certain minerals and radioactive materials."

"But I've seen lists of the artifact labels," I said. "The date ranges are quite wide. They intentionally avoided being specific...Okay, okay. So what's the worst case scenario? We correct some of the labels or pull the questionable objects and replace them with more of our own collection."

"Anita said things are a little complicated."

"Of course, they are."

"The New York curator who developed the new dating technique has an ego the size of an elephant...surprise, surprise. He decided to make a big issue of it instead of dealing with San Fran diplomatically. He ignited a feud between the two museums, and San Fran's so pissed now they're talking about pulling the exhibit from New York and Toronto and finding new venues overseas."

"They can't do that," I screamed.

"Do you have a signed contract yet?"

I slumped back in my chair.

"I take that as a no," said Brenda.

"I'm expecting the documents any time now."

"Fuck."

The blinking light on my phone was seriously distracting me, so I picked up the phone receiver and pressed a button. "You have twelve messages. Press one to play messages." Twelve messages? It wasn't even ten o'clock.

"Message number one," said the automated voice.

"Good morning, Kalena. It's Anita. I'm calling to give you a heads-up about a problem related to *Treasures of the Maya*. Call me as soon as you come in."

"Message number two."

"Kalena, are you there? What time is it? This is Richard. I need you to set up a meeting right away. It's about the exhibit. We should include Carson and Veronique. Maybe Stewart as well. I'm not sure you'll be able to deal with this on your own."

Piss off, Richard.

"Message number three."

"*Allo*, Kalena. This is Veronique. Richard said I should call you to set up a meeting. Please call me right away."

"Message number four."

"Hi, Kalena. It's Marco. Guess you're still not in the office. Oops, gotta' go. I'll call you later."

"Message number five."

"I forgot to mention Anita. She's key to this meeting." It was Richard's voice.

"Message number six."

"Kalena…it's Marco again. Have you figured out if you can sneak away for lunch? Or maybe you're busy with that Geoffrey guy."

"Message number seven."

"We should probably invite someone from Exhibits. Maybe Josie or Andrew."

Richard, you're a certified lunatic.

* * * * *

There was another message from Anita, and it seemed as though Richard had worn her down. The remaining voicemails included another from Veronique, one from Carson and two more from Richard, each subsequent one sounding more deranged than the previous one. I called everyone who needed to be at the *Treasures* meeting and had all the major players assembled within half an hour.

At the meeting, Richard sat at the far side of the table and interrupted me every time I spoke. Veronique was at his side. She had added ridiculous streaks to her bizarro haircut and wore a suit with padded shoulders and a Nehru collar. The Hermes head scarf was back. I surmised her brain was melting again, and she was attempting to keep it contained.

Carson chaired the meeting and advised everyone there was little any of us could do. He had already been in contact with San Francisco and New York, but their directors continued to be at odds with each other. Two hours of brainstorming various scenarios including the possibility the exhibit would be diverted from Toronto left everyone drained.

The tension we felt was evident on all our faces as we trudged from the meeting room. A substantial amount of revenue was at stake, and even worse was the risk of damage to the Museum's reputation. The unforgiving Canadian media would find a way to blame the ROM for the mess – 'the Museum should have been more vigilant before accepting the exhibition,' they were sure to report. And if the Museum lost *Treasures of the Ancient Maya,* it would fuel another round of diatribes against the Museum and impact on future funding from the government and donations from the public.

Along with all of that, my career could be destroyed in an instant.

When I returned to the office, it was empty. Brenda was likely in Stewart's office discussing the Lisbon crisis with Geoffrey. I picked up the phone and dialed.

"ROM Staff Entrance, Marco speaking."

"Hey, it's Kalena."

"Geez. You've been awfully busy today."

"I was in an emergency meeting with the Director."

"Speak of the devil. Carson's coming out of Malik's office. Gotta go. Bye."

The phone disconnected. Okay. Whatever. I reached under my desk and grabbed the Choccywoccydoodah bag and clawed it open like a crazed feline slashing at a package of gift-wrapped cat nip. Contained inside was a piece of chocolate in the shape of a voluptuous ballerina of exaggerated proportions and resembling a Fernando Botero sculpture. The hefty danseuse, garbed in a violet tutu and sporting purple lipstick, was positioned in a *passé* ballet pose with arms in fifth position. I mercilessly snapped off the legs and tossed them into my purse. It had dawned on me that I could sneak out and shop for something suitably sultry to wear to dinner with Geoffrey. Yorkville was just around the corner, and although purchasing something there would mean blowing two months' worth of my clothing budget on one article, it would be worth the investment. And the diversion would take my mind off the work crisis. The phone rang.

"Kalena, it's Marco. Can you meet me at Ned's in ten minutes?"

My smile flatlined and my gaze darted to the ominous clocks. Rats. I needed the ability to stretch time the way one could pull sun-softened toffee, but the dark side took over

113

my power of reasoning. "Sure." Did I really hear myself choose the option of getting dirt on Richard rather than shop for something with which I could impress Geoffrey? What was happening to me?

Once outside, I waited for the steady stream of traffic to clear on University Avenue and munched on the chocolate limbs of my precious Buxom Ballerina. The divine flavor and extraordinary texture fit for gods sent me reeling. The final morsels disappeared before I stepped inside the University of Toronto eatery. Ignoring the din of hordes of students conversing, I panned the room looking for Marco. The next thing I knew, someone had slipped their hand into mine and started tugging me.

"This way," said Marco. "Bob and I found an empty classroom. It's much more private."

"Who the hell's Bob?" I said, following Marco like a brainless lamb.

"He's the neighbor I told you about. I managed to convince him to talk to you. I think you need to hear this stuff directly from the source." Marco led me into a room where the lights had been dimmed and the blinds were closed. It smelled of smoke, and all I could see for a moment was the burning tip of a cigarette.

"I'm pretty sure you're not allowed to smoke in—" Marco squeezed my hand, and I stopped in mid-sentence. As my eyes adjusted to the light, we drew closer to a man sporting large mirror-lensed aviator sunglasses and his long, gelled grey hair was pulled back in a ponytail. His sallow skin and jaundiced tone betrayed a lifetime of heavy-duty smoking.

A skeletal hand reached towards me, and I reluctantly extended mine to shake it. "Bob, just call me Bob."

"Okay, Bob," I said emphasizing 'Bob.' "I'm Kalena."

"Bob doesn't have a lot of time," said Marco.

"Gotta get to Mississauga for a covert op I'm running."

It took every smidgeon of restraint to keep from bursting into hysterics. What was Marco thinking? This guy was clearly a nutcase, but I decided to play along. "So...I understand you have some information on the Museum's opal theft and Richard Pritchard's father."

"That's right," said Bob-just-call-me-Bob. "I was a veritable kidlet at the time, but I already had quite a reputation in the security biz. So, the insurance company called on me to reenact the theft."

Marco and I exchanged glances. Suddenly I sensed this guy was legit. "Wouldn't the police be the ones investigating the crime?"

"Doesn't sound like you know how these things work, little lady."

I separated my grinding teeth. "Tell me, how do these things work?"

"Insurance companies drive these kinds of investigations, not the police," said Marco.

"Oh right. I should have known that after all the movies I've seen about museum heists."

"Ha." Bob-just-call-me-Bob broke into a nauseating hack that sounded as if he would cough up both lungs. "Those Hollywood people don't know Jack," he said once the phlegm had cleared.

"I'm surprised they didn't catch the thief on camera."

"Camera surveillance equipment was pretty pricey in those days. Labor was cheaper."

"You're kidding. So, they depended on guard patrols."

Bob-just-call-me-Bob pushed his aviators down sufficiently for me to see him roll his eyes.

"They used passive infrared sensors."

"You mean like those red laser beam things?"

Marco shook his head no. "The Museum used passive sensors. That means they measured heat radiating from objects in their field of view. When the sensor detects a temperature spike, it throws a relay."

"Got it," I said. "Had the sensors been disarmed then?"

Bob-just-call-me-Bob's eyebrows arched above his ridiculous sunglasses.

"That's the point, little lady. They were workin' as per usual. We figured the thief must a' mapped the environment pretty darned precisely. He had to've checked out that space tens of times and figured out all the hot and cold spots."

"Uh, huh."

"But it gets crazier," said Marco. "The thief found a way to mask the infrared signature."

"Translation, Marco."

"The guy found some kind of material with the same signature as the walls in the gallery, like plywood or some kind of special fabric, hid behind it and then moved through the gallery as slowly as possible. Basically, the sensor thought the guy was just an extension of the wall."

"Floor is more like it. I figured he must a' crawled on his back with something covering him."

"That's bananas," I said.

"Not sure what fruit has to do with it, but he was brilliant. Brilliant he was. What this guy did sent a panic around the world. If it could be done at the Royal Ontario Museum, it could be repeated in any museum and anywhere that used passive infrared surveillance, like jewelry stores, banks, you name it. Every security company on the planet scrambled to develop more sophisticated technology."

It felt as if my eyes widened to the size of baseballs.

"Bob, tell her the other part."

I whipped my gaze back to the eccentric.

"There was a second level of security that this guy out-smarted."

"Like what?" I asked.

"The case holding those opals was wired too. The guy somehow bypassed the secondary system. We never did figure out that part. Stumped everyone, it did."

"Wow. But if he went to all that trouble why didn't he take something more valuable than the opals? There were diamonds and emeralds and–"

"Designer theft," said Marco.

I pretended I understood the term.

"Yup, somebody stole those gems for a specific client. Someone wanted them opals bad."

"Do you think it was *Il Gattopardo*?"

"Could've been. Could've been. The Leopard certainly had the skills. But we'll never know for sure. There was no such thing as DNA testing back in the day, and they never collected any samples from the scratch mark."

"Hmm. What about the idea of an insider accomplice?"

"That's where Richard's father comes in," said Marco.

"What, what, what?" I said.

"Like I said before," Bob-just-call-me-Bob said. "The thief either scoped out the gallery over and over and over again–"

"And someone would have noticed a repeat visitor who went into the gallery that many times," said Marco.

"Or it was someone who knew the Museum inside out – like the chief administrator," I said, feeling peacock proud.

"Things looked pretty bad on Benjamin Pritchard, 'cause

117

he'd just laid off a bunch of guards. Finances were pretty tight in those days, but Pritchard's security cutbacks raised some eyebrows. The union was up in arms, and even the papers were all over him."

"And besides that, Mr. Pritchard had an engineering background," said Marco.

"So?" I said.

"He could've had the knowhow about bypassing the wiring in the case."

"Holy smokes. What happened? Were they ever able to prove it? Did he go to jail?"

Bob-just-call-me-Bob pulled a packet out of his denim jacket pocket and tapped out a cigarette. I turned to Marco, but he gave me a best-to-keep-quiet look.

"Well, that's when things turned pretty ugly." Bob lit his cigarette, inhaled deeply, and with his head tilted upwards, blew smoke rings towards what looked like a smoke detector. "A couple of months after the theft, Pritchard turned up dead."

"Oh, no? Was he murdered?"

"Suicide.

I gasped. "How horrible."

"Did it in the Museum. A security guard found him hanging in the underground food tunnel—where they store the food supplies for the cafeteria still to this day. Under his dangling feet, they found pictures of his wife and his kid..."

Richard!

"And a note claiming he had nothing to do with the heist."

I felt sick to my stomach and was going to excuse myself when the building's fire alarm blasted. The three of us all stared at the cigarette.

"Shit. Run like there's no tomorrow. The coppers'll be here in two bits."

CHAPTER SEVENTEEN

The three of us spilled into the street along with everyone else reacting to the fire alarm. But just as I was about to ream out Bob-just-call-me-Bob for smoking, he disappeared into a vintage Lincoln Continental with black tinted windows and drove off into the sunset.

"Is he for real?" I said.

"He's probably been smoking too much dope for too long, but the guy knows his business. He's been trying to retire for years, but the RCMP, CSIS, you name it, they keep hiring him."

"Do you believe the story about the suicide?"

"Oh yeah. Some of the old-timer guards refuse to patrol the food tunnel because of the suicide. I just didn't know it was Richard's father who killed himself there."

"It certainly explains why Richard is so dysfunctional. But why would he want to work in the place that destroyed his father and his own childhood?"

"Redemption, maybe?" said Marco.

"Or maybe he's been biding his time to play his revenge card, you know, waiting in the wings to destroy the Museum's reputation."

"Like stealing the most valuable artifact from the Museum's biggest exhibition of the decade?"

"Can you think of a bigger FU moment?" I said.

"Listen, I hate to keep running out on ya', but I have to

get back to my post or I'm toast."

I peered down at my watch. How did that happen? I actually had time to dash to Yorkville to power shop. "Not to worry. I have to run a quick errand before I go back to the office."

I bid Marco farewell and, as I walked north past Bloor Street, I was still trying to process everything I had just learned about the opal theft and Richard's father. But it was time to change gears. Romance was in the air, and I needed to find something swedgy – a bit of swank and a bit of edge. And Cop-Copine was just the place. Its flagship store resides in Paris near the Centre Georges Pompidou where I stumbled upon it by chance a few years ago. When the French retailer opened a shop in Toronto, I thought I was in Shangri-La.

The clerk recognized me as a perennial browser and directed me to the sales rack. How flattering to be known as a thrifty shopper. But I took satisfaction in knowing the model wannabe probably could not afford to shop in the store herself. I panned through a small rack of clothing, and there it was – the ideal piece. The sultry, sleeveless ink black top had ribbed satin straps and edging along a v-neck. The front was ruched, and the form-fitting mesh fabric possessed just the right amount of transparency.

The piece was on sale for $250 – a bargoon, the clerk declared. I tried it on quickly and asked the clerk to ring it up, all the while hoping my credit card would not be declined. Relief. The charge was authorized. But if I had any urgent purchases in the next months, groceries for instance, I could be in trouble. At least I would look good eating mac and cheese.

I skipped out of the shop, paused at a railing bordering a group of mezzanined stores and drank in the endorphin rush resulting from the purchase of an unaffordable article of clothing. Down below, well-coiffed women with hypoaller-genic Cockapoos and Schnoodles escorted by magazine-perfect men in Gucci with cell phones glued to their ears, strolled past. I would be one of the 'entitled' this evening. As his hotel was just down the street, Geoffrey was sure to treat me to a meal at a high-end Yorkville resto.

Once more, I peeked into the Cop-Copine bag, and the sun reflected off the sateen trim. It was a glorious late Indian summer day and the rays were blinding. I put on my sunglasses, and with the glare reduced, the two figures that ambled on the sidewalk below came into focus. It was Richard and the woman I had seen with him at the ballet. Ms. X wore classic head-to-toe Chanel while Richard wore a ridiculously flamboyant fedora. Was it bad taste or was he trying to disguise himself?

I backed into the Cop-Copine entryway, and once Richard and Ms. X were a good ten meters ahead, I bounded down the stairs and morphed into a stalker. As the pair playfully sauntered ahead, I darted and crouched behind trees, sandwich boards and any other prop that blocked me from their view. They rounded a corner and entered Borovsky Fine Arts, one of many upscale art galleries for which the area is famous.

Not sure what to do next, I bolted to the edge of the bay window that fronted the gallery and stood against the brick wall bordering the glass. Passersby on the sidewalk threw me what-the-hell-is-that-woman-doing glances. Inside, Richard and his mate conversed with a statuesque man against a backdrop of prints, lithographs and small oils by the likes of Picasso, Chagall and Mondrian. Was the scene before me Richard and his accomplice interviewing a fence who might be able to liquidate a gold jaguar mask on their behalf?

With my eyes still fixed on the twentieth-century masterpieces on the gallery walls, I didn't notice Richard and Ms. X roam towards the entrance door until the last moment. Lord almighty. I had to fly at the speed of a Concorde jet and get off the street as quickly as super-humanly possible.

As I sped down the path, I angled a corner and tumbled onto the lawn of the building next door to the gallery. My Cop-Copine bag crunched under my body, but I bounced up almost as quickly as I had toppled. I turned and caught sight of a trousered leg emerge from the gallery. Without a second to spare, I pummeled through the doorway in front of me, the sign on the portal a blur as I passed inside.

The door gave way into a Zen-infused space filled with women who twitched in their seats upon my abrupt intrusion. The reception desk was vacant, and I tried to gauge the kind of operation into which I had stumbled. The women were all impeccably dressed and ranged in age from mid-twenties to mid-sixties. One of the more elderly women had a series of Band-aids dotting the exposed areas of her legs.

Within moments, a woman wearing an ultra-chic uniform materialized on the other side of the desk. We made eye contact, but a stunning beauty seated in the waiting area approached the receptionist and stepped in front of me. It was an ideal moment to escape unobtrusively except when I glanced out the window, Richard and Ms. X were in a heated discussion on the sidewalk out front. I was trapped.

"Can you tell me if there are any side effects when these veins are treated?" said the woman to the receptionist. She flipped up her fringed bangs and pointed to her brow.

"It varies," said the receptionist. "There's a possibility of bruising depending on the individual, but it can be effectively covered with a special foundation we carry at the clinic...And occasionally, but it's very rare...some people develop head-aches. They usually disappear in a few days. The doctor can tell you more about potential reactions when he speaks with you."

I examined the other women in the room more meticu-lously. In the corner sat a woman whose grotesquely bee-stung lips were painful to look at, while the skin on the face of another client was so taut, she appeared to be at the mercy of uncontrollable centrifugal forces. But another glimpse out the window confirmed that Richard and Ms. X were still outside. What could they possibly be discussing so vehemently?

"Welcome to the Yorkville Clinic," the receptionist said, turning her attention towards me. "Can I help you?"

"I'm not sure."

"Oh...you must be the woman who called earlier about the vein assessment?"

"Um, yes. That would be her...uh me."

"As I mentioned on the phone, the vein evaluation is covered by the provincial medical insurance, so I'll need to see your card."

"Sure." I handed my health card to the receptionist. Her flawless face could easily have graced the cover of any of the magazines lying about the room.

She swiped the card through a slot on her computer keyboard. "Here's your card. Now if you could fill out this form and hand it back to me, we can slip you in right away."

"But aren't all these other women ahead of me?"

"Not to worry. They're seeing specific practition-ers...And you inquired about liposuction as well? We'll in-clude that as part of the vein assessment. But I'll need you to fill out the second page too. We require a more substantial medical history if you're considering the additional procedure."

All the women in the room lowered their magazines and cell phones and stared at my butt and thighs. I shot a look out the window and was relieved to see Richard and partner take a few steps. But then they dead-stopped and picked up their discussion again. I breathed a heavy sigh.

"It's getting a little bright in here," said one of the clients.

"It's that time of day, isn't it?" said the receptionist. She pressed a button and opaque blinds lowered over the window, cutting off my view of Richard and his feisty paramour. I deposited myself in a high-backed leather chair and filled out the questionnaire as directed. Beside me rested a bowl filled with Godiva Chocolate Medallions and every few seconds I plucked one up and flung it into my mouth. Rather than cross the room to dispose of the wrappers, I dropped them into my Cop-Copine bag.

"Thank you very much, Ms. Boyko," said the receptionist when I returned the clipboard to her. "You can come right in."

I grabbed my belongings and as discreetly as possible transferred a gluttonous portion of Godivas into the mangled Cop-Copine sack. The receptionist led me to a dimly lit room decorated in subdued earth tones. New age music flowed from hidden speakers and water from a fountain befitting a Buddhist temple trickled in the corner. In the middle of the room stood a long table covered in luxurious velvet and beside it rested a stool hewn from a tree trunk. The receptionist handed me a piece of fabric that matched her elegant uniform.

"Remove your skirt and hosiery please. If the doctor

needs you to remove your under-garments, he'll call in one of the assistants."

The anxiety on my face must have been obvious.

"In case he needs to check the buttocks...for the lipo-suction procedure."

Over my dead body.

"Dr. Moynahan will be with you shortly. All of our clients love him."

"I'm sure they do."

"He'll turn the lights up when he's ready to look at those spider veins." The receptionist grinned and closed the door behind her.

How did I end up stepping out for a quick shopping ex-pedition to having my buttocks checked out by a Casanova cosmetic surgeon? I unfolded the chi-chi hospital gown and slipped it on. The shoes and skirt came off and then the pan-tyhose. Where could I hide the worn hosiery? Aha – the Cop-Copine bag.

As I jettisoned the hose into the bag, a glint from the Godiva Medallions shone at me. There was still no sign of Dr. Moynahan, so I gobbled up the remaining chocolates and pondered what to do with the accumulated mass of wrap-pers. A news bite played in my head. 'Toronto woman dies in freak accident. During one of the city's worst electrical storms on record, the twice-divorced and still single and cel-lulite-ridden employee of the Royal Ontario Museum was struck dead by lightning today. Although the investigation is still continuing, police postulate that her shopping bag—crammed to the brim with Godiva foil wrappers—acted like a lightning rod drawing the fiery bolt to her in, what one wit-ness described as, an unimaginably cruel act of God. She is survived by her cat...Correction...we've just received late-breaking word that her cat died over a year ago, but she kept a photo of the dead animal on her desk at work. A tragic end to a tragic life.'

I tossed the wrappers into the doctor's waste basket and delved into my purse for a mirror to ensure my face was free of chocolate smudges. My hand landed on a metallic tubular object – the can of Spray-On Stockings. It was a sign from the universe if ever there was one. With a quick spritz of the legs, my cellulite would become invisible, and Dr. Moynahan would send me and my unblemished gams away. Embarrassing evaluation avoided. Perfect.

As I sprayed my legs with the miracle sheen, a haze filled the room as though a fog had rolled in. I sprinted to the wall and turned the lights up high. Damn! The cellulite was still visible and, to my shock, I also spotted some spider veins. Where did they come from? This aging process was a bloody nightmare. What was next? Thick hairs growing from my chin?

I realized I hadn't shaken the container of Spray-On Stockings vigorously enough, so I whipped it back and forth as if mixing a can of paint. Before I knew it, streaks of orange-colored liquid streamed from the nozzle and splattered all over the floor, my gown and across the luxurious fabric covering the examination table. Uh-oh. I scrambled towards a box of tissues on the other side of the room and bumped into the trash can. The Godiva wrappers spilled out creating a blanket of metallic snow. I heard the creak of a door. Uh-oh. I was so screwed.

"What's going on in here?" said a voice from behind me.

The can of Spray-On Stockings slipped from my hand to the floor making a loud clang. One last spurt of orange glop spewed out from the defective spray top. I peered through the eerie haze that filled the room and made out the vision that had to be Dr. Moynahan. With the best puppy dog face I could muster, I spoke, "You'd think that by the twenty-first century manufacturers could produce a leak-proof can."

CHAPTER EIGHTEEN

The horrified look on Dr. Moynahan's face as he surveyed the scene of devastation will be embedded in my memory bank forever. He had never experienced anything like this in his twenty years in the cosmetic enhancement business, he told me. Lunacy, sheer lunacy, he kept repeating. Guilt-ridden and feeling foolish, I tried to explain my behavior. The discovery of cellulite in my thighs had been traumatic and compounded with my divorce, my cat's death, insurmountable pressures at work and financial concerns, I was very fragile. Eliminating my spider veins and cellulite, I thought, would give my spirit and self-esteem a boost, but when I entered the examination room, I had a change of heart.

Dr. Moynahan had witnessed about-faces before, but no one had ever turned the clinic into a wasteland of toxic fallout he said. Toxic fallout! I said. Oh no. I was certain if manufacturers had created a product that could be sprayed on one's legs, it was eco-friendly. The doctor appeared unconvinced and, for an instant, I toyed with the idea of telling the truth, how I had entered the building in an attempt to hide from my demented former boss and his partner in crime, but I feared the doctor would call for the men in white coats to come and take me away.

I swept the Godiva wrappers towards the center of the room with my feet and suggested to Dr. Moynahan he look on the bright side. What bright side would that be, he wanted to know. Telling the story at his next gathering of vein doctors and cosmetic surgeons would make him a big hit I said. The doctor was not amused. Would my insurance be charged for the visit? I asked. After all, the consultation was never completed. Dr. Moynahan glanced at my legs and advised me that I did not have varicose veins, so yes, I would be charged for the appointment. He asked me to leave as soon as possible and to never return to the Yorkville Clinic. But– I said. Never, ever, he interrupted. I had five minutes to get dressed and evacuate the building. Was there a rear exit? I asked. No, there wasn't. But surely – "Five minutes!" he screamed.

I slithered out of the examination room and into the reception area, sunglasses on and shirt collar pulled up as if that would make me invisible.

The receptionist was on the phone. "Yes, we need someone from maintenance to do a mop-up. It's an emergency. We have appointments booked in the room all day long...Oh, Ms. Boyko, here's your receipt."

"It's okay," I said and tore out the door.

It took me under ten minutes to hoof it back to the Museum, and I headed straight for the cafeteria to grab a bite.

"Lunch on the run again?" said a chipper voice as I picked up a salad. It was Deepa, Richard's assistant.

"Sort of. You too?"

"Sort of," she said.

"Is Richard still running around like a headless chicken?" I wondered if he had returned to the office from his outing.

"I don't think so? He took the afternoon off to drive someone to the airport."

"It must have been someone pretty important if Richard abandoned the Museum with all this controversy going on."

"The man does NOT think logically," said Deepa. "He left

for lunch as if nothing had happened."

"I suppose he has Veronique holding down the fort."

"Not today. She took the afternoon off as well."

Did she go to the airport with Richard?

"Join me for some tea?" said Deepa.

"Wish I could, but I must dash." .

"Ugh, I should too."

"By the way, I know it's none of my business, but did Richard mention where he stayed in Cincinatti?" I said.

"He said he and Veronique stayed with a mutual colleague."

"Richard doesn't strike me as a house guest kind of guy."

"Just thinking about him in a dressing gown creeps me out," said Deepa. "Anyway, I'll see you later." Deepa turned around, her long black hair swaying gently with her movement.

I paid for my salad and was heading down the corridor when I saw Marco ahead. "Marco, Marco."

"Hey, long time no see," he said grinning.

"I just saw Richard and his girlfriend in Yorkville and trailed them to an art gallery. Maybe the owner's into some illegal dealings on the side."

"Which gallery?"

"Borovsky...Borovsky Fine Arts," I said.

"That's a Russian name. I wonder if the dealer has ties to the Russian mob."

I gasped.

"I'll see what I can find out on the Internet," said Marco.

"Oh c'mon. Do you seriously think when you Google the gallery there's going to be a page on art fencing and money laundering?"

"Nooo. But you'd be surprised what can turn up. Mobsters are characteristically fearless and in denial about repercussions."

"O-kay." I was not totally convinced.

"Maybe we can regroup after work," said Marco.

"Today? Sorry. I have a commitment."

Marco's enthusiasm evaporated. "No probs. I'll check it out at home tonight...if I can kick my dad off the computer."

"You live with your parents?" I knew it. I knew it.

"Just my dad. My mom passed away a couple of years ago, so I moved back in with him. He wasn't doing well on his own."

"Sorry about your mother." I was such a heartless idiot.

Marco cranked his neck towards me. "Did you know you have some orange stuff in your hair?"

"What?"

"It looks a little like the color of my Gremlin...And there's some on the side of your face too."

"Oh, lord."

"Got a little carried away with your makeup this morning, did ya'?"

"I don't wear foundation. Crap. I thought I got it all."

"What is it?"

"Just some goop from a defective spray can." I whipped out a mirror and wiped the residue of the Spray-On Stockings from my face.

"I guess you didn't have a chance to say goodbye to Ogden."

"Geoffrey left?"

"Brenda escorted him out."

"He probably stepped out for a bite. I'm sure he'll be back this afternoon." I clutched the Cop-Copine bag in my

132

hand.

"I don't think so. He turned in his temporary ID and said he wouldn't need it again."

Where on Earth did Geoffrey go? Brenda would know. "I better go."

* * * * *

Back at home base, Brenda was at her computer with Stewart leaning over her.

"What brings you down to our humble office?" I said.

Stewart twisted around. "We're going over the Lisbon draft."

"Was Geoffrey able to help?" I said.

"The man's a wiz," Brenda said. "And he's on his way now to Lisbon to stall the clients."

"He is?" I said. WTF?

"All right then. You two seem to have everything under control. I'll talk to you both later." Stewart whizzed around and slipped out the door.

Brenda scrutinized my desk. "Is that what I think it is?"

"What?"

"It looks like a Cop-Copine bag. Did you rob a bank?"

"They had a super-duper end-of-season sale."

"Ya' right."

I felt a lecture coming on, so I picked up my phone receiver and tapped the rapidly blinking voicemail message button.

"You have eleven messages." Would this day ever end? I turned to my emails to see if there was anything from Geoffrey. Bingo. 'Kalena, I beg of you not to loathe me, but duty called, and I had to switch my flight. By the time you read this, I'll likely be in some tedious line at the airport. I'll make it up to you next time. Luv Geoffrey.'

Luv...luv, luv, luv...luv...luv, luv. I repeated the word a thousand different ways in my head. It was not the same thing as 'love,' but it was definitely more promising than 'cheers.'

I scooped up the Cop-Copine bag, flung it under my desk and ripped off yet another body part of my Buxom Ballerina.

CHAPTER NINETEEN

I stared at the door inching open a sliver at a time. It was ten PM, and I was alone in the office, the public having been ushered from the building several hours earlier. With Geoffrey bailing on our dinner date, I had decided to work late. Did I have a fever? Brenda had asked on her way out. No, I simply wanted to tidy up some paperwork after having spent most of the day in meetings and on the phone. I didn't allude to the fact that I'd wasted so much time in a Yorkville clinic destroying the offices of a cosmetic surgeon. Okay, she'd said, but had walked over and felt my forehead to double check.

The door advanced another sliver. Were phantoms capable of moving material objects? Patrick Swayze was able to do so in *Ghost*. But that was only after a lot of practice. But then Richard's deceased father had had several decades to master these kinds of things. My fear factor went off the scale, and I was catapulted into freeze mode. My breath halted, my legs went numb and my vocal cords tightened. "H-hello," I managed to squeeze out.

The door closed, and someone or something bounded away, their weighty footsteps echoing through the deserted atrium. I was pretty sure ghosts did not have heavy footsteps. Or did they? I poked my head out the door when a strong beam of light shone on my face, frightening me to lifelessness.

"Kalena, is that you?"

Still blinded by the glow, I shaded my eyes to cut the glare. Up ahead stood a security guard with flashlight in hand.

"What are you still doing here?" he said.

"Catching up on a mountain of work." I advanced into the dark gallery.

"Well next time you're working late and decide to leave your office for a spin, let the guards in the control room know. You just set off a whole series of alarms."

"That wasn't me. I've been glued to my chair since closing. Someone just tried to get into the office, and I stepped out to catch a glimpse of the intruder."

"That someone did a mighty impressive sprint through the Museum. None of the other guards has bumped into anyone else on this level. Shit. If we don't find out who the roamer is there's going to be hell to pay."

"Do you think ghosts are capable of tripping the alarms?" I lowered my chin and raised one eyebrow.

"For sure. And extra-terrestrials have the ability to set them off remotely. The paperwork lately has been a nightmare." The guard sneered at me.

"Just checking." I was clearly losing it.

"I wouldn't pay much attention to the stories about our resident ghosts," said the guard lightening up.

"Do you ever go down into the food tunnel?"

"Where that suicide took place? I don't pay attention to the mumbo jumbo you hear around here, or I couldn't work in a place like this at night."

"Do you know who committed suicide?"

"All I know is it was someone pretty high up. But there's an unwritten code around here that we don't talk about the incident. Apparently, the family's still pretty sensitive about it."

"That's understandable," I said.

"I've got to get back to rounds. Make sure you call us when you're ready to leave."

"I will. Shouldn't be much longer."

The security guard nodded, and as he walked away, his flashlight swung back, its light reflecting off something shiny on the floor ahead of me. I stooped down to pick up the mysterious object. It was a foil-covered Jeff de Bruges truffle.

* * * * *

"You're fucking kidding me," Brenda screamed after I had told her I had almost caught her secret admirer in the act the previous night. "I wish I'd been here. I would've snagged the guy, and we wouldn't be sitting here still wondering who he was."

She was right. Brenda would have tied up the coward and tortured him until he confessed ten times over.

"Whoever it was must have known you'd left the building, and they weren't expecting me to be here," I said.

"And security never found out who'd set off the alarms?"

"Nope. I checked with Marco this morning, and there was a big event in the theater last night. The list of people who signed out after the galleries closed was massive. None of the names jumped out at him."

"You certainly have him trailing close behind your heels these days," said Brenda.

"Who?"

"Don't give me that innocent crap. I've seen the way

137

that puppy swoons over you."

Brenda blathered on, but I tuned out the monkey chatter and panned my emails looking for one from Geoffrey. Since he stood me up on our dinner date, each day he emailed me a picture of himself from Lisbon. As I waited for word on the fate of *Treasures of the Maya*, his highly amusing photos were the only thing that helped cut the tension. In each shot, he sported crazy-mad hair and posed at various tourist sites in Lisbon: he leaned against the walls of the Palàcio da Pena as if supporting them, he stood in the rain underneath the Triumphal Arch holding two umbrellas and in Rossio Square he sipped a drink while seated on a chair on the verge of tipping over. I wasn't sure who the photographer was, but I presumed he had roped in one of the clients or charmed some passerby.

When I realized Geoffrey's visit to Lisbon coincided with the International Chocolate Festival in the Vila of Òbidos on the outskirts of Lisbon, I asked him if he would make the pilgrimage so I might live the experience through him vicariously. No one was more surprised than me when he obliged. He claimed it was his humble attempt to make up for the cancelled dinner the previous week. But there was no new email from him in my inbox. Rats!

The weekend passed quietly, but on Monday I received an email from Geoffrey with a series of new photographs attached. The shots of winding medieval streets in Òbidos were infused with romance and intrigue. I imagined myself wandering through the city with him, arm in arm, sampling the wares of the *chocolate artistes* competing for the title of Portugal's Best Chocolatier of the Year. Droplets of drool formed in the corner of my mouth as I poured over the pictures from the festival. The theme for the Chocolate Artistic Piece Contest had been cinema, and as I opened up the last photo, I burst out laughing.

"You're awfully cheery for a Monday," Brenda said.

I giggled again at a picture of Geoffrey standing beside a chocolate sculpture of Darth Vader of *Star Wars* fame. "My comedian brother's at it again," I lied. "He sent me another one of his silly emails." The message that accompanied Geoffrey's digital images read: 'I picked up some information on the *Salon du Chocolat* in Paris. Perhaps we could arrange a trip for you to the London office during the time of the *Salon*. Paris is just a hop, skip and a jump away from London thanks to the Eurostar train. Let's think about it, shall we?'

Paris with Geoffrey? Was he kidding? What was there to think about? My heart pitter-pattered.

"I have to meet this brother of yours sometime. Is he cute?"

"I guess so. He could charm anyone with a paper bag over his head."

"I guess that's why he does so well in sales. But it doesn't sound as if he gets home very much," said Brenda.

"Got that right. That's why my parents are always in my business."

"Forget it then. The last thing I need is a boyfriend with a woman in every port."

"I didn't know you were looking for a boyfriend," I said.

"I'm not."

"Hmm, I'll see if there's anything further Marco can do to find the Truffle Man."

"Oh shut up," Brenda said, shouting over the ringing of my phone. "Are you going to answer that damn thing?"

I scooped up the receiver. "Museum Consulting Services, Kalena speaking."

"Hey, it's Marco."

"Uh, hi. What's up?"

"Just wondering if you did anything exciting over the weekend."

"I went to a couple of OzFlix screenings."

"Oz what?"

"OzFlix. It's an annual Australian film festival held in the city. Just a weekend thing, but I caught some great stuff."

"Did you go with friends?"

"I went on my own. Foreign films, even Australian ones, are a hard sell to my friends." I heard a sigh on the other end of the line. "What about you, what'd you do?"

"I primed the Gremlin. She's almost ready for the new paint job."

"Cool."

Brenda turned her head sideways. I could tell she was dying to know who was on the other end of the line.

"I was calling to tell you I tapped out every possible source on the Borovsky gallery. On the surface it looks like the owner's clean."

"And below the surface?"

The office door popped open, and Aurelia strode in. Her ample bosom looked as though it was going to explode out of her clingy deep-v'd chenille sweater.

Brenda spun around to face her. "Can I help you?"

"I'm here to see Kalena," said Aurelia.

I raised my finger to indicate I would be with her momentarily. Brenda swiveled back to her computer.

"I'll talk to you later about this," I said into the phone. "Someone just stepped through the door."

"Okay," said Marco.

"Bye." I plunked the receiver down. "What brings you to this neck of the woods?" I said to Aurelia.

"I was told you've been having problems with the Internet."

"Yes, I have. I'd almost given up on anyone fixing it."

"We've been pretty busy in IT. I don't think we'll ever catch up on the back log of work that piled up before I was hired."

"And I guess you've had some new challenges too."

"Like what?" said Aurelia.

"I'd heard one of the Library's databases—"

"I don't know who created that system in the Library, but they should be shot."

"I think it was your boss...actually," I said.

"I need to check the settings on your computer. You'll have to get out of your chair?"

"Sure." I was barely out of my seat before Aurelia wedged herself into it.

"And I have to shut down your programs."

I noticed an email from Richard had popped into my inbox, but I would have to check it after Aurelia was finished with my computer. "Whatever it takes to fix the problem."

Aurelia tapped at my keyboard. "You should've asked Marco to help you with this."

"Why would I ask a security guard to fix my computer?"

"He's pretty handy with computers. And considering you're going out with him I would've thought he'd jump at the chance to come to the rescue."

Brenda stopped typing. I could sense her auditory faculties honing in on the conversation. "What gave you that idea?" I asked.

"Marco dumped me after a couple of dates because of some older woman."

"You must have me confused with someone else. I hardly know Marco."

"Some men are into cougars, especially when they're not interested in a commitment."

Brenda rotated her head towards me in slo' mo', probably hoping to catch me thwack Aurelia with a blunt instrument. But I held my tongue and my hands in check.

CHAPTER TWENTY

Brenda sauntered over to my desk as soon as Aurelia vacated the office. "Do you and Marco have a thing going on?"

"Are you bonkers?" I said.

"Why would Aurelia suspect you two—"

"I have no frigging clue."

"You know what they say about relationship rumors?" Brenda said.

"What?"

"They're usually based on truth."

"Oh, come on. That girl is off-the-chart cuckoo for Cocoa Puffs. You heard it in her voice. I know you did."

"She WAS being a bit of a dram' queen."

"Dram' queen? She's got Glenn Close in *Fatal Attraction* written all over her. She's the type that smiles sweetly at you after butchering your pet."

"Your cat's already dead," Brenda said.

"You know what I mean."

Brenda turned around and stepped towards her desk. "Oh shit," she screamed as she turned over on her ankle.

"Are you okay?"

"Yeah, yeah," she said, hobbling the rest of the way. "My bloody foot has never been the same since Walter stepped on it after the Lunch n' Learn."

"I'm sure you'll be fine." I logged into my computer and

opened the email from Richard. It was another message intended for Ms. Bouvier. 'Veronique,' it read. 'San Francisco and New York have finally come to an agreement. San Francisco has decided to pull some of the ceramics for further testing. But the damned tour will continue as scheduled. It toys with our timing, but things can still work in our favor. We need to brainstorm. And to answer your question – NO. Borovsky still hasn't come up with a price with which we can all live. Richard.'

I knew it. I knew it. Richard and his band were scheming large. But why would the fact that the exhibit was coming to the Museum affect timing. Timing of what? And what about the comment about the Borovsky gallery? Was that enough proof for the Director of Security to start a surveillance of Richard? Probably not. It was all still too circumstantial. But I was sure Marco and I could unearth some more dirt on Richard.

I was about to forward the email to Marco when I started to wonder if Aurelia might be crazed enough to monitor email correspondence between myself and Marco.

As soon as Brenda stepped out of the office, I dialed Marco.

"ROM staff entrance, Marco speaking."

"It's Kalena. What's your schedule like this week? Are you on days?"

"I'm double-shifting today, and it's afternoons the rest of the week."

"And the weekend?"

"I have Saturday off."

"Perfect. Can we meet for a couple of hours Saturday afternoon?"

"For sure. What time? Where? What do you have

planned?" Marco said.

"It's business. We have some undercover work to do. I'll call you later in the week with details. And don't talk to me in the halls, don't even nod hello, and especially don't email me," I said.

"What's going on?"

"Someone might be watching us...and could have access to our emails. I have to get off the phone before Brenda comes back. *Ciao.*"

* * * * *

I waited for Marco at the entrance to Dolce, the women's boutique on the south side of Yorkville Avenue. The stainless steel façade seemed at odds with its male counterpart, Gabbana, housed on the opposite side of the street in a classic old structure with painted beige brickwork. It was almost four o'clock on a Saturday afternoon that hinted of winter. Dolce's sheltered portico did little to keep the chill from penetrating my bones.

The last part of the week had dragged by more slowly than the rotation of Pluto around the sun. But now that *Treasures of the Maya* had been given the green light again all had ended well. Exhibition preparations were well under way despite almost a week of down time. The space had been painted and most of the millwork and electrical completed. Cases for the Museum's part of the exhibit were brought out of storage and touched up. Mounts to hold the artifacts were finished and the complicated paperwork for customs had been prepared. Graphics, press kits and other publicity materials had been signed off, and label translation

145

was in the last stages of being proofed. Orders for the Museum's shops had been placed by Gert, an extensive array of complementary programs including a lecture series on the Maya civilization was being developed, and a documentary film program was in the works.

I attempted to put the week behind me as I stood there in Yorkville, teeth chattering each time the razor wind maneuvered its way into Dolce's portico. The change of seasons in Toronto is often uncivil and manipulative. One moment you are convinced summer is here to stay and the next instant winter pounds on the door with a sledge hammer. I glanced at my watch. Where was Marco?

Across the street, I spied a figure step into the entranceway of the Gabbana boutique. Could that possibly be Marco? A second take confirmed it was. He looked at me with a similarly puzzled expression. Each of us had clearly done an excellent job of disguising ourselves. The plan was for Marco to infiltrate Borovsky Fine Arts by sneaking into the office to try to find some paperwork that might indicate the owner was a fence. I, on the other hand, would keep the proprietor distracted while pretending to be a jet-setting art collector in search of stolen works I might purchase for my private collection.

Marco raised his hand as if to wave then plunged both hands into his pockets. He must have remembered we had agreed that once we spotted each other, we would wait to ensure neither of us had been followed. My paranoia had escalated, and I feared Aurelia might be stalking Marco. After one last glance up and down the street, I crossed to the other side. Marco was clothed in a pin-striped suit, knock-off Gucci sunglasses and a heavy gold chain around his neck that gave him the air of an East European Mafioso.

"I barely recognized you. What did you do to your hair?" I said.

"My sister used some kind of iron on it, a crimper I think she called it." Marco stepped back and looked at the back of my head. "Your hair looks a lot longer when it's in a ponytail."

I shook my head. "It's a hair piece."

"Cool. I could've sworn it was your own hair...What do you think of this chain? I got it at Wal-Mart for $10.95."

"It's leaving green marks on your neck. You're going to have to wipe off the tarnish before we go into the gallery."

"Shit," he said rubbing his neck.

"I think you got it all."

"Did you go to a tanning salon?" said Marco.

"And ravage my skin? I think not. I used a dark bronzing powder on my face and hands."

"You look like an Italian Mrs. Peel."

"I'm surprised you know about *The Avengers*."

"I watched it in reruns as a kid."

In addition to large Sophia-Loren-like sunglasses, I was dressed neck-to-ankle in deep purple stretchy pleather, including skinny pants and a tight-fitting blazer. "Do you think this outfit is too much?"

"It's pretty hot, actually."

"Did you spot anyone trailing you?" I said.

"No. I can't believe you think Aurelia is that insane."

"How many times did you go out with her?" I said.

"I didn't. I had coffee with her once in the Museum's cafeteria. And I bumped into her at a café near the Museum after work one night. We talked for about ten seconds."

"She told me you two were dating and you dumped her for an older woman, who she thinks is me."

Marco turned pale.

147

"We'd better get going. The gallery closes at five," I said. "I'll go in first, and you wait a few seconds before you come in. You should try to get into the office as soon as possible."

"Roger. But I'll need to get a fix on the cameras first. I know we're in disguise, but the less time we're captured on tape the better," said Marco.

I took a deep breath.

"Don't worry, Mrs. Peel. It'll be fine."

After inhaling another big breath of air, I strutted down the street ahead of Marco and stepped into the gallery. The sky-scraping man I had seen with Richard and his lover sat at an ultra-modern desk made of glass and chrome. He was the type of man who had his suits custom-made in Singapore.

"Good afternoon," said the gentleman, rising to his feet.

"*Buon giorno*," I said.

"Can I help you with anything?" As the gentleman moved towards me, the ebony hardwood floors creaked under his weight.

"I'm just browsing," I said with an Italian accent. As I admired the plethora of paintings attached to an exposed brick wall, the door opened and Marco entered the gallery.

"I'll be with you shortly," said the gentleman to Marco. His Russian heritage was clearly evident in his rolled r's.

Marco nodded at him and perused the walls as I had.

"You have some wonderful paintings here, Mr...?"

"Borovsky. I am the owner of the gallery. Anatoli Borovsky."

"*Piacere di conoscerla, Signore Borovsky.* You have a better selection here than in some of the galleries in *Roma*," I said.

"Thank you. I lived in the Eternal City for many years before settling in Canada." The gentleman began to ramble in

Italian, and I panicked. I hadn't spoken much Italian since university. *"Mille grazie,"* I said, interrupting the man, "for not speaking in my native tongue, but I prefer to practice my English when I am abroad. But please excuse my clumsy accent."

"Of course. And your accent is quite charming." This guy was smoother than polished marble.

I surveyed the room and my throat dropped into my stomach as I observed Marco pass into a door marked 'Private.' My dread escalated when I spied a host of security cameras mounted around the gallery.

I sprang towards Mr. Borovsky. "I am looking for some very special works. Things you do not see hanging out in the open."

"I have some rare pieces by very collectible artists."

The door to the office propped open slightly, and Marco peeled across the room and out the gallery. Mr. Borovsky jumped at the crash of the door. He turned back towards me, but outside, Marco motioned to me to vamoose and then he disappeared. What the hell? Had Marco found the proof we needed?

"Can you provide me with some insights as to your tastes?" said Borovsky.

"To be more specific, I am looking for art not usually on the market." I lowered my Sophia Lorens and winked.

"I believe I understand Ms...?"

"Medici, Sophia Medici." Oh, lord. Could I not have come up with a more credible name?

"Ms. Medici. You won't find what you're looking for here. And I suggest that perhaps it is a good time for you to depart."

"I am very sorry if I have insulted you in any way. Perhaps you misunderstood."

"I think we understand each other very well. Goodbye, Ms. Medici." Mr. Borovsky almost seared my face with his piercing eyes.

I harrumphed, strode towards the exit and ripped open the door. There stood Veronique, staring straight at me.

CHAPTER TWENTY-ONE

With a split-second to act I one-eightied, feeling my fake pony tail swish against Veronique's face. I let my purse fall to the ground and crouched to scoop it up which was not an easy feat in my second-skin pants. Like a goose I hobbled past Veronique's lanky legs. "*Ciao Signore* Borovsky. *À la prossima, forse à Roma.*" Was that how one said 'until next time' in Italian. I bounced up and fled out the door.

Where was Marco? And why had he left the gallery at the speed of light? Had Veronique recognized me? Had I given myself away as a fraud to Mr. Borovsky?

In a flash, a taxi appeared in front of me and the rear passenger door exploded open.

"Get in."

"Marco? What's going on?"

"Just get in the cab...please."

Marco slid over, and I leapt inside.

"Where to, sir?" asked the driver.

"College Street," said Marco.

I looked at Marco perplexed as could be.

He leaned in towards me and spoke in a hushed voice. "We've got to get out of this area as fast as we can. Little Italy was the first place I thought of. But it's a good choice. We'll fade into the crowds there." I was thrown off guard when the rub of Marco's shoulder against mine sent tingles to my extremities.

"I don't get it," I whispered.

"I think it's better if we talk about this after we get out of the cab."

I settled in for what was sure to be a long ride through the traffic-laden streets of Toronto. Marco shimmied away slightly, and my hand dropped down between us. He gazed out his window and laid his hand on mine. The gesture was meant to reassure me, I presumed, but I snapped it away. I didn't want him to feel the sudden rise in my body temperature.

A fling with Marco could be just what the doctor ordered, but would it be fair to him? And then there was Geoffrey, the typical bad boy type I had been attracted to most of my life. Was a no-strings-attached affair with a playboy who lived overseas a more effective way to get my fix of romance without the complications of love and subsequent heartache?

"Up ahead at the next corner will be fine," said Marco to the driver, ripping me out of my introspective reverie. I delved into my purse for my wallet.

"It's on me. You can get the ice cream," said Marco.

"Ice cream?" A radiance filled my body as I spotted the Sicilian Sidewalk Café, one of the most renowned ice cream shops in the city. Its sublime homemade ice cream, gelati, milkshakes, and exclusive desserts had earned it a must-visit recommendation from the *New York Times*. I could taste the renowned chocolate *Zabajone Tartufo* already. Or maybe I would go for the *Tanti Baci*, a crèpe filled with Nutella and Baci chocolate ice cream.

"Thank you very much, sir," said the turbaned cabbie when Marco handed him a generous tip.

"You're welcome," said Marco. "Have a safe day."

We hopped onto the sidewalk, and I dashed through the intersection before Marco had a chance to blink.

"I take it you know this place," Marco said when he reached my side.

"It's just down the street from a great rep cinema. Before Hot Docs got its new home, I used to live in this place."

"I give up. What's Hot Docs?"

"It's Toronto's documentary film festival. It's considered one of the best in the world after Amsterdam."

"How many film festivals do you go to in a year?"

"Too many." As I spoke a police car patrolled past us.

"Let's get inside." Marco guided me into the café towards the back. The black tables and chairs with turquoise vinyl seats were garish against the clay-colored tile floor.

"Don't you want to sit by the window to people-watch?" I said.

"This table's better for now."

An energetic waitress in lethal heels handed us menus. "I'll give you a couple of minutes," she said and pranced away. I noticed Marco didn't even give her a second glance.

"We're trying to be inconspicuous," said Marco.

"Too late now. I ran into Veronique at the gallery."

"What? Why didn't you tell me?"

"I'm telling you now. You told me not to talk in the cab, remember? Did you think it was bugged?" I said.

"Of course not. But I didn't want to take any chances of the cabbie overhearing our conversation. So, what'd you do?"

"What any other respectable wannabe spy would do. I pretended I didn't know her and ducked before she figured out who I was."

"She's the least of our problems. If that Borovsky guy is

a legit gallery owner, we could be in trouble," said Marco.

"What do you mean if he's legit? Didn't you find any-thing?"

"His file cabinet was alarmed. I probably tripped a silent signal to the police station when I opened the drawer."

"No way. So, the coppers were probably on their way to the gallery."

"Uh, huh. And our entire visit was digitally recorded. Bo-rovsky probably has enough to put me away on a B&E."

"Breaking and entering?" My heart felt as though it had been swallowed by a black hole. What was I doing? I couldn't put this poor kid at further risk.

The waitress returned to the table. "Have you decided yet?"

"I'll just have a scoop of vanilla gelato," said Marco.

I scrunched up my face.

"Get whatever you want." Marco grinned and shook his head in defeat.

"In that case I'll have the *Montagna di Chocolate e una tazza di cioccolata calda.*"

"Do you want the hot chocolate at the same time as the ice cream?" asked the waitress.

"You can bring it before, thanks."

As the woman retreated to the counter, Marco gazed at me in disbelief. "Where do you put it all?"

"It's just an average-sized 'Mountain of Chocolate.' And the hot chocolate's just to warm me up. I've been bloody freezing all day."

"We can go somewhere that serves hot food if you pre-fer," said Marco.

"Are you kidding? This was a great idea. It's probably the last chance to indulge in ice cream before the cold weather makes it unthinkable." I leaned forward on my elbows. "But I have to say, the hot chocolate here could be turned up a notch. The best hot chocolate in the galaxy is in Torino, in Northern Italy. They make it with heavy cream and butter. I know it's *tanto decadanto*, but oh my, it's ambrosial."

I looked at the entrance door and shut up. Marco followed my gaze towards two police officers who had walked into the café. They scoped out the place, ambled to the counter and placed an order. "Do you think we could really be arrested?" I whispered.

"You might be for the criminal amount of chocolate you eat," Marco said.

"Seriously."

"Seriously? I don't know. But I suggest you burn that hair piece and destroy the outfit when you get home."

"I'm not getting rid of this suit. You can't find an eggplant suit like this just anywhere."

The waitress dropped off the hot chocolate.

"Have you been to Torino?" Marco said.

"*Naturalmente*. Torino's the birthplace of chocolate production in Italy. You can get this ChocoPass there. It's a book with about fifteen vouchers you can use at all the different *chocolatieri* in the city."

"My mom was from Torino."

"Shut up!"

"I spent my summers there as a kid. I think I know the city better than Toronto. You should come with me sometime. My grandmother still lives there."

Torino with Marco? Maybe there was hope for a May-September romance after all.

"By the way," said Marco. "I couldn't figure out why Borovsky would have a file cabinet alarmed—"

155

"Unless he had something to hide, like records related to stolen works of art!" The evidence against Richard, Veronique and Ms. X seemed to be stacking up heavily against them.

Chapter Twenty-Two

"Before we attempt vrksasana, engage your bandhas," said Vishnu, the yoga instructor.

Brenda turned towards me, eyebrows furrowed. "What the fuck? Does this guy not speak English?"

"Especially the mula bandha," continued the exotic yogi. His divinely long hair—of which any woman would be envious—hung loose past his shoulders. "Contract the anus and focus on your core."

"You should have warned me to brush up on my Sanskrit and anal contractions before coming to this class," Brenda whispered. "And if you'd told me how hot your yoga teacher was, I would've joined this class eons ago."

"Shh," I said. What was I thinking when I invited Brenda to accompany me to my Sunday evening yoga class? She had emailed me over the weekend complaining about her mother's rants regarding her sedentary lifestyle. When I mentioned my yoga class to her, I never expected her to take me up on it.

"Did you do anything exciting yesterday?"

I thought about my purple pleather suit sitting inside a used clothing bin on the other side of the city. Panic seized me. Did I wipe it down of fingerprints? "Nope. But, Bren, you're not supposed to chat in a yoga class."

"Okay, okay," she said. "Chill out."

"And if you are just beginning your practice…" Vishnu

smiled sweetly at Brenda…"you may want to begin with a less challenging variation."

Uh-oh. I knew Vishnu had pressed one of Brenda's buttons. As the template for Type A personalities, Brenda would never settle for the easier version of anything.

"Root your left leg into the ground and then gently plant the sole of your right foot on the calf of your standing leg. If the pose is familiar to you, try resting the instep on the inside of the thigh, near the groin."

Brenda whipped up her foot, slammed it into the side of her leg and teetered. For a moment, she had captured the pose, but then she lost her balance and slammed her foot to the floor at an unnatural angle.

"FUCK," Brenda yelled as she sank to the ground on top of her twisted ankle.

I ran to her side and was joined by Vishnu who had dashed through the forest of students still attempting to maintain their one-legged tree poses. "Take a deep breath," said Vishnu "and unravel those legs with serenity and mindfulness."

"Are you kidding me?" she said, wincing in pain.

"Let us immediately send a positive healing message to the universe," said Vishnu.

Brenda turned to me. "Is he on some kind of hallucinogen? Mushrooms maybe?"

I could feel my face flushing with embarrassment as the rest of the students gathered around us in a circle.

"Remain still. I will secure the first-aid kit from the office." Vishnu sprang up like a gazelle and leapt out the room.

"I just heard that in the States there were almost 4,000 yoga injuries treated in doctors' offices in the past year," said one of the students.

"Swell," Brenda said. "That makes me feel so much better."

"Can you put any pressure on your foot?" I said.

"The answer to that would be...NO."

Vishnu glided back into the room and unraveled a tensor bandage. "I'm not surprised this happened," said Vishnu tenderly wrapping Brenda's ankle. "Mercury is in retrograde."

"What the hell does that mean?" Brenda said.

"It's a kind of planetary discumbobulation" I said.

"A planet is described as retrograde when it appears to be moving backwards through the zodiac," said Vishnu. "Please attempt to place your foot down now."

"Planets don't move backwards." Brenda flinched as she touched her toe down.

"You are most correct. They only appear to reverse their motion. It is like an optical illusion in the heavens created by the orbital rotation of the Earth in relation to other planets in the solar system, a kind of cosmic shadow-play," said Vishnu.

"And all kinds of stuff goes wacky when Mercury's in retrograde," said one of the other students, "especially with communications, phones, computers, cars, buses, trains and anything electronic. We should all be careful for the next while. You should back up your hard drives and count on travel delays."

Vishnu and I hoisted Brenda up. "I never heard such bullshit," Brenda said supported on either side by myself and Vishnu. "I fell out of fucking tree pose. It's as simple as that."

Chapter Twenty-Three

"Good morning," said Aurelia. She leaned against the security desk counter at the staff entrance. Marco had pushed himself as far away from her as possible.

"Good morning," I said suspicious of Aurelia's chirpy demeanor. I slid my ID through the reader, ignored Marco and forged towards the door.

"Hold on," said Aurelia. "Marco and I are all caught up now." Marco looked as if he had just come face to face with a horde of ravenous zombies.

"I'll walk with you towards your office," said Aurelia.

Oh, joy. Aurelia's company was just what I was hoping for on a Monday morning.

"Have you ever been to the Sicilian Sidewalk Café?" Aurelia said after the door had closed behind me.

My throat closed up as if I'd had an allergic reaction to a deadly toxin. Was this a trick question? Had she followed Marco on Saturday after all? "Sicilian Café?" I said hoarsely. "I don't think so...Doesn't sound familiar."

"Oh, it's an amazing spot in the heart of Little Italy. Marco and I went there on Saturday."

"Really? I thought you two had broken up."

"It was just a misunderstanding between young lovers."

"I'm glad it all worked out." Clearly this psycho babe lived in her own alternate reality.

"It's actually an ice cream parlor. Marco had plain vanilla gelato. He's so predictable," said Aurelia.

How had this woman been hired? Did anyone at the Museum do a background check to see if she had ever been institutionalized?

"*Parla Italiano*, Kalena?" a voice said from behind me.

Rats. It was Veronique. I slowed to a crawl and turned around. "Veronique. Good morning...What did you say?"

"She asked if you spoke Italian," Aurelia said.

"Me? I can barely keep my French straight. But I'm fluent in Ukrainian. It's not a language that comes in handy too often—"

"I could have sworn I saw you in a gallery in Yorkville on Saturday. And there was a young Italian man, I think, who came out just before you."

A thousand arrows shot out of Aurelia's eyes piercing my body from head to toe.

"It must have been my long lost twin. I was in Richmond Hill all weekend doing a raw food cooking class. Well you don't really cook the food. It's all raw, but you learn how to prepare it."

"Perhaps I was mistaken then," said Veronique. "I saw a woman who looked...*ça n'a pas d'importance*. But this cooking course, it sounds *très intéressant*. Now that I'm a single woman again like you, I'm trying to take better care of myself."

Newly single? No wonder Veronique was experimenting with new looks. She was on the prowl again.

"And I'm debating whether I should return to my maiden name," said Veronique.

"What is it?" I said.

Veronique closed her eyes for a moment and tilted her

head as if I had sent her to another place and time. With her long narrow face and Mannerist neck, she could easily have been an artist's model in her younger days. She reopened her eyes. "Um...Landry."

"Veronique Landry," I said. "It has a nice ring to it."

"I'll let you two divorcées chat about life after abandonment. I have real work to do." Aurelia twirled about and left Veronique and me with our jaws hanging open. Aurelia had the emotional intelligence of a single-celled organism.

"You do that," I shouted at her down the hallway.

"Who is that viperous young woman?" said Veronique.

"The reincarnation of Lucrezia Borgia."

* * * * *

"Hey, I thought I told you to stay home today," I said to Brenda after entering the office.

"My foot's not that bad. I iced it last night and wrapped it this morning. I'm wearing the gimp shoes to prove it." Brenda raised her legs and flashed a hideous set of orthopedic footwear.

I raised my hand to shield my eyes. "Ohmygawd."

"I bought these clod-hoppers when I sprained my ankle during a field hockey game in university."

"Field hockey? This story gets better and better."

"Oh, clam up," said Brenda.

I noticed Brenda's computer monitor was dark. Had she not fired it up yet? "I'm surprised you're not working on the Lisbon report."

"The flipping computer network's down, the whole damned thing, email, network drives, you name it."

"Uh-huh," I said in an I-told-you-so tone.

"I knew you'd be on about that Mercury retrofit shit," Brenda said.

I was prepared to continue my gloating when the phone rang. The call display indicated it was from overseas. I scooped up the receiver with a little too much enthusiasm, catapulted it over my shoulder and then pulled it back to my ear. "Museum Consulting Services, Kalena Boyko speaking."

"So, speak to me, Kalena Boyko," said Geoffrey on the other end.

"How are you?" I said.

"Depressed. It was damned difficult to come back to the damp and fog of London after being in Portugal. I was meant to live in warmer climes."

"I can identify with that...So, did you survive the chocolate festival?" I lowered my voice in hope Brenda would not hear the question. She was bound to figure out I was speaking with Geoffrey.

"I did. In fact, I returned for a second visit."

"You're kidding," I said.

"I was quite surprised at how much I'd enjoyed myself. But the experience would have been complete had you been there with me."

My heart melted. "There's still the Parisian *Salon du chocolat.*"

"Indeed. But did you not receive my email?"

"'Fraid not. Our computer network's been down this morning." I whipped out my BlackBerry – no new emails since the weekend.

Brenda waved at me frantically. Her computer screen was lit up.

"Oh, hold on. Looks like we're back in business, but it'll take a few minutes to boot up the computer."

"While it's starting up, tell me how your search for *Il Gattopardo* is coming along. Any leads yet?" said Geoffrey.

"I've come to the conclusion it's best to leave such matters to the authorities." I dared not tell Geoffrey my suspicions about Richard. He would think I was completely daft.

"I'm relieved you're not wasting any more time on that. I must dash though. I have a tennis match I couldn't squirm out of and my fellow players don't look kindly on tardiness."

Visions ran through my mind like a film short of Geoffrey lobbing the ball with three stunning British socialites wearing stilettos, their satin-smooth thighs peeking out from the skimpiest of tennis skirts. "Sounds fun."

"I'll talk to you next week. Cheers," said Geoffrey signing off.

I returned the receiver to the phone and stared at it.

"I swear your mental age drops to the level of a tween when you talk to Geoffrey," said Brenda.

"Your point being?"

"I hope you have a copy of *How to Handle Heartbreak for Dummies*."

My eyes rolled back into the far recesses of my head.

"I'm going to grab a coffee. Can I get you something?" said Brenda.

"No thanks," I said frigidly. Brenda left the office trying to mask a limp.

I was plotting how I could lobby to have Monday mornings made illegal when the phone rang. "Now what?"

"So, what did she want?" It was Marco.

"Who? Oh." I started to sing the lyrics to Talking Head's *Psycho Killer*.

"Very funny. C'mon what did she want?"

"She grilled me about my weekend. And according to

164

Aurelia you two went to the Sicilian Sidewalk Café together."

"What a fruiterella. What do you think I should do?"

"Avoidance is probably the best strategy. Eventually she'll get bored pursuing you and move on to a new victim who might be more responsive."

"Do you honestly believe that?" Marco said.

"No."

"Oh, man, I've got another school group coming in the Staff Entrance. *Ciao*."

"Psycho Killer, *qu'est-ce que c'est,* fa, fa, fa, fa, fa."

Chapter Twenty-Four

When I arrived at the Museum the following day, I went straight to shipping and receiving to check on a package of samples I was expecting from Gert. I pressed the large red button that opened the heavy metal doors and was blasted by a cold wind. Yuck.

"Hi, Gaspar," I said to the shipping clerk. Any sign of the package I was expecting?"

"No, but something else arrived for you...from overseas."

"Really?"

Gaspar handed me a small package. It was from the London office.

"Thanks."

I pressed the release button to open the dungeon-like doors to exit. The motor driving the door mechanism hummed like a baritone exercising his vocal cords. The portals moved apart slowly, and I squeezed my way out as soon as there was enough space to slip through. I scampered down the hallway, ducked into a stairwell and ripped the box open. The outer layer of wrapping shed to the floor, and I slit open an envelope with my name on it: 'Kalena, you didn't think I would go to the chocolate festival in Òbidos without picking up a special treat for you, did you?' read the note. Holy cow. Geoffrey went to the festival a second time just to buy me something. I read on. 'I hope you find the Portuguese chocolate tarts as irresistible as I did. Luv, Geoffrey. P.S. I had these vacuum-packed and kept them frozen until the last minute. The pastry chef assured me they would taste as fresh as the day he made them.'

Portuguese chocolate tarts? Oh my. I sliced more deeply into the box and sure enough, amidst handfuls of Styrofoam chips were four magnificent vacuum-sealed tarts. With my teeth, I tore the thick plastic wrap and was struck by a sweet aroma. The delicate pastries appeared hand-molded with love, each being slightly irregular in shape. The tarts had a dusty cocoa sprinkling, and when I took a bite, I was jettisoned into paradise. The thick chocolate filling hinting of nuts was created with what must have been some of Portugal's best chocolate. Divine. I gobbled one down and then another.

The chocolate powder sprinkled over my mossy green coat, and I brushed off as much as I could before reentering the hallway. Zigzagging through the corridor, I encountered one of the preparators working on my exhibition team pushing a large crated box on a long dolly.

"Pretty soon you'll be pushing crates filled with ancient Maya treasures," I said still on a high from the sugar-loaded tarts.

She gawked at me with a peculiar expression. "Um, yeah. I guess so," she said, staring at me oddly for a moment and then she continued on her way.

Around the next bend, I chanced upon a curator from the Greek and Roman section of our Ancient Civilizations department.

"Good morning," I said.

"Good day," he said chortling. "Have you just come from

a Hobbit's birthday party?"

Huh? After I passed the Birkenstocked hippie throw-back, I glanced down at my stylish coat with its puffy sleeves and over-sized buttons. What would he know about fashion? I patted down the fabric on my arms and stopped to look in a fire hose cabinet with a highly-reflective glass covering. At arm's length from the mirror-like surface my mouth looked deformed. I drew my face closer and stared in disbelief at the thick border of chocolate powder around the perimeter of my lips. I looked like a baboon.

Footsteps echoed down the hallway, and fearing further humiliation, I sped to the nearest doorway marked 'Library Book Processing.' When the door wouldn't budge, I shoved with all my might until it gave way. I steamrolled inside and something whizzed past my face. A pinging noise sounded at the far end of the room. I turned and saw a target full of arrows and a large net draped behind it.

"Kalena! Are you all right?" Walter shrieked.

I stood there trembling and speechless.

"Did the arrow skim your mouth? Is that blood?"

"What's going on in here?" I screamed.

Walter threw down a crude bow and ran over to me.

I flung my hands up to ward him off. "It's not blood, it's chocolate."

"I, uh...I was testing an activity for the school break pro-gram."

"Archery in the galleries? You want to put bows and arrows in the hands of young children when the building is teaming with more bodies than at any other time of the year?"

"The station is aimed for children over twelve years of

age. And the netting appears to be very effective in containing the arrows."

"What does archery have to do with the library?"

"A Board member recently donated an extraordinary collection of books on Islamic weaponry to the library for the West Asian section."

"You almost killed me."

"And I'm very sorry about that. But I had locked the door. I'm not sure how you managed to break in. By the way, it's very distracting talking to you with your mouth looking like that."

"I came in here to clean myself off."

Walter pulled out an old-fashioned handkerchief from his pocket and handed it to me. I looked at it and hesitated. "I can assure you it's clean. Sterile, actually," he said.

"Thank you."

"How is it that you have chocolate powder all over your face?"

"I'd eaten some chocolate tarts en route to the office when I noticed I looked like a freak. That's why I ducked in here." I harrumphed. "Would you like a tart?"

"No thank you. Perhaps you could give my tart to Brenda."

"Brenda doesn't like sweets."

"But I thought she had an insatiable sweet tooth."

"Where did you get that idea?" I said.

"I'd heard that someone in your office adored chocolate. I presumed it was Brenda." Walter's expression transitioned to dour.

How could I have been so blind? "What do you know about truffles?"

"You mean the highly coveted species of underground

ascomycetes belonging to the fungus genus whose fruiting body is considered a delicacy? Some call it the diamond of the kitchen."

"No, I meant the type belonging to the chocolate confections genus, the kind customarily made with a ganache center."

"The chocolate ones...yes. They're named for their resemblance to the truffle fungus."

"Walter!" I stomped my foot and he jumped. "Are you familiar with Jeff de Bruges chocolates?"

"There appears to be some more cocoa on your face." Walter tugged the hankie from my grip and gently wiped a spot on my cheek. "That's the last of it."

"Jeff de Bruges?" I said.

"My...my uncle is in the chocolate industry."

"And he gives you samples?"

"On a regular basis," he said.

"And you've been trying to sweeten Brenda up."

Walter looked down at his feet.

"And it was you who tried to sneak into the office the other night? Do you know Security has been on the hunt for you?"

"I've been acting foolishly, I know. Please, please do not say a word to her. I'm prepared to do anything to keep your silence."

"Anything?" I lifted my eyebrows.

"What did you have in mind?" Walter stepped away from me.

"I'm just teasing. I can't imagine needing any kind of favor from you."

"You never know. Some sort of emergency might arise someday."

"Has it ever crossed your mind to just ask Brenda out on a date?"

"I don't actually have any experience dating."

Yoy! This man needed more help than I had suspected. "Do you mind if I make a suggestion?"

"Proceed."

"Get yourself a subscription to *Maxim*."

Walter's eyes widened. "Isn't that a top-shelf maga-zine?"

CHAPTER TWENTY-FIVE

Before Walter released me from his private archery range, he swore me to silence again both about the incident and his crush on Brenda. But as soon as I popped out the door, I flew to the office bursting to tell my colleague that Walter was the infamous truffle-dropper-offer. If I left things up to him, it would be another decade before he revealed himself to the love of his life. Certain if I used the right approach, still to be determined, I could convince Brenda to go out with the introverted librarian. Despite his geek streak, he was an attractive man and an intellectual equal to her. And, if it took playing Cupid to shave off at least some of Brenda's tough exterior, I was willing to give up my first-born in my next life.

I turned the office doorknob but it was locked. Odd. Perhaps Brenda had a meeting off site she had forgotten to mention. Once inside I dropped my gear and checked my voicemail box.

"Hey, Kalena. It's me, Bren," said voice on the recording. "I fucked up my ankle again, and I did a stellar job. I tripped over a box of exercise equipment my certifiable mom left in my hallway, and I heard something snap. I tried to suck it up, but it was bloody agonizing all night. I caved and called mum this morning. Big mistake. I'm sitting here in emerg with her. Actually, she's gone for some coffee. She thinks she's Florence Fucking Nightingale. Oh, for the love of– Here she comes with Big-Gulp-sized javas in hand. I'll give you another shout when I get the prognosis, if I haven't died of caffeine poisoning...Yeah, mom, it's a little excessive...no don't return it...Mom, come back...For fuck's sake, now I made her cry. Kalena, can you hold down the fort for the time being? But if I hear one reference to Mercury in retrograde, I swear, I'll have you snuffed. Gotta go." Click.

This was bad news. Brenda wouldn't have called her mom unless she was on the critical list. Crap! I had no time to cover her work right now. Crap! Why did Walter have to step on the back of her foot? Crap! Why did I take her to yoga class? Crap! Why had her mother left a box in her hallway. Crap! Maybe there was a cheery email from Geoffrey in my in-box. Crap! Nothing. He was probably waiting to hear about the tarts, so I decided to drop him a line.

'Geoffrey,' I typed. 'Your tarts arrived in tip-top shape only to be devoured voraciously and compulsively by the recipient. She managed to restrain herself and has saved two for later, though she doubts they'll survive past day's end. Yum! The Recipient.'

As I sent off the email, I noticed one had arrived from Stewart. He wanted to take me out to lunch. His noon meeting had been cancelled, but he decided to keep his reservation at Prego della Piazza. Prego's, huh? Nice treat. The la di da high-end Italian spot was located on the edge of Yorkville, tucked away on a small laneway off Bloor Street. During the Toronto International Film Festival the restaurant teemed with Hollywood celebs and even in off-season it attracted the odd star.

I puttered away the rest of the morning dealing with issues related to *Treasures of the Maya*. With the retraction of some of the artifacts from the San Francisco collections, new challenges had surfaced. A few new cases had to be ordered, the case layout reconfigured, different mounts created, labels modified and translated, and publicity materials revised. Since all these changes came with a price tag, the modifications ate up most of my contingency fund. I was not happy.

After I had finished with exhibit issues, I gave Gert another call to discuss delivery dates for the goods she had ordered for the shops, but her phone rang endlessly and didn't kick into any kind of messaging system. Had the woman ripped out her phone in a moment of pre-holiday-order-fulfillment rage or had she been abducted by aliens and whisked off to a far and distant galaxy? When I slammed my receiver down, my attention rested on the remaining tarts poised on the corner of my desk. What was the point of waiting to eat them later in the day?

* * * * *

At ten minutes to noon, I zoomed across the street to Prego della Piazza. The restaurant could easily double for an Italian design and furniture store. The dark red wood of the chairs, floors and room dividers was complemented by equally rich and deep-hued fabrics covering upholstered walls. Lighting was minimalist and it set off the ochre decor. The hostess, who was attempting to seat two men standing just inside the doorway, wore a white shirt so crisp you could probably snap off the collar.

"If you can bear with us just a moment, Mr. Byrne," said the olive-skinned Siren, "we're setting up a table in the back."

"It's my fault for not calling ahead. There's no need to fuss," said a man with an Irish accent, his back towards me.

Mr. Byrne? As in Gabriel Byrne? OH, NO! What were the chances? With a less-than fluid Michael Jackson moonwalk, I

174

was backing out when I stepped on someone's toe.

"Ouch."

I whipped around.

"You're supposed to be moving forward," said Stewart.

"Sorry about that, Stewart. I was feeling a little claustrophobic in here."

Stewart looked over my shoulder. "There are only two people ahead of us."

"Do you have a reservation?" said the hostess to us.

The man standing ahead of us twisted around.

"Yes...yes," said Stewart, nudging me in the back of the ribs at the sight of Gabriel Byrne. "Under the name of Anderson, for two."

The smiling greeter perused her list. "Ah, yes. We'll seat you momentarily."

"You look very familiar," said Mr. Byrne.

"Me?" said Stewart.

"No." Mr. Byrne looked me directly in the eyes. "I'm sure we've met somewhere."

"I...uh...I don't see how that would be possible. I don't travel in your kind of circles."

"Your table is ready, Mr. Byrne," said a man who had appeared from behind the hostess.

"I remember now," said Mr. Byrne. "You're the woman who followed me from a movie screening to the Museum...when I was here for the film festival."

"You must be mistaken, I don't think—"

"Kalena works at the Museum." I'm sure Stewart thought he was doing me a service volunteering the information.

"That's right," said Mr. Byrne. "When I spoke with a security guard, he told me you were an employee and not some

175

crazed fan off the street."

"Just a crazed fan from the Museum." I grinned at Stewart.

"But then you disappeared into the shadows of The Bat Cave." Mr. Byrne referred to the Museum's reconstruction of a Jamaican bat cave, complete with hundreds of mounted bat specimens, eerie lighting, sound effects and twisted pathways.

"You have a remarkable memory, Mr. Byrne." My face must have been redder than the ripest of peppers.

"A tool of the trade," said the Irish actor.

"Your table is in a private section in the back," said the hostess. "You won't be disturbed, I assure you."

"Excellent," said Mr. Byrne. He turned and whispered to me. "This is just a coincidence that we met again, correct? You haven't gone and bribed my personal assistant for information on my whereabouts?"

I shook my head 'no'.

"Then we will likely never meet again. A pleasure, Ms..."

"Boyko. Kalena Boyko." Great. Now Gabriel Byrne had a name for his Toronto stalker, and I would probably end up on some TMZ stalker-watch list.

Mr. Byrne followed his lunch guest towards their table, and the entire restaurant turned and peered at the understated celebrity.

"I can't believe you stalked Gabriel Byrne," said Stewart.

"He's one of my favorite actors," I said. "And who can resist that Irish accent?"

"I think there's a side of you I know nothing about," said Stewart.

"Your table is ready as well," said the hostess. She led us to our seats and handed us menus. "Your waiter will be

176

with you shortly."

"Wait until I tell Patsy about this. She loves Gabriel Byrne," said Stewart after we sat down at the table. "She was addicted to *In Treatment* and adores all his movies."

"So, what are you going to have for lunch, Stewart?"

"I think I'll have some Irish stew."

"Oh, stop. It was a moment of temporary insanity."

"I'm just teasing. I'll drop the subject."

"Thank you."

A waiter with a strong Sicilian look approached the table. "Can I get you something to drink?"

"Actually, I think we might be ready to order. Are you, Stewart?"

"Go ahead," he said.

"Organic greens and the grilled calamari. You can bring them together. And some spring water, please."

"And you, sir," said the waiter.

"I'll have the sea bass. And make that a large bottle of spring water. We'll share it."

"Very good," said the waiter as he took the menus from our hands.

"Did I hear right? No steak and no diet cola?" I said.

"Patsy's been after me. I swear she's had spies watching what I eat ever since my last doctor's visit."

"Good for her. With all the traveling you do, you should at least have a healthy diet when you're at home."

"Says the chocolate addict. I'm surprised you didn't order dessert," said Stewart.

"I'm cutting back too," I said while checking for traces of chocolate powder on my hands.

"Speaking of health, Brenda told me she left you a message this morning about her ankle."

"She did. Have you heard anything more from her?"

"I have," said Stewart. "She severed her Achilles tendon. Her doctor suspects she injured it beforehand and her stumble at home was the straw that broke the camel's back. But she hasn't lost her wry sense of humor. She asked me to tell everyone she came down the wrong way on her foot while making a spectacular save at a beach volleyball match."

"That sounds like Brenda."

"Unfortunately," said Stewart, "rupturing an Achilles tendon is worse than breaking an ankle. It's a very long recovery. She's been banished to bed rest for two weeks."

"For an Achilles tendon?" Two weeks! Two weeks of carrying Brenda's workload!

"Her mother's in the process of checking her into a private clinic."

"That's pretty extreme isn't it?" I said.

"Her mother doesn't believe Brenda will get the rest she needs at home. She decided private care was the only way to ensure her daughter's full recovery."

"Why doesn't her mother take her in?"

"Some kind of pet dander issue."

Lord, why was this happening to me? I hadn't noticed the waiter approach, and I jumped when he placed the dishes in front of us.

"Be careful with your fish, sir. Your plate is very hot."

"Thank you. It looks...healthy," said Stewart.

The waiter smiled and walked away.

"Not that any time is a good time to sever a tendon, but Brenda's absence is going to put a strain on things," I said.

"Especially since I'm heading to Hong Kong at the end of next week and then to Singapore."

"You are? Has the Hong Kong project been confirmed?"

"One last little hoop to jump through. They would like me to pitch it to the donor of the collection. I'm sure it's just a formality. But it will be strange seeing the Ogden opal collection on display at the museum in Hong Kong."

"The stolen opals? Ogden opals? As in Geoffrey Ogden? I'm confused."

"Have I not told you that story?"

"Noooooooo. I think I would have remembered something like that if you had."

"An inadvertent oversight. I must say, it is a bit of a tragic tale. Geoffrey's grandfather loved to play poker. Unfortunately, the Museum's founder was very fond of the game as well – and he was a more skilled player."

"Charles Trick Currelly?"

"Where do you think the nickname Trick came from?"

"I don't think it's in any of the authorized biographies of the man," I said.

"True, true. Well, Curelly had his eyes on the Ogden opal collection since the first time he saw it. But Geoffrey's grandmother absolutely adored the opals, her birthstone, you know, and she was not willing to part with them for anything. I suspect Currelly was just waiting for the perfect opportunity to acquire them for the Museum's collections. Unfortunately, it took one night of an abundance of drink and a poker hand that spiraled out of control and the Ogden family lost part of their heritage. And the opals quietly became part of the Museum's collection."

"Unbelievable." My hands trembled as I raised my fork to my mouth.

"Currelly was known to do anything when it came to building the foundations of the Museum, but that's how things were done back in the day," said Stewart.

I set my fork back down. "But when the opals were stolen—"

"You can imagine what a disgrace that was for us. Not only did we trick the Ogdens out of their family jewels, but then we failed to keep them safe."

"Yet Geoffrey is on such good terms with the Museum."

"The Ogdens are fine people," said Stewart. "I never sensed any of the family members held a grudge, except perhaps towards Geoffrey's grandfather who lost the opals in the first place."

"Interesting. Wow. This is the stuff movies are made of."

"Perhaps Geoffrey will show you the remaining family jewels when you're over there. Their entire art collection is an impressive one."

"What do you mean when I'm over there?"

"I'm sending you to London...to assist Geoffrey in presenting the Lisbon report to the clients in Brenda's absence."

I felt as if about to dive off a ten-meter platform into a bucket of water. "But I thought you bought some time on that presentation."

"We had. But there has been a change of plan. The British Museum Association is having its annual conference in London in a few weeks. The Portuguese contingent has decided to attend and Geoffrey was asked to hold the presentation at the London headquarters during the conference."

I sat on my hands to keep them still. "I don't mean to question the decision, but Geoffrey just spent a couple of weeks in Lisbon. I would've thought he was more than capable of dealing with the clients on his own."

"He is, but the Lisbon group is insisting someone from Toronto be at the table considering the bulk of the report was drafted here. And because I'll be somewhere in between

Hong Kong and Singapore..."

"That leaves me." I took a calming yoga breath, inhaling through the nose and exhaling making a sound as the air passed by the back of my throat.

"I am most cognizant that leaving the Museum at this time will be challenging for you," Stewart said. Translation: I recognize the timing sucks.

"We're coming down to the wire with *Treasures of the Maya*. The exhibit's scheduled to arrive around the time you'll be leaving for Hong Kong."

"I've taken that into consideration. I'll speak to Richard about taking a more proactive role in the exhibit."

Reality Check: Richard won't pull his weight on the project. I was so royally screwed.

I smiled at Stewart. It was an unconvincing smile.

"And there's Veronique as well," Stewart said.

My mouth fell agape.

"All right. I can see I am only making matters worse. Let's pretend I never said Veronique's name out loud."

"Yes, let's not mention the V-word again," I said.

"Trust me, I had no intention of dumping so much on your shoulders," said Stewart. "But challenges bring out the best in us." Stewart laughed from the depths of his belly. "We'll keep the trip brief. But I think we can add on a couple of days over the weekend, and I'll ensure Geoffrey frees up some time to play the good host and tour guide."

London with Geoffrey? But now? Did it have to be now? How was I going to manage everything? More importantly, who was going to keep an eye on Richard while I was away?

Chapter Twenty-Six

"On a scale of one to ten, how much do you hate me?" said Brenda on the other end of the phone line.

"For what?" I said.

"For abandoning you in a time of crisis."

"I keep reminding myself of that Chinese proverb, 'may you live in interesting times.'"

"Hah. That so-called proverb is actually the first of three curses."

"And great scholar of Chinese studies, prithee tell me what the other two curses are." I twirled an exquisitely delicate, long-stemmed rose between my fingers, its base embedded in a small vial of water.

"May you come to the attention of those in authority and may you find what you are looking for."

"Speaking of curses, how's the clinic?" A couple of days had already passed since Brenda had severed her tendon.

"As usual, my parental unit went hardcore. This lockdown place I'm checked into, against my will I might add, doesn't have phones in the rooms. I had to bribe one of the nurses to lend me her cell."

"I wondered why you hadn't called. Are you sure you're not in some drug rehab clinic drying out from a crystal meth addiction you've kept hidden from me?"

"I may as well be. Beats me how my mother found this asylum. It's some kind of spa-slash-retreat filled with high-level execs on the verge of nervous breakdowns. All outside communications are banned to keep the inmates' stress levels down."

"That is pretty hardcore."

"So, what's new at work? Anything exciting?" asked Brenda.

I spun the rose stem between my fingers again. "Your secret admirer's been at it again."

"Another truffle delivery?"

"A rose this time. It's gorgeous — pale yellow with frosted red edging."

"What the hell does that mean?"

"I suspect he finally figured out you don't eat chocolate."

"It's about fucking time. You'd think if someone were smitten, they'd do their research."

This wasn't the right time to out Walter.

"What's going on in here?" I heard a voice say in the background on Brenda's end.

"Shit," said Brenda.

"Where'd you get that phone? You're not authorized—" said the same voice.

"I'm busted. You're on your own," whispered Brenda. "I'll call you when I split this nut house."

"Give me that cell phone." I heard a scuffle follow.

"What's your computer password?" I screamed into the receiver. The line went dead.

Damn it. I needed that password for access to the current Lisbon file. Without it, someone from IT would have to crack her computer. And that someone would most likely have to be Aurelia.

* * * * *

Following my conversation with Brenda, I shot off an email to the Manager of IT and specifically asked that anyone other than Aurelia assist me in tapping into Brenda's files. I sent another email off to Stewart and carbon copied Geoffrey to let them know Brenda was in no position to finalize the report from her 'prison cell.' Just how long was Mercury in retrograde? If I was going to survive the next few weeks, I needed the planets and stars aligned in my favor. At least Gert had finally returned my calls and we had arranged a rendezvous off-site. Caligula had been traumatized during his last visit to the Museum and Gert did not want to risk him being 'emotionally damaged' again. I snatched up my black and white wool hound's tooth overcoat and headed out to meet the odd couple.

As I passed through the staff entrance, Marco's absence from his regular post and the sight of pouring rain visible through the glass doors darkened my mood, especially since I had left my umbrella on my desk. Once outside I dashed to a bus shelter for temporary cover. I twisted towards the backlit panel of the structure and saw my reflection superimposed over the image of a life-sized, scantily-clad young woman frolicking on a tropical beach. 'Bounty Chocolate Bars, A Taste of Paradise,' the slogan read above my reflection. Of course, it was paradise when one had a cellulite-free body and unlimited chocolate-covered coconut at one's disposal.

The traffic in my path cleared and I shot across the street to Ned's. The last time I was there was when Bob-just-call-me-Bob set off the fire alarm. I pulled up my coat collar and threw on a pair of sunglasses in case the campus police had my picture on file. Inside, the nondescript university cafeteria brimmed with people, but there was no sign of Gert or Caligula, so I took a seat and shed my coat.

"Hello, stranger," said a voice from the other side of the table.

I gazed up and my dour spirit evaporated into thin air. "Hello, Zeffirelli."

"Are we on formal terms now, Boyko?" Marco said.

I giggled. "No, I'm just being silly." The sight of the ever-cute Marco amid all the chattering university students had reminded me of *Love Story* and the star-crossed characters played by Ryan O'Neal and Ali MacGraw. They had referred to each other by surname throughout the film. "Are you getting lunch?"

"Just finished. I was about to head out when I saw you come in," said Marco.

"I'm meeting Gert and—"

"Caligula. I better watch out or that little mutt'll swallow me whole," said Marco.

"He probably could. Gert told me he's part boa constrictor."

"Ha, ha. So, what's new with you these days?" Marco plunked himself into the chair across from me.

"Chaos, utter chaos."

"I guess there's a lot going on with the big exhibit coming soon. You must be very excited."

"Over the moon." I stroked my index fingers across my wrists as if I were slitting them open.

"I better hide the real knives then. I just heard they won't have the new security cameras for the opening."

"You're kidding me, right?"

Marco shook his head slowly. "Apparently the purchasing department messed up the tender process, and they had to start over again."

"Why didn't anyone tell me about this?"

"No one wants to admit they screwed up."

"Do they not realize they're putting the exhibition at risk?"

"They're going to hire a lot more guards than usual for the exhibit," Marco said.

"I don't believe this is happening. I'm not even going to be around when the exhibit's being mounted. That means Richard's going to have free reign of the exhibit while I'm away. We may as well just hand him the jaguar mask."

"Wait a minute. What do you mean you're not going to be around?" Marco said.

"I'll be in London. I leave the day *Treasures* hits the loading dock."

Marco's expression turned mopey. "Business or pleasure?"

"Business. Geoffrey and I have to make a presentation to some clients together."

"I see."

Marco's expression shattered my heart into a million little pieces. "I won't be gone long."

"I could give you a ride to the airport. The airport limo drivers are on strike."

"You're kidding me, right?"

Marco shook his head slowly. "For a couple of weeks now and with no end in sight."

Out of the corner of my eye, I spotted Gert with Caligula in tow. And just two steps behind them stood Aurelia. WTF? "I'll get back to you," I said to Marco. "I have to scram. My lunch date has arrived. Good luck."

"With what?"

Aurelia's gaze locked with mine. Even from a distance, I could sense her black soul.

Marco rotated his head to see what I was staring at and he spotted Death Metal Chick. "Pleeeeeease, don't leave me now."

"Sorry, you're on your own, big boy."

CHAPTER TWENTY-SEVEN

During the next week and a half, I learned more about the terms 'ramp up' and 'sleep deprivation' than a person ever needs to know. Between polishing up the Lisbon report, ensuring everything was in place for the arrival of *Treasures of the Maya* from New York, prepping Stewart for his trip to Hong Kong and deciding what to pack for London, my brain turned into a wasteland of dysfunctional activity. Visits to the gym and yoga classes had gone by the wayside, and I transformed into one large bundle of unbridled kinetic energy. On the day *Treasures* was due to arrive on the Museum's loading dock I was especially hyped as I was also leaving for London that evening.

Museum employees are an unusual breed, driven to jobs in cultural institutions by a limitless passion for history or science and by an intense desire to work in a place filled with magnificent objects and specimens. Yet, being amidst such treasures, day-in and day-out and year after year, one often became oblivious to the magical surroundings. Just another ancient Egyptian amulet or one more Tyrannosaurus Rex femur, one would think. But occasionally some spectacular acquisition or piece on loan had the capacity to rekindle everyone's fire and set the place abuzz. In the case of *Treasures of the Maya,* this effect was magnified a hundred-fold. The Royal Ontario Museum was on the verge of receiving some of the most remarkable works of art created more than a thousand years ago by a civilization renowned for its monumental architecture and sophisticated mathematical and astronomical systems. Many of the objects the ROM was about to display had never been seen by the majority of the ancient Maya and here we were, the humble employees of the ROM, on the threshold of welcoming these breathtaking works of art and artifacts.

On the morning the shipment was due, Shipping and Receiving was as impenetrable as the Canadian Mint. The dock was sealed off, and no one had access to that part of the building for blocks. The Museum's regular suppliers and couriers had been forewarned to cease deliveries, and a squad of security guards patrolled all the Museum's perimeters. Richard and I planned to be present for the uncrating of some of the exhibit's key pieces, like the stelae (the large stone slabs with intricately sculptured surfaces), the world's oldest piece of chocolate and, of course, the sensational solid gold jaguar mask.

Stewart had already departed for Hong Kong and Geoffrey would join him for a few days following our presentation to the Lisbon planetarium project group. Stewart told me it would be the first time Geoffrey would see the Ogden Opals since they left the family vault. I so wished I could be there to witness that moment.

I was fiddling around reformatting the Lisbon document to European paper size, fulfilling a request Geoffrey made at the eleventh hour, when the phone rang.

"Museum Consulting Services, Kalena Boyko speaking."

"Houston, we have a serious problem."

"Marco?"

"Yeah, listen, I can't talk long. I know you'll be hearing about this really, really soon, but I thought I'd give you a heads-up."

"What's going on?" My stomach lurched. "Did the Gremlin die?" I had brought my luggage to work and the plan was for Marco to whisk me off to the airport at the end of the day in his newly-painted sub-compact.

"It's not that. She's purring like a cat. But I just over-heard there's a small problem with *Treasures of the Maya*."

"A small problem or a big problem?" I opened my desk drawer to see whether I had any chocolate within reach. No such luck.

"It depends on your perspective, I guess."

"Marco!" I shrieked into the phone.

"One of the crates is missing."

"That's impossible."

"It's the chunk of chocolate. It was in the tiniest case, and it's nowhere to be found."

"Ohmygawd! Are you thinking what I'm thinking?" I said.

"Richard and Ms. X scooped it. Maybe in New York. But why pick some dried-up piece of chocolate? How much could it be worth?" Marco said.

"Chocolate's big business; I mean really big business. Three and a half trillion beans are harvested a year, and there are cocoa magnates out there making more money than whole nations. Any cocoa bean baron would love to have that kind of artifact as part of a private collection of chocolate par-aphernalia."

"You think so?"

"Oh yeah," I said.

"What do we do now? D'ya think it's time for me to talk to my boss about our suspicions?" said Marco.

"Even though I'm positive Richard's involved in this

crate-gone-missing episode, we still don't have any concrete evidence."

"Uh-oh, here comes Malik, and he doesn't look very happy. Gotta go." The phone clicked.

CHAPTER TWENTY-EIGHT

I plucked up the phone receiver and dialed. "Hi, Veronique. It's Kalena. I'm trying to reach Richard, and he's not answering his cell. Do you know where he is?"

"I have no idea. We're not joined at the hip, *vous savez*."

I held my tongue. A wealth of information as always. I slammed down the phone.

Richard had to be down at the loading dock. Just how good an actor was he? I decided to find out for myself and zipped downstairs. Through a small window in one of the doors, I saw Richard barking at various individuals sifting through a container full of crates of every size.

"I see you've heard the news." Malik, the Director of Security, had appeared from behind me.

"What? That Richard is officially a raving madman?" I said.

I was hoping to get a chuckle out of Malik, but there was no hint of a smile.

"I'm trying to keep my sense of humor, but we've never been short-shipped an artifact as long as I've worked here. We've had instances where a whole shipment was stalled at a border, but there are so many checks and balances that this kind of thing just doesn't occur."

"Do you have any theories?"

"Not a one. We've being using this transport company for almost as long as the Museum's been in existence, and their reputation around the world for transporting works of art is flawless."

"I better cancel my flight to London," I said.

"There's no point. A theft of this magnitude, if that's what it is, must be dealt with by the top dogs. Carson will be the one to deal with San Francisco, and the rest of the work is mine to do. No offence, but you would be redundant."

"What about the jaguar mask? Is it safe?" I asked.

"Calm down. That case has been inventoried. And we're cracking open all the other crates as soon as possible to ensure the missing chocolate was not inadvertently packed with another object."

"Any chance I can still come by for the mask's reveal? I'm so dying to see it before I leave."

"I'll see what we can do." A guard tapped on the window and motioned to Malik. "Duty calls."

I peeked into the shipping dock as the door closed behind Malik. Richard was flapping his arms and turning blue in the face. He caught me spying on him and shot me an insidious smile. A shiver ran down the length of my spine.

* * * * *

That whole day the minutes felt like hours. I glanced at the clock, set to London time, yet again and wondered what Geoffrey was doing. Was he having his car detailed so it looked impeccable when he picked me up from Heathrow?

The office door popped open and Malik appeared.

"Don't even ask. Still no sign of the chocolate. But we're taking some of the crates up to the exhibition area to unpack. Would you like to join us for the unveiling of the jaguar mask?"

"Right now? Is that even appropriate under the circumstances?" The smile on my face reached from one ear to the other.

"Right now."

Malik and I beelined to the blockbuster exhibition space where security guards were circling everywhere. Inside we joined a small group of people who had gathered around a crate.

"We just removed the outer protective coating and the Pelican Case from the crate," said our chief preparator. He referred to the specialty polypropylene cases used to transport museum objects. They were waterproof and almost indestructible.

The group irised in on the crate, and as the huddle contracted, everyone in it shared a common sense of anticipation. The preparator raised the lid incrementally. "It's show time," he said as he exposed the precious contents.

We wowed in unison at the sight of the gleaming mask of gold. The jaguar was both feared and respected by the Maya, and its skin was often used as part of a costume during special ceremonies. This exquisitely detailed and crafted jaguar mask would have been the crowning glory of a costume worn by a Maya ruler to denote his power, authority and association with the gods. Goose bumps cropped up on my arms.

"What do you think, Anita?" Malik said to the Museum's registrar.

Anita donned her white gloves to prevent the corrosive acids on her hands from making contact with the metal, and she picked up the mask more gently than a mother would a premature infant. She pulled out a magnifying glass and examined every millimeter. "It's in excellent condition. After we've made some notes for the condition report, it can go directly into the display case. The case has been alarmed, and it's the safest place for it."

Anita carefully manipulated the mask and held it upright in front of my face so I could peer through the eye holes piercing the fragile gold. Quivers ran all the way down to my feet. At moments like this, you couldn't pay me millions of dollars to work anywhere other than at the Museum.

CHAPTER TWENTY-NINE

After Anita let me peek through the eye holes of the jaguar mask, she passed me a spare pair of gloves. "Are you friggin' kidding me?" I said. "You're going to let me hold it?"

"It's the least I can do after all the abuse you've taken as project manager over the past months," Anita said.

"Hear, hear," the group cheered in unison.

Expecting to hear an objecting jeer from Richard, I became cognizant of his absence. "Where's Richard? I thought he wanted to be here for the unveiling."

"He went to the airport," Malik said.

"What? Why?" I screamed. If Richard had that ancient piece of chocolate it could already be on a plane somewhere.

"He went to verify the customs documents with our broker. He was dropping someone off at the airport and said he could kill two birds with one stone."

This was not good news. Was Richard escorting Ms. X to her escape? Why wouldn't they just take the stolen chocolate to Borovsky? I felt helpless, and a huge lump formed in my throat. "I've got to go." I delicately passed the mask back to Anita and headed towards the exit.

"Kalena, wait," Malik yelled after me. He caught up to me and put his hand on my shoulder. "Is something the matter? You looked spooked when I told you Richard had left for the airport."

"Do you think Richard's capable—" I paused not knowing

whether to confess my suspicions to Malik.

"Capable of what?" Malik slivered his eyes.

"Do you think Richard might be involved with the disappearance of the artifact?"

"I'm going to pretend I never heard you ask that question. If you knew his family history, you would realize how absurd your accusation is."

"It wasn't an accusation. But you're right. I shouldn't have made that suggestion." I pursed my lips. This was not the time to tell Malik I knew about Richard's father and that was exactly the reason why I suspected he might be up to no good. "I'll never ever mention it again."

* * * * *

Malik's reaction had made me feel as if I was a cretin of magnificent proportions, but I couldn't shake the suspicion Richard was guilty of the theft and Ms. X was leaving the country with the contraband. Still, how would I ever regain Malik's respect? I should have kept my mouth shut, at least until I had caught Richard red-handed. Or was it too late? My body felt as if it was loaded with lead, but with just a few hours before my departure for the airport I had to step on the accelerator to finish up last-minute tasks – including picking up some chocolate for the flight. There were never enough cocoa products on airplanes.

With time at a premium, I wandered over to a small bulk food store down the street. Inside the shop, the narrow aisles were crammed with bins brimming with nuts, dried fruit, candies and, of course, chocolate. After overly analyzing the options, I settled for chocolate covered raisins as they could be eaten quietly and inconspicuously throughout the trip. Yes, indeed, these treats would serve me very well.

En route to the office I picked up the final Lisbon reports from a nearby print shop. The staff had done an exceptional job, and the reports looked spectacular. Like a proud mother or perhaps stepmother was a more appropriate analogy seeing that Brenda had done the lion's share of work, I left the shop with my head held high and a newly sourced energy coursing through my veins.

The traffic in Toronto seemed abnormally congested, and it was sure to be a madhouse leaving the city's core. It would be wise to check with Marco about escaping earlier than planned. Back at the Museum, Marco was absent from the desk at the staff entrance. Instead, I bumped into Aurelia.

"So, were you able to access Brenda's computer files?" said Aurelia.

"Uh, yes. I'm surprised Dave told you about the matter." Dave was the head of IT and Aurelia's boss.

"Dave shares everything with me. I think he might be grooming me to take over his position someday."

"Really?" Dave had confessed to me that the complaints about Aurelia's work were almost as numerous as the comments he received from the Museum's male population about her provocative clothing. I seriously doubted he would have mentioned my work request to Aurelia. She must have broken into my email box.

"Dave told me you specifically asked for him."

"We're old buddies. I thought a visit from him would give us a chance to catch up," I said.

"You seem to be old buddies with a lot of people around here," said Witchy Woman.

"I really must get back to the office," I said, sliding around her.

"Me too. One of the servers crashed. Email and the Internet are down."

"What? Again? How many days in a row is that?"

"We keep patching the server, but we haven't been able to find the root problem. We're doing a major overhaul over the weekend."

"Is the network going to be back on line this afternoon?"

"Not likely. Everyone'll have to survive a while longer."

My eyes bugged out of my head. I still had a gargantuan number of emails to send before leaving for England. "That's simply not acceptable."

Aurelia's expression turned dead cold at my officious retort. "Don't fuck with me, Boyko, or I'll tell people who care that you shut down the Museum's Internet with some stupid search on cellulite. Poor thing, is that bubbly fat getting you down?"

I plowed forward and ignored Aurelia. It was not a battle I had time to fight right now. Devil Girl could be dealt with upon my return from Britain.

At the office I double-checked my computer in hope that Aurelia had been bull-shitting me. No Internet service. I had no other choice but to ring up Geoffrey and confirm our rendezvous coordinates at Heathrow. "The cell phone you are attempting to contact is out of range of our service. Please try again later," said the automated message. Where is he, Timbuktu? I'll try calling him again later. Our meeting with the Lisbon group was scheduled for the day after my arrival, so there was no reason to panic.

I called Malik to check one last time on the status of the ancient piece of chocolate. The missing crate had not yet surfaced, he told me. Carson, Malik said, had decided if it did not turn up within a few hours he would contact both New York and San Francisco. Shouldn't the police be brought in? I asked. It was Carson's call, Malik replied, and Carson chose to delay.

Just moments after clunking the receiver down, Marco rang.

"Marco, Marco, Marco," I said. "Just put a bullet through my brain, will you?"

"Why would I want to do that?"

"This has been one of the worst days on record."

I heard Marco breathe a heavy sigh. "I don't want to put you over the brink."

"You're still driving me to the airport, aren't you?" I said, squeezing the life out of the telephone receiver with my tightening grip.

"Yeah, no problem. But I was watching the news in the staff lounge and it seems those striking airport limo drivers have blocked all entrances to the airport. They're not letting any vehicles in or out of the terminals. The highways outside Pearson Airport are at a standstill. It's one big parking lot north of the city."

"Uh-huh," I said faintly.

"Don't worry. I talked to Malik, and he said I could finish my shift early. I told him I had to drive my dad to the airport. How soon can you be ready?"

Every last life force in my body had been vanquished.

"Kalena...Kalena. Are you there?"

CHAPTER THIRTY

"Holy crow. Were you a racecar driver in a previous incarnation?" I said, gripping the Gremlin's dashboard.

"I used to street race when I was young and foolish," said Marco as he maneuvered with the precision of an Indy racecar driver through the dense expressway traffic.

"Like in *Rebel Without a Cause*?"

"More like *The Fast and the Furious.* And it's a good thing I'm experienced, or you wouldn't stand a chance of making your flight."

"As long as you don't do that Tokyo Drift thing on the off ramp," I said.

Marco turned to me for an instant with a huge grin on his face. "My mission, Kalena Boyko, as I've chosen to accept it is to deliver you to the airport, as fast as I can, and in one piece," said Marco.

"Good. I have no intention of losing my life sliding off some hairpin turn on a Toronto freeway. *Aye carumba*, Jim Phelps! Watch out for that transport!" I flung my arms upwards and covered my eyes.

"*Merda*," yelled Marco.

"What's the matter?" I said with my hands still obscuring my view.

"Look up ahead."

I opened one eye before dropping my hands like dead weights. "*Merda* is right." We were about to join four lanes of halted, bumper-to-bumper traffic that formed a sea of multi-coloured metal that stretched for miles ahead of us.

"I've never seen anything like this, not even in a blizzard," said Marco.

Sensing my eyes well up with tears, I shifted my gaze out the passenger window. The day had finally broken me. Via the window's reflection I watched Marco snag a cell phone from the visor and flip it open.

"You shouldn't be driving and using the phone."

"It's an emergency."

"Who are you calling?" I said, holding back the waterworks and still looking away.

"My sister's boyfriend. If anyone can get us out of this mess, he can."

"How can he do anything?"

"Hey, Vince. It's Mark. How's the cab dispatching biz today?"

Mark? He calls himself Mark?

"I bet. I'm in the thick of it myself. I'm driving a friend to the airport. What are you getting on the radio? Any cabbies found a secret passageway yet?...No kidding. That's the closest you can get?...I guess that's what we're gonna have to do...Thanks, man..." Marco snapped his phone shut.

"What'd he say?"

"Hold on. I've gotta' make the exit up ahead."

"No Tokyo Drifting," I screamed as we shot across three lanes of honking cars before sliding onto an exit ramp.

"Sorry. It was the only way I could get off the highway in time."

"Where are we going?" My heart pounded uncontrollably.

"Vince said to head down Dixie Road as far as traffic is

still moving. But once it slows down, he said to pull off, 'cause there's just no point after that. Everyone's dropping off passengers on Dixie and they're walking into the terminals from there."

My patent leather pumps gleamed up at me. I had to wear heels today, didn't I? I was going to wear a pair of pants and flats, but I had opted out of comfort clothing and wore a pencil skirt and sexy shoes so I would look smashing when Geoffrey picked me up. Damn you, universe. Couldn't you have cut me a break, just this one time?

"Traffic's really starting to slow down, so I think I better find a place to stop soon. And it'll be on foot from here. Vince said it's taking cabs two to three hours to get closer to the terminal buildings, but it'll only take you about an hour to walk it."

About an hour? I pushed up the sleeve of my coat to check the time. "At least we left really early. I should still be able to make my flight."

"There's a gas station up ahead. I'll pull in and see if they'll let me park for a couple of hours."

"Why do you need to park the car?"

"I'm not gonna make you haul your baggage three miles."

"Are you kidding me? I don't need a porter. I've got a Heys bag – you know, 'high-end designer luggage for today's fashionable traveler' and light as a feather. And, for once, I packed light too. It's ridiculoso for you to escort me."

Marco pulled into the gasoline station, and we hopped out of the car.

"I'm not listening to anything you're saying." Marco put his fingers in his ears and started to hum loudly.

I planted my hands on top of Marco's and lowered his

arms.

"This is a deal breaker for me," I said. "I am woman, I am strong. I can do this alone. Hell, I've crawled through mountains in the interior of Turkey, climbed the tallest pyramids in Mexico, snorkeled in barracuda infested underwater caves in Colombia. I even got to the top of a rock climbing wall with these nails." I let go of Marco's hands and showed off my manicure.

"You have?"

"Hard to believe, I know. But yes, I have...So I can do this, but I love you for offering to help."

Marco blushed a hot pink.

"It's so Walter Raleigh and I really appreciate it. But I'm going in alone."

"Is that a line from some movie?" Marco smiled.

"It should be." I advanced towards Marco, lifted up onto my tiptoes and pecked him on the cheek. His face felt even smoother than his hands. Damn, did he have to be so adorable? "Now, jimmy that trunk open and hand me my bags."

Marco ambled towards the rear of the car and hauled my suitcase out of the trunk. "I guess you like the color purple," Marco said, handing me the violet case.

I tugged at the extendable handle. "Doesn't everyone? Listen, I know there's not much you can do back at the corral, but—"

"I'll do my best to keep an eye on Richard." Marco slammed the trunk closed.

It occurred to me that if Richard was at the airport earlier, we probably passed him on his way back to the city.

* * * * *

Gawdamn skinny skirts. Lunatic limo drivers. Brainless shoe designers. I could not believe I hadn't packed a pair of flats or runners for that matter. With such a tight schedule, I knew there would be no chance to go to a gym, so I had not bothered packing any workout gear. Bloody hell.

I had already been walking for forty-five minutes dragging my suitcase behind me. Damn suitcase was damned heavy. I had lied to Marco. Packing light was not in my vocabulary. Most other travelers trekking towards the terminal buildings passed me as I stumbled down the middle of freeway ramps usually filled with speeding vehicles. The scene was straight out of some sci-fi flick about a civilization in which cars were made redundant after the world's oil reserves had been depleted. People of all races, sizes and ages traipsed across deserted freeways, transporting only the goods they could manage to heave. The situation was surreal, frighteningly surreal. I stopped for a moment and dug into my purse for the chocolate-covered raisins. If ever I deserved some chocolate, this was the time.

I ripped off a metal twist-tie, plunged my hand into the plastic bag and dropped a few of the orbs into my mouth. Eeeeew. The taste was hideous. These weren't chocolate-covered raisins. O.M.G. I'd stocked up on chocolate-covered coffee beans, otherwise known as the confection of choice for people high on drugs. I managed to swallow the mouthful and was stuffing the remaining cocoa-covered caffeine into my purse when I saw a police officer ahead. Thank the frigging heavens. The roadways I was traversing had never been intended for pedestrians and signs indicating the direction to various terminals were scarce. I was afraid I had taken an erroneous turn and was headed towards the wrong terminal.

"Hi there...Hi," I yelled as I scrambled to the policeman.

"Hello, ma'am. Guess you're having quite a day?"

Ma'am...whatever. "Yes, it's quite an adventure. Can you tell me if this is the right way to Terminal 2?"

"I'm sorry, but I can't help you with that information."

"Huh?"

"We're just stationed here to make sure people walk on the side of the roads and that no one gets hurt."

"And you can't tell me where Terminal 2 is because?"

"We belong to the same union as the limo drivers, and they've asked us to support their protest by remaining neutral – and that includes not giving out directions."

I looked at the officer incredulously.

"We shouldn't even be here at all, but we don't want anyone killed," he said.

"Well, hmm," I said. "Perhaps you can tell me this; when I'm walking down the middle of this particular expressway and I'm run over by a renegade van, when the media covers the story, will they say, 'Limo Protest Victim Run Down by Airport Shuttle Van While Trekking to Terminal 2'; or would it be, 'Limo Protest Victim Decapitated by Airport Catering Truck While Dragging Luggage to Terminal 3?'"

"It would be the first one, ma'am."

"Thank you. Thank you very much. Have a righteously good day."

"I'm sorry," the policeman said.

I kept on walking, raised my arm high and gave the officer the finger. But I dropped my limb immediately. How old was I?

Almost another half hour passed before I spotted signage for my terminal. I felt like doing the famous Rocky dance at the top of the stairs of the Philadelphia Museum of Art, but I didn't think I could pick my feet off the ground. Instead

I forged onwards, but noticed I had developed a limp. I halted, removed one of my shoes and discovered I had lost the rubber tip from one of the heels. It was probably stuck in that patch of tar I had stepped into earlier. Bloody hell. One heel was several millimeters shorter than the other. I glanced at my watch and observed that the trek had taken considerably longer than anticipated.

When I finally stepped into the terminal, utter chaos prevailed as screaming passengers formed long, snaking lineups. I glanced up at one of the television monitors and the words, 'Delayed, Delayed, Delayed' appeared after every flight number. With squinted eyes I found my flight information on the teleboard. Thankfully my flight had been postponed by an hour, but considering the length of the lineups, I was skeptical I would be checked in on time.

I rotated to grab the handle of my suitcase when I clocked a tall woman wearing a beautiful royal blue suit. The splash of color stood out amidst an ocean of beiges, grays and browns. It reminded me of the suit Richard's lover had worn the night of the ballet performance. Could it possibly be? I was darting towards the woman when I heard an airport employee bellow above the din, "Is there anyone here flying on Air Canada Flight 406 bound for London?"

"Me, me," I said, keeping my gaze fixed on the figure in blue disappearing into the masses. When the crowd parted slightly, I saw the lady in blue more clearly. It was Ms. X, and she was carrying a small Pelican Case.

"You need to get into that line over there," said the Air Canada attendant.

"But there's someone I need to speak to first," I said.

"You'll have to talk to them later," said the impatient man sporting a handlebar moustache. "We're doing our best to keep up with the international flights."

"But I—"

"Please, miss. It'll make life a lot easier if you just do what we ask. Everyone's a bundle of nerves. People are exhausted from the walk here, their flights have been delayed, and they haven't been taking too kindly to the way we've prioritized flights. Some people are getting downright nasty."

"Point me to the line," I said. There was no point chasing Ms. X. She had already disappeared into the throngs of passengers.

The queue which I joined moved more slowly than a wounded snail. People behind and in front of me recounted woeful tales about their journey to the terminal. I checked my watch every five minutes and hoped Geoffrey had the sense to check the update on my flight at his end. But just in case, I pulled out my cell phone and dialed him. I received the same message as earlier in the day, that his cell phone was out of range. Where was he?

Another half hour passed and my agitation level was off the Richter Scale. The airline employee with the crazy moustache whizzed past me, and I yelled out, "Excuse me, sir."

"You're still in line?" he said.

I shrugged my shoulders.

"Follow me and just ignore everyone," he said.

"Hey, hey, where are you taking that woman?" yelled someone who had been ahead of me in line.

With my head lowered, I trotted forwards like a horse with blinders on. My fearless escort led me to an open counter.

"There you go, miss. Enjoy your flight."

"Thanks," I said. "I hope you survive the night."

"Me too," he hollered back.

The counter attendant checked me through in record time, but gave my suitcase an odd once-over. Surely, he must have seen other purple valises before.

"You'll have to go to the gate immediately. Your flight's boarding."

"Already? Will my luggage make it on board?" My bag trailed away serenely on a conveyor belt running behind the attendant.

"You leave that to us. I recommend you make your way to your gate as fast as you can?"

Crap...crap, crap, crap. My bag would never get on my airplane on time. I galloped through the building as speedily as possible with one defective shoe. The agent at the security checkpoint insisted I remove my pumps, and I passed through the metal detector in stockinged feet. The floor was freezing, and I stepped into a puddle of liquid. Yuckeroo! Once past airport security, I pushed the fast forward button, and with my wet foot slipping inside my shoe, I hightailed it towards the gate. Once on the moving sidewalk, the heel-*sans*-rubber-tip kept catching in between the metal slats. People grunted and harrumphed each time I stopped and stooped to wedge my pump out of the horizontal escalator. When I hit the tile floor again, it was clear that the heel had worn down to the metal. I sounded like a one-legged tap dancer as I peeled my way through the echoing halls.

My departure gate was at the furthest end of the terminal, and upon arrival the airline staff was closing the door to the boarding tunnel.

"Wait," I yelled. "Please wait."

"You made it by the skin of your teeth," said an attendant. "You're lucky we held the flight a few extra minutes."

"Thank you, thank you." I handed over my ticket and passport. A flash of color up ahead caught my eye, but it disappeared around the final bend of the tunnel to the aircraft. It was probably the uniform of one of the flight assistants.

A gallant attendant with coal eyes and salt and pepper hair welcomed me on board and directed me to my seat. I turned the final corner into the center aisle of the plane and halted in business class when a man leapt out in front of me to put something up in the overhead locker. The section was full to the brim with a combination of suavely attired men, a few fashion plates and some rugged yahoos who seemed out of place. The man who had blocked my way resumed his seat wearing an apologetic smile, and I had a clear view of the passenger seated behind him. It was the woman in royal blue, Ms. X.

CHAPTER THIRTY-ONE

Since this occasion was the first in which I had been in such proximity to Richard's paramour, I studied her face as if examining a work of art in a museum. She looked fresh and relaxed, as if she had bypassed the airport mayhem entirely. Perhaps as a business-class passenger she had circumvented the enormous line-ups and had been pampered in some VIP passenger lounge. She was too young to be the infamous *Il Gattopardo* unless she had started her career as an art thief while a teen. What was the connection with the international art thief? Had she and Richard hired The Leopard to do the dirty work for them?

"Excuse me," someone said from behind me, but I ignored them.

Ms. X's cool eyes were a contrast to her tanned, glowing and well moisturized skin. This was a woman of means, but she looked subtly elegant and not opulent in her Prada. But how was it that a fud aging badly as Richard had attracted such a striking partner? Had their common passion for art theft drawn the two together? And why did I once again sense some familiarity as I examined her features? Had I seen her somewhere before, perhaps in *The Art Newspaper*?

"If you're not going to move, may I at least pass by," said the man whose passage I had blocked.

Ms. X looked up at me and our eyes locked. "Uh, sorry," I said, turning to the impatient passenger behind me. He wore a polyester suit that was so tight I thought the buttons were going to pop off like missiles.

"Is there a problem up there?" bellowed the attendant from the front of business class.

"I'm moving, I'm moving." I quickly inspected the perimeter around Ms. X's seat, and there was no sign of the Pelican Case. She must have stowed it in the storage bin above her head. If only I were sitting close enough to strike up a conversation with the mysterious femme fatale to at least determine the reason she was traveling to London.

I progressed through the cabin into economy to about a third of the way down the aisle. A female flight attendant sashayed towards me, and I leaned in towards her ear. "Can I speak with you for a moment?" I whispered.

"Certainly," she said with a perky English accent.

"What I meant was is there anywhere we can talk privately?"

"We're on a plane. I'm afraid there's not much privacy to be found."

"Well, it's just that ..." I let a passenger slide past us. "I have scoliosis and it's murder to sit in these seats for so long, especially after hauling my luggage for miles to get to the airport. It's in awful shape, and I was wondering if there was an open seat in business class. You know, with all the hullabaloo, maybe some of the passengers didn't make the flight?"

The flight attendant's Barbie Doll eyelashes and heavy blue eye shadow made her eyes pop. "There were a few no-shows, but we accepted passengers that had been dumped from other flights."

"Oh." I grimaced and placed my hand on my lower back.

"Let me know if you would like some extra pillows."

"Sure." I slipped down into my seat and feigned a wince.

A woman in her early twenties sporting dreadlocks and clothing that flowed into my personal space was seated beside me. Though we had not yet taken off, she already appeared to be in a deep sleep. Just as well as I was in no mood to chat with a stranger I would never see again. I pulled out my cell phone and attempted to call Geoffrey a final time before departure, but I received the same recorded message as earlier. Drat. I unzipped my purse and removed the chocolate-covered coffee beans and began to devour them one at a time. They didn't taste that nasty, after all. I consumed a few more. Who was I kidding? They were disgusting.

* * * * *

By the time supper was served, I had already strolled towards the front of the plane three times. I had explained to every attendant I encountered that my lower lumbar was seizing, and I needed to keep moving. In fact, the frequency of the jaunts was not only to spy on Ms. X, but also because the copious amounts of chocolate-covered coffee beans I had ingested had given me a serious case of the jitters and a knotted stomach.

During the meal, which consisted of an unidentifiable meat product, vegetable matter and shreds of fruit mixed in with sawdust, aka apple crumble, I managed to remain stationary. But following dinner my stomach was even more of a disaster, so I focused on getting my hands on Ms. X's Pelican Case. Once the meal trays were collected, lights dimmed and most passengers snoozing, it was an opportune time to sneak all the way into the forward section. But people didn't pass out as speedily as I had anticipated, and I wound up watching a Brit movie called *Wild Target* starring Bill Nighy

213

and Emily Blunt about art theft and forgery, hired assassins and sophisticated hijinks. As I watched I stewed in my seat thinking that the stolen piece of ancient chocolate might possibly be within my reach.

My body was wasted, but my mind was wired in on-position. Once the movie was over and the plane was finally a dead zone, I glanced up and down the aisle. I shifted out of my seat and in a crouched position I teetered down the row, twisting my head occasionally checking for flight attendants on the loose. I kicked an empty coffee cup that had fallen on the floor, picked it up and returned it to the tray of the polyestered passenger I had encountered earlier.

"I, uh, I'm looking for an earring," I said, turning my gaze towards the ground.

"I wouldn't go there if I were you," said the man.

"Where?"

"Business class."

"I have a friend seated up there."

"Sure, you do," said the busybody.

I ignored the remark and pressed onward. Who the hell was he, anyway? Once I reached the section where the attendants customarily rallied, I darted into a restroom and peeked through a slit in the door. No one to be seen. They must have all retreated to the rear of the plane for a talk fest. What luck! I squeezed out of the cubicle and lunged through a curtain into business class. The lighting was dim, but I could see everyone was in a reclining position including Ms. X. There were a few snorers in the crowd, and their cacophonous exhalations created an odd rhythmic drone. As I sneaked closer to Ms. X, I noticed she had rolled onto one side facing away from me. Double bonus.

I inhaled a deep breath, stretched my arm overhead and

was about to grasp the handle on the luggage bin when I heard a swoosh. A figure had passed through the curtain and was at my side. I tried to bolt, but the person grabbed my elbow and dragged me back to the other side of the drape. In the brighter surroundings, I could see it was the purser, and his stare was chilling.

"Just what were you doing in there?" he said in a hushed but stern tone.

"My back's still tormenting me. I went for a walk and was taking a big stretch when—"

"Save it," he said. "I'm not buying your cock 'n bull story. I don't know what you're up to, but if I catch you out of your seat one more time, I'll make sure airport security is on hand to greet you when we land."

My knees quivered. "What if I need to go to the restroom?"

The purser reached for a cart parked behind him and grabbed something. "Use this," he said planting a plastic cup in my hand then spinning me around.

I was treading forward when I noticed the busy body had poked his head into the aisle. He donned a malicious smile. O.M.G. The dork had finked on me.

"What'd I say?" said the man in polyester.

"Here," I said handing him the plastic cup. "You might need this."

He gave me a what-the-hell look, but I continued to my seat only to find the girl in dreadlocks was sprawled half-way into my chair. Great, just great.

CHAPTER THIRTY-TWO

managed to coax my slumberous neighbor back into her seat without waking her, but I envied her the sleep. The caffeine I had ingested took command of my central nervous system, and my stomach wound tighter and tighter over the course of the flight. I surrendered to the reality that I had a night of movie viewing ahead of me. Normally, I would have welcomed a marathon of movies, but I knew I would be a mess physically and mentally when Geoffrey picked me up at the airport. And what was I to do about Richard's lover? I couldn't just let her escape with the world's oldest piece of chocolate!

I was into my fourth movie of the flight when my fellow passengers began to join the land of the living, including my formerly comatose seatmate. She stretched out and pulled her hair from her face. She cast a sleepy gaze at my LED screen. "Anything worth watching?" she said.

"Plenty to keep any insomniac happy," I said.

Just as I finished my sentence, the pilot announced we had initiated our descent and would be landing shortly. My fellow traveler and I continued to chat, and I discovered she was a Canadian university student studying in London, but living with relatives in Wimbledon. I became animated as I shared with her the fact that I would be reuniting with my friend and former colleague, Tambra, who also lived in Wimbledon. Under other circumstances I would have stayed with Tambra, but I had decided to book a hotel in the city core near Geoffrey's office and close to London Bridge Station.

After the seatbelt light illuminated, the purser approached me. Uh-oh. What did he want now?

"Ms. Boyko? Kalena Boyko?" he said.

Uh-oh. "Yes."

"We've been advised that the luggage of a number of our late boarders failed to be loaded on time..." The purser's eyes gleamed devilishly. "And yours was one of them."

I knew it, I knew it. "What am I supposed to do now?"

"Your suitcase was placed on another flight. It'll be delivered to your hotel. If you fill out this form, you can avoid going to the lost baggage desk at Heathrow."

I snatched the piece of paper from the purser's hand, and he moved on.

"Bad stroke of luck," said my seat mate. "But at least you don't have to waste time waiting for your bag."

In fact, there was a silver lining to this piece of news. I was now free to follow Ms. X upon landing. The stars were working in my favor after all. I just needed to figure out how to convince Geoffrey to trail a complete stranger.

We landed smoothly, and the instant the aircraft stopped, I sprang from my seat with my portfolio containing the Lisbon reports in hand. I made it to the front of the line just outside business class where Richard's paramour stood a few people ahead of me. I was in excellent position for my sleuthing activities.

"Have a pleasant stay in London," said the purser to each of the passengers as they disembarked. He grinned at me insincerely and turned to the next person with another affable goodbye.

My shoe-heel-sans-rubber-tip tapped loudly on the airport's tile floor as I barreled towards passport control. The customs officer seemed intrigued when I mentioned I was in the UK on museum business. A few other people attending the British Museum Association Conference had passed through earlier, he remarked. When I mentioned my bag had been left behind in Toronto, he was sympathetic and waved me straight through. Ms. X must have sailed past as well as she was nowhere in sight – she was likely already at baggage reclaim.

I fled passport control and headed downstairs, pummeling through Heathrow's heavy crowds like a linebacker opening up the field for the quarterback. The shops I raced past were a blur. Shops? There were no shops on the way to baggage reclaim as I recalled from previous visits. Rats. Somehow, I had ended up on the departures level.

In search of some signage, I spun about like a whirling dervish and caught a whiff of something ambrosial in the air. It was the unmistakable aroma of chocolate, but the scent was infused with the even sweeter bouquet of toffee. I scanned the area and spotted the source of the chocolate perfume. It was Heathrow's Thornton's boutique, the shop Stewart frequented.

No, no! I couldn't stop. There was no time. But all those Thornton's treats: the dessert gallery, the fudge, the ice cream. Why did life have to be so complex? I pressed my nose to the window and saw a clerk milling about the store with a tray full of samples. Hallelujah. Perhaps there was no time to shop, but there WAS time to sample. I scurried towards the white-gloved server, my eyes the size of saucers.

"May I interest you in the tasting of some of our white chocolate smothered toffee, miss?"

"Sounds dreamy." To the clerk's astonishment I scooped up a hefty handful of the tidbits. "Which way is the baggage hall?"

"That would be downstairs, miss. But—"

"Thank you. And thank you for these," I said, raising my hand as I took off at full gallop.

I was scuttling through the airport popping little chunks of Thornton's into my mouth when I finally came upon the reclaim area. With a mass of luggage carousels before me, I was reminded of a program I had seen on Heathrow's labyrinthine baggage conveyor network and sorting system. Somewhere lay a room occupied by operators monitoring equipment almost as complicated as that found in air traffic control towers. I noted an overhead television screen listing the incoming flights and corresponding carousel numbers, but I didn't need to read it because up ahead I spotted a splash of royal blue. If Ms. X only knew how her ultra-chic outfit made her such a visible target.

From behind a pillar, I spied Ms. X snatch an expensive-looking suitcase from the carousel. She turned and moved towards the exit clutching the small Pelican Case in the other hand. I followed the perp through the airport and headed into open air in time to see her step into a cab. I scanned the passenger pick up lanes for Geoffrey's car, a classic Mercedes that I would recognize instantaneously, he had told me, but there was no sign of the posh vehicle – and Ms. X's cab was driving away. I made a split-second decision and hopped into a taxi. "Follow that car," I barked at the young taxi driver.

"For real, miss?" said the cabbie.

"For real."

"I've been waiting five years for someone to say that to me."

"Well now's your chance. It's a matter of life and death, of international importance, that we keep up with that taxi."

"Is it a terrorist we'll be following, miss?"

"Something like that."

The tires screeched as we pulled away. "Wow. That was a beauty," said the cabbie, looking into his rearview mirror.

"What's that?"

"A 1950 Mercedes Cabriolet just pulled into the spot we vacated."

1950 Mercedes Cabriolet? "Was it silver?" I said, slouching down into the seat.

"Yes. Are you on the lam too?" said the driver.

"Not really." I spun my head around, but we were already on a ramp exiting the airport environs. It was too late to turn back, so I pulled out my cell phone to dial Geoffrey, but the screen was black. Rats. During the flight I must have left the phone on and drained the battery. I would make it up to Geoffrey somehow.

"Do you mind if I ask what kind of business you're in?" The cabbie kept a close watch on Ms. X's taxi.

"I work in a museum...in Canada."

"Is this some kind of *Da Vinci Code* escapade? I hope you don't expect me to crash my car for you."

"No one's been murdered, and I'm not after the key to one of the biggest mysteries in the Western world. And please don't smash up your taxi on my behalf." We were just following a woman I believed had stolen the oldest piece of chocolate in the world.

I gripped the edges of the seat as we zoomed along the motorway maneuvering through heavy traffic. Over the years I had experienced many a harrowing taxi ride in cities like Cairo, Naples and Athens. But those spins paled in comparison as we swerved around countless hair-raising roundabouts tossing me from one end of the seat to the other.

"Bloody hell," cried the cabbie. "Pardon the language, miss."

"What's the matter?" I looked out the window and observed a throng of identical cabs circling a traffic circle.

"It could be any one of them. I don't know which one to follow."

"She's given us the slip." I sighed deeply.

"Sorry, miss."

"It's not your fault. It's probably a sign for me to go to my hotel and get some rest. I haven't slept in about thirty hours."

"Would that be Claridge's Hotel, miss?" The driver winked in the rearview mirror.

"I'm not exactly in Kate Moss's league. This particular super model is staying at London Bridge Hotel."

"London Bridge it is," said the driver.

With the car chase at an end, my body stopped pumping adrenalin through my system, and I crashed fast and furiously. I was slumping into the back seat when I was almost blinded by a sudden flash of light. Within seconds a thundering boom followed and rain crashed down on the car like artillery fire.

"The weather men called for thunderstorms, and here we go. I'm not sure if my windscreen wipers can keep up with this downpour," said the cabbie.

My eyes followed the hypnotic swiping of the blades on the windshield and my lids grew heavy. I leaned my head onto the backrest. Rain, rain, go away...

* * * * *

I must have nodded off, because when I next glanced at

my watch, some time had passed.

"Did you have a good rest then, miss?" said the cab driver.

"I did. But where are we?"

"Not too far from your hotel. The traffic is wicked for this time of morning. I suppose the storm's the cause of this havoc."

The rain had stopped, but water flowed heavily along the street gutters.

"You could walk to your hotel from this spot in two minutes, but it might take us another fifteen to pass through this bottleneck."

I peered at the meter. "I think I'll get out here if you'll point me in the right direction."

"Are you certain, miss?"

"The walk will wake me up."

"Whatever you think is best. I noticed you didn't have any luggage."

"It took a separate flight."

The cab pulled up to the curb, and I handed the driver a large handful of £20 notes, an amount that equaled my taxi budget for the whole trip. I wasn't sure how I'd explain the hefty fare in my expense report. There was no budget for tailing an international art thief on Britain's motorways.

I hopped out of the cab, and the driver handed me a receipt before driving off into the dense traffic. The sun peeked out from behind some clouds, and I breathed in refreshingly clean air purified by the earlier cloudburst. Cars swished past as they drove through monstrous puddles, and I heard an ominous splash of water behind me. I turned to see if anyone had been struck by what sounded like a tidal wave and was startled by the appearance of a sopping wet sheep dog at my heels. The creature was attached to a retractable leash, and its owner was quite a number of steps behind. It halted beside me, and the doused dog began to shake faster than a can of paint in a hardware store mixer. Within seconds my wearied and wrinkled outfit was covered in large splotches of filthy water. Expecting an apology from the beast's owner, I spun around, but the culprits had vanished down a laneway.

I pulled a mirror out of my purse and wiped the sludge from my face. But it was the least of my worries. The bags under my eyes looked hideous, my hair was in need of serious attention and my skin looked positively sallow. My first instinct was to click my heels like Dorothy in *The Wizard of Oz* and ask the universe for speedy transport home. Instead, I dug deep for some strength and marched towards the entrance of my hotel in true Bridget Jones fashion. Pee-u, I smelled like wet dog.

A doorman attempting to suppress a laugh drew the hotel door open for me. I was heading towards the reception desk when I saw a disgruntled-looking Geoffrey seated in a plush wingback chair. He sprang up as though ejected from the seat of a fighter jet and landed by my side.

"Geoffrey, I am so glad to see you."

Without saying a word, our man in London threaded his arm through mine and shuffled me off to a small sofa. His face was almost blue, as if he had been holding his breath.

"I am trying very hard to remain calm," Geoffrey said, "but where have you been?" he said quite loudly.

"My flight was late. Toronto was a disaster zone. I don't know if you heard, but access to the airport was cut off. I've been trying to call you since yesterday afternoon, but–"

"Didn't you get any of my messages? I have a new mobile. I emailed you the number."

"Our computer network was down before I left. I haven't been able to access my email for over a day."

"Well that explains why Stewart hasn't been responding to me either. But I've been dialing your mobile for several hours. You still have phone access, do you not?"

"The battery was depleted during the flight...Sorry."

"I still don't understand. Why didn't you wait for me as we had arranged?" Geoffrey sniffed the air and scrunched up his face like a pug nose dog.

"With my plane being delayed, when I didn't see you at the curb, I presumed you weren't able to wait. Honestly, I thought I was doing you a favor grabbing a taxi."

"What is that odor?"

"Essence of wet dog. I was the victim of a canine splattering while walking to the hotel."

Geoffrey's demeanor softened. "It appears you've had a bit of a dreadful journey. But, there's no more time to waste. You must freshen up immediately."

"What's the hurry?"

"There's been a change of plans. Our meeting with the Lisbon clients is in less than an hour."

"But my luggage is still over the Atlantic somewhere. This is all I have until the airline delivers my bag to the hotel." I looked down at my grime-spattered body in despair.

"Do you have the reports?"

I clutched my purse and realized the small portfolio I was carrying was missing. "I...I think I may have left them in the cab." The satchel must have slid to the floor of the vehicle during my nap.

Geoffrey covered his face with his hands.

CHAPTER THIRTY-THREE

It felt like an eon passed before Geoffrey released his hands from his face. "Did you receive a receipt from the chauffeur?"

"From the cab driver?" I whipped out a stub from my purse and handed it to him.

"I'll call the company and track down the reports. Now scoot to your room and..." Geoffrey gave me a quick up-and-down, "do the best you can. I'll head back to the office and keep Dr. Ravasco and his colleagues occupied until your arrival." He gave me a peck on the forehead, twisted me around and gently propelled me towards the elevator. "Oh wait. Here's your room key. I checked you in while I was waiting for you."

"You're always a step ahead." I snagged the plastic swipe card. "By the way, why was the presentation time switched?"

"I believe the client wants to see how we respond under pressure. Some dissenters on the team think Dr. Ravasco made the wrong choice recommending an English-speaking consulting firm based in North America. They're looking for any excuse to exclude us from the next stages of the project which, as you know, involve lucrative fees. If we don't knock their socks off, this will be the end of the road for us."

"Fab," I said, weakly. "Just fab."

I rushed to my room and headed straight for the bathroom. With no time to shower, I washed my greasy fringed bangs with hotel shampoo, clipped my hair up and put three layers of cover-up on the dark circles beneath my eyes. I dabbed my soiled coat with a damp face cloth and dunked my pantyhose in the sink to remove the splotches of dirt that covered them. With the pantyhose still soggy I donned them cringing at the sensation of moist synthetic against my skin. Fortunately, the room was equipped with an iron and I gave my deeply wrinkled clothes a quick press. While putting the ironing board away, I noticed a red light flashing on the telephone. Voicemail, already? But the phone hadn't rung since I entered the suite. I pressed a button accessing the message and pulled on my coat as I listened.

"Hi, Kalena. I know you haven't checked in yet, but the hotel promised this message would get into your voicemail box. Hope they're right." It was Marco's voice. "I hope you don't think I'm stalking you, but I wanted to let you know that the case with the chocolate turned up." I dropped into the sofa as if I weighed a ton.

"You won't believe what happened," Marco continued. "Some birdbrain from New York, an assistant curator or something, decided to drive the case to Toronto. He claimed he wanted to save the chocolate from the ravages of air pressure changes from yet another flight. But it didn't take Malik long to find out the guy's got a girlfriend who works at the University of Toronto, and he used the delivery as an excuse to visit her. After that, it was one screw-up after another. He forgot to change the shipment's manifest, and he claims he sent an email to Richard informing him of the change of plans. But it must have been lost in cyber space when our

226

server crashed. But the biggest beef is with customs at Pearson Airport. Someone marked the small case as having arrived and being inspected. I imagine heads will roll there. But Richard and Ms. X are off the hook. I have to admit—" Marco's last words were cut off by the sound of an electronic beep.

Ohmygaaaaaaaaaaaaaaaaawd. I had made a complete ass of myself on the plane, chased a stranger around London and jeopardized the meeting with our clients – all for nothing. But what did Ms. X have inside that Pelican Case? I would have to get back to that thought after I was finished with the Portuguese firing squad – that is, if I survived.

* * * * *

Geoffrey's office was within walking distance of the hotel, but I hopped a cab to save time. It dropped me off at a delightful Victorian building whose bottom level was occupied by a popular café and other sundry businesses. Its numerous arched doorways were painted fire-engine red contrasting with the alternating light-clay and ochre-colored brickwork that striped the building. Once inside, since there was no evidence of an elevator, I proceeded to the stairwell. My mutilated heel tapped against the worn stone stairs, and as my thighs rubbed together during the upward climb, my damp pantyhose created an annoying hum.

My lack of sleep and food and a bad case of nerves took their toll on my constitution. By the time I ascended to the third floor, I was winded. I dragged myself down the hallway and entered a door with a familiar sign on it – Museum Consulting Services – identical to the one beside our office at the Royal Ontario Museum. But when I passed through the door, the atmosphere was a stark contrast to the Zen-like tranquility of our space in Toronto. The office here was a bee-hive of activity and the noise level was almost deafening. In one corner an exotic-looking man with striking features spoke loudly on the phone in Arabic. In another section of the open space, a petite woman in her fifties unplugged a whistling tea kettle. And in the farthest reaches of the office, several people had gathered for a meeting and appeared to be arguing.

The woman brewing the tea lifted her gaze and ran over. "Kalena?"

"Phillida?" I said. She nodded. "How did you know who I was?"

"Geoffrey described you to me – pretty with big eyes."

Geoffrey said I was pretty?

"Plus, I looked up your picture on the website."

"Of course," I said. "Very efficient."

"You can call me Philly. Everyone else does."

"Thanks, Philly," I said, slipping my coat off. With her flipped-up do and retro suit she reminded me of a prim and proper Doris Day.

"Let me take that for you," she said, taking my soiled coat as though it were infected with some kind of virus. "Would you like me to send this out for you while you're in the meeting?"

"Oh, would you? I mean, if it's not too much trouble."

"There's a cleaner just below us. Leave it to me. But I need to deliver you to the conference room. The Lisbon team just arrived."

My stomach twisted back into a knot, but I followed Philly obediently as she steered us between desks and tables and past shelves overflowing with books and documents. As we skirted a small huddle of people, a large hulking mass on the other side of the room caught my eye.

Philly noticed my gaze. "It's an old safe. It's been here since the building was constructed. But it's so monstrously heavy, no one's ever dared try move it."

"How interesting? Did it ever hold the Ogden Opals?"

Philly gave me a Medusa look that almost turned me to stone. "If I may give you one good piece of advice to follow while you're with us, I would make this the last mention ever of the opals."

"But —"

"There's no time for 'buts'." Philly eased me towards an overly wide dark wood door and tapped on it. She turned the knob and poked her head in. "Kalena's here," she whispered.

Geoffrey appeared and drew me inside. Philly responded to my look of terror with a comforting smile and secured the door behind us. The room was claustrophobic, far too small for eight people. Feeling completely wired I found it impossible to focus on anyone's face.

"It is my pleasure to introduce you to Kalena Boyko from the Toronto office," said Geoffrey.

"*Boa tarde*," I said to the group. Geoffrey appeared impressed with my Portuguese.

"But where is Miss Lockhart?" said an elegant woman with a bronzed complexion and her hair pulled back severely. Her unnaturally taught skin reminded me of Greta Garbo past her prime.

"I'm afraid she had an accident and was unable to travel. Ms. Boyko will represent her here today," said Geoffrey.

What? Geoffrey hadn't warned the group that I would be here in Brenda's place? What was he thinking? I surveyed the room again. There were two women and five men of varying shapes and sizes all sporting the same grim expression.

"Kalena, please sit down over here and we will proceed with introductions," said Geoffrey, "followed by a Power-Point presentation." Geoffrey didn't have to say anything else to cue me about the gravity of the situation. There was no sign of the reports anywhere in the room.

"I've been to Portugal several times," I said as I shifted towards an empty seat. "*Eu amo seus pés.*"

Everyone raised their gaze and smiled. I even discerned a giggle. The room's heavy gray air dissipated, and I knew I had them in the palm of my hand.

Geoffrey pushed my chair in underneath me and whispered into my ear. "Where did you learn your Portuguese?"

"An old Portuguese boyfriend," I said out of the side of my mouth.

"That would explain it," said Geoffrey. "You just told everyone you love their legs."

CHAPTER THIRTY-FOUR

"Ohmygawd," roared Tambra. "It's too Ripley's. I can't believe you actually told your clients you loved their legs."

"Oh, be quiet," I said. "It was just a matter of mispronunciation. The Portuguese word for country is *país* and the word for legs is *pés*. I meant to say I loved their country."

Tambra burst into another round of laughter as she sat across from me at a table in Pret a Manger, a trendy little spot that served up top notch, fresh, healthy food. Her chocolate-colored skin was flawless. Had she been a little bit taller, she could easily have given model Naomi Campbell a run for her money. She had escaped her high-octane job at one of London's major art auction houses to join me for a quick lunch. She was dressed in a gorgeous tailored suit with pointed shoulders and a pleated skirt whose folds moved like delicate ribbons. As always, she paired her outfit with the most whimsical of shoes, a pair of black and white checkered wedges with a peep toe.

"At least your reports turned up part way through the meeting," Tambra said.

"Oh, the clients were really impressed when a cab driver waltzed into the meeting and handed over the confidential documents. And the fact that I looked like the Wicked Witch of the West coming down from a heroin high as I handed them out completely won them over."

"I'm sure it wasn't as bad as you've described. But why didn't you call me after the meeting? I would've gladly gone to the Tate Modern with you last night."

"I was in such a state after the presentation, I wouldn't have been good company, trust me." I adjusted myself on the tall polished metal bar stool. The backs of my shoes slipped off my heels as my feet dangled.

Tambra grinned and wiped away the tears of laughter that had rolled down her creamy, dark cheeks. "I do miss working with you. Your antics always kept me in stitches."

I stabbed into my tuna salad bowl and glanced up at Tambra. "How's your crayfish and avocado sandwich?"

Tambra took a nibble. "Delish," she said. "I'm glad you hijacked me. It's a treat to get away for lunch for once."

"Your job sounds absolutely whirlwind."

"It is, but it's crazy good. I absolutely adore it. And I'm in love with my flat in Wimbledon. My life is brilliant."

"I'm so happy it turned out this way — in spite of Richard."

"Are you sure this vendetta you have against Richard has nothing to do with the fact that you're still angry he fired me?"

I put my elbows on the small bar table and stared into Tambra's dark eyes. "This is no vendetta. Richard's a thief, a reprobate, a—"

"I get the picture. What about Veronique? I don't think she's clever enough to be a criminal, do you?" said Tambra.

"She might not be a willing player. Richard seems to have Svengali powers over her. Oh, let's drop this. I don't want to spend our time together talking about Richard."

"Capital idea." Tambra's effervescence reappeared. "So this young security guard sounds sooooo sweet."

232

"Young is the operative word."

"Why are you so fixated on his age?"

"Oh, c'mon. How many successful May-December relationships do you know?" My eyes wandered to the dessert board. "We'd be like Jane Wyman and Rock Hudson in *All That Heaven Allows*, without the happy ending. Marco and I are a recipe for disaster."

"And Geoffrey and you aren't?"

"I'm not worried about hurting Geoffrey," I said. "His little black book is probably bigger than the London white pages."

Tambra grabbed my hands and smiled.

"Are you finished with that?" asked one of the café staff who had appeared at the table.

"Uh, yes. Thanks," I said. The young man cleared our table of plates.

"You never did tell me what Geoffrey's feedback was on the presentation," said Tambra.

"He said I did a fine job fielding questions, considering he kept poking me in the ribs to keep me awake. Afterwards, he sent me back to the hotel to get a good night's rest while he went off to some big charity event at Leeds Castle."

"Quite posh. Where's Geoffrey now?"

"At the BMA Conference. He's schmoozing all day, hoping to drum up some business for the Museum."

"Why aren't you attending?"

"I'd rather stick needles in my eyes. All those museologists in one place – I would crack. I'm much happier doing some sight-seeing today. And tonight, Geoffrey's taking me to the 'thee-tar'."

"*Menopause the Musical*?"

"Geoffrey tried oh so hard to get us tickets for that

show," I said facetiously, "but he settled for fifth-row centres to *Billy Elliot*."

"You'll swoon over it."

"La Maison du Chocolat is near Victoria Palace Theatre, isn't it?" I said.

"At Piccadilly. I can't believe you know so much about London chocolate shops. Well, actually, I can believe it," said Tambra.

Once again, my gaze was drawn to the dessert listings on the wall behind Tambra. "I may have to have a Chocolate Brownie Bar. Care to join me?"

"I would love to, really I would. But I have to make a mad dash back to the office. They're so lost without me."

The grin on my face turned into a sour pout.

"I know, I know. This visit's been far too short," Tambra said. "But I know just the thing that'll put a smile back on your face. Take a pass on the brownie. There's a shop around the corner that's to-die-for."

My eyes lit up like sparklers.

"It's called Patisserie Lila...in Borough Market. Their *pain au chocolat* is made by French elves, I'm sure of it. Pass me your map, and I'll show you where the bakery is."

* * * * *

Outside the café, I gave Tambra a huge hug and both of us were misty-eyed. When we finally let go of each other, she darted off, and I buttoned up my coat to the neck to keep the dampness at bay. I pulled out the map, and with my pathetic navigational skills, wandered through the winding streets taking what was likely the longest route possible between the café and the shop. When I finally spotted Patisserie Lila's colorful awning, I accelerated my pace. As I drew closer, the glorious pastries came into view sending my heart aflutter. Rose meringues were heaped high on ceramic cake platters embellished with zebra-striped stems, fairy cupcakes were artfully arranged on translucent glass plates with accordion-like folds, cookies the size of saucers flowed off antique dishes and the scent of treacle tarts wafted into the street as a steady stream of customers opened the door. This was pa-tisserie Shangri-la.

Once inside I was overwhelmed by the selection, but I opted for a supremely decadent chocolate cupcake sealed with a lava-like layer of dark chocolate icing and crowned with gossamer curlicues of white chocolate. The tiny café whose walls had been stripped down to the original stone structure brimmed with people, and I decided to eat the dessert en route to my first stop.

Although St. Paul's Cathedral was nearby, I had visited it several times before and instead chose to stop in at South-wark Cathedral located on the south bank of the Thames, close to London Bridge. Near the entrance of the church, an old gentleman created a flurry of avian activity as he flung pieces of bread onto the sidewalk. Pigeons descended en masse and one swooped directly in front of my face. Startled, I dropped the Patisserie Lila's masterpiece to the ground.

"Bloody hell," I screamed staring at the mound of mouthwatering chocolate on the pavement in front of me. One of the birds meandered towards my cupcake. "Oh, no you don't," I said, stomping my foot and scaring it away. If I couldn't have the cupcake, no damn pigeon was going to feed on it either. I knelt down, scooped up the pastry into a napkin and looked for the nearest garbage can. Hmm, I won-dered...would anyone notice? I did a quick three-sixty. The only people nearby were a young couple locked in an embrace. Even the grizzled bird feeder had disappeared. I wasn't that desperate, was I? I dashed towards the cathedral, tossed the cupcake into a trash bin and scurried inside.

The repugnance I felt for almost having eaten a grounded cupcake soon dissipated as I strolled down the cathedral's magnificent nave. The humbling expanse of the vaulted ceiling, the splendor of contrasting light and dark stone, and the experience of walking upon floors eight-centuries-old melted my soul. When someone invisible from sight began to play a sublime piece on the cathedral's mellifluent organ, I was overcome with emotion and the tears poured as if from a faucet.

"Can I offer you a tissue?" said a woman who appeared from behind a pillar. She rolled up a newspaper, tucked it under her arm and pulled a packet of tissues from her dress pocket.

"Thank you," I said.

"Have you lost a loved one recently?"

"Oh, no." I mopped up the salty residue on my face. "I'm Canadian."

"I don't quite understand the connection." The sweet woman, in her early thirties, possessed the radiance of a Raphael angel.

"I was born in Canada, but I've always felt I was European. Every time I come here something inexplicable happens to me. I feel more in sync with life on this side of the pond, and when I step into places like this cathedral..." More tears streamed from my eyes, and the woman handed me another tissue. "Have you ever heard of Stendhal Syndrome?" I said.

"I don't believe I have," said the British-accented

woman.

"I hadn't either until it came up in *The L-Word*. I don't know if that television program aired over here, but it's a lesbian version of *Queer as Folk* – maybe not quite. The dialogue in *L-Word* is very literate, and the music is kick-ass, but some of my gay friends have issues with the show's content. They don't think it portrays authentic lesbian life."

I realized I was rambling, but I couldn't stop myself. The flood of thoughts inundating my brain could not be contained. "A main character in the show was the director of an art museum for a while, and in one episode she succumbs to Stendhal Syndrome. It's a condition where a person's heartbeat quickens or they become dizzy or confused, even hallucinatory when they overdose on beautiful art."

"Is it contagious?" The stranger had a smile on her face.

"I...I don't know. But it's been written up in psychiatry textbooks. I think after seeing the exhibits at the Tate Modern last night...and now this stunning cathedral. It's just too much."

"Perhaps the cure is to move to this side of the pond."

"You're probably right." I tried to decrease the rate of my breathing.

"And perhaps you'll meet a dashing Londoner who will win your heart."

"Perhaps." This was not the time to discuss Geoffrey, I decided. My nose dripped profusely, and I honked into a tissue. "You must think Canadians are flaky."

"Not in the least. My name's Haley."

"Like Haley Mills. I just loved her in *The Trouble with Angels*."

"That was one of my favorite movies as well." The woman set her newspaper on a pew, and I spotted a headline that instigated a body jolt. '*Il Gattopardo* Live at Leeds Castle: Items of Interest Disappear from Britain's Top Charity Event.'

"Holy shit!" My words echoed through the cavernous cathedral.

CHAPTER THIRTY-FIVE

"Do you mind indulging a desperate Canadian woman?" I said to my angel of mercy as I scooped up the paper, "by donating this section of the newspaper to me?"

"It would be remiss of me to deprive a victim of Stendhal Syndrome of London's arts report."

"Thank you so very, very much."

"I hope you will come back to the cathedral again. I'm here most days of the week."

"You work here?" My head twisted robotically in every direction. "In the cathedral?" I scanned the woman from head to toe. Her Ivory-girl face was free of makeup, her hair was devoid of artificial highlights and was tied back and her colorless outfit bordered on drab. What a dolt I was.

"I'm a nun, an Anglican nun...and what you North Americans might call a meeter-greeter."

"That explains your patience of a saint. Sorry about *The L-Word* banter." I lowered my head. "And the 'holy shit' thing. And all the other inappropriate language."

"I'm a nun, not a saint. And I have heard far worse language from my brothers. I do hope you have a pleasant stay in London and that you sort out your displacement issues."

"I think my confusion stems from being conceived here, in England, in Ashton-under-Lyne, in the Borough of Tameside in Greater Manchester." I edged towards the exit, backwards, newspaper in hand. "But my parents moved to Canada just before I was born."

"It all makes so much sense now," said the smiling nun.

I thanked the sister one last time for the paper and dashed from the building and to the front where I had previously spotted a garden with some benches recessed between the cathedral's buttresses. The flowers in the enchanting spot had lost their blooms, but the shrubbery and perennials were still a vibrant green. It was a veritable oasis tucked beside a bustling street and busy railway line.

I whipped out the paper and pored over the news report:

> 'As Britain's high rollers and glitterati wined and dined at the former residence of Henry VIII and no less than six of England's queens, little did they realize they were being stalked by the continent's most infamous art thief, Il Gattopardo. While guests sat down to a magnificent £1,000 a plate dinner...'

£1,000 a plate! No wonder Geoffrey hadn't invited me to the event. I'll forgive him.

> '...the cat prowled the castle in search of worthy prey. Although the Banquet Hall was filled with treasures donated by the castle guests in hopes of raising record funds for one of Britain's most worthy charities, the stealthy Leopard bypassed the jewels, paintings and sculptures designated for auction. Instead, the jungle cat pounced on the Lady Baille collection of eighteenth-century porcelains. To add insult to injury, Il Gattopardo left his tell-tale signature scratches in the castle's oak panel doors.'

Was it possible that Geoffrey had seen something while attending the event? I glanced at my watch. Drat. It was still hours before I would be able to pump him for information. I panned down the page to the photograph accompanying the story, a shot of actress Elizabeth Hurley, looking exquisite as always, with her latest squeeze on the red carpet. Wait a minute. I drew my face closer to the newspaper. The woman behind the celebrity. O.M.G. It was Ms. X. Was her presence at the scene of the crime coincidental? Was she *Il Gattopardo* after all?

* * * * *

Once I came to grips with the fact there was nothing I could do for the time being, I pushed the theft to the recesses of my mind, at least for the time being, and returned to my sight-seeing agenda. London possessed a plethora of museums, and I had a dearth of time to do them justice. But Geoffrey had once mentioned he had whiled away his youth in the Victoria and Albert Museum, so I decided to make it my top priority. It would have to be a quick visit, however, as I still wanted to pop into La Maison du Chocolat before meeting him.

As I arrived above-ground from the Tube station, my phone rang. It was Geoffrey. "Hello there," I said. "My phone's charged up."

"I am relieved and delighted." I could hear Geoffrey chuckle under his breath.

"How's the schmoozing going?"

"The schmoozing, as you call it, was most successful. I made some excellent contacts, and I've landed a meeting

241

with a group representing a consortium of museums in Cairo. There is a huge pool of money available from the World Bank to renovate the aging galleries. Even if we get a small slice of the work, it will finance Museum Consulting Services for years."

"What a score. If it works out, Stewart'll be ecstatic."

"Most definitely. This does mean, however, the timing for tonight will be tight. I thought we might meet up at the theatre bar and proceed directly to the production from there."

"That sounds like an awfully good plan," I said.

"I'm awfully glad you think so. Where are you, by the way?"

"At the V & A. I can't believe how massive it is."

"Don't miss the Music Room. It's one of my favorite spots. I used to spend hours there as a child."

"I'll be sure to check it out."

"I must dash. Cheers."

Geoffrey disconnected before I had chance to bring up Leeds Castle or ask him about his one-day-later thoughts on the Lisbon presentation. Perhaps I was better off not knowing.

I proceeded to the museum's galleries and stumbled upon the Medieval and Renaissance rooms. As I read every label of the Renaissance decorative arts objects, I relapsed back into Stendhal Syndrome. This time I was able to control the waterworks, but I had to dab my eyes a few times. Next, I moved on to Miniatures, the British Galleries, Ironwork and Silver, Glass, Fashion, Jewelry and Accessories and to countless other galleries. It felt as though I was living one of my recurring nightmares where I try to escape a building filled with an infinite number of rooms. This museum required at least another ten visits. I checked my watch, and it was approaching five o'clock. My stomach grumbled, and I had yet to visit Musical Instruments. I couldn't leave the V & A without seeing Geoffrey's favorite childhood haunt. What if he grilled me about it?

According to the floor plan the gallery was on Level 3, but I became completely twisted around and resorted to asking a security guard for directions. His Cockney accent was so indecipherable as to require subtitles. I thought I had followed his instructions properly, but I ended up circling around a large grouping of galleries and landed in the spot I had started from and encountered the same guard. Oh, you again, he said. That way, he said, pointing. Thank you, kind, sir, I said and ripped past countless stunning objects until I reached my destination. I tugged at the doors, but they were locked. How could that be? It wasn't closing time. A panic seized me, and I accosted another security guard advising him that someone had inadvertently locked the Musical Instruments Gallery. If I didn't get into the gallery, I said huffing and puffing, the last hope for love of a quickly decaying forty-year-old was at stake.

The officer looked at me as if I was a survivor of a massive lobotomy and indicated no mistake had been made. The V & A closed off sections of galleries one at a time at the end of the day as it was the only way to clear visitors from such a grandiose structure. They were being particularly vigilant following the theft at Leeds Castle the previous evening. Oh no, I screamed, *Il Gattopardo* would be the death of me yet. Did I know anything about the infamous art thief? the guard asked me most curiously. He had once victimized my city, I explained. The guard softened and escorted me to a spot where I could get a good view of the Musical Instruments

243

Gallery from behind closed doors. Thank you, I said, and the officer left me with my nose pressed against a glass portal.

The room was filled with harps and lutes, violins and harpsichords and so much more. At least now I would be able to tell Geoffrey I saw his beloved gallery. When I left the Victoria and Albert it was dark, but the shadows could not cloak the majesty of the grand architecture. The building was colossal and sacred, humbling and accessible, all at once. Tears formed in my eyes again. I had to compose myself.

The city's traffic looked horrendous, and I gambled on the underground for a speedy return to the hotel. Wrong choice. The system was plagued with delays and unimaginable crowds. Once at the hotel, I had a quick splash under the shower and changed into my theatre attire. Fortuitously, I had brought along a killer dress — a unique deep purple number. A series of eight intricately crisscrossed spaghetti straps were attached to the bodice, creating a dazzling web-like pattern on my upper back and leaving my shoulders bare. To complete the outfit, I slipped on a pair of Manolo knock-offs, seeing as the real deal was beyond a working girl's budget. But the shoes were still awfully sweet. They were black suede slingbacks with two straps across the top of the foot with small pompons hiding the clasps. They were oolala-fine and made my legs look oolala-sexy. Perhaps the ensemble was a bit flash, as Tambra might exclaim, for *Billy Elliot*, but not for Geoffrey. Perhaps next time he wouldn't think twice about inviting me to a la-dee-da charity affair.

I was ready by 6:30, and on my way towards the hotel lobby, I noticed a few heads turn. When I stepped outside the building, the doorman's jaw almost dropped to the pavement. It was the same fellow who had tried so hard to suppress a laugh at the sight of me upon my arrival at the hotel.

It was a bit of a Julia Roberts moment from *Pretty Woman*, except I had transitioned from war-weary traveler rather than from a hooker. Evidently, I cleaned up well. The doorman promptly called a cab and grinned while opening the taxi door for me.

"Piccadilly, please," I said to the cabbie. "La Maison du Chocolat."

"La what?"

"It's a Parisian *chocolatier*."

"Shock of what?"

"It's a chocolate shop...on Piccadilly, number 45." I had looked up the address in my hotel room.

The driver zigzagged in and out of traffic with great skill. "Is there something special about this shop, miss?"

"They blend the best chocolate beans in the world, and all the products they use are natural and untreated. And they never, ever substitute vegetable fat for cocoa butter."

"That makes a big difference does it, miss?"

"It's like comparing a bottle of Château Margaux to wine in a box."

"Blimey," said the driver.

"And La Maison still makes their chocolate by hand, the traditional way. They're true artisans, and they refuse to bend to modern production techniques."

"That must be rare in these times."

"It sure is. But I just hope the shop's still open."

"We'll find out soon enough. It should be just ahead."

We pulled up in front of the store, and my heart palpitated when I saw the lights still illuminated. "Can I ask a humungous favor?" I said to the driver. "I have to run to Victoria Theatre after this stop. Would you mind waiting for me? You can keep the meter running...And I'll bring you a sample."

"I'll do better than that," he said. "I'll stop the meter and come inside, if you don't mind, miss. I've never been to a real cho-cla-tee-ay before."

"You're on," I said. The driver opened the door for me, and the two of us advanced to the entrance. I noted the hours posted on the door. "It closes at seven. We just made it."

The cabbie and I seemed an odd couple, he in worn trousers and an oversized leather jacket and me in my stylish coat and frou-frou shoes. The shop was empty of customers, and the two clerks dressed in über chic uniforms greeted us with a smile and a nod. The driver put his hands in his pockets and shuffled along polished granite floors towards the wooden counters trimmed in black. At the doorway I hesitated a moment, closed my eyes and inhaled the scents of vine peaches and mirabelle plums intermingled with those of roasted almonds, Madagascar vanilla, and chocolate, chocolate, chocolate. Pure ecstasy.

As I perused the shelves dressed with confections and pastries, memories of my aunt and uncle's corner store in Hamilton came flooding back to me. Each time we visited my relatives, my first stop was the candy counter. From BB Bats and wax cigars filled with some mysterious liquid to Tootsie Rolls and sponge toffee, the store carried a selection of treats that would delight any child. Somewhere in time I graduated to Chunky Chocolate Bars, Crunchies and Fudgsicles, but with the delicacies before me, I knew I had reached a confectionary pinnacle.

"So, what do you think?" I said to the cab driver. "Caramels, coated fruits, bars, truffles?"

"They all look bloody amazing. Oh, excuse me." The cabbie whipped off his cap and glanced around as if he were in

246

church.

"I know. It's impossible to decide. Definitely some champagne truffles...and corollas...and a few macaroons and rochers suisses."

"You've been to our establishment before, madame?" said a suave clerk behind the counter.

"Only in New York. This is my first time in your London boutique." I studied the counter before me. "I'm astounded by the new associations and flavor balances of your offerings."

"I'm very pleased to hear that."

I spotted a clock on the far wall and noticed it was after seven. "It looks as if I'll have to make my selections rather quickly."

"Please take your time," said the clerk. "It is always our pleasure to serve you at your leisure."

The cab driver looked at me with raised eyebrows, apparently impressed with the exemplary customer service. I selected a variety of pieces - as many as I thought I could stuff into my purse, and a few for the driver. We bid our goodbyes to the gracious staff, headed back to the cab and, while in transit to the theatre, I transferred the chocolates from the beautiful milk-chocolate-colored bag with dark chocolate brown accents into my handbag. Although it broke my heart to leave the exquisite La Maison du Chocolat bag behind, I had no intention of flaunting my chocolate addiction in front of Geoffrey. He needn't know my love of chocolate bordered on a substance abuse problem.

"Here we are, madame," said the driver mimicking the shop clerk.

"Thank you ever so much." I handed him the fare and his tip of chocolates. "Let the chocolate melt in your mouth a few moments before you begin to chew it. The primary aromas will release during the first few seconds. Then let it rest on the roof of your mouth to experience the full body of flavors."

"I'll do my best." The driver tipped his hat and sped off the instant I closed the door.

Inside the theatre there was no sign of Geoffrey in the crowded lobby. I tucked my hand into my purse, removed a truffle and hoovered it without anyone noticing. So much for listening to my own advice regarding slowly savoring the delicacy. But my, oh my. Chocolate this divine should be illegal. While the chocolate rush rippled through my body, I became cognizant of the grandeur of the lobby, its elegant pale marble contrasting against the rococo-inspired carpet. My roaming gaze halted at a small sign on the bar wedged in the far corner. 'Ask about our chocolate martinis', it read. Were they kidding? I bounded towards the counter.

"I wanted to ask about your chocolate martinis," I said to the freckled-faced red-haired young man behind the bar.

"I'm glad to hear that," he said. "The vodka company has a special promotion here this evening, but it doesn't appear to be stirring much interest in this crowd."

"I'm actually not much of a drinker myself, maybe the odd glass of wine at Christmas."

"Is that an accent I detect?" said the bartender as he whipped up the cocktail with the speed of a seasoned mixologist.

"I'm Canadian, from Toronto."

"Have you seen many polar bears?" said the man in all earnestness.

"Only in captivity." I chuckled. "It's a little too warm for them in Toronto." The server slid a jumbo martini glass filled to the rim towards me. "How much is that?" I said, pulling out my wallet.

"£2," he said.

"But this drink must be a double."

"It's the promotion, miss."

"You should advertise the price on your sign. There'd be a stampede," I said.

"I am sure you are correct on that account. Best of the evening to you." The bartender grinned and moved to the next customer.

The lobby-bound patrons, most of whom held wine glasses and noshed on chocolate-covered strawberries, stared at my Texan-sized drink as I meandered about. The bells signaling the pending start of the performance rang, and I took larger slurps of the beverage. But where was Geoffrey? Was he going to stand me up again? I swigged the rest of the drink, devoured one more truffle and crossed the lobby. Still no Geoffrey. I bit my lower lip and proceeded through the theatre doors.

My ankles felt wobbly, and as I looked down, my feet seemed to disappear into the ornate rug upon which I cautiously treaded. The floor grade steepened, and I grabbed onto the corners of the aisle seats to keep my balance. Once seated I was overcome by a wave of fatigue and a mild dizziness. I was still jet-lagged, seriously under-nourished and also over-martinied. In retrospect, I realized I should have eaten dinner.

I had just closed my eyes when someone's finger tips caressed my bare shoulder.

"Hello, my lovely." Geoffrey plunked himself down beside me and kissed the nape of my neck.

Za-za-zing. An electric-like current ebbed through my

body. "You made it." I wiggled myself back to an upright position.

"Is that a faint smell of chocolate I detect?" said Geoffrey.

"I don't think so." Geoffrey must have had bloodhounds in his family tree. Either that or the chocolate liqueur in my drink was stronger than I had suspected.

Geoffrey winked and threaded his arm through mine. Did life get any better than at this moment?

CHAPTER THIRTY-SIX

As the thunderous roar of applause subsided, Geoffrey and I headed to the lobby for intermission.

"Is that big grin of yours an indication you're enjoying yourself?" said Geoffrey.

"I'd always thought *Billy Elliott,* the movie, was a high-voltage experience. But seeing the dance performances live – there were shivers running up and down my spine."

Geoffrey peered over my shoulder. "And a beautiful spine it is."

I found it impossible to suppress the smile that had floated all the way up from my toes.

"One hears all this nonsense," said Geoffrey, "that the midriff is the new erogenous zone. But I don't think anything's as alluring in the universe as the gracefulness of a long neck and the gentle curves of a woman's back."

Geoffrey's comment was in stiff competition with the swoon factor of Kevin Costner's line to Susan Sarandon in *Bull Durham* – the one about believing in long, slow, deep, soft, wet kisses that lasted three days. But then I wondered if Geoffrey found cellulite as seductive as the curves of a woman's back. I doubted it.

Geoffrey's gaze drifted away from me as he scoped out the lobby. "I'll try to propel my way through this feisty crowd to the bar. What can I get you?"

"A bottle of water would be heavenly," I said.

"Just water?"

I nodded.

"You really are a woman of simple needs," said Geoffrey.

After a few minutes of milling about the space, I spotted Geoffrey heading towards me. Surely my eyes were deceiving me.

"You must be a chocolate magnet. The bar has an offer on chocolate martinis tonight. I didn't think you'd be able to resist," said Geoffrey.

"You're right on that count." My tongue felt as though it were coated in fur.

Geoffrey passed me one of the glasses and clinked his with mine. "Besides, congratulations are in order."

"You've heard from the Lisbon team already?"

"I'm afraid not. Dr. Ravasco's not returning my calls."

I was so cooked. Stewart would never trust me again with the level of responsibility he had bestowed upon me on the Portuguese job.

"Congratulations are in order because the meeting with the Egyptian contingent went very well. Now drink up. The bells will be ringing soon."

Afraid I might insult Geoffrey by not partaking in a celebratory drink, I sipped the martini. "Nectar of the gods." With my empty stomach, save for a few truffles, I imagined the liquor coursing straight into my bloodstream. "You haven't mentioned the event at Leed's Castle?"

"You know those charity events, they're all the same."

"What about the special appearance?" I said.

"Elizabeth Hurley? It did cause quite a stir."

"I meant *Il Gattopardo*."

"You heard?"

"It was all over the papers – the Chinese porcelains gone missing and the damage to the doors with the claw marks. Weren't you going to tell me about it?"

"I didn't want to fire you all up again. I must say though, I'm even more convinced someone is impersonating The Leopard. Back in the day, he never intentionally vandalized property."

"You 'sheem' to know a lot more about *Il Gattopardo* than you let on."

"And you sound like you're developing a bit of a 'shlur'. Did you have any supper?"

"Not exactly."

Geoffrey took the drink from my hand and deposited it on a nearby table. "Let's get you that water."

* * * * *

"Kalena...Kalena."

"Huh, what?"

"Your phone's ringing. Please turn it off before they toss us out of here," said Geoffrey.

It took me a moment to clue in where I was and that I had fallen asleep in my seat. "I'm so sorry," I whispered. "I'd left it turned on in case you tried to reach me after your meeting." I ripped the phone out of my purse, noted the caller on the illuminated display and turned it off.

The people around us grumbled.

"What a nerve," someone said.

"How very rude," said another irate patron.

"She must be American," said a person seated behind us.

I turned to Geoffrey. "It was Carson. I better call him

back." I stood up and crawled past Geoffrey, but before advancing to the aisle, I spun around and said, "I'm European, but I'm trapped in a Canadian body."

CHAPTER THIRTY-SEVEN

I burst into the lobby and drew the cell phone towards my face. Carson wouldn't have called me in London unless it was an urgent matter. I pressed the button to access my voicemail and listened.

"Hello, Kalena, Carson here. Sorry to disturb you so late in the evening, but could you please return my call as soon as possible. It's critical I speak with you about some issues that have surfaced. Don't hesitate to call, no matter how late."

I was about to dial Carson's number when Geoffrey hurtled through the doorway, allowing the sound of applause and whistles to escape the theatre. "What's the matter? Is there some kind of emergency?" he said.

"I'm not sure yet. Carson left a cryptic message."

"It's a shame you missed the finale. Mind you, you were dead to the world for the last half hour of the performance."

"That's not true. I might have nodded off for a second."

"You were snoring, Kalena."

I certainly knew how to impress a guy.

Geoffrey smiled. "It was kind of a cute snore. I didn't have the heart to wake you up."

"You're so considerate." I grinned. "But I really, really need to call Carson."

Geoffrey gently grabbed my wrist, pulled my hand towards him and peered at my phone. "Hmm, you should give your mobile a bit of a wipe before it's permanently choco-latized."

I noted specks of chocolate, precious La Maison du Chocolat chocolate, on my cell and whipped my hand behind my back.

Geoffrey leaned in towards me and brushed his lips against my ear. "Frankly, I'm a little miffed you didn't share some of your cache with me. I may not be a chocolativore, but I do enjoy a fine piece of chocolate."

I turned my head and my lips almost touched Geof-frey's. It felt as though a magnetic field had enveloped us and was drawing us closer and closer towards each other. "I'll have to find a way to make it up to you." Did I just say that? What a brazen hussy.

"I'll hold you to that." Geoffrey tickled his cheek against mine.

I was desperate to throw my arms around him and melt into his aura.

"Go ahead and make your call." Geoffrey stepped back and shattered the force field that had shielded us from the rest of the world. We tuned in simultaneously to the boister-ous crowds streaming into the lobby like cattle. "Maybe I can find something to clean up that chocolate." Geoffrey pulled away sporting a smile that could have thawed the polar ice caps.

I planted myself in one of the lobby's corners and caught another heart-stopping glimpse of the most delicious man on the planet. I had finally found something, or rather someone, that was better than chocolate.

"Hello. Carson James speaking," said a voice startling me out of my delirious bliss.

I must have hit the 'dial last number' button on my cell

without being aware of it. "Oh. Carson. Hello. It's Kalena."

"I was hoping it was you. I do hope I have not caught you at an inopportune time."

One of the patrons who had made a comment about my cell phone ringing inside the theatre passed by, and I pivoted to face towards the corner. All I needed was a dunce cap to complete the punishment. "Not at all. How can I help you, sir?'

"Have you not heard from Richard?"

"Um, no."

"He does have his hands full and not a moment to spare these days."

Hands filled with what?

"It seems that *Treasures of the Maya* is cursed," said Carson. "No one's died, knock on ancient wood, but ever since we uncrated the exhibit, it's as though we'd unearthed Tutankhamun's tomb."

"But I thought the missing piece of chocolate surfaced?" I said.

"Yes, indeed, yes. It was our one bit of fortune. But now I'm afraid the basketry is infested with pests."

"Basketry? I don't recall any baskets on the artifact list."

"Not in the exhibition. The baskets were part of the Mexican craftwork your buyer purchased and one of the shipments wasn't properly fumigated before being stocked on the shelves."

I was puzzling about how this situation affected the exhibit, when it dawned on me. "The textiles!"

"Precisely," said Carson. "With the satellite retail area set up outside the exhibit space, there's been a danger of the bugs spreading to the display hall and devouring the textile artifacts."

257

"Have the Entomology staff been able to localize the infestation?" I picked up a *Billy Elliot* program book someone had left behind on a nearby chair and fanned my face.

"I have never seen a group of insect specialists move as quickly as they did. They swept through the area faster than a swarm of soldier ants."

"That's a relief."

"But the roof over Exhibition Hall is another matter."

My stomach clenched. "Was there a bad storm?" Some of the roofing over the older parts of the building had proved to be rather unreliable as of late.

"We were about to pull the ark out of storage," Carson said.

"Was anything damaged?" I held my breath.

"Some water damage to a few of the case bases, but it's repairable."

"Have the letters been sent to the SFMA?" I referred to the written notice we were obliged to send to lending institutions when their materials were endangered in these types of circumstances.

"The letters went out today. The dirt will be hitting the fan shortly."

There was a huge lump in my throat. "I should return to the Museum as soon as possible."

"It would be advisable, especially with the exhibit security situation at jeopardy."

"I'm not following, sir."

"The water damage went beyond the exhibit itself. The new security wiring Malik had installed was compromised. The flooding triggered some kind of electrical loop that shut down the entire Museum's security system and crashed the security company's interface with the police station."

I thumped my forehead against the wall and closed my eyes. "I'll see about booking a return flight departing first thing in the morning."

"Thank you very much, Kalena" said Carson. "We could use your trouble-shooting skills around here. We look forward to seeing you shortly then."

"I'll be back at the Museum before you know it. Enjoy the rest of your evening, sir." I deposited my BlackBerry into my purse and turned around, coming face-to-face with Geoffrey. "How long have you been standing there?"

"Long enough to realize I should cancel the reservation I had made for us tomorrow evening at an utterly charming B&B outside of London."

"You didn't?"

"Followed by brunch the next morning with my Choccywoccydoodah friends. They've closed their shop on Harrowby Street in the city, so I was going to surprise you with a little side-trip to Brighton."

* * * * *

I finally had the opportunity to ride in Geoffrey's immaculate classic Mercedes, but the trip back to the hotel was somber.

"I did manage to view the music room at the V & A," I said, breaking the silence and startling Geoffrey.

"My father donated several of the harpsichords to the collection," he said.

"Seriously. That was awfully generous of him."

"I was hoping you might have a chance to meet him before you left London, but I see that is not going to happen."

259

Meet Geoffrey's family? Get out of town! Oh, I was getting out of town. Life sucked.

Geoffrey took a sharp turn off a roundabout. "Can you share what the urgency is for you to return to Toronto?"

"Besides an insect infestation and a freaky breach in the security system, nothing much. It's nothing much at all. Just Mercury in retrograde fallout," I muttered.

"What was that?"

"I was mumbling about planetary alignments. Just ignore me."

Geoffrey leaned towards me and grinned. "You make it almost impossible to do so."

We pulled into the hotel, and the doorman opened the car door for me. Geoffrey thrust open his door, dashed towards the uniformed employee and whispered something to him.

"What's up?" I said.

"I'm just going to pop upstairs with you and use the loo, if you don't mind."

"Uh, sure. You can check out my chocolaty room. The chairs are a milk chocolate color, and the drapes and bed cover are dark chocolate. And the creamy sheets remind me of white chocolate."

"Only you would equate a hotel room's décor to different varieties of chocolate."

I led Geoffrey to my suite in silence. Only the sound of our deeper breathing was audible.

"I suppose this will be the last time I see you before your opening," said Geoffrey after we had entered the suite.

"What do you mean?"

"Stewart and I intend to return in time for your shining moment. You didn't really think we would miss it, did you?"

"I was hoping you might be there, but—"

"Well, you better fire up that laptop and book yourself a flight for the morning. Best to keep that Director of yours happy." Geoffrey gave me a quick peck on the cheek and retreated towards the door. "I'll see you very soon."

"But I thought you needed to use the loo."

Without a moment for me to bat an eyelash, Geoffrey disappeared. I stood there for a moment as if in a vertical coma. What the hell just happened there? That was the quickest exit I had ever witnessed. I shlepped over to the dresser and slid open the top drawer. Inside rested some sassy lingerie from Smart Ass's EuroTrash line. The French-inspired black and white filigree patterned fabric was trimmed with pink lace comprised of delicate hearts. I crumpled the soft 'finally long enough camisole' and 'jolie bee-keenee' in my hand and was about to toss them across the room when I changed my mind. Someone, namely me, should test whether the lingerie lived up to its promise of combining 'ooh la la and ahhh comfort.'

I stripped off my clothing, changed into the lingerie and pranced in front of the mirror. It needed two last touches, so I put on my ever-so-sexy high-heeled Manolo knock-offs and my reading specs. It was the perfect outfit for web surfing, I decided, and I sat down in front of my computer. I logged into the Air Canada website and found an outbound flight leaving at eight o'clock the following morning. It wasn't likely Marco would be able to pick me up from the airport on such short notice, but I shot him a quick email letting him know my change in plans just in case.

With my laptop tucked under one arm, I was sashaying towards the phone to arrange the required 3:30 am wakeup call – argh – when there was a knock at the door.

"Room service." I heard the swish of a card and then a familiar voice say thank you to someone on the other side of the door. The door opened and in rolled Geoffrey pushing a cart loaded with jumbo shrimp, smoked salmon, cheeses and biscuits, a bottle of wine in a cooler, a couple of long-stemmed wine flutes and a silver platter loaded with a delectable array of chocolate truffles. Geoffrey halted and stared at me as though he had never before seen a woman wearing lingerie and high heels while clutching a computer.

I felt a flutter of giggles rising up from my belly. "I didn't order any room service."

"Compliments of the hotel," said Geoffrey. He sauntered towards me and my knees quivered. "The staff of the London Bridge Hotel wanted to ensure you received the proper send-off."

Haaal-lelujah...hallelujah, hallelujah.

Chapter Thirty-Eight

Geoffrey and I had said our goodbyes several times over about half an hour before I received the call from the hotel lobby that my cab had arrived. I left Geoffrey sleeping soundly and with a note asking him to complete the hotel checkout when he was done with the room. In the bathroom I had left a lipsticked message on the mirror reading. 'Thanks for the great ~~sex~~ night" and underneath the text I signed it with a lipstick kiss. Oh dear. I hoped Geoffrey would be sufficiently discreet to wipe the mirror clean before the hotel staff came in to make up the room for the next guest!

I had called the venturesome cab driver with whom I had chased Ms. X through Britain's motorways. Despite the ungodly hour, I was a chatterbox during my transfer to Heathrow. I nattered on about how morose I felt about abandoning London prematurely – the city, the *joie de vivre,* the razzmatazz, the museums, the theatre, Tambra, and the chocolate. However, I kept the romantic episode to myself, as well as the fact that I felt I was leaving home to return to a strange land. I wondered if there was a support group for people with my kind of personality disorder, namely screwballs who considered themselves displaced persons in the country in which they were born and raised.

During the flight home, I felt like Diane Lane in an unforgettable scene in the movie *Unfaithful.* After her first tryst with an irresistible Frenchman, played by Olivier Martinez, she rides the commuter train from New York City to her home in the suburbs. On this otherwise banal voyage, she alternates from discreet smiles to soft weeping, from writhing in her seat to covering her flushed face with her hands. The excitement of the liaison, the touches, the pleasure, the whispers, the promises, the laughter, all must have been as evident on my face as they were on Diane Lane's. I fell asleep on the plane only after recalling every delicious moment spent with Geoffrey the previous night a thousand times over.

A few hours of sleep during the trans-Atlantic voyage were not sufficient to make up for the lost night, and I arrived in Toronto wiped to the core. At Canada Customs I received a strange look when I announced the only purchase I had made abroad was chocolate (my carry-on bag was full of Thornton's products I had picked up at the shop in Heathrow), but I was whisked through quickly. Baggage Claim was not as successful an experience. My suitcase was one of the last pieces to fly down the chute onto the carousel. I trundled towards the last security checkpoint with my luggage and handed in my forms just before exiting through a set of sliding doors.

"Kalena, Kalena!" I hadn't made visual contact, but Marco's voice was unmistakable. I twisted my head and saw him, his boyish smile stretching from one ear to the other. "I'm over here." Although glad to see him, I was unexpectedly inundated by a wave of guilt as though Marco would somehow guess I was consumed with memories of Geoffrey in my arms the night before. "What are you doing here?"

"You emailed me and told me you were coming home early, remember?" Marco looked so very young in his bomber jacket.

"I'm just surprised. I didn't expect you'd actually be able to pick me up."

"It turned out I had the day off, so it all worked out."

I was flabbergasted. Marco certainly got an A++ for effort. We traipsed through the indoor parking, and I gazed around.

"If you're looking for the Gremlin, I didn't drive her here. I've got a potential buyer, so I'm trying to keep her out of the rain and slush."

"Slush?"

"We had a bit of snow while you were away. It melted almost right away, but the city had salters on the streets. Can you believe it?"

"Unfortunately, yes I can. Welcome to Canada."

We walked a few more rows and stopped in front of a vintage turquoise Karmann Ghia, a two-seater sports car marketed by Volkswagen from the late 1950s to the mid 70s. Marco opened the trunk located at the front of the car.

"Shut up! Shut up!" I screamed.

"What is it now?"

"I've always dreamed of owning a Karmann Ghia."

"No kidding."

Marco opened the door, and I hopped in with great gusto. He circled around to the other side and climbed into his seat slowly. "The only thing is there's not a lot of room for a guy my height, but this car is just too sweet to let go."

I caressed the black dashboard.

"I had to do a lot of work on this one."

"You're an artist," I said. "This car looks brand new."

"Are you buckled in?" said Marco.

"Roger, Houston. Take me to the moon."

Chapter Thirty-Nine

"Is it true that the Brits really love their cars?" said Marco as we zipped along.

"Every word of it. You never see any jalopies or rundown cars on the road like you see in North America."

"I wonder what kind of car our infamous Leopard drives."

"I guess you heard about the latest heist?"

Marco nodded. "Just outside of London."

"Well, guess what? Richard's partner was on the same plane as I was on the way to London. I tried to trail her once we landed, but I lost her. And she was at Leeds Castle the night of the theft. I saw her in a picture of the event in the London papers."

"I saw that picture too, on the Internet, and I thought exactly the same thing. Actually, there were a whole bunch of pictures posted from that night. I printed them off, and they're in a folder behind the seat."

"I should've known you'd be on top of this." I unfastened my seat belt and reached back for the file. Most of the pictures were celebrity and socialite shots, but I stopped when I came to another picture of Ms. X. "Well, she was definitely there?" I said flashing the page at Marco.

Marco glanced at the photograph. "For sure."

"You know. There's still nothing we can do with these shots unless there's a picture of her lifting the porcelains."

"'Fraid not."

I skimmed through the remaining pictures and was stunned by the last one. It was a shot of Geoffrey with his arm around the waist of a drop-dead gorgeous woman. The caption underneath read 'The Stunning Lady Sahara Leamington Arrives at Leeds Castle with Geoffrey Ogden.'

* * * * *

Lady Sahara Leamington. How bloody bombastic. What kind of people named their daughter after a desert? Did she have siblings named Gobi and Mojave? No wonder Geoffrey hadn't invited me to Leeds Castle with him. He already had a date. And a very sexy one at that.

"I guess you saw the picture of Geoffrey?" said Marco.

"Yeah," I said feebly. "It's a nice shot of him and his girl-friend."

"She's quite a stunner, isn't she?"

Why not just thrust a stake through my heart?

"I guess that's his usual type. Long blond hair..."

Probably hair extensions.

"A killer shape..."

Plastic makes perfect.

"Rich..."

An accident of birth.

"Young–"

"Slow down," I yelled. "We should get off at the next exit. It's usually faster than going all the way to Spadina." If Marco said one more thing about Sahara, I would spontaneously combust.

"He's a jerk." Marco turned the wheel sharply hugging the curved exit ramp.

"Yup." If only Marco knew how much of a jerk Geoffrey was and how much of a fool I was.

"He's one of those guys who relies on cookie-cutter high society types to make himself feel better about himself."

We merged into city traffic, came to a red light and halted.

"Zeffirelli..."

"Yes, Boyko?"

"I think there's an old soul in that young body of yours."

"I'm not sure what that means, but I'll take it as a compliment." The light turned green, and we sped ahead.

Marco tried to keep the conversation going as best he could, but I had shut down. My ego had been dashed to pieces and there were a few bits of my heart in there along with the rest of the debris. How could I have been so emotionally dyslexic?

The Karmann Ghia pulled into a parking bay in front of my building. Marco leapt out of the car and scooped my luggage out of the trunk. "Are you going to be all right?"

"Sure. Things at the Museum can't be that bad," I said.

"That's not what I was talking about."

"I know."

"Well, if you need anything, like a giant tub of Häagen-Dazs Mayan Chocolate Ice Cream perhaps?"

"You're sweet. But I'm fine." I started to grab my bag then stopped. "I almost forgot." I rummaged through my carry-on piece and withdrew a box of Thorntons Continental Chocolates. "I know you're not the chocolate lover I am, but the shop clerk said this assortment was suitable for those who like 'the finer tastes associated with the Continent'."

"Cool. But you didn't have to get me anything."

"It was the least I could do for the ride to the airport and picking me up today." I gave Marco's hand a squeeze and sent him on his way.

Once I had landed in my living room, I plunked my bags down and sank into my couch. The unpacking would have to wait until that evening. I had promised Carson I would haul myself to the Museum as quickly as possible, and he would be expecting me to be true to my word. But I decided to check my Museum voicemail before I headed out just to make sure the exhibit hadn't been inundated with any new plagues.

"You have thirty-two messages. Press one to play messages," said the recorded voice. Thirty-two? How was that possible? I had cleared my voicemail box just before I left London.

"Message number one," said the automated voice.

"Uh, hello. My name is Kevin Spencer, and I go to Flesherton Creek Public School. Me and my friends, Abdul and Roger, we were diggin' around outside the school and we found a pair of really big teeth and part of a bone. We think it's really old, maybe even dinosaur teeth. Could you please call me back so I can talk to you about this some more? My number is..."

Every now and then, I, like many Museum staff, receive stray calls from the public that bypass the main switchboard.

"Message number two: Hi, my name is Nicole, and I'm calling from the Map Division at the National Geographic Society in Washington D.C. I'm hoping you can pass this request to someone who can help me. We're looking for an image of ivory snow goggles to use on a map supplement about Native Americans. Do you have such goggles in your collection? Please call me at your earliest convenience at ..."

What the hell was going on?

269

"Message number three: Hey, Kalena. It's Dave from Computer Services. I heard you'd be back at the Museum in the next day or two, and I thought I'd better give you a heads up about something. Your phone number accidentally got posted to the website as the Museum's general information line. It was only up for a few hours this morning before we discovered the mistake. Hopefully you didn't get too many wacky calls."

Too bloody late!

"I'm really sorry about this," continued Dave. "I sent Aurelia to help the web designer with a problem she was having, and we think the number accidentally got switched when they were sorting things out. We owe you one."

Aurelia. That vixen. If I found out she put my phone number on the website deliberately, I would have her tossed out of the Museum on her keister.

"Message number four: Kalena, it's me, Gert. I don't know if you heard yet about the baskets I purchased. I do not believe my products were infested. I am certain they picked up the bugs once they arrived at the Museum."

Oh, brother. Are you kidding me?

"Message number five: Hey gorgeous, it's Geoffrey." Oh, brother. He had some nerve. "Thanks for letting me get my forty winks, but you should've awakened me before you left. And thanks for the message you left on the mirror. Wink, wink."

Bottom feeder. I should have poured a bucket of ice water over him when I left.

"Message number six: Hello. My name is Violet Baker and I was wondering if admission to the Museum is still free for seniors on Tuesdays. I've been ill, but I'm finally getting back to my old routine. Please call me when you have a chance, dear. I'm at..."

The woman sounded darling, but I decided to forward the call, and all the other messages intended for the Museum's main switchboard, to Aurelia's line. That would teach her a lesson.

No sooner had I hung up the phone when it rang. "Hello," I said.

"Oh. Kalena, you are home. It's Veronique."

My eyes rolled into the back of my head. "Yes, I just got in, and I'm about to make my way to the Museum."

"*Excellente*," she said. "The staff at the SFMA went into a bit of a *panique* and they put the exhibit curator, Dr. Perry, on a plane to Toronto. He's expecting to meet you at 3:30."

"That's in less than an hour. Why isn't Richard meeting with him?"

"Poor Richard. He's come down with a cold, and he's not up to it."

"This is ridiculous. Certainly, you realize that."

There was an awkward pause before Veronique spoke again. "Richard asked me to call you, and I felt obligated—"

"Is Richard threatening you with something?"

"No! Of course not."

"Then why do you do all of Richard's dirty work? It must be demeaning for you."

"Richard has been very good to me and my family."

Family? What on Earth did that mean?

"I must sign off now," said Veronique. "I'm sure you've communicated with Dr. Perry countless times so introductions won't be necessary. He'll call you when he arrives at the Staff Entrance." The phone disengaged.

"Veronique! Veronique!" AAAAIIIIEEEEE!

271

Chapter Forty

I opened the office door and saw Brenda seated at her desk. "Hul-lo, stranger."

Brenda pressed the heel of her cast into the ground and rotated her chair to face me. She was fortressed by walls of boxes in every available space in the room.

"Well, it's about time you showed up here," she said.

I trotted over and gave her a big hug.

"Okay. That's enough. It's not as though I've risen from the dead."

"It seems as if you have to me," I said. "I wasn't expecting you back yet. I trust your mother gave you the thumbs up to return to work."

"Not exactly. I was into the middle of my second week at the clinic when I realized so-called clients could check themselves out, a small detail my mother forgot to mention. When I packed my bags and hightailed it to the city, Mum went postal, but I put my foot down...the good one that is, and told her enough was enough."

"I'm glad you're here."

"Now what the fuck are you going to do about all these boxes?"

I was completely daft. "What are they?"

"Your Mexican baskets. They can't go into the shops yet and shipping and receiving ran out of room, so pea-brained Richard made the executive decision without consulting us to dump everything here until they can be fumigated."

"So our office is going to be teeming with bugs. Ohhhhhhhhhhhhmygawd. You know I have this thing about bugs." I started to scratch my arms.

"Yeah, be careful. I thought I saw some critters scampering around."

Crikey! I jumped up on a nearby stool and scanned every inch of the floor around my desk.

"Oh, chill out. I was just kidding." Brenda started cackling like a crazed hyena.

"Ha, ha. You're always a barrel of laughs." I stepped off the stool as if descending into a pool of frigid water. "How are you doing by the way? Is that cast coming off soon?"

"Are you kidding? I have to gimp it for another month. I would've been better off with a broken foot. At least then I could've put pressure on the heel of the cast. But I have to keep my weight off the whole foot. And these fucking crutches are rubbing my arm pits raw."

"Sorry you're having such a rough time of it." I exaggerated a pout.

"My mother says there's some life lesson in this episode for me. But I'll have to consult the Dalai Lama, because I sure as hell don't see what it is." Brenda pushed down on her good foot and slid sideways in her chair revealing a beautiful bouquet in a vase.

"Wow. Those flowers are gorgeous. Who are they from?"

"Walter, of all people."

"Really."

Brenda's neck and upper chest broke out into pink splotches.

"Have you heard anything from Lisbon?" I said.

"Not yet. Just how badly did you fuck it up?"

My stomach felt as if someone had kicked a soccer ball into it, full force from a meter away. "Why? Did Geoffrey tell you I blew the presentation?"

"He didn't have to. The fact we haven't heard from Dr. Ravasco is a tell-tale sign."

"I did the best under the circumstances."

"What circumstances would those be?"

I raised my eyebrows. "It was a real piece of cake running the office and all the projects the last couple of weeks. Peachy keen, as a matter of fact." I flung open my desk drawer and rummaged around as though searching for something. Clearly Brenda had no appreciation of what I had experienced during her absence. "You'll have to excuse me. I have two minutes to prep for a meeting with the curator from San Fran. He flew up a few days early to see how badly I fucked up here."

Brenda glowered at me and spun around towards her computer monitor.

* * * * *

"So, do we have the SFMA's stamp of approval?" I said to Dr. Perry as we strolled away from the exhibition site. I had tried to gauge his reactions during our walk-through of *Treasures of the Maya*, but it was almost impossible to see his facial expressions behind his thick beard and untamed hair that hung over his eyes. I trembled in my flare-heeled boots in anticipation of his reply.

"The report I file to San Francisco," Dr. Perry said methodically as if dictating his response, "will indicate, as I had suspected, that the ROM handled the 'plagues' promptly and effectively."

"I was hoping you'd arrive at that conclusion." I grabbed Dr. Perry's hand and shook it. He pulled away looking a little embarrassed by my enthusiasm and buttoned up his suit jacket. The outfit looked as if it belonged in the Museum's collection of 1970s men's wear.

"I'm not at liberty to discuss the problems we encountered in New York," said Dr. Perry, "but I can assure you the issues there far surpassed anything I've seen here."

It just dawned on me that it was Dr. Perry's research and dating techniques that had come into question regarding the ceramics in the collection.

"I don't understand why Mr. Pritchard insisted I come to the Museum so urgently."

"Pardon me? Richard requested you come here for an inspection?" WTF? What was Richard up to?

"Highly irregular, actually. But seeing as the Museum was paying for my flight, it was a good opportunity to come up and do some research at the ceramics museum across the street."

"I'm glad it worked out for you." I wondered if anyone would notice if I strung Richard up on the flagpole outside the Museum.

"Will you stay until the opening?" I said.

"Yes, of course. Mr. Pritchard offered to cover the expenses of my extended stay."

"How gracious of him." This expense was NOT, NOT, NOT coming out of my budget. I would make sure Richard paid for this from his own department's coffers.

"I hope you won't find my presence intrusive," said Dr. Perry. "Since I'm here I'll take advantage of being present for the last days of installation."

"An honor," I said. I'm fucked.

I grinned at the visiting academic and imagined removing Richard's fingernails and toenails one by one...with a pair of pliers...and then attaching his Armani suit with him inside of it and hauling him up the flagpole.

CHAPTER FORTY-ONE

Following the walkabout with Dr. Perry, I returned to the office, dealt with my more urgent voice and email messages and decided to call it a day. I was burnt out, and all I could focus on were Richard's latest machinations. If he and *Il Gattopardo* were planning to hit the exhibit, why would he want Dr. Perry in the wings watching our every move until opening? Was it possible Dr. Perry was in on the scheme too?

Despite my exhaustion, I slept restlessly that night tormented by visions of Geoffrey entwined in the arms of that cellulite-free Lollipop Head who was named after a geological formation in Africa. I wondered if Geoffrey had noticed my cellulite before we turned off the lights in my London Bridge Hotel room? Oh, brother. I really needed to get over my obsession with my lumpy thighs.

Sleep continued to evade me as I obsessed over my conspiracy theories regarding Richard and the ever-expanding band of art thieves that had grown to include Dr. Perry. In the early morning hours, I finally recognized that perhaps my imagination had overtaken reality, but I was certain of one thing – Richard was intent on damaging my reputation at the Museum. And it was possible he aimed to have me tossed from the institution in the same brutish manner he had used with Tambra.

When I reached the office puffy-eyed and face drained

of color from lack of sleep, I was jumpier than a frog on amphetamines. It didn't help matters that we were still in a holding pattern with the clients from Lisbon. The only good news upon arrival was word from Stewart that his pitch to the Hong Kong museum's Board had been greeted with enthusiastic applause. But the announcement from Stewart threw Brenda into a rampage. She stomped around the office on her crutches ranting about all the research she would have to conduct and complained about having to work with the 'fucking impossible' curators in our Mineralogy Department. Considering the Mineralogy crew consisted of some of the most benign staff in the Museum, I chalked Brenda's caustic conniption up to frustration with her limited mobility.

I slogged through the next few days like a soulless android performing my duties efficiently but robotically. Dr. Perry and I crossed paths a few times but, for the most part, I stayed under his radar and prayed no more plagues barraged the exhibition. I also managed to avoid any encounters with Aurelia who seemed to have disappeared off the face of the Museum map since my return from London. There was no way of knowing for certain why she had inappropriately posted my phone number on the Museum's website. However, I speculated she had read the email I sent to Marco from London. And with evidence that Marco and I were more than colleagues, she probably came unglued and lashed out.

Richard was also sequestered in some secret hiding spot. According to Deepa and Veronique, he was in the building, but no one seemed to be able to track him down. And I received no calls from Geoffrey. With a half-day time difference between Toronto and Hong Kong I hadn't really expected to hear from him. Still, what a pill!

I had no idea that the amount of work required to

mount an exhibition was so staggering. The Facilities Department was still trying to complete the work on the roof covering Exhibition Hall, and Malik and his security staff continued to struggle with the new security system. Coordinating members of the department of volunteers as well as teachers from the education department who were gearing up to do public and school tours was a logistical nightmare in itself. Simultaneously, we were attempting to accommodate previews with 'friendly' journalists.

In addition, a technical glitch had been discovered in some of the audio-guide equipment, and I was battling with the rental company to replace the defective pieces. I was also waging war on various members of the Conservation Department who were being overly meticulous with several exhibit artifacts being cleaned and repaired. Information- and activity-overload zapped my brain and body, but when a brief lull surfaced in my frenzied schedule, I took refuge in my office. I was leaning back in my chair, my arms hanging off to the side like limp vermicelli when Walter poked his head into the room.

"Good afternoon, ladies." He stepped into the office.

Brenda turned around, curled up one end of her lip in a half-hearted smile and swiveled back to face her computer. Walter looked as though he wanted to throw himself off a precipice.

"Hi, Walter," I said in as upbeat a tone as possible. "The flowers you gave Brenda were positively 'gorge'."

Walter turned bright pink. Brenda stopped typing, but refused to turn around.

"Yes, well, yes. It was my pleasure. Brenda is such a valued employee."

Walter was sinking fast, and I wasn't sure if I would be

able to save him. "Is the library ready for the onslaught of visitors expected during the run of *Treasures of the Maya*?"

"Yes, indeed. I began adding books to the library collection on the Maya the instant I learned we would be hosting the exhibit."

"Excellent, Walter. We're lucky to have such a proactive librarian on staff." What a dork I was. I wasn't doing much better than Walter at making him look good.

"You must be very excited with the opening approaching," said Walter. "Will both of you be attending the gala opening festivities?"

"Not at $150 a pop." Brenda started typing on her keyboard again, but at least she was following the conversation.

"What about you, Walter? Will you be going to the party?"

"I was gifted with a pair of tickets. The donor of the books on West Asian weaponry passed them onto me when he realized he and his wife would be out of town."

"Two tickets?" I said.

"Yes."

"And have you found someone to accompany you?"

"I thought, perhaps, if you were in need of one—"

Oh, Walter. What were you doing? Offering the ticket to me was the wrong maneuver.

I shook my head like a manic cat trying to shake a mouse to death.

"That's very considerate of you, but one of the Board members purchased my ticket for me. One of the perks of being the exhibit's project manager, I suppose. Maybe Brenda could go with you. I don't think you've been to one of these events since you came to work for the Museum, have you, Bren?"

Brenda swiveled around and gave me a look that could have fried an egg in the Antarctic. "And I'm happy to keep it that way."

"Oh, c'mon," I said.

"Yes...perhaps–" Walter said.

"I really have no intention of going to my first Museum gala as a peg leg." Brenda pointed at her cast.

"You'll already be on site and working late anyway. You may as well get a delish dinner out of it. I could join you two, and we can roll our eyes at each other when Carson thanks Richard for all his hard work on the exhibit."

"It could be a more pleasant experience than you might expect." Could Walter have been any more sheepish?

"I'll think about it," said Brenda.

"I'm sure Walter needs an immediate response."

"Oh, no. It can–"

"Don't be silly," I said. "Consider it done. I'll find out who's doing the table arrangements and make sure we sit together. It'll be a blast."

"Groovy." Brenda gave me the evil eye.

"Do you have a favorite flower, Brenda?" said Walter.

"Flower?" she said.

"For a corsage."

Brenda looked stunned.

"It's not a prom," I said. "There's no need for a corsage."

"Thank you for clarifying the protocol. I would not want to perpetrate any faux pas."

"No, we wouldn't want any perpetrations," said Brenda.

"I think I'll leave now," said Walter.

"While you're ahead," I said.

Walter scrambled out, and the door slammed behind him sending a breeze through the office.

Brenda hopped towards me like the lead contender of a three-legged race and stopped in front of my desk.

I lifted my gaze slowly towards hers. "Yes?"

"Walter's the truffle freak, isn't he?"

"Yes."

"You knew all along?"

"I found out only recently, while you were laid up at the clinic. I swear."

"You just hooked me up with my stalker?"

"I honestly think you two might make a good couple," I said.

* * * * *

During the next couple of days, Brenda's iciness made me feel as if I had a case of full-body frostbite. It was almost a relief that my working hours were what Stewart called 'frentic,' a combination of frantic and hectic. But Stewart's absence during such a stressful period was difficult for me. I missed his support and his ability to distract me from my woes with his tales of past adventures. Stories such as how he had been shot at by *bandidos* while working on an archaeological dig in Central America always helped me put things in perspective. And I still had to figure out what I was going to wear to the gala. I had not had time to shop for a new dress, but Geoffrey would be at the fête, and I was determined to look killer. I wanted him to regret every second he had wasted on Lady Sahara blah, blah, blah.

Despite my best efforts, I departed the Museum very late on the eve of the exhibit opening and gala dinner. At midnight I found myself splayed out on my bed squinting at the incandescent light bulb in the middle of the dated fixture above my head. When I stared at it long enough, prismatic rays of color appeared to emanate from the center. All around me clothes were scattered in my normally tidy boudoir. I had spent the last hour trying on every dress I owned in combination with every pair of shoes. I looked from side to side at the shredded gold chocolate bar wrappers that surrounded my head like the sun's corona. In my deepest funks I had a habit of turning to my childhood chocolate bar of choice – Crunchie, 'the fun, feel good chocolate bar'. The amount of sugar in my system must have approached toxicity, but my body was stoned from fatigue. My eyelids grew heavy, and I switched off the lights.

CHAPTER FORTY-TWO

It seemed as though I had been out only a few minutes when I was awakened by a grating creeeeeeeeeeeeeeeeeeeeeeeak and a startling THUD. What was that? What time was it? Was there someone in my condo?

I was paralyzed in freeze mode, but a voice in my head was hollering I was in grave danger. There was an intruder in my space, and I needed a weapon. I mobilized my arm and fumbled for the lava lamp on my bedside table. It was a vintage piece, purple in color, and I could undoubtedly knock someone unconscious with it. I tugged at the lamp, but the plug refused to release from the wall. Perhaps if I just turned the light on? But I thought of Audrey Hepburn in *Wait Until Dark* where she played a blind woman terrorized in her apartment by a trio of thugs in search of a heroin stuffed doll. If a blind wisp of a thing like Hepburn could defend herself, so could I, I reasoned. And like her, I decided to keep the lights off as an advantage over the trespasser who would be stumbling in the dark in an unfamiliar suite of rooms.

"Ouch!" I whimpered after smashing my leg against the nightstand. Maybe maneuvering in the dark was more of a liability. With nothing to lose, I ripped the cord out of the wall, jumped to my feet with lamp cylinder in hand and turned the bedroom lights on. There was no one in sight. The closet. Maybe they were hiding in the closet. I felt as if I were in a B horror movie. 'No! Don't open the closet door, you moron,' the audience would be screaming. Good advice. The closet could wait.

With lava lamp still in hand, I tore into the small hallway outside my bedroom and illuminated all the lights. I leapt into the living room and hurdled over the coffee table into the sunroom and back into the living room. From beside the fireplace, I picked up a poker in my left hand and awkwardly jabbed it up the fireplace flue. "Come out you coward!" I yelled at the top of my lungs. "Come out, I dare you!" There was no response to my challenge. What was I thinking? Whoever had entered my condo, it surely wasn't Santa Claus, so I charged into the bathroom. 'Don't pull that shower curtain open,' said the voices of my imaginary film-viewing audience. My knees started to buckle, but I had to do it. I shoved the plastic drape to the side. No one. That left one last place.

I returned to the bedroom and reached my trembling hand to the edge of the sliding panel of my closet. Damn nerves. The universe would protect me, the universe would protect me. I ripped open the closet door in one fell swoop. Oh no! This couldn't be happening to me! I bolted to the kitchen. There was one more Crunchie chocolate bar stowed away in my cupboard.

* * * * *

When I had gazed into my closet, I realized there had been no nocturnal visitor after all. The creaking I had heard was the sound of the wooden closet rod bending before it snapped in two places. The resounding thud was the noise created by hundreds of articles of clothing making impact with the closet floor. For months I had noticed the bar supporting my extensive wardrobe was sagging. With each new

285

skirt, shirt, pair of pants or dress it bowed even more, but I just ignored it. The repetition earlier in the evening of removing and replacing different items I was considering wearing to the gala must have weakened the rod even more.

The closet looked like a tornado zone and although it disturbed me to see all my beautiful, previously perfectly pressed clothes lying in heaps on the floor, I returned to bed. When the alarm went off a few hours later I was a groggy shambles. The time I had spent the previous evening selecting an outfit was all but wasted as I scooped up the dress that had landed on top of the mountain. It was a v-necked/v-backed chocolate brown velvet piece with a sheer flounce edging the skirt. It wasn't expensive, but it looked it, and it had a classic elegance to it. I slid the frock into a garment bag along with some gold, open-toed Christian Louboutin clones and headed for the office. If I survived the day, it would be a miracle.

The trip into work was a huge blur. I suppressed a yawn when I swiped my ID at the Museum's security desk. It wasn't until after I had passed by that I wondered where Marco was. Oh, right. He was working the late shift. I contained another yawn as I stumbled down the hallway, but got creeped out when I noticed a pair of beady eyes peering through the slit window of the Information Technology Department's door. As I scurried along, I heard a door fling open.

"Hey, Kalena," said Aurelia.

"Good morning," I said without turning around.

"Wait. Hold on."

I stopped in my tracks and shut my eyes for a moment. My garment bag was slung over my shoulder.

"Looks like you're going to that big party tonight."

"I'm not sure yet," I said.

286

"Too bad Marco couldn't be your date."

I sighed profoundly. "Was there something you wanted, Aurelia? I don't have any time for chitchat today. My exhibition is opening."

"I guess you and Marco did lots of chitchatting on the way home from the airport."

Aurelia's comment was all I needed as final proof she was monitoring my email as well as Marco's. I sighed again. "Seriously, I'm drained. Can we do this another time?"

Aurelia paused and stared directly at me with her laser beam eyes. "I can recommend a good cover up for those dark circles."

"Not the one you're wearing, I hope? It doesn't seem to be doing the trick."

"Kalena," someone yelled down the hallway.

Aurelia and I turned around simultaneously and watched Walter scamper towards us.

"May I escort you towards your office." Walter was a little breathless. "That is, if you two are done—"

"We're done like dinner." I passed my arm through Walter's and tugged him forward.

"Thanks for forwarding all those phone calls to me," Aurelia said with a bitterly facetious tone.

"My pleasure. I thought you might want to deal with them personally seeing as you were the one who made that tiny error on the website."

"I just deleted the calls," she said.

"Stellar response. Your customer service training always shines through," I said.

"Does Marco know how close you are to that Geoffrey guy?" Aurelia bellowed down the corridor.

What a piece of work she was. She was reading ALL of

my emails.

"I'm not so sure about that young woman," said Walter once we were out of earshot.

"In what way?"

"She doesn't appear to be very competent in her field. She made a mess of our databases."

"I'm sorry to hear that." Her days were definitely numbered at the Museum.

"Ms. Alberti seems to have what some psychically-endowed individuals might call dark energy."

"Like a black aura? I'm surprised you know about such things," I said.

"You'd be surprised at the type of literature that crosses my desk."

"Walter," I screamed.

Walter nearly jumped out of his socks. "What is it?"

"I just noticed you're wearing new glasses."

"Yes, yes I am. That was my motive for stopping you. I wanted your opinion of them."

"Very sharp, Walter. Very sharp." I peered down at Walter's feet. "Ohmygawd! Are those new shoes?"

"I wasn't certain that Wallabies would be appropriate footwear for the gala, so I purchased these at Harry Rosen."

"You made the right choice. Is this effort all for Brenda?"

"Both you and Brenda have hinted I was in need of one of those makeovers."

"I hope I wasn't too insulting. But there's nothing wrong with keeping current."

"I suppose not," said Walter. "But I must admit I have been experiencing some anxiety. Since we pressured Brenda into attending the gala with me, she's been avoiding the library. I haven't seen her in several days."

"Don't take it personally. She hasn't been able to get out and about much."

"I never thought of that."

"Don't worry. Everything'll be fine," I said.

"I'm not sure how to thank you."

"There's nothing to thank me for. Besides, the rest is up to you. You'll have to win her over with your charm and wit."

A panicked expression overcame Walter's face.

"I know it's in you. Just relax."

"Should I come with you to the office now and bid hello to Brenda?"

"She's at the airport this morning."

"Is she leaving town? Where's she going? Will she be back by this evening?"

"She has a meeting there. The Museum's just signed a contract to develop a series of rotating exhibits for the new terminal at Pearson. Our department's taking the lead and Brenda will project manage the venture."

Walter's shoulders, which had risen towards his ears, descended a few inches. "Oh, hmm. Interesting concept. A kind of teaser, I imagine. Hit the tourists as soon as they arrive in the city."

"Exactly. Stewart 'borrowed' the idea from the San Francisco International Airport and Schiphol Airport in Amsterdam."

"Stewart's an excellent borrower."

"Yes, he is. But I really must get moving. I have a full day...and night ahead of me," I said.

"I shall see you later then." Walter turned and trotted off towards the library.

When I arrived at the office, there was a huge handwritten sign on one of the stacks of boxes of Mexican basketry. It read, 'We cannot move these right now. Hang in there. Still nowhere to put them. But maybe later today. Gaspar, Shipping.'

I threw my dress over one of the mountains of cardboard and started to repeat a mantra. "I trust in the universe to protect me to everyone's greatest benefit. I trust in the universe to protect me to everyone's greatest benefit. I trust..."

CHAPTER FORTY-THREE

ours and hours later, I was slumped over my desk when the door suddenly swung open. Veronique entered and perused the room. *"Oh, la, la. Quelle catastrophe."*

Immediately behind her, Brenda limped in. "What are you doing here?" said Brenda to Veronique. "Shouldn't you be steaming the creases out of Richard's party pants?"

"I didn't know Richard steamed his trousers?" Veronique jerked her head side to side like a nervous bird. "Stewart has just arrived upstairs, and he asked me to find you. Everyone will be sitting down for dinner shortly."

"Why didn't Stewart come himself?" I said.

"He and Carson are keeping some of the dignitaries entertained. He was unable to escape."

Walter entered the doorway and ran into Brenda who stumbled into Veronique. I couldn't help giggling at the human domino effect.

"Brenda, go ahead and get changed and head up with Walter. I'll do the Cinderella transformation in a bit." I darted towards the closet, pulled out a beautiful aquamarine silk dress and held it in front of Brenda. "Go put this on right now, or I'll...I'll..."

"You'll what?" said Brenda.

"I'll call your mother and tell her you're working late again."

"Oh, for God's sake." Brenda snatched the dress from

me, retrieved a cosmetics bag from her desk and hobbled out the door.

"I don't understand what is happening," said Veronique, "but I must go back before Richard realizes I have left the party without his permission."

"Go ahead. We wouldn't want Richard to think you might have a mind of your own," I said.

Veronique began to sputter, but when she couldn't form any words, she fled the room.

"Richard appears to have some kind of Svengali-like control over that poor woman," said Walter.

"Ya' think? Have a seat, Walter. I have a few more emails to shoot off."

A few minutes later, Brenda returned to the office. Walter and I dropped everything and stood there with mouths agape. Brenda, who had swept her hair back and pocketed her glasses looked as though the fairy make-up artist had waved her wand over her head. At this moment it appeared as if the Earth had stood still for Walter. When he regrouped, he edged towards her removing his specs. "A Pre-Raphaelite artist's muse exists in the flesh before me."

"Let's not go overboard, Walter." Brenda scrunched her clutch purse in her hands.

"I'd sell my soul to have someone pay me that kind of compliment," I said. "Now skedaddle. Tell Stewart I'll be out in a few minutes."

"You better be," said Brenda. "Or I'll come back and drag you out of here. And I'll bring Geoffrey with me, if I have to."

Geoffrey – I had almost forgotten he would be at the party. "That won't be necessary."

The debonair pair floated out of the office as though

they had just been crowned king and queen of the prom. Cupid himself could not have enabled a better match, and for a few moments, my heart tingled. But the sweet sensation dissipated as I honed back in on my surroundings. The room was horribly silent, and I felt claustrophobic amidst the mountain of boxes that loomed around me.

I darted around the boxes to the closet, nabbed my chocolate brown dress and slipped it on. The elegant gold shoes, delicate gold drop-earrings and thinly-carved dark wood bangle bracelets were the perfect finishing touches. Despite the dark circles that peeked out from behind the freshly applied cover-up, I thought I had cleaned up relatively well. But was it enough to make Geoffrey eat his heart out?

I left the office, stepped into the atrium and could hear the buzz of the party in the distance. Just a few more minutes and I would be rubbing shoulders with Toronto's social elite and enjoying my much-deserved moment of glory. As I passed by the ominous artificial volcano in the Earth Gallery, I stopped expecting to see Richard and Veronique whispering in the shadows. Would *Il Gattopardo* make an appearance this evening? Was the jaguar mask at risk?

Something cold grazed my arm and I jerked away.

"Did I scare you?"

"Marco!" I put my hand over my heart and took a deep breath. "You should think about becoming a cat burglar. I didn't hear you sneak up."

"It's these crepe-soled shoes we have to wear – they're regulation footwear for the security guards."

I smiled. "How are you? I've been so busy since I came back from London that–"

"I know. That's why I haven't bothered you. I figured you had a lot on your plate."

"I've barely had enough time to breathe."

"And I guess with Geoffrey in town—"

"Is he with Stewart?"

"Um...I don't know. I saw him yesterday."

"That's impossible. He didn't arrive from Hong Kong until late this afternoon."

"He came through the public entrance yesterday. I saw him shmooze his way into *Treasures of the Maya*."

"You must be mistaken."

"Then the guy's got a twin."

The sound of applause sounded in the distance, and we both turned towards it.

"I should probably get going before Stewart sends out a team of bloodhounds to track me down. You're here all night, right?"

"'Til the wee hours of the morning. I've been keeping my eye on Richard, but so far he's been hobnobbing with the mayor and some of the local politicians."

"I'm not surprised," I said.

"And I saw Aurelia skulking around."

"What's that about?"

"Don't know. She was hiding behind a pillar, but when she spotted me, she took off. She's probably working overtime and snuck out to check out the shindig."

That young woman was certifiable, in my opinion.

"You look pretty awesome. Like one of those women in a Renaissance painting, except your dress is shorter, and I don't think they had shoes like that back then."

"Have you been talking to Walter?"

"About what?" Marco looked adorable when he was puzzled.

"Nothing. You just reminded me of something Walter

said to Brenda earlier. Anyways, I'll catch up with you later."

As I made my way to the gala, the clickety-clack of my shoes reverberated off the monumentally tall walls. When I reached the end of the tube-like space, the atrium opened up into a huge expanse buzzing with activity. Wait staff dressed in black and white maneuvered around large replicas of Maya stelae and collected empty wine glasses and brass trays now emptied of hors d'oeuvres. A man wearing an extravagant feather Maya headdress and sporting little else but traditional Maya ceremonial body paint trumpeted a Giant Conch shell signaling the official start of the gala dinner and ceremonies. People everywhere sauntered to tables covered with brocaded chestnut fabric, fine white china and gold-colored flatware. The centerpieces, imitation Maya sculptures carved out of foam core and spray-painted gold were a stunning touch to the opulent table settings. The Museum's events department had spared no expense on the function, the cost of which undoubtedly had been picked up by a sponsor.

I zigzagged my way through the guests, about five hundred I speculated, and scanned the crowds in search of my colleagues. A whiff of sweet chocolate floated past me capturing my attention. I looked about but couldn't see the source of the heavenly aroma. Instead, my eyes landed on Richard who was seated with the Director, the Chairman of the Board, two couples who had recently been identified by Forbes as the 'richest of the rich Canadians.' Joining them was Veronique wearing a sequined Nehru jacket and in conversation with a woman sitting across the table. It was Richard's paramour – the elusive Ms. X.

CHAPTER FORTY-FOUR

The moment I saw Ms. X I panicked. Marco had disappeared from view, but security guards were everywhere. I was about to retreat and check the exhibition area for suspicious activity when I heard someone calling.

"Kalena...Kalena." Stewart was standing at a table and motioning to me.

I hesitated.

"Kalena," Brenda yelled. "Get over here."

I proceeded towards the table, hands clenched. Stewart pulled out an empty chair wedged in between his seat and Brenda's. "Hi, everyone." I plunked myself down.

"Didn't you hear Stewart calling you?" Brenda whispered into my ear.

"Just barely," I said under my breath. "Welcome back, Stewart."

"Thank you. I hear you've been burning the midnight oil. I'm sorry I haven't been around to assist," said Stewart.

"It all came together in the end." There were two empty chairs beside Brenda and Walter. "Where's Patsy?" I said.

"She's come down with the flu. I wanted to stay home with her, but she insisted I attend. She sends her best."

"I'm so sorry she couldn't make it," I said.

"What have you done with our man Geoffrey?" said Stewart.

"What do you mean?"

"He made such an effort to fly to Toronto a day early, and he's still late. I haven't been able to reach him on his mobile, and there's no answer at the hotel."

I glanced at Brenda, and she shrugged her shoulders. Marco hadn't been imagining things after all. "I'm sure he'll turn up."

A server approached the table and began pouring wine. My thoughts turned to keeping a vigilant eye on Richard and Ms. X. I covered the bowl of my glass with my hand. "None for me, thanks."

"Do you abstain from alcohol?" said Walter.

"It puts me to sleep," I said.

"Oh, look." Walter twisted his head sideways. "Carson's heading towards the microphone."

Carson ascended a small platform and approached the podium. The crowd began to clap even before he uttered a word. "Thank you, thank you all." He bowed graciously.

"You've all listened to my banter enough these past months," said Carson, "so it's my sincere pleasure to turn the microphone over to Richard."

"It's not like Geoffrey to be late for an event like this," said Stewart. "I'm a little concerned."

"Good evening." Everyone in the room leapt out of their seats as Richard's voice boomed over the P.A. system at full volume. "Oops, sorry about that." Richard backed away from the mic. "I would like to welcome you all to one of the grandest evenings in the history of the Royal Ontario Museum. Let me first of all extend the Museum's deepest gratitude to our sponsor and host of this most splendid event…"

I tuned out Richard's annoying drone and looked curiously at the dish the waiter had deposited in front of each of us.

"Kalena, what is this?" said Stewart.

"A quinoa and avocado salad." I couldn't help giggling at Stewart's befuddled expression.

"Quinoa is a species of goosefoot grown for its edible seeds," said Walter in a hushed tone. "It originated in the Andean region where the Incas held the crop to be sacred. Although the crop is grown in Mexico, it's not a Maya dish. The catering company has clearly confused the two cultures—"

"Shhh," said Brenda. "Richard's thanked everyone in the entire world. He should be mentioning Kalena any moment now."

"...to the volunteers who will be conducting tours this evening," said Richard. "And finally, I could not live with myself if I failed to mention, my most dedicated of colleagues. Without her endless hours..."

"Here it comes." Walter winked at me.

"...and brilliant spirit, this exhibition would not have opened on time...and on budget, I might add..." Someone in the hall clapped loudly and the guests chuckled. "...the indomitable, Veronique Bouvier. Veronique, please stand up."

All eyes turned to the gangly beanpole as she rose from her chair to a thunderous round of applause. Stewart and I clapped politely, but Brenda and Walter were frozen. I panned the tables around us and noted that various exhibition team members in my sightline had abstained from clapping.

The plaudits subsided, and Richard cleared his throat before continuing. "Thank you. Thank you, one and all. Please enjoy your dinner and take note that dessert will not be served at your tables, but will await you at the end of your exhibition tour." Richard left the platform and returned to his seat beside Carson and Canada's elite.

"What a f...fop." Brenda whipped her cell phone out and pressed some buttons.

"Who are you calling?" Stewart said to Brenda.

"It better not be Richard." I knocked the device from Brenda's hand.

"I was trying to call Carson," said Brenda.

"I'll speak to Carson at an appropriate moment," said Stewart. "Kalena deserves her thirty seconds of fame."

"Honestly, it's no big deal. C'mon, let's dig into this yummy dish." I poked at my salad and took a few bites. Despite the odd mixture of flavors it was surprisingly tasty. But I had lost my appetite. I had not anticipated much recognition from Richard, but I had not expected him to give all the credit for my work to Veronique. "What was that comment about dessert?"

"Didn't you see the chocolate fountain on your way over from the office?" said Brenda.

"Apparently it's the largest ever erected at an event in Toronto," said Walter.

"I caught the scent of it," I said.

"It's a surprise from the sponsor," said Stewart.

The wait staff removed our salad plates and returned with the next course, a medley of fish, lobster and shrimp accompanied by a colorful combination of squash and beans.

Stewart pondered the dish before him "Don't they have steak?"

We all giggled.

"At least I recognize the components on this plate," said Stewart.

"Traditional Maya staples," said Walter. "I'm relieved they passed on serving iguana or dog for that matter. Monkey and turtle were also common proteins consumed by the

Maya."

Both Stewart and I rested our forks.

"It might be wise to save the running commentary until after dinner," said Brenda.

"Certainly," said Walter.

"I, uh, I'm going back to the office for a sec to check on something," I said.

"But you haven't even touched your entrée," said Walter.

"I've lost my appetite."

I pushed myself away from the table and stood up.

"This exhibition would have been doomed to failure if it hadn't been for your participation and constant intervention," said Stewart. "I couldn't be more proud of you."

"That means a lot to me." I glanced over at Carson's table and Ms. X had disappeared. WTF? Where was she? I tossed my napkin on the table. "I'll be back shortly."

"Kalena," the whole table said in unison.

"Calm down, everyone. Gaspar said he might be able to move the boxes out of our office. I'm not going to miss this opportunity."

Stewart made a comment, but his response was swallowed up by the din of the boisterous crowd. I advanced through the room and strode past Richard and Carson as though inhabited by the spirit of a deadly Ice Queen.

* * * * *

Richard had plunged a knife deep into my belly by failing to give me credit for my work. Furthermore, he had twisted the knife by publicly declaring Veronique the project's 'savior'. Veronique! Of all people! She had contributed nothing

300

to the mounting of *Treasures of the Maya* and, if anything, had been a serious liability. As I sat back in my chair trying to chill an email from Richard marked urgent was delivered into my in-box. What did he want now?

'Kalena, please meet me in Prep Lab 1B7 immediately. I'm shutting off my BlackBerry, so don't bother replying to this message. I only have a few moments. Richard.'

Hah! Stewart or Carson must have reprimanded Richard for his 'minor' oversight and insisted he apologize to me. But why did he want to meet in a Prep Lab? Maybe he had decided to humble himself in privacy and the Prep Labs were remote but not too far from party central.

I bolted from the office and passed through the doors on the other side of the gallery. Once I had descended the staircase, I realized I had forgotten to advise Security I would be setting off an alarm or two. Oh well. It was too late. They had probably dispatched a floater to check the area already so I would have to apologize later for the breach.

Upon arrival at the underground level of the curatorial center, I headed towards the Prep Labs. There were various rooms dedicated to everything from carpentry and welding to taxidermy. 1B7? Where was it? It had to be up ahead. There it was. '1B7 Ornithology Prep Lab.' Why would Richard pick the bird preparation area? But since when did Richard do anything logical?

I twisted the knob, and the door opened. It was as black as road tar inside.

"Richard? Are you here?"

There was no response. Great. Not only did he order me to meet him in these bizarre surroundings, but he was late. I located a switch on the wall and a single dim light was illuminated. As my eyes adjusted, I noticed a bag suspended above my head. I gazed up and saw a stuffed stork gripping a diaper bag in its beak. Ornithologist humor, I guessed. Beside it, hung a vulture – one of Richard's predecessors. I snickered.

It was impossible to avoid banging into things in the tight space. The room was jammed with fume hoods, desks, filing cabinets and boxes. I walked over to a storage unit and pulled out a tray. Yech! It was filled with countless specimens of small birds. I had heard the Museum was a repository for the 5,000 plus dead birds collected annually by FLAP. The Toronto animal rights group gathered birds that had crashed into skyscrapers that were illuminated at night, and the Museum took most of the skykill off their hands for research purposes. But I never realized the Museum had such an extensive and morbid morgue on site. I shoved the tray back in and noticed more ornithologist humor up ahead. Someone had cut out an image of the Grim Reaper and attached it to a dark blue metal door labeled 'Members' Lounge'. Above it a sign written in calligraphy read 'Abandon all hope ye who enter here.' If that wasn't an invitation to enter, what was?

I slid the bolt across, cracked open the door and stepped inside. A ghastly smell blasted me, and I turned to escape. But as I rotated, the door slammed in my face, and I heard the faint sound of metal scratching against metal. I reached for the knob, but the door refused to budge. Something scampered across my feet and I let out a blood-curdling scream.

CHAPTER FORTY-FIVE

"Is anyone out there?" I pounded on the door. "Richard! Richard!"

Nausea overcame me from the horrible odor that coated my nostrils and seeped into my lungs. I clutched the walls in search of a light switch, but they were clammy from the room's dense humidity. Finally, my fingers made contact with a small plastic lever and my horrific surroundings were illuminated. Beside me rested a large filing cabinet and atop it stood a white cross constructed of cardboard. The letters R.I.P. were emblazoned on the cross and someone had further embellished it with crude drawings of insects. I peered around and felt energy draining from my body as though it were being siphoned off. Down at my feet boxes held decaying bird carcasses, dead rodents and severed limbs of mammals. Masses of beetles fed on the rotting flesh while others flitted about looking for their next meal. I was imprisoned inside the Museum's infamous Bug Room.

I had heard about the Bug Room, but until this moment had not known where it was situated. I did know, however, that it was inhabited by tens of thousands of carrion-eating insects used to turn animal carcasses into pristine skeletons. The three different varieties of bugs could consume a small bird overnight while larger animals such as a deer could take up to a month to be cleaned. I had also been told that staff never spent more than five minutes in the impermeable container as the bugs would begin to fly when the light was left on too long. The thought of a room filled with airborne flesh-eating beetles amplified my panic. I struck the light switch blanketing the room with darkness.

"Goddamnit, someone help me." I clobbered the door with my fist all the while doubting my cries and pounding were audible beyond the room, let alone in the hallway. For a moment I stopped to swipe my arms and legs. It appeared that if I kept in a state of motion the bugs avoided me. The lifeless flesh in the boxes was likely an easier meal ticket. But how long could I keep up the frenetic movement before passing out from the foul reek?

As I pummeled the door again, it flew open unexpectedly. I lost my footing and fell into someone's arms.

"Kalena, are you okay?"

"Marco. If ever there was a knight in shining armor."

We both jumped as we heard a number of zaps.

"Shut the fucking door," I hollered.

Marco pulled me forward and slammed the door. The zapping continued. "What is that?" "An electric bug zapper," I said. "It kills the escapees. If any of these suckers get into the collections, the Museum's doomed. These beetles eat carpets and fiber as well as meat."

"No kidding?" said Marco.

"How did you find me?"

"Brenda told me you'd gone back to the office, so when a call came over the radio that an alarm was set off in your area, I volunteered to check it out."

"But the Bug Room's nowhere near my office. How'd you end up here?"

"The email Richard sent you was open on your computer monitor...and well, I kind of read it. I'm really sorry. I didn't mean to snoop."

I gave Marco a big squeeze. "You can snoop through my emails anytime."

"I thought it was weird that Richard asked to meet you here, especially since he was still at the party working the room as though he was running for office or something."

"But if Richard wasn't down here, who was?"

"I don't know. But someone locked you in there." Marco forced the door bolt back into its fastener.

"Maybe it was Ms. X."

"How's that possible?"

"She's at the party. Didn't you see her?"

"No. Are you sure it's her?"

"She was sitting with Veronique," I said. "She and Richard must've wanted me out of the way."

"We've got to get back to the party, pronto, and check on their whereabouts."

"Wait a minute. Do I smell like a corpse?"

Marco drew me near him. "Let me put it this way, it might be hard for you to find a dance partner tonight."

* * * * *

Marco and I stormed down the hallway together. I kept slipping in my barely-there sandals, so Marco grabbed my hand to keep me upright. Once within view of the party, two security officers approached us, and I dropped Marco's hand.

"Marco, where've you been?" said one of the officers.

"What's up?" said Marco.

"The alarm system's rebounding again," said a grim-faced officer. "Malik thinks water from one of the cooling system pipes is leaking into the new security wiring."

Marco shot me a glance. "I didn't hear anything about that over the radio."

"The boss doesn't want the world finding out the whole damn exhibition's unarmed," said the younger of the two guards.

"But the jaguar mask – and the other artifacts," I said.

"They're safe. Everything's been triple-checked, and no tours are entering the exhibition until the system's up and running again," said the senior guard. "Come with us, Marco. Malik wants us floating closer to the exhibition." Both officers turned on their heels and shuffled off in the opposite direction.

"Something's up. I just know it," I whispered to Marco.

"Go back to the party and keep your eyes peeled for Richard and his partner."

"Comin', Marco?" one of the guards yelled back.

"I'm with ya'." Marco sprinted and caught up with the two guards.

I edged my way back to the main event. Although dinner had ended some time ago and tables had been cleared of dishes, most guests were still seated, sipping wine and chatting. I surveyed the room, but couldn't see anyone I knew. As I continued to pan the space, I caught a glimpse of Richard standing behind one of the imitation Maya stelae, in conversation with Ms. X. I started inching my way towards them ducking behind the monuments scattered throughout the grand hall when I felt a hand land on my shoulder. Startled, I turned about and came face to face with Brenda and Walter.

"Where the f...frig have you been?" said Brenda.

"We checked the office, but you'd already left." Walter

306

raised his nose and sniffed the air. He must have picked up my Bug Room cologne. "We were rather concerned."

"When Geoffrey finally turned up, Stewart asked me to track you down. I feel like I've been herding cats all night," said Brenda. "And Carson's been looking for you too."

"He was?" I said.

"Just as dinner was coming to a conclusion," said Walter, "he returned to the podium and gave you that much deserved pat on the back."

"He called out for you to join him on stage and then realized you weren't in the room," said Brenda.

"Someone yelled out that you were probably dusting off the cases in the exhibition," said Walter. "The comment stirred up quite a bit of laughter from the staff."

I grinned, imagining the scene in my mind. "So why was Geoffrey so late?"

"Jet lag," said Brenda.

"He lay down for a cat nap and woke up three hours later. He was quite embarrassed by it all," said Walter. "Very charming fellow, however."

"Yeah, whatever," I said. "Listen, I better go do my rounds."

"I hope you have some perfume," said Brenda. "Did you just walk through a dung heap?"

I waved both my hands as though they were Spanish fans. "It's the moth balls. I hauled this dress out of storage."

"Hmm. I detected an unusual essence as well," said Walter, "but it's not naphthalene."

"You're right. I use cedar chips – more ecofriendly. I'll give you the supplier's name later. You two enjoy yourselves. I'll be back in a bit."

I trotted away from my favorite oddball duo and

combed the area for Richard and Ms. X, but they had disappeared. Frustrated and still reeking of *Eau de Bug,* I decided to retreat to the office and douse myself from head to toe with Christian Dior's *J'adore* before I offended anyone else. I was wading through the walls of gauzy draperies lining the perimeter of the room when a figure darted through a small crossroads just ahead of me. The area was poorly lit, but I could have sworn it was Geoffrey. What was he doing here and where was he heading?

I crept forward, but instead of encountering Geoffrey, the silhouettes of two people resembling Richard and Ms. X came into view. Almost simultaneously I caught the fragrance of melted chocolate lingering in the air. It dawned on me that the artificial alley created by the reams of ceiling-to-floor curtains was a back route to the exhibition and, in particular, to the chamber that housed the jaguar mask. Were Richard and *Il Gattopardo* on their way to steal the priceless object?

A shudder ebbed through my body when I realized my instincts had been right all along. The heist was unfolding before me and something had to be done. The priceless artifact had to be saved, and I was the only one who could do it — whatever the cost.

I raced beside the towering granite walls, the drifting odor of chocolate serving as my beacon. As I approached the passageway to the exhibition, Richard emitted a sickening chortle which echoed to the top of the atrium and bounced down to the stone floor. Outraged by his reckless brazenness, adrenalin pumped through my body. The courage I needed to attack the deadly cat and her contemptible accomplice rose from an unknown source within me. My base instincts had been accessed, and I was in fight mode.

I ripped off my shoes and dove ahead emerging beside a table supporting a skyscraping chocolate fountain and bountiful trays of exotic sliced fruit. Richard and Ms. X, their backs turned to me, were about to enter Exhibition Hall when I stampeded forward and screamed like a banshee on Angel Dust. The two spun around, their faces filled with terror at my frenzied cries and wild gesticulations. I sprang towards the table supporting the fountain and lifted the edge with all my might. The pumping reservoir of rich, dark liquid slid to the ground along with the metal platters, creating a crash so loud I thought my ear drums were going to implode. In a split second a tidal wave of liquid and fruit washed over Richard, Ms. X and myself leaving us splattered with chocolate goop.

Before any of us had a chance to react, a confused-looking security guard barreled out of the exhibition doorway and radioed an all-points alert. As he finished his transmission, Geoffrey appeared out of nowhere and ran to the officer's side.

I pointed at Richard and Ms. X with my chocolate-slathered finger. "Cuff these two and arrest them immediately."

"Have you lost your mind, Kalena?" Richard screamed. He stooped down, picked up a pile of napkins from the floor and handed a few to Ms. X.

"We don't carry handcuffs," said the guard. "And we don't have the authority to arrest anyone."

"Detain them then. They were about to steal the jaguar mask," I said.

"She must be on some kind of medication or perhaps she forgot to take some," said Ms. X.

"She's not on any medication." Geoffrey picked up some of the strewn serviettes, maneuvered through the mess towards me and sponged up the chocolate on my chin.

"Are you?" he said under his breath.

"Of course not." But my answer was drowned out by the commotion of a crowd approaching the area. Malik appeared from behind a curtain with two-way radio in hand followed by Carson and Stewart. Within seconds a posse of security guards, including Marco, turned up. The numbers escalated even more as Brenda, Walter, Veronique, Dr. Perry and a number of other staff joined the throng. Most were unable to suppress their guffaws at the sight of the chocolate disaster zone before them.

Malik replaced his radio into its holster. "Could someone explain what's going on?"

"I'd like to know myself," said Ms. X.

Stewart strode forward and stopped beside Malik. "Kalena, please tell me there's a rational explanation for this scene."

"There is an explanation. I'm not so sure it's going to sound rational," I said.

Marco charged towards the front of the crowd, but I interjected. "Richard and his accomplice – sorry, I don't know her name – were about to steal the jaguar mask. This stranger, Richard's lover, is *Il Gattopardo*, the notorious international art thief."

"I've never heard anything more preposterous in my life," said Richard.

"That's a very serious allegation," said Carson.

"I know, sir. But I've been following their scheming for months." Out of the corner of my eyes, I saw Geoffrey shaking his head.

"Wait a minute. I've seen you before." Ms. X's gaze was frozen on me. "You're the maniacal woman who was on my flight to London...when I went to the British Museum Association Conference. Richard, do you remember me telling you the story? The purser warned me she was stalking me."

"I wasn't stalking you. I was shadowing your Pelican Case," I said.

"Pelican Case?" said Richard. "What are you on about now?"

"I thought she had the piece of ancient chocolate that had gone missing from the exhibition shipment."

"This statement alone proves how ridiculous Kalena's accusations are. The chocolate was in the hands of an assistant curator from New York, as we all know," said Richard.

"The case I was transporting to England was filled with some valuable crystal specimens. One of my museum's benefactors pledged a gift to a charity event at Leeds Castle. And since I was attending the conference in London, I volunteered to deliver the pieces, personally."

"Kalena," Carson said, stepping to the forefront, "allow me to introduce you to the Director of the Cincinnati Museum of Science and History, the distinguished Dr. Alexandra Landry."

Landry? Where had I heard that name before?

"Why would you suspect Richard and Dr. Landry of plotting to steal the mask?" said Stewart.

"It's my fault, sir," said Marco.

"What involvement do you have in this matter, young man?" said Malik.

"Marco simply loaned me some articles on *Il Gattopardo*." I twirled towards Malik. "I swear. That's all he did."

"And they've been consorting with a fence in Yorkville?" said Marco.

I glared at Marco. It looked like I was going down, and I

didn't want to take him along with me.

"What fence?" said Dr. Landry.

"The owner of Borovsky Fine Arts," I said.

"This conversation has surpassed slander," said Richard. "I'd heard you have an active imagination, Ms. Boyko, but this is beyond comprehension. Borovsky Fine Arts has an impeccable reputation, and the owner's been assisting me in selecting some artwork for my new home."

"Well what about the email you sent me less than an hour ago, luring me to the Bug Room so you could sneak into the exhibition through the back door while the security situation was compromised?"

"Who had time to email anyone about anything?" said Richard. "When I finally did have a spare moment, I offered to take our esteemed guest on a tour of the exhibition before the gala crowds made it impossible to view anything."

"What was that about a compromised security situation?" Carson turned towards Malik.

"We've had a recurrence of the system failure we experienced several weeks ago," said Malik.

"But we haven't had any rain," said Carson.

"One of the cooling system pipes burst resulting in a similar pattern of water damage in the ceiling. A barrage of signals from the Museum recreated the electrical loop we witnessed before. It crashed our system again as well as that of the security company and cut their connection to the police. But thanks to the previous episode, we were able to do a much quicker patch."

The door to the Exhibition Hall almost blew off its hinges when a burley security guard flung it wide open. He hesitated a moment, staring at the congregation like a moose mesmerized by a car's headlights and then shouted towards the crowd. "Malik...sir. We received the go-ahead from the security company. Everything's back in order."

Chapter Forty-Six

Carson shifted towards Malik and mumbled, "Get a few of your officers to round everyone up. Stewart, Richard, Dr. Landry and Kalena stay put. I want the rest taken directly to one of the Education Department's classrooms."

"Yes, sir," said Malik.

"Next," said Carson, "see if Linda Ababwe is still at the party."

"The head of HR?" said Malik.

"I need to meet with her immediately about drafting a confidentiality agreement. No one goes home tonight without signing one and that includes the senior staff and every last guard. If Linda's gone home already, call her and send a cab to pick her up."

"Roger," said Malik.

"We'll need a few of the Facilities staff to clean up this mess, and when they've finished, they're to be escorted to Education. And I need someone from PR. We'll tell the sponsor that at the last minute we were advised to nix the chocolate fountain because of concerns related to the exhibit...you know, food in the area was unacceptable to the lending institution...or something to that effect. Let PR figure out the party line." Carson paused to take a deep breath. "I think I have everything covered. But let me make it clear, nothing and I mean nothing about what happened here this evening is ever leaving this building. There will be no reports filed, no email exchanges, no paper trail whatsoever."

Like what happens in Vegas stays in Vegas I wanted to shout out, but I didn't want to let on that I could hear every word of Carson's and Malik's barely audible conversation. Malik approached two of the guards and spoke to them in a hushed tone. The officers corralled everyone, except for the individuals Carson had asked remain with him. As the guards guided the troupe towards the building's rear staircase, Brenda kept looking back at me. Marco attempted to turn back, but Walter gripped him by the arm and pulled him along.

Geoffrey managed to break loose from the group and ran to my side. He put his hands on my chocolate-covered shoulders and whispered, "Why have you been incommunicado since you returned to Toronto? Did I do something wrong?"

"I can't compete with Ms. Desert Storm," I said. "And I don't want to."

"Who's Ms. Desert Storm?"

"Lady Sahara blah, blah, blah. The woman you took to the charity function at Leeds Castle. And don't tell me she's your cousin or something. That would be too Hugh Grant."

Geoffrey's expression turned quizzical. "Kalena Boyko, I'm not sure what language you speak sometimes. I have no idea what that means."

"It doesn't matter." My exhale was so deep my lips fluttered.

"I really wish you had shared your suspicions about Richard and his friend with me. I could've told you Landry isn't The Leopard."

I jolted away from Geoffrey. "How? What?"

"Geoffrey," said Stewart. "You need to follow the rest

315

of the group immediately."

Geoffrey shrugged his shoulders and walked away. The look of desperation on his face when he glanced back just before disappearing down a stairwell, will be emblazoned in my mind forever. What did he know?

* * * * *

After the bulk of the crowd outside exhibition hall dispersed, Carson, Malik, Richard and Dr. Landry carried on a discussion beyond earshot. When they finished up, Richard and Dr. Landry followed Malik to his office I presumed, leaving Carson, Stewart and myself on our own. The facilities staff arrived to mop up the chocolate sludge and sweep up the fountain fragments, so Carson suggested the three of us move to Brenda's and my office.

"What are all these boxes?" Carson said as we stepped into my office.

"Baskets," I said.

"God help us," Carson moaned. "As for what just happened, I'm not really sure where to begin. It does appear your imagination took a walk on the wild side."

"Do you mind if I check one thing, sir?" I said to Carson. "I know it may seem insignificant, but I'd like to show you the email Richard sent me this evening about meeting him in the lab. If he's lying about that, he could be lying about other matters as well."

"Very well," said Carson.

I walked around to the other side of my desk fully expecting to see the message displayed on my screen just as I had left it and as Marco had found it earlier. To my bewilderment, the message had vanished. "Just give me a second. I know it's here." I checked around my folders maneuvering my mouse with shaky hands as if I had a case of the DTs. But it was nowhere to be found. "Sorry, sir. It was here earlier. I swear."

"Kalena," Stewart said, "is there anything going on in your life we should know about? Are you getting enough sleep?"

Did I dare confess the traumatic discovery of cellulite in my thighs? Or the fact that I had had a humiliating one-night stand with his best friend? "No, nothing unusual on the home front."

Stewart turned to Carson. "I may have burdened Kalena with too many responsibilities. And with Brenda and myself absent for a period of time, the pressure of running the office on her own must have taken its toll."

"There's no reason to apologize on my behalf," I said. "I take full accountability for what happened this evening, and I know what I have to do."

"I suggest you don't say another word," said Stewart, "until you have spoken with someone in Human Resources."

God bless Stewart for always looking out for my best interests. He knew Carson would likely have to fire me. But if I beat him to the punch and quit, the Museum wouldn't pay me a cent in compensation. "It's okay, Stewart. I think the best thing for everyone concerned would be for me to leave this evening and never come back."

"Let's consider the options here," said Stewart.

"Don't worry. I'll provide Brenda with a complete briefing on my outstanding projects. And I'm sure you'll find a replacement for me in no time."

* * * * *

Carson informally accepted my resignation. There would be much paperwork to follow. I quickly packed up as many of my belongings as I could carry. When I found a couple of chocolate bars stashed in the recesses of one of my file cabinets, Stewart and I had a good laugh. He told me not to worry about taking all my personal effects as I would be able to return to pick up any remaining items, but someone would have to be present. Standard procedure, he said, to prevent disgruntled employees from committing corporate sabotage. I explained I wasn't disgruntled, but that I understood and there was no reason for him to be apologetic. My computer would be locked down immediately, passwords would be disabled, home access lost, he said, and I had to turn over my BlackBerry. Argh, Aurelia would be one of the first to find out I had been canned. I knew the drill, I said to Stewart, from Tambra's experience.

Stewart escorted me to the staff entrance, and I tried to keep things light. I joked about how much better off he would be without me working for him. He cracked a smile and said he would miss me. He regretted, he said, that he hadn't taken a picture of Richard, Dr. Landry and me sopping in chocolate and dotted with fruit debris. It would have been a good shot, I said, for *The Art Newspaper*. We cracked up one last time, but I was dying inside. I headed out into the cold air and even before I had a chance to raise my hand to hail a cab a vehicle halted in front of me. Geoffrey popped out, grabbed the things in my arms and deposited them in the cab's trunk before I had a chance to run.

Still silent, Geoffrey motioned for me to step inside the taxi. It wasn't until I told the cabbie where to take us that he began to speak. "What happened after we left," he said.

"I quit."

"I was afraid of that. You didn't let Stewart do the talking, did you?"

"Nope."

"He could have done some back-pedalling and saved you."

"I didn't want to be saved."

"Kalena, Kalena, Kalena. What are we going to do with you?"

"I've never been so humiliated in my life. How could I ever face any of those people again? I could never live it down."

"We can discuss this further when we arrive at your place?"

"Can't this wait?"

"Nope."

"You've never said 'nope' before tonight, have you?" I said.

"Nope." Geoffrey flashed a sly, yet reassuring grin.

Moments later we arrived at my building and entered the lobby. "I think we should just sit here. It's fairly private."

Geoffrey looked puzzled.

"I don't think it's appropriate that you come upstairs with me tonight."

"I see."

We settled into a couple of desert-hued faux leather cubed chairs some distance from the building's security desk and traffic. An oversized mirror in front of me reflected an image that wasn't very pretty. The bright lights were cruel indeed.

"Let's get one thing straight," said Geoffrey nudging me into the present.

"Huh, what's that?"

"I had made a commitment to attend the event at Leeds Castle long before I knew you would be coming to London."

"Uh, huh."

Geoffrey grimaced and dipped his head to one side.

"Okay, okay I get it."

"I know it's going to sound cliché, but my date that night really was an old family friend."

"And you've never slept with her?"

"Well, I can't honestly say that I haven't. But we were kids. Both of us have long moved on. She only asked me to attend the function that night because she had recently been unceremoniously dismissed by a long-standing boyfriend."

I was fried, and I had had enough. Sleep was the only thing I could focus on.

"As for what happened tonight, what I am about to tell you I have never shared with anyone, not even Stewart."

Suddenly my ears perked up.

"My grandfather stole the Ogden Opals from the Royal Ontario Museum in 1981."

"O.M.G. Your grandfather's *Il Gattopardo*?"

CHAPTER FORTY-SEVEN

When I finished lifting my jaw off the ground, I sank back into my chair. My vocal cords felt paralyzed.

"Now, Ms. Boyko, you're jumping to conclusions again."

I was unable to emit any kind of sound from my throat.

"Do you know any of the history of the opals?"

I cleared my throat and a version of my voice that sounded like one of the animated Chipmunks characters came out. "I'm aware that your grandfather lost them to the Museum's founder in a card game."

"I see Stewart filled you in."

I nodded yes.

"The loss of the gems almost ended my grandparents' marriage. The jewels had been in my grandmother's family for over a century, and she was devastated by the transfer of ownership."

"Why didn't they try to pay out Charles Currelly with something else or cash even?"

"Trust me, they tried. But there had already been some bad blood between Currelly and my grandfather, and Currelly refused to negotiate. He had once been in love with Grandmother Arabella, but my grandfather James crushed Currelly when he stole grandmother's heart and married her."

"But your grandmother must have been half Currelly's age."

"That didn't seem to make a difference to Currelly. He was used to getting what he wanted. And Currelly saw the appropriation of the opals as payback."

"So your grandfather was a heartbreaker and a thief." I said.

"It's not what you think. My Grandfather James was NOT The Leopard."

"I'm totally befuddled."

"Understandably. It's a complex story. Long after the opals went over to Canada, Grandfather inadvertently walked in on *Il Gattopardo* in the middle of an attempted theft of other treasures at Arabella's family manor."

My eyes tripled in size as Geoffrey's story played out in my mind like a movie. I envisioned The Leopard, who of course looked exactly like Cary Grant in *Alfred Hitchcock's To Catch a Thief*, in a dark room removing the contents of a safe when Geoffrey's grandfather suddenly walks in and turns on the lights – both men equally stunned to find themselves in each other's presence.

"Grandfather agreed not to report The Leopard to the authorities if he conceded–"

"To steal the opals from the Museum and return them to your grandmother," I said completing Geoffrey's sentence. "Oh my God. This can't be true."

"Most times truth is far more intriguing than fiction."

"But Richard Pritchard's father became the fall guy."

"Is that a Canadian expression?"

"Sorry, I guess I picked up the lingo from watching too many detective movies. So, Richard's father got blamed for the Museum theft." When I looked at Geoffrey, I was startled. A layer of water had coated his eyes, and he fluttered his eyelids to hold back the tears.

322

"No one, and I mean no one, anticipated the suicide."

I drew my hands to my mouth in prayer position, and my stomach felt as though it had been coated in lead.

"My grandmother never forgave her husband. Richard's father's death weighed on her a million-fold more than the loss of her opals. Once grandfather received the gems back, she wanted nothing to do with them so Grandfather employed The Leopard one last time to dispose of the hot jewels."

"And that's how they ended up in Hong Kong," I said.

Geoffrey dipped his head down.

"Do you know who *Il Gattopardo* is?"

Geoffrey jerked his head back up. "That information rests with Grandfather James in his grave." There was a quiver in Geoffrey's lips that reminded me of a poker players' tell when bluffing. This was the only part of Geoffrey's story I questioned. He continued. "What I do know is that neither Richard nor Dr. Landry could be *Il Gattopardo*."

Oh, lord. Not only had I lost my job, but Richard was in a position to sue the shoes off me. I was doomed to hell.

* * * * *

Geoffrey was flying directly to Lisbon the following day for the much awaited debrief with the clients, and so he left my building shortly afterwards. There was minimal fanfare upon his departure, and I dragged my dog-tired body upstairs. I dropped my heavy load of office files and noticed I had a couple of phone messages. The first message was from Marco who mentioned he had tried to call my BlackBerry — no longer in my possession — but when he received no answer had called my home phone. The second message was from my dear brother.

"Hi, sis," began the message. "According to my calendar, it's your big night tonight. Really wish I could have been your date. What happened to that British guy anyway? Well, it's day two for me in Barcelona, and I'm lovin' it. I'm not sure if I'll make it to the Chocolate Museum here, but I owe you one honkin' chunk of chocolate. Love ya' and miss ya'. We'll talk soon."

I pressed one of the speed dial buttons on my phone and spoke. "Hi, Mom."

"Kalena, I was thinking about you tonight," she said in Ukrainian. "I was going to call, but I thought it might be too late."

My mother never failed to amaze me with her sixth sense. She always seemed to know when one of her offspring was in trouble. I replied in Ukrainian. "It's never too late for you to call me, mom."

"Your brother telephoned from Spain, from some city."

"Barcelona," I said.

"Yes. Isn't that the place you visited when you were in high school?"

"I was seventeen, and it was my first trip to Europe."

"And you earned the money to pay for the trip yourself. You wouldn't even take any spending money from us. You were always such an independent child."

"Yes, mom."

"Were you calling to tell me something, Kalynechka? You don't sound right."

"I had a crazy day. I'm just exhausted."

"You get some rest tonight, then. You don't want to be tired for work tomorrow."

"I will. How's dad doing?"

"He's eating too much these days. I may have to put him on a diet."

"I don't think he'll like that."

"No. No he won't." The two of us chuckled. "Good night, little flower. Call me again soon."

"Good night, mom."

I had wanted to tell my mother what went down at work, but after she commented on my independence, I lost my nerve. When I set the receiver down, I noticed I still had some chocolate on the back of my hand. I raised it to my mouth and took a lick. What a waste it had been to dump such ambrosia all over the Museum floor.

CHAPTER FORTY-EIGHT

That night I suffered from a case of what the French call *nuit blanche*, a term which literally translates into 'white nights'. It's a very romantic sounding expression for the not-so-romantic condition of insomnia. Fortunately, I was well-entertained for at least a couple of hours while viewing a witching-hour telecast of the program, *Iron Chef America*. To my delight the 'secret ingredient' featured in this segment's 'battle' between the two top chefs and their crews was chocolate. The drool factor was exponential as I observed the chefs whip up appetizers, such as pumpkin and chocolate soup, and concoct main dishes that included chocolate encrusted bison and cocoa and espresso seasoned duck. But the desserts were beyond yummy, and I sat at the edge of my sofa with eyes eating up the screen as the competing kitchen magicians served chocolate and goat cheese beignets, chocolate-dusted plantains and blue cornmeal and chocolate Johnnycakes to the jubilant judges.

After only about an hour's worth of sleep, I rose and immediately disconnected my phone. There wasn't a single person I wanted to speak to – not Brenda, not Walter, not Marco and certainly not anyone from the Museum's Human Resources Department. Everything could be settled the subsequent Monday, I had decided, after I had a few days to regroup.

I spent the day languishing on my couch devouring

chocolate goodies I had delivered to my home from Dufflet Pastries, a patisserie located nearby in the trendy Queen West neighborhood. The bakery wasn't in the habit of delivering non-commercial orders, but I was a regular customer, and they must have tuned into the desperation in my voice when I rang them. The pastries were the perfect accompaniment to viewing a slew of shows on the Oprah network I had taped on my digital Personal Video Recorder. Between happy cries and sad sobs, depending on the show, I was a tearful mess and went through a hefty supply of Kleenex. But by the sixth show, I felt guilty for having felt sorry for myself. There were women in the world who had watched their children be murdered by their husbands and young girls in South Africa who risked their lives daily just traveling to and from school. I watched shows that featured tweens who had become their families' primary caregivers and episodes on war correspondents who struggled to recover from a shower of shrapnel. Hell, my life was paradise compared to the lives of most people on the planet. By evening I was convinced I needed to start a gratitude journal and to move forward with my life.

The following day the phone was plugged back in, but I wasn't quite ready to answer calls. One step at a time, I figured. Instead, I let my old-fashioned answering machine record the stream of messages from people like Walter and even Malik asking about my well-being. Marco dropped by my building, but when he buzzed me from the lobby, I let the call go to my answering machine as well. Later, I shot off a brief email to everyone via my home Internet service and informed them I wasn't planning on putting my head in the oven (especially since it was electric), that I wasn't gorging myself with chocolate (though I was) and that I was slowly becoming accustomed to the fact that I no longer worked at the Museum (not).

My day was filled with updating my resume, doing an Internet job search and registering on various cultural and government job sites. In between these tasks, I completed an on-line aptitude test to determine what kind of work would allow me to 'follow my bliss.' Perhaps a vocation in the film industry would be more fulfilling. Maybe I could make a living writing screen plays or I could become a certified yoga instructor and help others find their bliss. My head spun, and the non-stop mind-chatter propelled me back into a dark funk. I pulled out all my old break-up tunes like Johnny Cash's cover of Nine Inch Nails' *Hurt*, Sarah McLachlan's *Hold On*, Ute Lemper's *You Were Meant for Me*, Siouxsie & the Banshees' *Tearing Apart*, and Adele's *Rolling in the Deep*. When I ran out of morose singles, I turned to the albums of Dead Can Dance, This Mortal Coil and David Sylvian. Could one die listening to sad music?

The results from the aptitude test I had completed earlier in the day impacted me several hours later, and I lamented how much I had loved my job with Stewart. Challenges were bountiful, but routine was not part of my workday vocabulary. Brenda was erratic, but she was entertaining to the core, and though I joked about the number of misfits who worked at the Museum, my colleagues stimulated me intellectually and creatively. I was proud to work at the ROM, to be part of a place whose research work was globally recognized and which was the pilgrimage site of almost every child in the province. The only object acquired in my youth to which I still clung was a paper weight I had purchased at the Museum during a school field trip at the age of ten. The Museum was my life and my soul. And there was the matter of the men at the Museum. I had met both my ex-husbands while working there and more recently Geoffrey and Marco. The Museum, I realized, was my primary source of romance. Would I ever find love in the real world, or would I have to resort to Internet dating?

Frustrated, I decided to spend the day in movie theatres living off my favorite organic dark chocolate bark topped with nuts spiced with coriander, cayenne and sea salt and handmade by the Toronto-based company, Delight. The bark's rich, velvety texture was unsurpassable even in comparison to chocolate created by exceptional European chocolatiers. But during the third movie of the afternoon, I became overwhelmed by thoughts of my impending inability to pay my mortgage and support my movie and chocolate habits. At the end of the screenings, I raced home and checked my email, hoping that some diligent employer had checked their Internet job applications over the weekend and had requested an interview with me. But my email box was a void and the reality of my predicament settled into every crevice of my psyche. What was I going to do?

Too distraught to attend my Sunday evening yoga class, I retired early. But I slept restlessly again and intermittently turned on the television to drown out the monkey chatter in my head. I found myself beguiled by infomercials that plugged everything from ultrasonic toothbrush cleaners (the levels of bacteria found on the bristles of tooth brushes was alarming), PIYO exercise DVDs (perhaps it was time to move on from yoga), natural cures they don't want us to know about (I wasn't sure who 'they' were), Bonzai Choppers (even though I rarely cooked) and Robo Maid (despite the fact it took me five minutes to vacuum my place with a conventional vacuum cleaner).

It was around six AM when I finally drifted off, but a few

hours later, I was jarred out of an alpha state by the sound of my phone ringing. Still in a stupor I let the answering machine pick up. It was Carson's assistant leaving a message.

"Good day, Kalena. It's Naoko calling. I was wondering if you were available for a meeting at five PM with Carson, Stewart and Malik. Carson asked me to apologize for the lateness in the day, but he's booked up as usual, and it's the only time I could get the three of them together. They'd like to discuss a number of issues that have arisen since Thursday. He said you'd know what I meant – exhibition stuff I gathered. No need to call me back unless the time is inconvenient for you and we need to reschedule. Hope you're having a good day off. Personally, I think they've got some nerve asking you to come in on a vacation day, but I guess it's important. Talk to you soon."

Vacation day? Was that the story Carson was spinning? And why did I have to be interrogated again? Was it really necessary to prolong my humiliation and torture? Couldn't I come in, fetch the rest of my stuff quietly and deal with Human Resources directly? What more could they want from me?

I bolted upright in bed. Richard was going to sue me for libel or defamation of character or whatever the appropriate charge was. Why had I acted so recklessly? Why hadn't I listened to Brenda and Tambra. They had both warned me about going after Richard. Maybe I could plead temporary insanity claiming that some of the fat cells that had recently settled in my thighs had become detached, traveled to my brain and created a series of mini strokes. Would anyone buy that argument?

I flopped backwards onto my bed and heaved the covers over my head.

* * * * *

At the end of the day, I mustered up sufficient courage to make my way to the Museum on the public transit system. I descended the subway one stop earlier than usual and snaked my way to the ROM through the back laneways and paths of the University of Toronto campus. Most Museum staff would be on their way home, and the fewer I bumped into, the better. I scurried towards the staff entrance and peered through the glass doors, my heart skipping a beat. Aurelia stood at the security desk with Malik. She handed him something and snatched up a shopping bag that had been sitting at her feet. Terrific. I wasn't out the door two days and Aurelia was already best friends with the Director of Security.

She turned to exit the building, and I retreated faster than an Indy racecar finishing its last lap. Aurelia was the last creature in the universe I wanted to encounter. I fled in the direction of the university campus and ducked behind a brick wall bordering a parking area reserved for the Director and other Museum executives. When I heard the clacking of stilettos on concrete, I knew Aurelia was headed my way. I could only pray she would keep her gaze straight ahead and wouldn't see me cowering to the side.

Aurelia's footsteps drew nearer and nearer. She passed by the wall against which I had pressed my back, stopped, dropped her big bag to the ground and lit a cigarette. Two fine pipelines of smoke filtered through her nostrils, and she gazed around as though she had sensed someone was watching her. She didn't even flinch when her eyes chanced upon mine. "What the fuck are you doing there?" said Aurelia.

I popped my purse open and scrounged inside. "I, uh. I think I may have left my keys back in the office." I prayed she had not been informed that I was no longer on staff.

Aurelia snickered. "Alzheimer's setting in already?"

"Just what is your problem with me?" I stepped out of the shadows into a streak of light from the setting sun that had peeked through the buildings.

"I feel sorry for women like you."

"Just what is a woman like me?" I said.

"You're like my sad excuse of a sister. You go to work every day to your cushy, little job. You do your work and everyone adores you. Then you go home to your apartment, clean out the litter box and eat your Healthy Choice frozen dinner while watching some pathetic Audrey Hepburn movie. And just before going to bed, you check the mirror to see if your grey roots are showing."

"My, my," I said "You have life all figured out, don't you? I guess that's why you spend your days clawing at everyone who gets in the way of what you want?"

"Oh, you mean the way you've been pushing me out of Marco's reach, and all the while you have that Geoffrey guy wrapped around your finger?"

"You don't know anything about my life," I said.

"And you don't know anything about mine."

"I do know you're going to end up with a black heart."

Aurelia took one last drag from her cigarette, cast the butt to the ground, and extinguished it with an exaggerated twist of her foot. After grabbing her shopping bag, she sauntered forwards. "Time to move on," she yelled back without turning around.

She must have heard about what happened to me after all. I gulped down some air. At least I would not have to see that demon spawn ever again.

CHAPTER FORTY-NINE

I raised my hand and tapped on an intricately carved oak door that had once graced the Museum's entranceway.

"Come in, Kalena, come in," said Carson in a disarmingly cheery tone. Unlike Richard, Carson avoided ostentation and his office was simply appointed. He possessed a handsome antique desk that had served numerous directors before him, but the walls were almost bare, with the exception of a few framed posters of previous Museum exhibitions. The expanse of windows that stretched along one side of the room looked out onto the former planetarium dome and university campus. The view was a little drab at this time of year, but still impressive. Malik was already seated, and he nodded at me. "Stewart should be along any minute...Oh, speak of the devil."

Stewart turned up behind me and shot me a grin. Why was everyone so damned jolly? Was this how executioners behaved before dropping the guillotine blade?

"Sit, sit. Let's get this meeting underway," said Carson.

Stewart and I took our seats across from Carson and beside Malik.

"I'd like to thank you for coming in so late in the day, Kalena. I believe Naoko explained my scheduling challenges."

"It was no problem, sir. It was the least I could do after..." My voice started to get shaky, and I couldn't complete my sentence.

"I'm sure you've had a trying few days," said Carson.

Was he kidding me? SOMEONE GET ME OUT OF HERE, I screamed in my head.

"There have been a few interesting developments."

"Very interesting, in fact," said our head of Security.

I squirmed in my seat. "I imagine Richard wasn't too thrilled about the accusations I made against him...in front of all those people."

"No, he wasn't," said Carson.

"I'm so, so sorry about that, sir." Nervously, I looked around at the cast of senior directors that surrounded me. "I know my apologies can't undo anything..." I looked down towards the floor.

"It behooved us to do some investigation into the events that led up to the gala and we were astonished at some of the results," said Malik.

What results? We had already clearly established that Richard, Veronique and Dr. Landry were not plotting a heist.

"We've uncovered a considerable amount of subterfuge that's been occurring right under our noses," said Carson.

"Not quite the subterfuge, you suspected, Kalena," said Stewart, "but still rather insidious."

I didn't have a bloody clue what they were talking about.

"We have evidence that for some time Richard had been plotting a coup of sorts," said Carson.

Richard was planning to take over the government of Canada?

"He had gone to great lengths to undermine my authority in recent months," said Carson, "and has been working diligently at having me ousted from my position."

"Are you saying Richard had his sights set on the Museum's Directorship?" My head was spinning as though I had just downed five tequila shots.

"In a manner of speaking," said Malik. "You were most correct that Richard and Dr. Landry are involved. What you are not aware of is that Dr. Landry is Veronique's sister."

Landry? I knew I had heard that name before. Veronique had let slip her maiden name during the conversation we had had about her being newly single. Richard's lover and Veronique were siblings! No wonder Richard had promoted Veronique to the position of Head of Exhibits. It was an act of nepotism, a favor to his paramour. But how could I have missed the family resemblance? I was such a dolt!

"No one at the Museum knew about the connection," said Carson. "They managed to keep it very hush-hush. They had been quietly setting up house together in Toronto preparing for the day when Dr. Landry would find a position in the city," said Stewart. "It seems the only job Dr. Landry felt worthy of someone of her stature was Carson's position."

Numbness shot through my body. Was I going into physical shock?

"Richard was using *Treasures of the Maya* to undermine my credibility with the board of directors," said Carson. "He suggested we take on the exhibit and, at the same time, he attempted to sabotage the project from day one."

"Like planting that piece in *The Art Newspaper* before the Board had given their approval on the exhibit," I said.

"It began even before that. We have documentation indicating Richard and Dr. Landry knew long ago that the dating of some of the pieces in the exhibit was suspect," said Malik.

My mind flashed back to the day I collided with Richard in the hallway and his photographs of the exhibition artifacts

335

scattered all over the floor. He had those photos in his possession before we received the official package from San Francisco.

"Dr. Landry went so far as to deliberately alienate the main sponsor that had been lined up for the exhibit in Cincinnati," said Carson. "She intentionally forfeited *Treasures of the Maya* at a great cost to her museum, I might add, so that the exhibition would come to Toronto instead."

"Richard intended to expose the irregularity of the artifact dates once the exhibit arrived at the ROM," said Malik.

"But the curators in New York beat us to the punch and put a wrench in Richard's plans," said Stewart.

"Unbelievable," I said.

"Richard, Veronique and Landry were temporarily stumped by the turn of events," said Stewart. "But when the oldest piece of chocolate went missing, there was a new opportunity to make the Museum and Carson appear incompetent."

"But how did Richard orchestrate that?"

"We found emails indicating Richard knew all along that the chocolate was being transported by ground," said Malik.

The evil gleam in Richard's eyes the morning the exhibit landed on our shipping and receiving dock now made complete sense.

"And when the Museum was struck with further misfortunes – the insect infestation, the flood and the compromised security system – Richard was back in his element again. He gave Carson the impression he was doing extensive damage control, but all the while he sat back and watched the Museum crumble, and he inappropriately publicized the events."

"Like to Dr. Perry in San Francisco," I said.

"Precisely," said Carson. "There was no reason for Dr. Perry to be called in other than to rustle up some controversy. And I do so regret having to recall you from London early," said Carson.

"You couldn't have known, sir," I said. "But I still don't understand the logic of the plan. The selection of a new Director is a long and complicated process. How could he ensure Dr. Landry would be selected as Director if you resigned or were forced to leave?"

"Astute observation but it's based on an incomplete picture," said Carson. "It was confidential information that Dr. Landry was a candidate during the Museum's last search for a Director, and I beat her by a single vote. Since then Richard has been conducting a secret campaign for his partner, chatting her up to the Board members and curatorial heavyweights at every given opportunity."

"Our Machiavellian threesome was very creative," said Malik, "but they weren't very savvy about computer forensics."

"How do you mean, Malik?" I said.

"They could not have left a more perfect email trail for us. Richard was foolish enough to believe that just because he deleted an email there was no longer any trace left of it," said Malik. "The IT staff and I spent all weekend going through their email communications dating back as far as a year ago."

Did Aurelia help to dig up the dirt on Richard? Is that why she was speaking to Malik at the staff entrance when I arrived at the Museum?

"By Sunday evening Malik had gathered all the evidence we needed to construct a case that would stand up in court," said Carson.

"Are they being charged with something, sir?" I said.

"We decided to take a different approach to avoid negative publicity to the Museum," said the Director. "We confronted Richard and Veronique and they have tendered their resignations. In addition, Dr. Landry will be stepping down from her post in Cincinnati."

"Just before I came to this meeting," said Stewart, "I read a press release issued by her museum. The deed is a fait accompli."

No way. No way. No way.

"And Richard and Veronique have signed a release form which prevents them from seeking any kind of compensation from the Museum," said Carson.

Haaal-lelujah...hallelujah, hallelujah.

"Given Richard's family's tragic history with the Museum, we have in turn agreed to keep silent about the circumstances surrounding the departure," said Carson. "We owe it to him."

My eyes met with Stewart's in acknowledgement that Richard's dismissal was sufficient punishment.

"We have a document you'll need to sign before you leave," said Stewart, "the same one signed by all the staff who were present at the big kafuffle outside the exhibit the night of the gala. After this meeting we will no longer be discussing these events amongst ourselves, not even in privacy. You'll come back to work tomorrow as though nothing had happened. An official statement about Richard's and Veronique's sudden exodus will be issued by Human Resources in the morning. The party line will be that following the mounting of the exhibition, the division was restructured. The duo is not well liked, as you are aware, so the decision will not come as a surprise to most staff."

I nodded.

"We apologize for keeping you in the dark until this meeting, Kalena," said Carson. "But all the steps had to be put in place and all bases covered from a legal perspective before we could share this information with you."

"I'm sure it was a complicated process," I said.

"I would like to add that had it not been for your suspicions about Richard, I would most likely have lost my position at the Museum," said Carson. "Please accept my deepest gratitude for saving my neck, as some would say."

I beamed more brightly than an exploding supernova.

"However, in future, it would be prudent for you to discuss matters of such a consequential nature with a superior." Carson glanced at Stewart. "One who might advise you on a more appropriate course of action should you suspect a colleague of nefarious behavior."

My bursting star imploded. "Noted, sir."

"I'm glad we understand each other," said Carson. "Now, I believe Stewart has some issues he would like to discuss with you in the privacy of his office."

There was more?

CHAPTER FIFTY

After I signed the confidentiality agreement, Carson and Malik shook my hand. I could tell Malik wanted to give me a hug, but he restrained himself in front of the Director.

"What a difference a few days makes," said Stewart after we entered the corridor.

"I'll say," I said. "But, Stewart...I know I messed up big time and although everyone seems to have forgiven me my wacked-out behavior, if you have any qualms about my continuing to work for you, I really need to know."

We stepped into Stewart's office. "Have a seat, Kalena."

Uh-oh. I wasn't out of the clear yet.

"When I said, what a difference a few days makes, it was in reference to some additional developments. Our Lisbon colleagues finally made some decisions."

I puffed up my cheeks and exhaled the air slowly.

"It seems they made up their minds some time ago about the project, but Dr. Ravasco has been on vacation and no one told us. Geoffrey phoned this morning to inform me we've been granted the lead on the project's next stage."

"Holy smokes."

"Despite a few hiccups during the presentation, Dr. Ravasco's team was so impressed that you handled the interrogation with such competence and grace after having flown all night and managing without your luggage."

Would wonders ever cease?

"So, to answer the question you asked when we entered my office, I have no qualms about you continuing in my employ. I do, however, believe you should channel your imagination in more productive ways. But I couldn't be more delighted that you're still a part of my crew."

"Really?"

"Really. And so is Geoffrey. As a matter of fact, we agreed to implement some work exchanges starting with an assignment in London. It would be excellent experience for you and Brenda to work in London, on a short-term basis, that is."

Me? A European trapped in a Canadian body in London? It sounded like the opportunity of a lifetime. "You can count me in, sir. I don't know how to thank you."

"You can thank Geoffrey. It was his brainchild. But enough of business. Go home. And I insist you take another day off and get some much-deserved rest."

"Are you sure?"

"We'll manage." Stewart picked up a BlackBerry from his desk and handed it to me. "I think you'll be needing this."

"Thank you." There was something about having the BlackBerry in hand that made me feel validated. "By the way, Stewart. Who made the decision to probe into Richard's emails? After all, when I left here on Thursday evening you all thought I was loony tunes."

"It seems you have an angel in your corner. Malik started the investigation after receiving hard copies of some of Richard's incriminating emails."

"Who gave them to him?"

"They were dropped off on his desk – anonymously."

CHAPTER FIFTY-ONE

As I left Stewart's office, he returned my Museum ID and told me never to leave home without it again. I chuckled and entered the Director's private elevator to the staff entrance. The antiquated lift reminded me of the grand old elevators in department stores back in the day. When I landed on the ground floor, I pulled the folding metal grate to the side and pushed at the swing-door, but it refused to budge.

"You have to push the grate all the way over," said a voice on the other side of the door.

I forced the brass mechanism as far as I could and pried the door open. Brenda and Walter stood on the other side.

"We're your welcoming committee," said Brenda as she wrapped her arms around me. Her crutches started to fall to the floor, but Walter caught them in time. "We've been waiting here forever. I knew you'd get stuck in this elevator." Nothing ever got past Brenda. "We wanted to see you before you went home. Are you okay?"

"I am now. But I guess we can't talk about anything that's happened," I said.

Brenda and Walter nodded.

"I must rush back to the library for closing. Brenda's agreed to accompany me and observe the procedure," said Walter.

"The highlight of my week." Brenda's cheekiness was

overridden by a warm smile. "Just one second, Walter." She brushed up beside me and whispered. "Carson took Richard and Veronique off site for lunch this afternoon and he came back alone."

"Brenda," said Walter.

"I'll see you in the morning," Brenda said to me.

"I won't be in until Wednesday. Stewart told me to take another day off."

"Excellent idea. Wednesday, then." Brenda winked and hobbled off towards the library with Walter.

I walked around the corner and ended up at the window to the security control room. The security guard behind the glass panel spoke into the microphone as I signed out. "Hope you have an umbrella. It's pouring out there," he said.

"At least it's not snow." I grinned and passed through the door stopping under the granite archway to scrounge for my umbrella when my BlackBerry vibrated. I pulled it out, and the notification icon indicated I had close to 200 unread emails. Oh, lord! But the last email that arrived in my inbox was from Geoffrey. 'Welcome back, kiddo,' it read. Boy, news sure travelled quickly. The email continued. 'Below is the link to the *Salon du chocolat* in Paris. Looks like you'll be able to make it after all. Geoffrey xox.' I smiled and returned the electronic device back into my purse and continued rummaging for my umbrella. While doing so, it dawned on me that Geoffrey had never explained what he had been doing the day before the gala and why he hadn't told me he had arrived early. Weird. Oh well, I'm sure he had a logical explanation.

"Are you looking for something like this, Boyko?"

Up ahead stood Marco swinging a large umbrella like Gene Kelly in *Singing in the Rain*.

343

I plowed towards him and pulled him by his elbow escorting him towards Philosopher's Walk. "How'd you do it? How'd you get your hands on those emails?"

"What emails?"

I tilted my head and sported a give-me-a-break look.

Marco lifted the umbrella, pressed a button and it shot open above our heads. "We could get into a lot of trouble if we talk about–"

I continued to drag Marco away from the Museum. "Just this one issue and then I'll drop it. I swear. I just have to know?"

"Well, when you asked Richard about the email he sent you telling you to go to the Bug Room, he denied having sent it."

"Richard lied about a lot of things."

"But it didn't make sense. He knew something like that could easily be verified."

"What can I say? Richard's a tool and not very computer savvy."

"Or maybe he didn't send the email. What if it was sent by someone who had access to staff passwords and could make it look like the email came from Richard?"

"O.M.G. Someone like Aurelia!"

"I had a sneaking suspicion she was up to no good that night," said Marco. "After Malik finally let us leave the Education Department, I headed straight to Aurelia's office. She was reading *Cosmo* while supposedly monitoring a server upgrade that night. I took a chance and confronted her about cracking into your emails and cyber-impersonating Richard."

"What did she say?"

"She denied it, of course. But then I kind of lied and told her that her boss had been tracing her keystroke activity for the past several weeks."

"Good one, Marco."

"But then she turned drama-queen and started shedding major crocodile tears. You should've seen the mascara running down her face."

"You've got to be kidding." I rolled my eyes.

"I told her to fess up or I'd radio Malik to come join the conversation, and she started to spill the beans. She said she'd been reading your emails and knew you and Richard were on the outs. She admitted she was jealous you were at the party while she had to work overtime in a freezing server room. She used Richard's email address, sent off that phony message and went to the Bug Room. She claimed she didn't really have a plan and when you turned up, she panicked and locked you inside."

"Oh, give me a break."

"I pretended I believed her and told her she could redeem herself if she gave me access to Richard's email history. It didn't take long for us to come up with some dirt on Richard, Veronique and Landry. Malik must've dredged up a lot more because the rumor mill has it that Richard and Veronique were tossed out on their cans today."

"They were, but we won't be able to tell anyone why," I said. "But I can live with that."

"Me too."

"What about Aurelia? I ran into her on my way into the Museum, and she was acting more bonkers than usual."

"She quit the Museum today."

"What?"

"You didn't think I'd let her get away with everything she did to you, did you? After she gave me the evidence I needed on Richard, I suggested she'd be better off if she left the Museum on her own terms."

"Her terms? That woman deserves to be drawn and quartered – or better still, head shaved and tar poured over her."

Marco chuckled. "I told Aurelia if she stayed and got caught for what she'd been doing she'd never get another IT job again. She thought it over on the weekend and resigned this afternoon. She just packed everything up at the end of the day and told her boss she wasn't coming back."

I flashbacked to my encounter with her a little over an hour ago. The object she handed to Malik upon her departure had to have been her ID and the shopping bag she carried was filled with her personal items.

"I've got my new project parked over there. Can I give you a ride home?"

"You're not going to talk about this anymore, are you?"

Marco shifted his eyebrows upwards. "So, can I give you a lift?"

"It depends." I grinned. "What kind of clunker have you got on the go this time, an Edsel?"

"Something like that."

Marco guided me towards a car with a brushed stainless steel body and opened the vehicle's gull-wing doors.

"Holy Batman. You got a De Lorean?"

"Pretty sweet, eh?"

* * * * *

As we drove along Bloor Street, the rain turned into a soft drizzle, and my thoughts turned to the last conversation I had had with Geoffrey. "Marco, did you know that the opals that were stolen from the Museum so long ago once belonged to Geoffrey's family?"

"Yup. Bob told me."

"Bob-just-call-me-Bob Bob."

"Yup."

"Did Bob say anything else?"

"He said there was a nanosecond when Geoffrey's family was under suspicion, but the investigation was terminated due to a complete lack of evidence."

"Why didn't you ever say anything to me?"

"You weren't in a frame of mind to believe anything negative I said about Geoffrey."

Marco was right. I would have just thought he was trying to tarnish Geoffrey's shiny reputation and allure. But I was in no position to share Geoffrey's confession with Marco. That would have been an unforgivable betrayal of Geoffrey's confidence.

We drove a few blocks in silence when Marco suddenly piped up. "Stewart seems like a pretty good guy."

"He is. But what makes you say that?"

"I could tell he tried to give you the benefit of the doubt."

"I couldn't ask for a better boss. Tonight, he asked me if I wanted to work in the London office for a while."

Marco slammed on the brakes sending us both flying forward to the limits of our seatbelt reach. "Are you okay?" he screamed.

"You just scared the freaking daylights out of me. But other than that, I'm fine." Except for the whiplash! I leaned back in my seat carefully.

Marco peered upwards towards the red traffic light. "I'm really sorry about that. I didn't see the light turn."

I tilted my head up and saw the light change to green. We slowly advanced.

"So, when are you leaving?" said Marco.

"For where? Oh, London. I'm not sure yet."

"How long will you be gone?"

"Don't know. Maybe a few months."

"So, it's not permanent?"

"No. It's just a kind of work exchange. We'll do a swap with the London staff."

"Sounds cool." Marco could not have sounded any less enthusiastic.

We drove further along and then we turned south towards the Lakeshore. Within a few blocks, Marco pulled over to the side of the street and parked.

"I know for a fact there's no Rocky Mountain Chocolate Factory Store around here." I was puzzled.

"There's something better." Marco grinned. "There's a place up ahead where you can buy ChocoSol Traders chocolate bars. The two guys who make them import organic and solar-roasted beans from ecofriendly farmers in Mexico. And get this, they pulverize the beans with a bicycle-powered grinder. They're one hundred percent green energy bars."

"Are they one hundred percent calorie-free too? After all the chocolate I ate this past weekend, my cellulite's going to explode out of my legs."

Marco burst out laughing. "You women worry about cellulite way too much."

"That's because the media bombards us with the notion that women are supposed to have the same kind of thighs at forty as they did when they were pre-teens."

"You should ignore that crap," said Marco. "You know,

348

my mom was real feisty and had a great sense of humor. Before she died, when she was in the hospital with tubes sticking out of her everywhere, she turned to my sister and me with a huge smile and said she wished she hadn't spent so much time in her life worrying about her weight."

"She sounds like a woman of substance," I said.

Marco stared into the centers of my eyes, straight through to my soul. "You mean like you?"

"Hardly. A woman of substance wouldn't have been so hell bent on a mission of revenge to the point of not seeing what was really going on around her."

"But Richard was a bad guy. Your instincts were right all along."

"But I was after him for the wrong reasons, and because of that I messed up badly."

"It takes a woman of substance to admit that," said Marco.

"Does it also take a woman of substance to have three people fired and put out on the street?"

"I wouldn't be too worried about that. Veronique and her sister are loaded thanks to a hefty inheritance. That's how Richard and Landry were able to afford to shop at Borovsky Fine Arts," said Marco.

"And explains the house they bought in Rosedale. But if they were rolling in money, why did Landry want Carson's job so badly?" I said.

"I suspect that through Landry, Richard was planning to drive the Museum to ruins as payback for his father's death."

"You could be right. Well, I hope they all live happily ever after. C'mon. Let's open up these wacky doors and get ourselves some green energy chocolate bars. Then we'll scoot up the street."

"What for?"

Marco opened up the doors, and we hopped out onto the street.

"There's a little organic market around the corner. I need to pick up some groceries if I'm going to cook us dinner."

"You cook?"

"Hard to believe I know, but I'm actually a decent cook?"

"I thought you lived on chocolate. You know, a chocolativore." Marco winked.

Marco laced his arm through mine as we walked towards the café. "You know this London work exchange of yours."

"Uh-huh."

"It sounds like the perfect gig. The whole world's waiting for you. You're a smasher."

I halted and gawked at Marco in amazement. "Sidney Poitier to Judy Geeson in *To Sir with Love*. I can't believe you know that line."

"It was one of my mom's favorite movies. She made me watch it every time it was on TV."

"O.M.G. I love that film. I've seen it at least forty times," I said.

"Why am I not surprised?"

THE END

"Life should not be a journey to the grave with the intention of arriving safely in an attractive and well preserved body. Rather aim to skid in sideways, Chardonnay in one hand, chocolate in the other, body thoroughly used up, totally worn out, and screaming Woo Hoo! What a ride."

Kamhi, Ellen, Alternative Medicine Magazine's Definitive Guide to Weight Loss: 10 Healthy Way to Permanently Shed Unwanted Pounds, Celestial Arts, 2007, p. 241.

ACKNOWLEDGEMENTS

Immeasurable thanks to:

Andy Kulchyckyj and Zenon Kulchisky for being the most supportive of brothers and just being who they are (even spelling their names differently).

My grade four English teacher, Mr. Dalton, for recognizing decades before I did, that I had the potential to spin an amusing yarn.

Craig Pyette at Random House Canada for telling it like it is.

Lise Creurer for directing me to the new starting point of my journey.

Nika Rylski of George Brown College for rekindling my passion for writing.

Nancy Kilpatrick of George Brown College for teaching me about structure.

Antanas Sileika and The Humber College School for Writers for warning me that writing and publishing a novel is a marathon.

Kim Moritsugu of The Humber College School for Writers whose invaluable mentorship went above and beyond the call of duty.

Judith Lavin and Florence Russell for giving so generously of their time in proofreading my drafts and for their unwavering support.

Nick Whittington for the visioning tools and encouragement.

Bob Ramik and Stephen Ball for digging into the past and triggering some new inspirations.

All my earthly angels who gave me moral support, in particular those who suffered through reading my early drafts – bless you!

The Royal Ontario Museum and all the eccentric, loveable, brilliant, funny and dedicated staff who made my more than 20 years there feel like a nanosecond.

Robert Barnett, Linda Pearcey and the rest of the staff of Cultural Innovations for giving me a few more awesome years and experiences in the museum world.

Elizabeth Jennings and the Women's Fiction Festival in the sublime town of Matera, Italy for providing such an incredible forum for writers of women's fiction.

All my survival job employers who kept me gainfully working so I could pay my bills and write without having to resort to eating cat food.

Mike Uhlmann for being my center of gravity until I found my own.

The Maya for inventing chocolate.

Anselm and Eloise Aston at Attica Books for getting it.

About the Author

Soon after finishing her graduate studies in history, Luba Landed on the doorstep of Canada's largest museum, the Royal Ontario Museum where she worked for more than 20 years. Moving from positions in the Education and Programs Departments to the Museum's consulting branch, she concluded her career in the office that managed the Museum's controversial architectural renovation. After leaving the Museum, Luba worked for several years in an administrative and research capacity for a private museum consulting firm with offices in Toronto and London (UK). She currently works in the educational sector and teaches yoga in her home town of Toronto.

Theft By Chocolate is Luba's debut novel, though she has been amusing people with writing since the age of eight. Her love of chocolate precedes this age and she has been in and out of chocolate rehab for most of her adult life. When not writing or looking for her next chocolate fix, Luba can be found in dance classes, trekking to remote waterfalls in the mountain rain forest of Puerto Rico, jogging through the streets of Paris or any other number of calorie-burning activities that help offset her chocolate intake.

COPYRIGHT INFORMATION

ISBN (print): 978–0–9936054–0–6
ISBN (epub): 978–0–9936054–1–3
ISBN (mobi): 978–0–9936054–2–0

First published by Attica Books, 2012
This edition by Luba Lesychyn, 2019
Cover artwork and design by Fitzpatrick Maloney

eBook conversion and typesetting by Anselm Audley

Made in the USA
Las Vegas, NV
04 December 2022

61114284R10208